THE PATH TO HE
THROUGH

THE PATH TO HEAVEN RUNS THROUGH ISRAEL

First edition. April 4, 2024.

ISBN: 979-8224467327

Written by Luis Gomez and Mauss Barna (Pseudonym of Luis gomez).

THE PATH TO HEAVEN RUNS THROUGH ISRAEL

MAUSS BARNA

The path to heaven runs through Israel

© Mauss Barna, 2024

First Edition

Author-Editor: Mauss Barna

lmgomezv72@gmail.com

Cover Design: Marisol Villarraga

marypublicista@gmail.com

Translation: Jack Beeching

Style correction: John Beeching

Author's Note

This is a novel based on various real historical events that are part of the development of the Jewish people. The events narrated here permanently cross that very thin line between reality and fiction. In other words, based on real facts, documented events, the literary perception of what could have happened, and the author's imagination are recreated.

It could be said that some characters are fictitious, and the truth would not be lacking. However, it can be stated that each one of them existed, perhaps with other names and different physical characteristics but surely with the same Jewish soul and spirit.

This is the first part of a novel that compiles the life of several generations of a Jewish family, whose members are not only witnesses, but also direct protagonists of various historical events in Europe, Asia, the United States and Israel, over a period of century and half.

In sublime and eternal tribute to the brave people who for four thousand years have endured persecutions and injustices, but who have overcome them all. *"The sons of Israel could fall a thousand times and they thousand times they will get up".*

1

"Grandpa, I wish I wasn't been a Jew".

The boy, nearly a youth, had spent a long time in thought. It was as though it pained him greatly to put into words that which occupied his mind. He breathed deeply and slowly exhaled the air from his lungs. He sat expectantly, looking sidelong at his grandfather.

The old man felt a shiver run down his spine. For a moment he was still, as though considering his grandson's words. Suddenly the memory of a forgotten event entered his mind. He tried to quash the thoughts that had engulfed his head. In a fraction of a second, the memory took him to that distant day when his own grandfather had told him of a situation so similar, it seemed unreal. The story took place at the end of the 19th century, when a boy, perhaps as young as his grandson, expressed the same words and caused the same discomfort.

After a few moments, without having looked at the boy, he slowly rose from his armchair, took the walking stick that lay against the table, and hobbled toward the window. The pain in his left leg flared up. The same always happened whenever he tried to walk after sitting for a long while. It was not an ache typical of one who had lived for more than eight decades. No, it was the consequence of an injury left untreated for too long, that still after so many years brought him, recurrently, to the memory of the action which saved the lives of his comrades in the war of '73. He was decorated as a hero, but his leg paid the price.

"How ironic" the old man thought to himself "the Yom Kippur war, where I atoned for an untold number of sins."

A few more moments passed, which to the boy seemed an eternity. The old man looked through the window towards the bay. He stood watching the cars that had already turned on their lights, and were driving down the Avenida de los Italianos, towards Dársena Sur. Beyond, the sea of an intense and deep blue shone under those last rays of the sun, in that southern summer of 2019. Then he slowly turned, his sad eyes meeting the expectant gaze of his grandson.

"Tell me David, why do you say that?"

"Grandpa, I can't explain it. It's not that I think it's bad to be a Jew, it's just..."

The boy had risen and was walking around the room somewhat nervously. His grandfather watched him fixedly. David touched the palms of his hands, searching for the right words. Eitan, seeing his grandson's uncertainty, supported himself with the walking stick, bowed towards the boy and asked him:

"Why does it pain you so much to speak? Maybe I could help you express it. Sometimes, it's hard for a twelve-year-old to find the right words. Especially when you think they won't much like what you have to say."

"Yes grandpa, it's just that there are many things."

"Maybe there aren't as many as you think, and maybe they aren't as bad. Can I help you? Are you trying to tell me that at school, or in the neighbourhood, they've made you feel different?"

"Something like that, how did you know?"

"Maybe they've also said hurtful things about Jews, or about being a Jew?"

"Well, it's ... yes, something like that. They make me feel bad. And I see myself as like them, I do the same things, live the same way, I don't know..."

The old man Eitan regarded his grandson. His gaze softened, as he motioned for the boy to sit again. He did the same, resting the walking stick against the table. Then he said to him:

"I know you have spent half your life outside of Israel. Perhaps every day that passes, your memories of living in the home of the Jews fade. But know this; we carry our homeland in our hearts. *Wherever in the world there lives a Jew, you will find a piece of Israel.*"

"I understand. And I have not forgotten my time in Israel, I miss those days. There, I felt normal, exactly like the other boys. All my friends wore the Kippah, just like me. But here ... I don't know. It's different, I don't like it."

"Life is full of unpleasant things, there always will be, just as there will always be those who know how to confront and overcome them, and those who will be knocked down and defeated by them. No people like ours better understands the meaning of those words."

Eitan sat in thought for a moment, letting his head fall slightly to one side. He then continued:

"I think the time has come for you to know more of the history of the Jews, so you can understand our path on this earth, and the legacy left by your ancestors over the ages. There are many truths you will not find even in the Torah or the Talmud."

David signed deeply, indicating that his grandfather held his attention. The old man continued:

"Perhaps what you learn today will turn your discomfort into something else. But we will go in parts. I'm going to tell you of things that happened many, many years ago."

The boy widened his eyes, showing his interest:

"I'm listening, grandpa."

"But first, I want you to know that this uncertainty you feel, that invades your spirit, has been felt by your ancestors as well. One could say that it is not something new amongst our people. Actually, what surprised me most about your words is that they remind me of an identical case, that my grandfather Yosef told me of many years ago."

"I don't understand, what are you talking about?"

"He told me once that when he was about your age, he spoke the same words to his father that you said to me."

"What? I'm confused. The same words?"

"Yes, once he also wished not to be a Jew."

David regarded his grandfather with mixed feelings, partly regretting what he had said, but also somewhat relived to know that he was not the only one of his family to feel such discomfort.

"Of course, those were hard and fateful times for Jews. "Continued the old man" however, according to my grandfather's story, despite his father's surprise and fierce character, he did not scold him. Just the opposite, he ran his hand through the boy's hair and promised that he would take him on a journey and tell him a story much like the one I will tell you."

"What story grandpa?"

"The story of your people, which is no small thing. Did you know that we Jews are the most ancient people on the face of the earth?"

"I didn't know that."

"It's true my boy. Our story goes back nearly four thousand years. No other people or race in this world can presume to have a story so old. Already you have one reason to feel proud to be a Jew."

The boy narrowed his eyes and watched somewhat thoughtfully.

"But that's not all David, you carry in your blood the heritage of the men that many years ago, began the process that allowed the forging of Western civilisation."

The words *blood* and *Western civilisation* didn't make sense in the boy's mind, but he understood that they were something very important. Meanwhile Eitan breathed deeply, saying to himself: 'the boy is a Jew, his whole world knows what he is, and I treat him as such, but neither my son nor his wife have bothered to teach him the doctrine of our religion. They haven't shown him what it means to be Jew. No wonder he feels so confused. Oh Lord, what has become of our new generation?'

He shifted in his seat, and told his grandson:

"I'm going to tell you a fascinating story that belongs not only to the Jews, but to all humanity. But first I'm going to repeat some of the things that, I'm sure, you've been told at school or in the neighbourhood."

The boy regarded him with great curiosity. Eitan continued:

"They've told you that the Jews are arrogant, and think themselves better than everyone else, yes?"

"Yes, grandpa, exactly that! How did you know?"

Eitan smiled, shook his head, and went on:

"You've heard it said that Jews only think of making money. Am I still correct?"

"Yes grandpa."

"They've also said that it was the Jews that killed Christ, or am I wrong?"

The boy's eyes were wide open.

"That's not all, they've also implied that the Jews stole the Palestinians' land and left them without a home. Is this also true?"

"It's incredible grandpa, it's like you were there!"

"It is not necessary to be there, it is just that these are the same accusations as always. However, it is important that you understand that not all Christians speak badly of the Jews, rather the great majority are respectful and tolerant of our beliefs, just as we are of theirs. Do you follow?"

"Of course. In fact, most of my fellows have never said anything against the Jews, rather they treat me well and don't look on me as if I were different. It is just the few that do that bother me."

"Well, for those few I am going to explain to you who the Jews are, so that you will have answers to your doubts and arguments with which to respond to the mistaken ideas that you have heard about the Jews."

The boy listened intently.

"They label us arrogant, my son. But did you know that we are the oldest people on Earth. We built our own identity while the other peoples roamed the world without a fixed course. But most importantly, we have conserved our identity throughout all adversity. While other peoples either disappeared or were obliged to transform themselves. We have maintained our homogeneity. That is something that no other people can claim."

"Our what, grandpa?"

Eitan smiled, gazing at his grandson with great tenderness, and continued:

"We have always been the same. We adapt, but we don't change. Therein lies our strength. It's because of this, David, that they persecute us, but have never beaten us. Well, this is the first thing I wanted you to know. We are not only the most ancient, but we have maintained our own identity, unlike other peoples. Do you understand?"

"Yes, of course."

"So, from now on don't forget that if someone, no matter their race or religion, calls you proud or arrogant, you can say that while you are not like that, you have many reasons to feel that way. Because you belong to the first organised people who inhabited the world, that still exists. I think that's one plus for us Jews, don't you agree?"

The boy smiled sincerely, and then laughed:

"Yes grandpa! One-nil!"

"Good, let's continue. This country you live in today is mostly Christian. In fact, the whole Western world is. I assure you that those young Catholic boys from the neighbourhood and school that try to humiliate or mock you for being a Jew, don't know that the basis of their religion is the history of our people."

"I don't think I understand."

"I'll explain. Those boys, in their ignorance, don't know that the Bible from which they hear so much at home, at school, and in church, is actually the history of the Jewish people."

"Really Grandpa?"

"It's true David, the entire Old Testament is about the history of the Jews. No other people possess a book that recounts with such accuracy the historical events that developed their nation. Do you think any of those who mock you can say the same? Of course not, only the Jews can claim it, we have the most ancient history of humanity."

"Of course, grandpa, only us. I guess that's two-nil."

The boy's face reflected joy and, more importantly for Eitan, pride as well.

"We're on the right track", he thought, then continued.

"Yes, two-nil. But that's not all when it comes to the Bible, you know that the New Testament, which is the basis for the Christian faith, is no more than a continuation of the Old. And that, Jesus was a Jew. In other words, without Judaism, Christianity would never have existed. Do the boys who mock you know that?"

"Definitely not grandpa!" David enthusiastically exclaimed, noting that fact in his mind. "I'll tell them when I have the chance."

"Good, so we're up to three-nil, right?"

"Yes grandpa!"

"It's good to see you so enthusiastic about this. Perhaps you should have known this sooner, but it doesn't matter, better late than never."

"It's true grandpa, I'd never thought about these things you're telling me. I really like talking with you."

"My boy, it delights me that you're interested in this subject."

At that moment they heard a noise at the front door, and some female laughter. David's older sisters and Martha, his mother, had arrived.

"Hello, is there anyone home?" Exclaimed Martha.

"We're here mum." Replied the boy from the study.

Martha entered with the shopping bags and amiably greeted them.

"Hello, my child. How are you, Eitan?"

"Hello." Replied the old man. "How was the shop?"

"Good, good, I'm going to tidy the kitchen and prepare dinner. David, come and help me. I'll have to borrow him for a few minutes, Eitan."

"Don't worry Martha, we have been talking awhile. We'll continue later."

"Yes." Interrupted David. "Wait for me, I'll be back soon, and you can continue, right?"

"Of course, my boy, I'll wait here. You'll discover a lot of interesting things about Judaism. But first I'll tell you the history of your family, of your ancestors. It's also important that you know that."

Mother and son left the study and headed towards the kitchen. Eitan was left thinking about the conversation with his grandson and, also, about his daughter-in-law.

"Martha is an extraordinary woman." He said in a low voice. "She's a good wife and mother, and she has many good qualities. I'm pleased my son chose her to be his life's companion. It's a shame she wasn't born into a Jewish home. Maybe that's why David hasn't been able to immerse himself in the essence of our people."

Indeed, Martha had not been born in the bosom of a Jewish family. While her father was certain that they were descended from Sephardic Jews that had emigrated to America in the 17th century, establishing themselves by the Plate River. The truth was that when she knew Moshé in Tel Aviv, she was a Christian, or as she referred to herself, a *'non-practicing Catholic'*. Before marrying she converted to Judaism. For Eitan, it was compromise rather than conviction. While they lived in Israel during the first years of their marriage, he could see for himself that the *'non-practicing Catholic'* had become a *'non-practicing Jew'*. And the same had been true since they established themselves in Argentina. It was as though Jewish customs were disappearing from Moshé and Martha's home. Eitan felt a great affection for her, not only because she was a great woman, but because she had made his son very happy, and nothing pleases a parent more than seeing their child happy. However, he always felt that small annoyance in his heart. The importance of a woman in creating a Jewish household and raising children according to traditional customs is no secret to anyone.

"I've already taken charge of putting David on the right path." Eitan said to himself. "He'll be a good Jew, just as I have been, and my father, and my grandfather, and his grandfather before him."

2

He was very small, and the intense cold chilled him to his bones. Instead of footwear, his tiny feet were wrapped in pieces of cloth that his mother had torn from her own skirts. It had only been a day since his fifth birthday, but given the tragic circumstances, he had not seen the celebration promised by his parents. The cake and presents that Sara had neatly wrapped, imagining her little one's shouts of joy upon opening them, remained forgotten at home.

At his side was his mother, completely downcast. She had cried so much that her tears had dried up. She wasn't the only one; in the stable's semi-darkness, the little Gabriel could make out various women who quietly prayed and wept. They sometimes talked amongst themselves, but only through murmurs.

Suddenly, with a loud noise, the gate that connected the stable to the cellar opened. A Russian official entered, flanked by two soldiers. His features were harsh, his gestures rough. The Sergeant shouted:

"You can all leave now Jewish bitches!"

Some of the women tried to approach the official, but one of the soldiers pointed his rifle at them, threatening them with the bayonet attached to its point.

"Get back!" Those who had approached scattered immediately.

"At my command, you leave the stable, let's go, let's go!" The Sergeant roared again, before signalling to his men to evict the women.

Gabriel's mother, keeping her distance to avoid his fury, implored him:

"I beg you; my husband has nothing to do with the rebellion! He is innocent!

The Sergeant let out a laugh, then spat in her face and scornfully replied.

"He's a Jew! That alone makes him guilty."

He then ordered the soldiers to remove the women.

Sara took Gabriel in her arms and, with the other women, some of whom also clutched children, exited the stable. The bitter cold of that

February 1863, cut through the folds of their clothing. The snow went on as far as the eye could see. The Russian soldiers continued to shout and yell curses at them. Gabriel couldn't have known what they were saying, he didn't speak their language. The women continued to beg, but the soldiers were implacable. The Sergeant shouted again:

"All of you get out of here! You will never see your husbands again! You should have told them better. Who ordered you to raise filthy arms against Mother Russia?"

The women, despite the bayonets and curses, desperately approached the Sergeant. Exasperated, he unsheathed his sabre. At that moment, they heard the neighing of horses. From the corner of the stable appeared four Russian soldiers. One of them wore a great leather hat decorated with a plume, and a grey coat that reached his boots. Leather straps crossed his chest, revealing gold buttons on either side. One could immediately see that he was of a higher rank. The Sergeant stopped his blade in mi-air, lowering it quickly when he saw his superior.

"What's happening here?" Asked the official.

"We're ridding the stable of these dirty Poles, Captain."

"And is it necessary to unsheathe your sabre to evict women, Sergeant?"

"They weren't obeying me, Captain. They insisted on seeing the prisoners."

"I assume these are the wives and mothers of the prisoners?"

The Captain, from atop his horse, looked at the dozen or so women, who looked back with pleading and fearful eyes. His own gaze was filled with a certain sadness. Perhaps in that moment, he thought of a wife and mother who awaited him in Moscow or St. Petersburg. After a moment he approached the Sergeant and said, in a gentle yet firm voice:

"Our war is not with them. Their men leave today for Siberia, they have the right to say farewell."

The Sergeant did not hide his contempt for the words he had heard.

"Damned Captain." He thought to himself. "He comes showing mercy to these Polish bitches. Damn him a thousand times! He's making me look ridiculous."

However, he had to obey, and so he snapped to his men:

"Bring the prisoners!"

The soldiers reluctantly headed towards the barn. Meanwhile the Captain, in a rough Polish, told the women:

"You may see your husbands one last time. Five minutes and then you leave the house. Despite the circumstances, I wish you luck. "

He bowed his head slightly, turned to his mount, and galloped off, followed by his escort of soldiers. The mounts kicked up snow from their hooves as they disappeared. At that moment the prisoners exited, with chains around their ankles. The soldiers pushed them, making it difficult to walk. The women ran to them, embracing them while crying. Gabriel's mother ran towards her husband, leading the boy by the hand. They hugged each other fiercely, then his father lifted him to the sky, held him in front of his face, and gave him a kiss on the cheek.

"My son, dream of my soul, you don't know how much I love you. You are very small, but you will grow. You will be a good Jew and take care of your mother. I will always keep you in my heart." Then he said to his wife. "I will love you for the rest of my life, and still after death, tell the same thing to the girls."

The Sergeant, still red with anger at the shame his Captain had brought him, took it out on the poor men and their wives, not allowing them more than a minute to say goodbye.

"Let's go, you damned Jews! Your rotten souls will freeze in Siberia. It's time you faced the consequences for those who attack the Holy Empire."

With the soldiers, he pushed the men back towards the barn. Gabriel watched his father with sad eyes, until he reached the entrance. At that exact moment, the man turned his head and met his gaze with that of his little boy. Gabriel felt a lump in his throat. Despite his young age, he knew he would never see his father again. Sara wept inconsolably; she knew full well that Isaak was being taken to a place from which there was no return. The boy looked back at the countryside and watched the Captain as he galloped into the snow, flanked by his men. Gabriel hated the Russians for the rest of his life, but he never forgot that Official's gesture, which allowed him to see his father for the last time.

Isaak, Gabriel's father, was a good man and a good Jew. He had overcome many personal and economic hardships. With great effort, he had managed to establish a small shoe repair and sales business in Ostrow. His father was Polish, but his grandfather came from Austria; they were pure Ashkenazim, from whom he inherited the love of work and discipline. His name, Rothman, while very German, was also Jewish. He had always felt proud of his ancestors, his religion, and his race. He never stopped attending the Synagogue and celebrated Jewish holidays every year. He faithfully observed the Shabbat and the Jewish dietary laws.

He was not wealthy, but lived relatively well with his beloved wife Sara, a virtuous and simple woman blessed with great beauty. She stood out due to her light grey eyes and perfect face, framed by abundant blonde hair which she almost never covered with a scarf. The couple were very happy, although their happiness was clouded by one thing: The Lord had not given them the pleasure of having children. They had tried for a long time, but Sara could no longer conceive. They visited many doctors, even in Warsaw, but the specialists, to the best of their knowledge, could not find any reason why. More than once, Isaak thought of the paradox of his wife's name, thinking to himself:

"The Lord gave Abraham and Sarah a son, despite their age. I'm certain that sooner or later he will grant the same for us."

With faith that they would one day have a child, they continued their modest but happy life. The pair worked tirelessly, he in his shoe shop and Sara in the cafeteria of a Jewish merchant on Sielska street, in the heart of town. They lived in a small and plain wooden house, decorated with good taste, within their means. They had made a name for themselves within the Jewish community, and Isaak's renown as a shoemaker already extended to the surrounding farmhouses. He did not only repair footwear, but also made it to measure, in which he was highly skilled.

However, one day things changed. The Russian's defeat in the Crimean war inspired Polish liberation and encouraged nationalism.

Tsar Alexander's response was to impose yet more restrictions on occupied Poland. He also initiated the process of *russification* throughout his kingdom, which involved the removal of Polish officials, to be replaced with Russian representatives. In many places officials remained Polish, but under strict Russian supervision. This was the case in Ostrow, where the mayor had been deposed and replaced with a Russian puppet.

To the pair, these political machinations were alien. They thought, not without good reason, that they would not be directly affected, as two average citizens who maintained an anonymous existence. Thus, they continued their lives, he through his business and she in the cafeteria. Sara, however, could sense that something was coming. Despite there being no logical reason, one night she told her husband.

"My love, I can't say for certain, but I feel that hardships are coming."

"What are you talking about?"

"Nothing in particular, but this *russification* people speak of, I don't like it. I don't believe it bodes well, especially for us Jews."

"You're exaggerating Sara! These political changes concern only those in power, we're not important, neither for the Russians or the Poles."

"Maybe, but I don't know. I can sense something strange and I don't like it."

"You can't live life based on premonitions. Nothing will happen, especially in a town as unimportant as ours. It wouldn't even exist on a map were it not for the crossroads."

"Well, if you say so."

"Yes, my love, don't worry. Let's go to sleep, tomorrow I must get up earlier than usual."

Sara couldn't go straight to sleep, she lay thinking about what might happen, but she could not picture it. Perhaps her husband was right, what could happen in such an insignificant town? Finally, she fell asleep.

The new mayor was an impulsive and fickle man. He had never done anything important in his life, but as soon as he was appointed to rule the people's destinies, he was filled with such arrogance as if her were the owner of Ostrow. He was rumoured to have a criminal record in

Warsaw, but nothing was ever proven. The only certainty was that he served Russian interests, for which he was appointed. Now that he held power, he liked to walk the streets of the town, with his secretary, every summer evening. It so happened that on one of these walks, he passed the cafeteria where Sara worked. Upon entering, he was captivated by her. The beautiful young blonde, with large grey eyes, struck him deeply. When she approached to take the men's orders, he watched her closely and without modesty. She, of course, was annoyed by the customer's attitude, but hid it as best she could, taking their order.

"I haven't seen you before around town." Said the mayor, still staring at her.

"What would you like, Sir?"

The man, whose manners were far from gentlemanly, simply told her:

"I'd like for you to sit with us."

"I'm sorry Sir, I'm working, and it is not my job to share meals with customers."

"Look! The blonde has spirit." He said as he took her hand.

She immediately pulled it back and headed for the counter, standing behind it. From there she said to the man:

"If you want to eat, I will gladly serve you, but you will not be disrespectful to me."

"Oh! Very dignified as I see, don't you know who I am?"

"I don't know, and I'm sorry, but it doesn't interest me."

"Well, let's go." Said the mayor, getting up and addressing his secretary. "She will soon find out who I am."

The two men left the cafeteria, but the problem didn't end there. This unpleasant character became obsessed with Sara. He made a habit of visiting the cafeteria every day and flirting with the woman, harassing her with offensive attitudes and improper proposals. The situation became unbearable for her and began to affect the cafeteria's owner. One evening he told her how pleased he was with her work but asked her to do without her services to avoid any more problems with the mayor. He feared that scorning him would have consequences for his business. However, the opposite occurred, the next day when the burgomaster arrived on a usual visit, he found the woman no longer there. He simply said to the owner, that if she did not return, he would close the cafeteria.

She reluctantly returned, as she needed the work and hoped the situation could be dealt with. She had not spoken to her husband about it in an attempt to avoid a problem. She had already seen what the mayor was like and was sure that he would take out his anger on Isaak and his shoe shop. So, she tried to get used to it, keeping the annoying man at bay. The mayor, however, was used to getting what he wanted without regard for decency or legality and decided that he would have Sara no matter the cost. One afternoon in the cafeteria, he forcefully took her by the waist. She screamed, but the man drew her closer and reached down to her buttocks. The woman struggled free. She threw her apron to the floor and ran from the shop. She went straight to her husband's shoe, which was three blocks away.

She entered weeping and told her husband everything. He held and comforted her, wiping away her tears. Then, he calmly took her hand and led her out of the shop, locking the doors. Without releasing her hand, he took her to the cafeteria. Sara begged him not to go, to return home instead, but the man ignored his wife's words. Upon arriving, they saw that the mayor had left. Isaak spoke with the owner, reproaching him for allowing the customer to harass his wife. The old man merely said that he had been unable to help. After all, the mayor was powerful, and he wanted to avoid problems.

Once again, Sara urged her husband to return home, to leave things as they were. She knew the mayor's character and feared that there would be consequences. Despite her begging, Isaak walked toward the town hall.

"Let's go home, my love. We shouldn't look for trouble."

"Troubles come and go, if you must have them, better go for something worthwhile."

"That's why it's better to avoid a problem with a man like this."

"If a man can't defend his own wife's honour, he does not deserve to be called a man, nor to be married to his wife."

They arrived at the town hall and when straight to the secretary's office. Isaak didn't bother to greet him.

"The mayor?"

"Who's asking?" The secretary replied with another question.

"Is he in his office?"

"Yes, but who are you and why do you wish to see him?"

At that moment the secretary noticed Sara and realised what had happened. He tried to block the pair from entering the office.

Isaak had heard enough, still holding his wife's hand, he pushed past the secretary into the mayor's office. Inside, the mayor was talking to a couple, seated behind a desk. The violence of Isaak's entrance shocked him, his wife practically dragged behind.

"Secretary!" He shouted, calling his assistant as he rose from his seat.

He noticed Sara, immediately understood the situation and lost his composure. The secretary entered but did not know what to do. Isaak approached the desk which the mayor sheltered behind. Shakily, the mayor said:

"You should know, Sir, that I hold power in Ostrow."

"And you should know!" Isaak replied as he slowly walked around the desk, nearing the mayor, "that I am this woman's husband, whom you have harassed!"

"No, no, I, I ..."

"No excuses, you coward!" Isaak shouted at him. He was close enough to feel the little man's ragged breathing and see him trembling. Isaak was a tall and well-built man, at least a half-head taller than the other, who now appeared as a fawn before a bear. Fear could be seen in his eyes. Meanwhile the secretary was motionless, the other couple had moved to a corner of the office and Sara clasped her hands over her chest. Isaak took the mayor by his coat and snapped at him:

"Listen well to my words!" He exclaimed fiercely. "you may be the mayor but come near my wife again and I will return to break your skull!"

As soon as he had finished, he released the mayor, took Sara by the hand, and walked towards the door. Before leaving, he turned and added:

"And if you dare lay a finger on my wife again, it will be the last thing you do in your life!"

The event soon became the talk of the town. Rumours spread quickly, and peoples' opinions were divided. Many hated the mayor and were glad to hear that someone had finally put him in his place. Others said that the Jewish shoemaker had overstepped the mark. However, he had the support of the entire Hebrew community. Isaak's friends stopped by his shoe shop to congratulate him. Others were more cautious, advising him to leave town for a while. They knew the mayor's vindictive character.

"Don't forget he was in a criminal gang back in Warsaw" said one neighbour, "you should watch out".

Many warned him to be careful with the man. They were certain that he would take revenge for insult. But Isaak refused to be intimidated. He knew that he was admired and respected in town, not only by the Jewish community, but also by those of other faiths. However, they began to see that not only his integrity was at risk, but also his safety and business. They knew the mayor had the support of the Russians. One night, the town's Rabbi came to the couple's house, urging them to leave as soon as possible, as the mayor had arranged for a mob of men to rob their house. In effect, that heartless man had recruited a group of bandits, promising to look the other way as they took whatever they wanted from the house and shop.

Left without options, Isaak did not delay. He hurriedly took a few changes of clothes, the little money he had, and his most precious possessions: The Menorah, Chanukah chandelier, the Tefillin given by his father on his 13th birthday, and the Tallit given to him by Sara on their wedding day. Other Jews provided a cart for their flight. They left town just as the bandits broke into their home. Rather than steal, they destroyed everything they could. The mayor, furious that he had not found Isaak and could not have Sara, ordered them to burn both the house and business.

The couple went to Bialystok, where they knew people with whom Isaak had done business. They arrived as refugees, carrying the few belongings they had. They were literally out on the street. Fortunately, the city's Jewish community provided them with support. They found temporary accommodation and Isaak quickly found work as a saddler. Piece by piece, they rebuilt their lives. Sara managed to join a family-owned bakery. Every day she collected the bread, loading the loaves into two sacks and delivering them all over the city. Before long, they were able to rent a room, which was a relief for Isaak. His pride could not bear to live on charity.

He, with Jewish resilience and entrepreneurship, was not disillusioned by the circumstances. He was determined to establish a shoe shop in Bialystok, to replace the one he had lost in Ostrow. With the support of other Jews, he took out a loan with which he bought leather and some tools. He was also able to rent a small place. It was tiny, but he managed to set up a small repair shop and started making children's shoes. The business slowly grew, thanks to quality of his repairs and shoemaking. Through his skill he became well known, to the extent that he was soon overwhelmed with the number of orders. He rented a bigger shop and hired two employees, one was a boy of only 14 years, but with talent and enthusiasm for learning the trade. The other was an older man, grey-haired and wrinkled, but with a great work-ethic. The community noticed his kindness in supporting the man, who was working to support his disabled wife.

In addition to growing his business, he was known for his generosity and willingness to help those in need. He gained recognition for the quality of his shoes and kindness of his character. Sara also gained respect. She took an interest in preparing bread and quickly learned how to knead and bake it, so when the baker passed away from scarlet fever, the owners took Sara on in her place. She was no longer engaged solely in deliveries but arrived at four-thirty every morning to prepare the bread. Once the batch was ready, she filled the counters and left everything ready to distribute with the saleswoman on her arrival.

Within a few months, they had saved enough to rent a small two-room house, with a kitchen where they could resume their home life. One month after moving into their new home, Isaak arrived one Spring night, exhausted. He had returned from a long trip to Grodno, where he had carried several boxes of shoes. He took off his coat and hat, hanging them on the stand, and greeted his wife:

"Hello, my love, how are you?"

"Very well, my husband!"

"I'm starving, my love, what do we have for dinner?"

"A delicious stew, but first I have news for you."

"What news?"

Sara walked to the centre of the room, so that she could be seen more clearly under the lamplight. She stared at him intensely, then placed his hands on her stomach. Tears instantly formed in his eyes. He smiled and held his wife, then put on his Tefillin and began to pray, thanking God for blessing his Sara, four-thousand years later. After finishing his prayers, he sat at the table, took his wife's hand, and wept.

Sara's pregnancy was a great risk, and she had to always be careful, looking after herself throughout. Yet not for a moment did she neglect her duties at the bakery. Her husband took charge of distributing the bread, to prevent the long walks that could harm the baby. To make up for the time, he would wake at two in the morning and repair shoes by candlelight, until dawn. Sara dedicated herself only to preparing and selling bread in the shop, avoiding sudden movements, and remaining as calm as possible.

Gabriel was born in February 1858, and brought more joy to his parents' home. From a young age he was a lively and curious child. He came into the world without a single hair on his head, but after a few months he had beautiful blonde hair, just like his mother's. He also inherited her light grey eyes, which by sunlight were as blue as the sky. From his father, he took tenacity, discipline, and strength of character. He arranged things precisely, always smiled, and endured pain stoically. Gabriel remembered that he had not reacted to his circumcision, although after a few moments he screamed so loudly it was heard throughout the neighbourhood.

Gabriel inspired them to work hard and give the best to their son, especially after the doctor had warned Sara she could not conceive again. They gave the little one all their love.

The pair worked tirelessly; thanks to their discipline they progressed little by little. When Gabriel was only one year old, they had saved up enough for Isaak to buy the property in which Isaak had his shop.

His skill and ingenuity had already earned him recognition beyond the borders of Bialystok. Their repair business also grew, to the extent that they built a large workshop behind the establishment, divided into sections for repair and manufactures. The front of the warehouse was completely remodelled, giving it a more modern and elegant look.

Things gradually improved, and within a year, Sara opened her own bakery. It was a humble place, but it slowly grew. She was very thrifty, and when they decided to buy a plot of land outside the city to build their home, Isaak was in awe that his wife, after two years of saving, had collected more than 80% of the land's value. Thus, they bought it immediately and began constructing their house, which they both designed themselves.

They had more than recovered all that they had lost, because of their hard and constant work of course.

"Look how life turns out, Sara." Isaak said to her one night. "Perhaps had we stayed in Ostrow we would not have achieved so much."

"Certainly, my love." She answered. "Now what matters is that we give Gabriel all we can."

"Of course, but life is strange sometimes." He chuckled and then continued. "In the end that mayor did us a favour."

"Whether there, or here, we would have succeeded." She spoke. "God never forgets the children of Israel."

Isaak loved to hear Sara talk like that. The greatest dream of his life was to go to Jerusalem. His great-uncle had once gazed over Mount Zion and since he had told him, it had become an obsession for Isaak. He knew it would be difficult, but nothing could stop him from trying.

Isaak built their home with his own hands and the help of the Bialystok Jewish community. Before it was fully finished, Sara and Gabriel moved in. From her first entrance to her new home, she decorated it with great care. Its decorations were simple, and mostly made by hand, as she had a great gift for making them using inexpensive materials.

From the beginning, the house was designed so that more rooms could be added. At first it had only the necessities: one room and a kitchen. Before Winter's arrival, the house had already been expanded with little Gabriel's room, a hall, and a dining room. It was not an elegant house, but it was beautiful and filled with colour, reflecting the modesty of its inhabitants. Isaak had resolved that they would one day have a brick house, but in the meantime, although built of wood, making it very cosy. The comforts of home filled their dwelling, where they lived happily with their small son. Love and thanks to the Lord were given daily in the small Rothman house.

Every day, early in the morning, Isaak went to his shoe shop in Bialystok's centre, and Sara went to her bakery, where she would light the ovens and knead bread with two young girls. They were Jewish sisters who had been orphaned in "59, when their parents had been killed by a mob in the Odessa pogroms. Their story was tragic and all too familiar to the Jewish race. Their father had emigrated from Vienna, in a few years becoming one of the most successful entrepreneurs of this port on the Black Sea, displacing several Greek merchants. Some of these did not forgive him and took advantage of the disturbances, inciting the mob to storm the Austrian Jew's properties. The crowd broke into his home, murdering him along with his wife and two of his children. They then looted his residence and warehouses. The girls, by chance, were not at home and managed to flee. After a month of hardship, they reached Bialystok in search of an old relative who had already passed away. The two girls were left on the street as beggars, living off of public charity.

Isaak found them one Winter night, lying on the pavement wrapped in rags, the younger one shivering with cold and the older one burning with fever. Immediately, the kind man helped them up and took them home. When Sara saw them, she exclaimed in shock:

"My God, Isaak! Who are these girls?"

"I found them by chance, returning from the shoe shop, I had never seen them before."

She noticed that, beneath their rags, they were half-starved. One was so weak she could not stand on her own, and so she leaned on her sister. She took them to the dining room and sat the girl on a bench, indicating for the other to do the same. She took out a piece of linen and had Isaak soak it in snow. She applied it to the forehead, face, and neck of the girl, who could not speak in her weakness. She thanked her with her eyes.

She heated some coffee and offered them bread and cheese. The younger girl ate gratefully, the older could take only liquids, which Sara helped her swallow. She then took two of her dresses and, removing the rags, dressed the girls. They were too big for them, but it was that was the least of their worries. She quickly put blankets over their shoulders and held them close to the fireplace. Isaak put two logs on and fanned the flames. He then asked the girls:

"Who are you? And where are you from?"

The girls stared at him, obviously not having understood. One then said in Russian:

"I don't understand."

Isaak was more surprised, and repeated his question in the same language:

"What are your names? Where are you from?"

"My name is Aliza; this is my sister Jana. We are from Odesa."

"Odesa is very far; how did you get here?"

"We have been travelling for several weeks."

Of course, the couple gave them a place to stay and fed them, taking special care of Jana, who was only eleven years old. Within a few days, she had overcome her illness. Both she and her nine-year old sister bought new clothes from Old Jacob's shop, who gave them a substantial discount when learning their story, to support the homeless Jewish girls. A couple of weeks later the colour had returned to their cheeks. The girls were very charming and helpful. They had lived a comfortable life in Odessa, but the tragedy they had endured tempered their character. They were humble and dutiful. Both Isaak and Sara took great care of them, practically adopting them as daughters.

Sara taught them the art of baking and the girls not only learned quickly but also, as good Jews, came up with new recipes. They could soon bake many different types of bread: sweet, salty, with cheese, raisins, seasoned – a great variety. The bakery slowly gained prestige. Meanwhile Sara, at mid-morning, left one of the girls in charge of the bakery and took the other with Gabriel and the baskets of bread. They got into the small cart pulled by her black horse and travelled several miles delivering to their clients. They did one round in the morning, and another in the afternoon.

The girls had an immense affection for Gabriel, and they pampered and cared for him all day, playing with the boy as if he were their younger brother. They liked to sit with the child and pinch his cheeks, although he shook his head in protest, he always ended up laughing. It was obvious that he also had a special fondness for them, and he loved playing with them. The girls were fascinated with the little boy's beautiful blond hair and grey eyes, inherited from his mother, who Jana and Aliza thought the most beautiful woman in the world. Sara laughed at this, blushing at their flattery and telling them that they exaggerated, although they were certain it was true. As well as her extraordinary hair, eyes, and figure, she always carried a charming smile that captivated all those who knew her. The girls professed their affection to her, seeing her both as a mother figure and an older sister. In turn, she considered them her own daughters, and always called them 'her girls'.

Isaak also saw them as his own charming daughters, Gabriel's older sisters. With each passing day his fondness grew. He gave them a Jewish education, so that they would never forget their origins. They organised the girls' Bat Mitzvah with as much elegance as they could afford. The tragedy they had lived through in Odessa was left in the past; the couple took care of them as though they were their parents. The girls were beautiful in their dresses, and Sara remembered that it was thanks to a dress she had made for Isaak's sister's Bat Mitzvah, that she had met him.

With the neighbours' help, Isaak built a room connected to the hall for the two girls. With his own hands he made them beds as well as a chest of drawers for their few belongings.

"Without realising it, our family has grown." He said to his wife one night after dinner.

"You're right." She replied with a smile. "But I'm so happy, Jana and Aliza are wonderful girls, they fill our home with joy. To hear Gabriel laugh with them, when they play with our boy, is the greatest music to my ears."

Thus, the Rothmans passed their days. It was a modest life, but they were happy. Gradually, they built some economic stability, allowing them to collect some savings. Isaak, with his generosity and willingness to help those in need, earned the affection of many of Bialystok's inhabitants. Sara, in addition to her beauty and charisma, became known amongst Jews and Catholics for her support for those who were suffering.

One day when Isaak was leaving his shop, he was approached by two acquaintances, who invited him to have a drink at the bar, as they wanted to discuss an important matter. A little reluctantly, he accepted. He had already refused two of their invitations this week.

"Well, I am tired, but since you have insisted so much, I won't turn you down again."

"We're glad you've finally accepted our invitation." Replied Noam, whom Isaak hardly knew.

They went to a small bar, Noam and Moshe each ordered a beer. Isaak opted for a glass of wine. He had never had a fondness for drink.

"What is this important matter you wanted to discuss?"

"Isaak," said Noam, after checking that nobody was listening, "you have known for several months the events that are occurring in Poland."

He knew exactly what Noam referred to. Since Russia's defeat in the Crimean War and Tsar Alexander's abolition of serfdom in the Empire, Polish nationalists had been spreading anti-imperialist sentiment and wishes for independence.

"I know what you speak of, Noam, and you also know my position."

"Isaak, within a short time you have become an influential member of our community. You also have good relations with the Catholics."

At that point Moshe interrupted, also after checking for eavesdroppers:

"Poland is an oppressed nation, enslaved by the Russians. We are Jews, but also Poles."

Isaak looked down at his glass. He didn't share their nationalism. His ancestors had emigrated from Austria only two generations ago. But he didn't admit this to his interlocutors. He simply said:

"This independence movement is absurd; do you really think that the Russians will lose Poland without lifting a finger?"

"Of course not, Isaak, we know it's more complicated than saying: listen Tsar Alexander, from now on Poland will be free. But if we don't unite to fight for our country we will die as slaves to the Russians."

"That sounds very nice, Moshe," Isaak said firmly, "but I will repeat my position to you and Noam; revolution always brings blood and suffering."

"We know that!" snapped Noam, "But the alternative is slavery to a foreign power that imposes its law and taxes on us."

"A revolution has no chance of success!" said Isaak, wondering why two Jews would care so much for independence, supporting Christian Poles who had discriminated against them. Why were the Jews important for their planned freedom? He continued:

"You must abandon these notions of independence for Poles in the capital. We are too far from Warsaw and too close to the Russians."

"I don't understand you, Isaak." Said Noam. "It seems like you're afraid to face the reality of what is happening in Poland."

"No, my friend, I have no fear. What I have is a wife, two daughters, and a young son."

"We all have children. That is precisely why we fight for a free country."

Isaak finally grew frustrated, seeing his interlocutors would not see reason. Setting his glass down on the wooden table, he exclaimed:

"You are meddling in matters that don't concern you! It is not a Jewish problem. An uprising may seem romantic when for a good cause, but your enemies would not see it as a simple Polish revolt. The Russians would see it as an affront against them and their Tsar, and believe me, they could easily crush any revolution in Poland. For them, it will be war, and they will treat it as such. The only difference will be that they have well-trained and armed soldiers against civilians with farming implements. It's absurd!"

"Isaak, your attitude is exactly why Jews are discriminated against. Yes, we are Jews, but as I've said, we are Poles as well, just like everybody else. Only our religion distinguishes us, Poland is our homeland.

"Above all, I am a Jew, and I dream of Eretz Israel every night. And I tell you now, if there is a revolt, the Russians certainly will distinguish between Christian Poles and Jewish Poles. You have forgotten the sad history of our people in the land of the Tsars."

"That is precisely why the time has come for us to change our history."

"I am sorry to disappoint you, but that hour has not yet come. For that, we would first need political power, which we currently do not possess."

"If we do nothing, we will continue in slavery."

"Life is not easy for us in Russia, we Jews suffer discrimination because of the Empire's laws. But worse still would be the prisons or forced labour camps. I'm sorry, friends, I will not help in this plan that cannot succeed."

He took one last sip of his wine, stood, and bowed to the men as he told them:

"Thank you for the drink, I wish you a pleasant evening."

He turned and left the bar.

On his way home he pondered his conversation with the two men. For months, almost all of occupied Poland had been tense with longing for independence. Although the Russians ruled with an iron fist, he knew perfectly well that the Poles did not have the means to break their cruel yoke. As he had told the men, Russia would not lose Poland without putting up a fight. What could the Poles do against the imperial army? He began to fear that this tension would end up rebellion which the Russians would surely crush. Poland had no army, and there were Russian garrisons in every major city, and the public offices were held by Russians or Polish puppets. Transportation, industry, nearly everything was under their control.

Isaak worried things would get out of control and fall into a cycle of violence that would destroy his world, everything that he had built through so much work. Despite a certain amount of discrimination and abuse, they lived relatively well in Bialystok, something other inhabitants of the area, who suffered continuous persecution, could not say. After all, Poland had the largest Jewish population of the Empire, so the imperial authorities allowed some freedoms that other communities elsewhere did not enjoy.

When he arrived home, these thoughts were still on his mind. His worries showed on his face, which gave him away instantly. His wife understood that something was wrong and watched him as he hung his coat and hat.

"What happened to you?" She asked him. "Why do you look so worried?"

"I had a drink with Noam and Moshe earlier, do you remember them? They work in the furniture factory."

"Of course, Moshe's wife is a teacher at the Hebrew school. I sell bread to their cafeteria every day. Tell me, why did this drink leave you so worried?"

"What concerns me is their attitude towards recent events, and the Russians."

"Do you mean these so-called 'claims for justice'?"

"I mean much more than that, they do not simply want greater autonomy. They have greater demands and threaten revolution. They spoke of Polish independence."

"I've also heard talk of that, although according to what I've been told, everything seems concentrated in Warsaw."

"It may be more intense in the capital, but it will have repercussions throughout the country. I fear for the vulnerable, who will suffer first if anarchy spreads and the Russians crush the revolt. It would be us; we are too close to the border."

Sara considered this, looking towards the dining room where Gabriel played innocently with a wooden sledge. Isaak following his wife's gaze and a shudder ran through his body. He was conscious of their weakness, doubly vulnerable as Jews and Poles, knowing very well the persecutions his people had suffered in the Tsar's empire. Because of a damned Russian puppet, they had had to flee Ostrow, leaving everything they owned. Would they have too so again? He took a deep breath, then exclaimed:

"Oh Lord! How much longer must we suffer!"

"My love..." Sara said to him.

He realised he had been thinking aloud, a saying came to his mind: 'next year in Jerusalem.' His mind went back in time, to the day that his great-uncle, who had served under Napoleon, told him of the Egyptian campaign. He had taken the great journey to Palestine and could see Jerusalem in the distance. He had always said that for that one moment in which he contemplated the sacred city, his whole life was made worthwhile. Until the day he died, he repeated that the Jews would one day return to the land of Israel. We will always have our dream: 'next year in Jerusalem.'

Isaak left his thoughts and went into the dining room, following Sara who had already prepared dinner. As he saw him enter, Gabriel's eyes lit up.

"Father, look at my sled! Jana painted it for me today!"

"My son, come over here."

The boy approached with small jumps. When he was within reach, Isaak lifted him over his shoulders and spun him through the air, the boy screamed in excitement. His father then hugged him tenderly, saying:

"You and your mother are two wonderful gifts from God." he then addressed the two girls who were helping serve dinner "and, in his infinite generosity, also gifted me two beautiful angels who bring even more joy to my life."

The girls smiled and looked at him with affection, he returned the look. They had changed so much since that night he had found them lying in the alley. They had recovered their beauty, wearing simple but elegant dresses, their brown hair attractively tied-up, their rosy cheeks and blue eyes. But above all, they had charming smiles. He saw them as part of the family, almost as his own daughters. He couldn't imagine his home without them.

The girls had demonstrated great resilience in their strength to overcome tragedy. They were also already excellent bakers; with their initiative and imagination produced many varieties of bread. They were industrious and helped with all household work, including Sara's small garden. They were talented seamstresses, thanks to their previous skill and lessons given by Maretska, a neighbour and friend. They were intelligent, speaking Russian and Yiddish perfectly, as well as having acquired some knowledge of Polish. Finally, they were artistically talented: Jana played violin and Aliza the piano. They did not have these instruments in Isaak's modest home, but the girls had demonstrated their gifts one day when they visited the Rabbi's residence in the city. At that moment, his wife interrupted his thoughts:

"Come on, my love, dinner's getting cold."

This life and this home are paradise, Isaak thought, "I hope it will last."

The situation in Poland was getting increasingly tense, the Jews of Bialystok were divided. One side strongly supported the independence movement, longing for a free and independent country. The other, which included Isaak, preferred to maintain the uneasy peace. They continued to try to recruit him to the side of insurrection because they knew of the influence he had within the Jewish community. However, he always rejected their proposals, stating his belief that confronting Russia was suicide.

By the early Autumn of 1862, the atmosphere was so heated that Isaak considered emigrating. However, he soon gave up the thought. He knew the trauma of abandoning one's home and beginning anew elsewhere. Furthermore, his family had grown. It was no longer just Gabriel and Sara, but also Jana and Aliza, for whom he wanted stability. The business was succeeding, and he could now afford small luxuries. They were able to buy new mattresses for Gabriel and the girls, as well as rent a violin and piano so that Jana and Aliza could practice their skills. They performed small concerts which were attended by a good number of neighbours. Sara, always thrifty, had managed to save a few Roubles, with which they hoped to improve their home and eventually begin building the brick house.

He hoped that, if the rumoured insurrection occurred, it would be confined to Warsaw and the other major cities. It did not seem likely that it would consume the entire country. Truthfully, those who lived in poverty, starving and illiterate, cared little for whoever ruled them. They felt that both the Polish aristocracy and the Russians exploited them equally. Isaak was convinced that even if the Poles revolted, it would not last, as the Russians would crush them quickly. What worried him was their retaliation, which would surely affect everyone equally, regardless of whether they had taken part in the rebellion. And there was no doubt that the Jews would suffer most. What else could one expect from the Russians?

"Don't worry about it anymore, my love." Sara said to him one morning, as she served him a hot drink, "It only serves to depress you more."

"I can't help it, my love, I'm afraid it will affect us. Not only our business but also our safety."

"Well, I've heard that the Russian police are aware of the insurgents' movements. If so, we will avoid trouble before it begins."

"Yes, in fact there have already been some arrests in Warsaw, from what I've heard. I stay on the side-lines, and everyone knows my position, but I'm still worried about you, Gabriel, and the girls. I've been thinking that it might be safer to move elsewhere. Sometimes circumstances change quickly"

"And where would we go my love? Our home and businesses are here, and we are known and respected. If we leave, we would lose everything again. However, your worries have had me thinking; we must not ignore these rumours as they could soon become reality. I agree with if there is an insurrection the Russians will crush it without mercy."

"Yes, I think the same."

He then stood, and began to put on his coat, scarf, and hat. Isaak said to his wife:

"I think the coming winter will be harsh, October has barely begun and already the snowfall has started. You should wrap up well before delivering the bread."

"Of course, I will. now give me a kiss to get rid of your worry. We will be careful, my love, the most important thing is the safety of Gabriel and the girls."

Isaak kissed her and left the house thinking on his wife. God had gifted him a wonderful woman. Stood in the doorway, Sara was thinking the same thing: "*God has given me a great man.*"

Isaak kept thinking on the events which, sooner or later, would take place. "How much would this affect us?" He thought on the way to his shop, when he was approached by Noam and his brother Ramel, who was visiting Bialystok from Warsaw.

"*Shalom Aleichem*, Isaak."

"*Aleichem Shalom*, Noam. How are you Ramel? I thought you had returned to Warsaw."

"No, I will stay here a while."

"How goes your work?" Noam asked him.

"Well, very well. We have quite a few orders, which is good."

"Congratulations. And I assume you remain doubtful about the coming events?"

"If you're referring to my position, then yes, it is the same. You know I will never change my mind."

"Think about it, Isaak, maybe later you will come to regret your stance. I tell you this as a friend, when the wind changes, the people will judge where we stood.'

"And if the wind doesn't change, will we still be judged?"

"It's your decision, we will see what happens. I'll see you soon."

Isaak was bored of Noam, Moshe, and the others' insistence. He couldn't understand what made him so important to the conspirators. It felt like they needed him for more than his influence in the community. Obviously, he was respected amongst the Jews of Bialystok, or at least so he thought. But with the Catholics, he only had a few acquaintances, of which Piotr was the only one he'd call a friend.

Winter came, and it was indeed one of the coldest in memory. The Jewish community in Bialystok celebrated Hanukkah with much rejoicing, and the new year began.

'Soon my Gabriel will be five years old.' Isaak thought, one day in early January, 'I'll have to start teaching him Jewish customs this year.'

He and Sara had been teaching him some Yiddish words for a long time. The boy was smart; his intellectual development was well ahead of any other boy his age. This filled his parents with pride.

As the days passed, Isaak heard more and more of the rumoured insurrection against the Russians. His concern grew, he remained convinced that Poland did not have the strength to face the Empire and its forces. He also knew that in a confrontation, the Jews would bear the brunt of the suffering, especially in Bialystok where it was no secret the many conspired against the Tsar.

Again, he considered packing his belongings and taking his family far away, at least until the trouble was over. However, he soon abandoned the idea. Where would they go? What would they live on? It was in Bialystok where they had their livelihoods. Regardless, his anxiety persisted.

His fears were confirmed towards the end of January, when news arrived from Warsaw. He was in his shop, saying farewell to two customers to whom he had sold boots made in his workshop, when he heard a row in the street. The ladies hurried away, and Isaak felt himself shiver. He looked onto the street, and saw a crowd of people, waving the Polish eagle and chanting pro-independence slogans.

A few minutes later Noam arrived, running. He couldn't hide his excitement. In a jovial voice he exclaimed:

"Finally, Isaak, the time has come! The National Government has been proclaimed in Warsaw, independence has come, now we can be free! I told you, thank God."

Isaak looked at him sorrowfully, Noam stopped, confused.

"Why are you not happy? This will be a new beginning for Jews, we will be given rights equal to those of other Poles. Do you not understand?"

"*It is you who doesn't understand.*" Isaak thought, but he said only: "I hope things turn out alright for us."

"Oh, my friend! You don't change your mind, even when you are proved wrong."

"You can't imagine what I'd give to be wrong."

"You'll see, things will change quickly. This will be the start of a new life for us."

Indeed, things changed very quickly in Bialystok, much more quickly than Noam would have liked. Before fifteen days had passed, his corpse swung from the beam from which he had been hanged.

All of Poland would suffer for the uprising, as the Russians quickly took control of Warsaw and the other major cities, from which they began to persecute the insurgents. Although they fought on for more than a year, they inevitably imposed brutal measures, as Isaak had predicted, especially against Jews.

Unfortunately for the Rothmans, and the rest of the Jewish community, Bialystok was the first city that suffered Russia's vengeance. It not only had a strong military garrison, but it was close to the heart of the empire, and so imperial reinforcements arrived there first. Within a few days, the insurrection was under control and the Jews began to be persecuted.

At first, it seemed that the Jews would not suffer alone, however intelligence sources from the garrison and Tsarist police were informed that several leaders of the uprising had been Jewish. They were arrested one by one, within a matter of hours rumour had spread that it was an entirely Jewish plot. Neighbours and citizens began to attack their businesses and homes. Moreover, the Russian military began a propaganda campaign against them, which sought to arrest Jews so they could loot their properties.

This whirlwind of events quickly got out of control. Isaak continued to stand on the side-lines, hoping the community, Jewish and Catholic, remembered his neutrality. He had long since established a good relationship with Bialystok society, despite his religious and social position. He was respected for his generosity and willingness to help others. His renown even reached the Polish and Russian authorities; he was even known by the garrison's officers for whom he had made and repaired boots. He had designed a special process for treating leather, which produced particularly light and comfortable boots that even withstood the Winter snow. They were popular within the Russian military, which had started to use them. Since then, they had stopped calling him by name, instead referring to him as 'botinki', that is, 'boots.

His good association with the Russians, strengthened by the fact that he could fluently speak the Tsar's language, had made him popular even amongst the rank and file, and he repaired their boots at no extra cost. This had earned him the esteem of Colonel Ulyanovsk himself, the commander of the regiment, who had, on occasion, invited him for Vodka in the barrack's casino.

Despite this, Isaak's anxiety persisted as events unfolded in the city, he always arrived home with a look of worry that Sara noticed immediately. She could sense her husband's concern.

"What has happened to you, my love?" She asked on more than one occasion.

"It's nothing in particular, I'm saddened by what has happened to the city, and country."

Sara knew her husband well and could tell that it wasn't simply a matter of sadness. Nor was it nationalism; Isaak had never felt completely Polish, he was a Jew first and foremost.

"Tell me Isaak, do you think these events will affect us? I have heard about this campaign against the Jews."

"I don't know, my dear. You always know how these things start, but you can never tell how they end."

"I think we should be cautious. We've done nothing wrong; they cannot blame us. But we are still Jews."

"You're right, I will be careful. Where's Gabriel, and the girls?"

"The boy is in bed; he played all day and is very tired. I gave him dinner and he went straight to sleep. Jana and Aliza are at Maretska's for their sewing lessons."

He went up to Gabriel's small room. It was simple, but Sara had decorated it with great care. It was almost an extension of the main bedroom. By the lamplight, he gazed at his son; his blond hair was bright, his small eyes were closed, and his gentle breathing indicated that he was sleeping peacefully. He looked at him tenderly, his heart full of love. He then stroked the boy's head lightly, before kissing his forehead. His wife entered the room, putting her arms around his shoulders, and the two continued to watch the boy.

"His birthday is the day after tomorrow." Sara said in a low voice.

"Yes, you're right." Isaak almost whispered. "Five years old, time goes by so quickly."

"I'm preparing a small celebration with a cake and gifts. He already knows about it and is excited for the day to come."

Isaak smiled lovingly, but at that moment felt a chill run through his body, like a premonition. His wife felt him tremble.

"What's wrong, my love?"

"Come." He said, taking her by the arm and leading her into the hall. Sara looked at him in surprise.

"Tell me, what's happened?"

"Sara, our Gabriel is an innocent and defenceless child, I couldn't bear it if something were to happen to him."

"What do you mean? You're scaring me."

"These recent events in the city, I don't know what's going to happen, but we can't take any chances. You said it yourself, we are guilty of nothing, yet we are still Jews. I don't want to endanger the children, or you."

She looked at him, considering his words. Isaak continued.

"We have to go! We must leave, we cannot take this risk. We cannot remain in Bialystok."

She said nothing but nodded at her husband's words.

"Tomorrow I will close the shop. My friends can look after the tools and goods until we return. It's as my grandmother Martha used to say: *'these are the kinds of things we can't predict, we'll to things better next time.'*"

"Where will we go?" Sara asked.

"I don't know yet, we'll decide later. Maybe Austria, my uncles still live in Vienna, although I have not seen them for many years and have lost contact, we can ask for them in the Jewish community."

They were both silent. Soon Jana and Aliza arrived; they immediately noticed the worry on Isaak's face, who usually greeted them affectionately. He invited them to sit at the table.

"Jana, Aliza, we have to talk."

"I think we know what about," exclaimed Jana, "the insurrection."

Aliza nodded, confirming their awareness of the situation.

"Exactly." Said Isaak. "You must understand that things could soon get out of hand and become dangerous for us. We have decided to leave Bialystok."

The two girls looked at each other, then turned their eyes to Sara, as if waiting for confirmation. She simply nodded.

"Where will we go?" Aliza asked.

"We don't know yet, but somewhere far from here."

"And when do we leave?"

"Tomorrow, you must pack your things early in the morning. Take only the essentials."

"We understand." Jana said, then continued, "we will be happy wherever we go, as long as we're by your side. We just don't want to leave you."

Isaak's gaze softened. He opened his arms and exclaimed:

"Come here, my dear girls."

They came closer. Sara did same and the four of them shared a tender embrace.

"We will never part." Said Isaak. "The five of us will always stay together."

They then sat at the table while Sara and Aliza served dinner. No one spoke a word while they are. They went to bed straight after they had finished, but the couple could not fall asleep. Isaak was planning their flight from the city in his mind, deciding on the best exit. Noticing his wife was still awake, he quietly said to her:

"Tomorrow, before dawn, I will go to the warehouse to organise my things. I will speak with Piotr and have him keep the goods and tools from the workshop. As soon as the bank open, I will withdraw our savings. In the meantime, sort out everything with the girls, and pack the most important things from our home that will fit in our cart."

"I'll do as you've asked."

"As soon as I return, we will leave. We'll go South via the Lublin road."

At that moment Sara got up and put on her shawl, her loose blonde hair almost reached down to her waist, and she was resplendent in the dim lamplight.

"Where are you going?" Her husband asked.

"To pray."

He got up and they prayed together, then got back into bed. Even though the hearth was lit, the cold was bitter, so they hurriedly covered themselves with the blankets. Neither slept well.

As he had decided, Isaak woke early, long before dawn. He dressed quickly, as Sara got out of bed and made him a strong coffee. He went to see Gabriel. The boy was still fast asleep; he watched him tenderly and did something universal to parents: tucked him into bed. He blew him a kiss and headed to the girls' room, who also slept. He then returned to the kitchen, finished his coffee in three gulps, kissed his wife, and made for the door.

"It's time to wake the girls and start packing." He said, turning his head.

He opened the door, and immediately shut it again. An icy blizzard blew snow into the room. Sara looked at him questioningly.

"Wait." He said.

He returned to the main bedroom, pushed the bed aside, and knelt down. From beneath the floorboards, he took a metal chest, and he took the money that was kept there, most of Sara's savings. He then put the chest back in place, covering the cache, and handed the money to his wife.

"Keep this in a leather bag, hidden under your clothes. On the way I will take out my savings from the bank, and you will keep what we had at home. It's better not to put all our eggs in one basket.

He kissed his wife once more, then stepped onto the icy street, heading towards his warehouse. It was still dark when he entered; he lit two lights and began organising the goods.

"When dawn comes, I will go to Piotr's house and ask him to help move these goods to his warehouse." He murmured aloud.

He then continued packing the shoes, women's boots, and children's shoes. Once finished, he went to his workshop and packed his best tools and leathers. He was so absorbed in his work that he did not notice that the sun had risen, nor the commotion building at the end of the street. At that moment, there was a loud knock at the warehouse door. He was about to open when the knock sounded again.

"Isaak, open, open quick!"

"I'm coming, I'm coming! He opened the door and there stood, out of breath and looked distressed, Joshua, Noam's brother.

"What is it?" Isaak asked.

"It's terrible! Last night the Russians arrested Noam, by dawn he was hanging from a beam in the square."

He started to cry, then continued:

"We must flee, Isaak! They are arresting every Jew. The citizens have gone mad, our own neighbours are pointing out Jewish homes to soldiers, then looting them after they are arrested and taken away."

Isaak realised there was no point in looking for Piotr anymore, nor in going to the bank to withdraw his savings. He had to return home and flee as soon as possible with Sara and the girls.

"Come on!" He said to Joshua, going out into the street. He saw a crowd approaching, led by Russian soldiers. "Come on," he repeated, "We must flee!"

He saw that the people were pointing at them, and they started running. The soldiers fired and Joshua stumbled and fell. Isaak could see the snow turn red, but he could not stop. He ran with all the strength his legs could muster. He turned the corner, only to find another mob with soldiers. One of them shouted:

"He's a Jew! He's a Jew!"

A soldier aimed at him; Isaak knew he could do nothing. He stopped and raised his hands.

There was a loud knock at the door, Sara and the girls were still packing their few things, first of which was, of course, the silver menorah. The last things she packed were the gifts she planned to give Gabriel for his birthday tomorrow.

"Sara, Sara!" They yelled from behind the door.

She ran to open it, there stood Maretska and her son, a boy of about 14 years. Her neighbour was a Catholic, but she had always shown great sympathy for the Jews. Sara felt distress:

"What's happened?

"Sara, it's a disaster! The soldiers are arresting and killing Jews, Isaak has been captured!"

Sara felt the ground open beneath her feet and she felt like she was falling into a pit. Maretska took her arm before she fell, and the boy helped hold her up.

"Help me!" Maretska said to her son, as she took Sara into the house and sat her in a chair. She then said to Jana, "Bring her a glass of water!"

When Sara could finally speak, she asked, full of anguish:

"Where is he? Do you know where they have him?"

"No, Sara, the news just came to me from my son. Many Jews have been arrested and the people are looting houses and shops. The soldiers and police are not only allowing it, but they are participating in the looting."

"This cannot be, my God! It cannot be true; I must look for my husband." She tried to stand from the chair, but Maretska stopped her.

"No, Sara, that's impossible. It's as if the people are possessed, pointing our Jews. It would be suicide."

"But I have to look for my husband, Maretska, do you know where they took him?"

"No, I don't know, but the worst you do is run into the street. It's like a revolution out there, you must think of your child."

Sara began to cry and looked towards the hall where Gabriel was standing, looking upon the scene with confusion. She called to him, taking him in her arms whilst crying inconsolably.

"The best thing to do is wait for the frenzy to die down," Maretska said, "then we can try to find where your husband is."

Sara nodded and took a deep breath, then closed her eyes and continued to weep. Her friend approached and ran her hands over the woman's shoulders, for whom the world had just fallen apart. The two girls approached as well.

'My Isaak,' Sara thought, 'has never hurt anyone, just the opposite; he always tried to help. And now they've arrested him and who knows what they will do to him, Oh, God, why is life so cruel?'

In the afternoon, once the situation had calmed a little, Sara called to Gabriel, dressed him well to protect from the cold, took him by the arm and, accompanied by Maretska and the girls, went to the Russian headquarters. By the barracks entrance was a crowd of mostly women, pleading for information about their loved ones. Sara learned that several Jews had been killed, including Isaak's acquaintances, Noam and Moshe. Her despair enveloped her.

Despite their begging, the women could find out nothing. The soldiers at the entrance were like statues, undaunted by the crowd. Night fell and they had gained no news of Isaak. Maretska had to return home, since her two little girls were left alone. Sara sent Jana and Aliza with Maretska but kept little Gabriel with her. She then went to Piotr's house, to plead for his help. He was not a Jew and could easily search for news. Piotr and his wife welcomed the heartbroken Sara in, offering her and Gabriel a hot drink.

"Piotr." she said, "You must help me, I beg you."

"Sara, the situation is complicated, but I promise I will do all I can."

"You can talk to Prefect Marinowsky, Isaak saved his son's life, remember? He covered the cost of transportation and surgery for the boy in Warsaw. You remember, right? At the time Marinowsky wasn't a prefect or anything, he was poor and if it hadn't been for my husband, that boy would have died."

Piotr turned his head to the side and placed a hand on his temple, then ran it through his hair. His wife, Malka, stared at him, waiting for him to speak to Sara, rather, to tell her.

"What is it, Piotr?" Sara asked, "Why don't you talk to him?"

"Oh, Sara ... Marinowsky advocated these arrests of Jews. He not only betrayed Isaak and the others, but also directed the soldiers to their properties and incited the crowd to loot the warehouses, including your husband's."

Sara collapsed into the seat, if it wasn't for Malka, she would have fallen to the ground.

The next day, of course, they couldn't celebrate Gabriel's birthday. Sara left Jana and Aliza with Maretska and returned to Piotr's house, who had heard from Isaak. He had managed to speak with a lieutenant from the garrison, who informed him that some detained had been sentenced to death and would be executed that day, while others would be deported to Siberia.

"We have to go to the barracks!" Sara said, "I must speak with that lieutenant!"

Piotr's face indicated it would be useless, but he said nothing and accompanied her. After trying for more than an hour, they managed to speak with the officer. He was so young that his face was still covered in spots. Sara begged him to let her speak with Colonel Ulyanovsk, as she knew that he liked Isaak.

"I'm sorry, ma'am," replied the officer, "Colonel Ulyanovsk and his general staff left urgently for Warsaw, the command is now held by the officers who arrived two days ago from Minsk."

"Please, help me lieutenant, I beg you!" Sara implored him. "My husband is innocent; he never did any harm or conspire against anyone."

"I'm very sorry, ma'am, I can't do anything. I'm just a lieutenant."

Sara was powerless. The next morning, she learned that Isaak would be deported to Siberia, along with eight other Jews from Bialystok that they could not prove had participated in the uprising. However, as put by the ruthless Colonel, recently arrived from Minsk: *Because of these warnings, the Poles will never think of rebelling again. We will send them to a labour camp in the Motherland, far away from this backward place.*

The prisoners were chained and led through the snow to a stable on the outskirts of Wasilkow. There, they were joined by seven other Jews from neighbouring towns. Sara, with Gabriel in arms, went with the other women to the stable, to try to see her husband. It was a hellish journey through the snow, they were harassed by villagers who attacked and robbed them, taking what little they had. They did not even take pity on the little ones, Gabriel had his tiny shoes taken from him, so Sara was forced to tear strips from her clothes to wrap around the boy's feet.

3

David remained silent. His grandfather looked into the distance, towards the Puente de las Mujeres, occasionally sipping the mate that Martha had prepared for him. When he had met her, the drink had seemed horrible, but he now liked it more than he could say. The sky was blue, and an aeroplane flew high above, leaving a trail in its wake which slowly faded.

"What do you think, son?" Eitan said.

"Life's so sad sometimes, right grandpa? Poor Gabriel..."

"Yes David, life is often sad and unfair, but in the end, God never forgets his people. Now you know of your ancestor, Isaak, a good man and a good Jew. He was married to a good woman, Sara."

"And her name was beautiful, very Jewish."

Eitan was glad to hear his grandson say that, and replied:

"Very well, now I'll tell you more of the origins of our people."

"Yes grandpa! I'm really interested to know."

The old man went to the study's library and, from a lower shelf, took a heavy book with a green cover. David looked at him in surprise, and asked:

"Grandpa, is that a Bible?"

"Yes, my son, you remember I told you that the Bible tells the history of the Jewish people. The sacred book of the Christians tells of the lives of the sons of Israel.

He sat, and called David to him:

"Come here to my side. I want to show you some things from this book."

David approached, curious. Eitan opened the Bible and began to search, turning the pages and tracing paragraphs with his finger, until he reached Genesis 15:18, and read:

"Then the Lord made a covenant with Abram and said, 'To your descendants I give this land, from the Wadi of Egypt to the great river, the Euphrates."

He put the Bible aside and addressed his grandson:

"You know, as all Christians should know, that Abram or Abraham is the father of the Jewish people. And you have just heard from the same Bible shows how God decided to gift a part of the land to his descendants to the Jews. That part of land was even greater than that which we have received on which to found the state of Israel."

David thought for a moment. The boy, very intelligent, understood what his grandfather was trying to tell him. He looked him in the eye and said firmly:

"I understand grandpa, the Christian Bible itself clearly shows that God gave the land of Israel to the Jews. It isn't true that we have taken it from other peoples, it always belonged to us."

Eitan felt great satisfaction and smiled broadly.

"You are an intelligent boy, you've understood perfectly. That paragraph is irrefutable proof that you can use next time someone dares to tell you that the Jews robbed other peoples of their land."

"Yes, grandpa!"

"But there's more, David. We will read more of the Bible, so that we aren't limited to Jewish texts. Look for yourself in the Fourth Book of Kings."

He passed the heavy book to his grandson, who began to search.

"I've found it grandpa."

"Now, go to chapter 17, verse 24, and read."

David read:

"And in the place of the children of Israel, the king of the Assyrians, the people of Babylon were brought and put in the cities of Samaria."

"Do you see, David? Other peoples took the territory from the children of Israel."

"Yes, grandpa, I understand."

"Well then," Eitan continued, "powerful empires took our land from us, but the Jews would return because we never renounced it, nor will we ever renounce it. The book of Ezra, from that Bible in your hand, shows how, before Alexander the Great conquered Asia, the Jews returned to Jerusalem, to Judea and Samaria. We recovered what belonged to us many centuries before."

"What a beautiful story, grandpa."

"I'm delighted that you like it, my boy. Especially now that you understand the importance of what you read in this book. Learning the history of your ancestors should put your doubts to rest."

Eitan motioned for the boy to put the Bible back in its place. As David did so, he continued:

"I've given you a few examples, but you should know that the Bible is full of references just like them. Not only did God give Israel to the Jews, but we never abandoned it. Even though we were violently forced from our home, we never stopped to dream of returning. That thought has always given us hope, and for that reason we have always found our way home. Don't forget that we call ourselves Jews because we are the original inhabitants of Judea."

"Grandpa, I really like talking to you about these things. You know so much about our history and it interests me to learn it through you."

"Well, I am pleased that you are interested in your origins. Knowing them, you should never feel inferior to others, rather you should feel proud of your roots."

"Of course, grandpa! I will no longer let them humiliate me for being who I am."

"Exactly, you can see that what they tell you about Jews isn't true. So, let's review; you now know that we are the oldest people on the face of the earth, that also we are the only people with a written history from our origins, and that those Christians who mock you for being Jewish would have no religion were it not for Judaism. Do you agree?"

"That's right grandpa!"

"Now you also know that it's not true that we have taken the land of Israel from other peoples, in fact, it has always been ours from the beginning. Rather, others have taken it from us, but we have always recovered it. You cannot steal what belongs to you, you are only recover it from those who took it from you. That is your right, don't you think?"

"Of course, grandpa!"

"So, what's the score now?"

"Four nil! Four nil, grandpa!"

"Excellent!" Eitan exclaimed enthusiastically, "As you can see, we're on the winning team, nobody can look down on us. Now let's continue with the story of your ancestors. Yes?"

"Of course," said the boy, sitting next to the old man.

4

Sara moved like a sleepwalker, amongst the other women returning to Bialystok. The snows had stopped, but their march was hindered by the thick layer that covered the field, hiding the road from view. They were guided by the wooden houses in the distance, some of which were burning, sending clouds of smoke towards the sky. All the women were weeping, from despair and injustice. With swollen eyes and red noses, several carried children, including Sara who held Gabriel in her arms, trying to give him warmth.

As they approached the town, they could smell burning wood and smoke which made them cover their noses. A few hundred metres further, several houses were burning, including Sara and Isaak's. She took the boy in her arms and quickened her pace, approaching the remains of her house, from which flames showed over the bushes in front which she had planted years ago. The heat stopped her from getting too close. She lowered Gabriel to the ground, covered her face and began to cry inconsolably. Seeing the home, she and Isaak had built with so much effort and sacrifice was very painful. It had been a happy home and she felt as if the bond with her husband had been cut at its root.

"Sara, Sara!" She heard someone call out to her. It was Maretska, her kind neighbour, who was hurrying towards her.

"Come with me!" Maretska said, taking Sara and Gabriel's hands.

She let herself be taken away, like a spirit that simply drifted onward. Maretska led them to her house, which was more modest than that of Isaak and Sara, but also decorated in good taste. Maretska sat her on a bench in the living room and placed Gabriel on the carpet, near a small stove that provided the room with some heat. Their neighbour brought a blanket to cover the child's body, then put a kettle on the stove and started to heat some water. Sara remained motionless, staring fixedly at the opposite wall. Her tears had already dried, and she sat as if she were completely dumb.

Maretska offered her a porcelain cup of hot tea, but she remained static. Suddenly, she blurted out:

"The girls! Where are the girls?"

She looked both ways, as though searching for them and then exclaimed:

"Jana, Aliza!" She turned to her friend in anguish, "Maretska, where are my girls?"

"Calm down Sara, I don't know. I think they fled. We were all together here, then we heard angry voices. I looked out and saw a crowd approaching along the path, in fear I hid my two little ones under the bed. When I returned here, Jana and Aliza had disappeared. I went out looking for them, calling repeatedly, but I did not see them, nor did they answer. At that moment those maddened savages entered your house and began to destroy it and setting it alight. I had to lock myself in until they were gone."

"You don't know where they went?"

"No, I looked around for them around here, asked for them, but nobody could tell me anything. One thing I'm sure of is that those bastards that destroyed your home didn't find them, the neighbours assured me of that."

Sara collapsed and began to weep again.

"Have your drink, it will do you good," her friend said, offering the tea.

She looked up, sad and melancholic, at Maretska while she insisted that she drink. Finally, Sara took a sip, and said:

"How can this be? What's happened?"

"Oh, my dear friend, it's terrible! Hordes of barbarians came and attacked Jewish houses, including yours and Wosolvsky's. They completely looted them and then set them alight. They seemed mad, we had to hide in fear. Some neighbours fled in terror and their houses were ransacked as well. Can you believe it? Despite being poor and having little worth stealing, they still came and took chairs, tables, and straw mattresses."

Sara began to picture all their belongings at home, they were trivial, but had been collected with Isaak. She would miss most of all the religious items and gifts she had carefully packed to celebrate Gabriel's birthday. Thinking about them, she burst into tears again. Maretska put her arm around her friend's shoulders, while saying:

"I'm sorry, I know this isn't fair. I don't understand how this could happen to people as good and honest as yourselves."

Sara looked at her with deep sadness, "I don't know what I'm going to do, I don't know how to survive this," she said, lowering her head even further.

"I wish I could help you, my dear friend, but the only thing that I can recommend is that you must leave Bialystok as you're not safe here. A wild hysteria has been unleashed against the Jews, they blame you for the insurrection and all the region's misfortunes."

All Sara could do was listen.

"You have to leave Bialystok as soon as you can," Maretska continued, "at least until things calm down."

"I have nowhere to go, Maretska, I'm all alone."

"All I know is that you must leave. The people have lost their reason and their principles. You are Jewish, and at them moment they are merciless against you.

"But what else can they take from me?" she said between sobs, "I've lost everything, my husband, my girls, my home..."

"You must understand," Maretska said seriously, "you are Jewish and are therefore at risk, but you are also a beautiful young woman. They will not hesitate to take advantage of you. This may sound harsh, but it's true. Not just the Russians but look at what your neighbours have done to your home."

'*And my husband*', she thought, remembering Piotr's words when he told her Marinowsky, the very man Isaak had helped so much, had been the one to hand him over to the Russians.

"You understand me, Sara? You can't take any chances," Maretska continued, "think of little Gabriel."

"Yes, Maretska, you're right. But perhaps Piotr and his husband can help me?"

"You must go to them immediately."

"I will," she exclaimed, getting up from the bench.

"My son will accompany you to his house." Maretska said.

"Thank you, Maretska," she said, hugging her friend, "I will never forget what you have done for me and my little son,"

"Don't worry, I greatly appreciate how much you and Isaak supported me, especially after my husband's death."

Sara tidied her clothes a little, then remembered that Gabriel still had no shoes. She checked the strips of cloth that covered his feet. Maretska noticed and fetched a pair of dancing shoes from another room.

"I've kept these since I was a child, and dreamed of becoming a dancer," she said to Sara, "they aren't the best for the winter cold, and they may be a little big, but they're better than cloth."

They both fit them for Gabriel, inserting pieces of wool so that they would fit.

"Thank you, my friend," Sara said again, embracing her. "I just need one more favour, if you learn anything of my girls, please let me know, I beg you."

"You can be sure I will."

"Thank you for everything."

"Wait!" Maretska said, "I have something to give you." She turned and took a cloth bag from the table, which Sara had not noticed.

"In the disorder before they started looting your house, my son salvaged this." She stretched out her arm, handing Sara the bag.

Sara recognised it immediately; inside the sack were Isaak's Menorah, Tefillin, and Tallit. She couldn't hold in her tears; she could have had no better reminder of her husband.

The two friends embraced for the last time and said a reluctant farewell, hoping to meet again in less turbulent times. Leaving, Sara felt an icy blast which made her shiver. It had begun to snow again, and the street was quickly being covered. She shielded Gabriel as best she could and quickened her pace. Maretska's son led the way. It was past four, the pale sun was setting, and the dark made the journey more difficult.

By the time they reached Piotr's house it was almost completely dark. The street was deserted, and one could see dim lamplight from a few of the houses. An icy breeze was blowing through their clothes, Gabriel shivered with cold, despite Sara holding him tightly to her.

"We're here, ma'am," Maretska's son said, "I have to return home before it gets even darker."

"Yes, my son," Sara replied, "go home. I will never forget what you and your mother have done for us."

"My mother asked me to give this to you," said the boy, taking a bag out of his beneath woollen coat. He handed it over and turned, leaving quickly. Sara opened it, inside there were some loaves of bread a sponge cake, plums, and dried apples. She looked toward where the boy had gone to thank him, but he had already disappeared into the darkness.

That night when she opened the bag to share the food, Sara noticed a small pouch inside. There she found a crucifix with a chain, and a note. She unfolded the paper and read its contents, her eyes brimming with tears.

'My dear friend, I know that you will never use this crucifix, but please keep it as a token of my gratitude and so that you do not forget the many Christians who love Jews. Our religions are sisters. I will always remember you with love.'

Maretska.

Sara treasured that crucifix for the rest of her life. That object, a Christian symbol, has remained in a Jewish household for generations, occupying a special place. It serves to remind how, just as all men are brothers, so too are Judaism and Christianity.

Piotr and his wife were very generous to Sara and Gabriel. They were grateful to the Rothmans as two years ago, they had supported them when their sawmill was destroyed by a chance fire. Isaak raised funds from the entire community of Bialystok to enable them to rebuild their business. He also organised a group of men who, with Piotr, rebuilt the sawmill. Sara also donated 10% of the profits from her bakery for three months, so that they could recover the tools they had lost during the fire.

The persecution of Jews continued in the city. The Russian authorities had also imposed a strict curfew, so Sara remained in the house without even looking out of the door. Malka, Piotr's wife, had a great affection for her friend and tried to take her mind off her loss by talking with her, but Sara could not recover from the loss of Isaak and the girls. For days, Piotr had tried to find news of them, but nobody could help. He had gone to Maretska's house, hoping that Jana and Aliza had returned there, but was surprised to find the place empty. He asked the neighbours what had happened and discovered that the night after the destruction of Isaak's home, the vandals returned to attack the houses of those who were thought to have helped the Jews. Maretska, her adolescent son and two little girls had managed to take refuge in a friend's house, just before the mob arrived. Although they did not set fire to the house, everything inside was stolen or destroyed. The following day Maretska and her family had fled. No one had seen her since.

Piotr kept looking for the girls but found nothing. It was as though the earth had swallowed them. Sara feared the worst, but he told her that if they had died, he would certainly have found out by now. He tried to comfort her by reminding her how smart and resourceful they were, and that they already knew what it meant to flee and save themselves. More than likely, he said, they would surely reappear when things had settled down.

Sara was not comforted. At night she found it hard to sleep at night and cried silently so as not to wake little Gabriel. The boy was wise beyond his years and could understand his mother's suffering. Once, she was crushed to hear him say:

"Mother, I too miss father a lot and would love to see him again."

She felt a knife in her heart and burst into tears. Malka came in running and hugged her. Sara said:

"Malka, my dear friend, you can't imagine the pain I feel. I will never recover from the loss of my loved ones. I don't know why it has to be this way, I've lost the kindest man in the world and the most beautiful and tender girls on earth."

"I know, Sara, but you must not lose hope. You don't know for certain that your husband is dead, there is no confirmation of it."

"Oh, Malka! You know as well as I do that those taken to the Siberian camps never return alive."

Malka knew it, having seen it happen first-hand to one of her brothers. In Russian-occupied Poland, everyone knew that those taken away to Siberia never came back, much less if they had been accused of opposing the Empire.

The days passed and, although Sara did not recover from her grief, she understood that she could not stay there forever. She did not want to abuse Piotr and Malka's generosity and was aware that her presence put them at risk. If the Russians discovered that they were sheltering the Jewish wife of a convicted rebel, they would be in great danger.

More than a month had passed since she had been welcomed into their home. She tried to stay on, in the hope that Jana and Aliza would reappear, but knew that she would have to start a new life far from Bialystok. This was not because of the persecution, in fact, having realised that they were a community essential for commerce in the city, the Russians had softened their anti-Judaism. It was because Sara could not bear to live in the place, she had shared with her beloved husband for the past five years.

One night, she broached the subject with Piotr and Malka. After dinner they sat in the living room, where Sara addressed her hosts.

"I've been meaning to talk to you about something which can wait no longer."

The couple's expression indicated that Sara would not have to say much, they knew what she meant. She went straight to the point.

"Gabriel and I cannot stay in this house forever. I'll never be able to pay you back for the kindness you have shown us, but I think that the time has come for me to continue with my life, and I want it to be far from Bialystok."

Piotr finished lighting his pipe, took three puffs, and exclaimed:

"Sara, you know you can stay with us as long as you want. This is, and always will be, your home. It's no secret that we had a great love for Isaak. I would have wished to be, as a Christian, half as good as he was a Jew."

His words in the past tense were like needles to Sara, as they confirmed, so casually, that her beloved husband had ceased to exist. She managed to reply:

"I know, Piotr, that you were always a good friend to my husband."

"You can stay here as long as you like. If you decide to leave, then you are always welcome to return."

"Thank you, Piotr, and you Malka. You can't imagine the gratitude I feel for you, but I hope you understand when I say that I want to leave the city."

"We understand you perfectly, you don't owe us an explanation. But where are you planning to go?"

"I'll go to Lublin, there's a bakery on Okopowa Street. It's Jewish, and I'm sure they will give me work delivering bread, just as I did here."

"But are you sure they will give you a job?"

"I can't be, but as I am a Jew, I hope they'll help me."

"And in the meantime, what will you live on?"

"I have a small amount saved up. I'll also go to the bank; Isaak had an account that has the rest of our capital. In his absence, as his wife, I and our son become his beneficiaries. It isn't much, a few days before he was arrested Isaak had bought supplies for the whole summer, but even a few roubles will be a great help to us."

Piotr took a deep breath, then exhaled gently. He approached the poor woman.

"Sara, things have changed since the insurrection. The Russians have occupied the city, and one of their first acts was to confiscate Jewish savings. You can be sure that the money Isaak had in the bank is already in their hands."

Upon hearing his words, Sara rose and looked towards the window, as if gazing at the pattern on the curtain. She murmured:

"Why are the Russians doing this to us?"

"Unfortunately, Sara, it's not just the Russians. The truth is that unscrupulous individuals have taken advantage of the situation to steal the possessions of Jews, and even from Christians, you ..." Piotr hesitated, before continuing, "You should know that Isaak's warehouse and workshop have been appropriated."

"What? Who owns it now? The Russians as well?"

"No, Sara, sooner or later you were going to find out ... it was Marinowsky."

"Marinowsky? That damned rat!"

Piotr and Malka were surprised by Sara's words, she usually spoke in an elegant way.

"Yes, the warehouse was looted by the mob, but the workshop and tools were saved, as well as the supplies from the warehouse. It was because of Marinowsky and his accomplices, without a doubt. That beast wanted your husband's business.

Sara clasped her hands, held them to her face and remained silent. Her hosts did not want to interrupt her thoughts. At that moment, Gabriel entered. He had been in the next room playing with a little wooden cart that Piotr had given him. The boy approached the man, showing how a wheel had come off his toy. As he became the centre of attention, Sara and Malka watched as Piotr mended the toy while tenderly stroking the boy's hair.

Piotr and Malka had become very fond of the boy. The couple lived alone, despite having had two children. Their beautiful daughter had died aged 14 from cholera, and their tall and strong son wanted to study engineering, but the Russians had forced him into the army at the outbreak of the Crimean war. He fell in action of the Battle of Almá River when he was merely 19 years old. His parents were not even able to give him a decent burial.

Finally, Sara rose from her seat. She approached Piotr and Malka, took them both by the hand, and said:

"You will always be in my thoughts and in my prayers. You have been so kind to Gabriel and me, but I must leave you. I will start preparations for my journey."

Having said this, she left the room and began to pack the small case Malka had given her with their few belongings – a dress and some other things of hers and Gabriel. Of course, in a special place, she also included the religious items including the small crucifix Maretska had given her.

Sara had planned to leave three days later, after Shabbat, since she had someone, she wanted to visit before leaving the city. She knew it was a risk, but felt it was necessary out of duty.

The next morning, she got ready, putting on the dress that Maretska had given her which she had altered to her size. She put on her shoes, covered her blonde hair with a scarf, took her coat, and headed towards a house on Zamenshofa Street. Once there, she rang the bell and a servant soon came to the door.

"What can I do for you, Madam?" The man asked her. He ran his eyes over her, lingering on her face. He could clearly see that her coat was not particularly elegant, but her bearing and beauty were not unnoticed. As such, he treated her as a young lady.

"I wish to speak with Mr Marinowsky."

"The prefect is not at home, Madam."

"Would you be so kind as to tell me where I could find him?"

The servant was overawed by presence of the woman. He stared at her, dumbstruck.

"Sir?"

"Yes, of course, he went out a few minutes ago to the shoe shop."

"Which one?"

"The one on Lipowa Street."

Sara felt like she had been stabbed through the heart. What Piotr had told her was true, the wretch had seized Isaak's warehouse. She wanted to cry, but her rage overcame sadness.

"If you want, you could come in and wait. I can offer you tea."

"No, thank you, and good morning." She replied, turning, and heading towards the shoe shop which was five streets away.

It was hard for her to enter the shop; she couldn't help feeling Isaak's absence. She paused a moment before going through the door, taking a deep breath. Behind the counter was a boy, who turned pale at the sight of her. He had evidently recognised her, but she could not remember having seen him before.

"Good morning." She said dryly and with a certain haughtiness. "Is Mr Marinowsky here?"

"Yes ma'am, he's in the back room. I'll call him."

It wasn't necessary; at that moment Marinowsky entered the room. Upon seeing Sara, he was paralysed with shock. However, he quickly regained his composure.

"Hello, Sara! How are you?"

"Please, don't mock me."

"What a surprise, I didn't expect to see you here," Marinowsky replied, ignoring her plea.

"Yes, I imagine you weren't expecting it, especially after everything that's happened." She said, looking at him with contempt, "Or should I say, after everything you've done."

"Wait, Sara, let me explain," he replied, and then addressed the assistant, ordered him: "go for a walk, leave us alone, and close the door when you leave."

Clearly very nervous; Marinowsky was a physically unpleasant little man. Shorter than Sara, extremely thin, with a receding forehead, hooked nose, and ridiculously thin moustache which almost gave him the appearance of a caricature.

As soon as the clerk man left, Marinowsky went to the door and released the latch, then turned to Sara who stood by the counter.

"Look, Sara, you may not think it, but I'm glad to see you."

"The pleasure is all yours, Mr Marinowsky."

"You don't have to be so aggressive. Really, I am pleased that you are here."

He directed his beady eyes towards the woman, looking her over from head to toe, slowly and deliberately. Sara felt uncomfortable, and decided to get to the point:

"My visit here is not a courtesy."

"All right then, let's talk, but sit down first." Said the little man, pointing to a chair.

"This won't take long, I just want to tell you one thing, Mister prefect the thief."

"Wait, wait!" he reacted, "I'm no thief! How dare you!"

"Are you not?"

"What you have been told is a lie, nothing more than common slander."

"If it's a lie, then why are you here? It's obvious you've taken over my husband's business."

"It's not what you think, my dear Sara."

"Don't call me 'dear'!" Sara shouted back, "I already told you not to mock me!"

"Please, calm down, this meeting should be pleasant."

Sara laughed; she couldn't believe this man's attitude. *Pleasant meeting? Could he be any more cynical?* Meanwhile Marinowsky came closer, and said to her:

"I only saved your husband's business."

"Ah, you saved it?"

"Yes, so that it did not fall into the hands of the Russians."

"Do you take me for a fool? What is certain is that you did not save the business, rather you appropriated it, which is very different. The only one to have saved anything was Isaak, who had saved your son's life. What a lovely way to pay him back."

"For which I am grateful to him."

"And how you show it! You are despicable to have committed such a crime against the man who helped you in the past. You should have shown gratitude and sympathy towards my husband rather than treat him so appallingly!"

Marinowsky looked at her fixedly, then approached closer the woman standing next to the counter, whispering sweetly:

"The truth is all I have ever had for Isaak was envy. I have always envied him his woman."

She was aghast, she couldn't believe what the man was saying.

"How dare you say that!"

"I say it because it's true, I have always liked you very much, Sara."

"Who do you think you are, to disrespect me like that?"

"Don't be naive! Look at your position, you are a Jewish widow without the means to support yourself, much less your son. I can provide you with everything you need."

He came so close that Sara could feel his breath against her face, she stepped back, repulsed, and stumbled against the counter. Marinowsky came even closer to her, losing all composure. He pinned her against the furniture and put his arm around her waist, then lowering his hand even further. With the other hand he held her face forcefully. She struggled as best she could.

"Let me go, you brute! How dare you!" She said as she tried to break free, scratching at his face. But the man seemed not to care, he was possessed.

"Ah! I find you irresistible, Sara, I have always wanted to caress you and kiss you. Come, don't be silly," Marinowsky replied, trying to kiss her lips.

She could feel that the man was deceptively strong beneath his thin frame. He had her trapped her tightly with one hand, whilst with the other he unbuttoned her coat, groping her breasts through the dress. Sara felt like she was being suffocated.

"Enough, enough, let me be, you beast!"

She struggled to break free but was powerless. She fought to free her hands and threw her head back, turning it this way and that to prevent him from kissing her. Marinowsky drew her towards him and pressed his repulsive body against hers, attempting to untie the ribbons from the top of her dress. In the struggle Sara's scarf came off, and beautiful blonde hair fell down her shoulders. Marinowsky was incensed by the sight of it and began to stroke it with one hand. She saw the opportunity and balled her fist, reached her arm back and, drawing upon an unknown strength, struck the wretch on the nose. Marinowsky stumbled, releasing her, and brought his hand towards his face, from which blood began to flow. In that second Sara took advantage of his confusion and, without hesitation, kneed him hard between the legs. Marinowsky gasped and hunched over. Sara knew she would not get another chance, and aimed a kick at his face, the heel of her shoe colliding with his nose, causing him excruciating pain that knocked him to the ground.

"You are an evil beast, and one day you will pay for your crimes!" she shouted at him. "Now you will hear what I came to tell you. Yes, I may be a Jewish widow, but you are the most heartless man ever to walk the earth and I swear that the day will come when I make you pay for what you have done. I will return for what you have stolen from my husband."

Marinowsky tried to stand, but she grabbed the wretch's own walking stick, and struck him twice at knee height. The man collapsed between groans and curled up on the floor, still clutching his broken nose. Sara knew she couldn't stay a moment longer; the assistant could return at any moment or someone could have heard the man's groans. She made for the door, leaving the shop, but not before turning to the pathetic man and shouting:

"You cruelly gave my husband to the Russians; you are the reason for our misfortune. I will make you pay for this. Never forget this every day of your miserable existence, that I will return to reclaim what belongs to my family."

She made for Piotr's house, cradling her right hand as her knuckles ached from the hard blow, she had given Marinowsky. Her heart was still pounding and she was breathing heavily. At one point she realised that her coat was still open and the ribbons of her dress were untied, revealing her corset. She tied them as best she could and buttoned up her coat. As she had lost her scarf that had covered her head, her abundant blonde hair was flowing in the early spring breeze, which caught the attention of passers-by. Sara noticed this and tucked her hair into her coat in an attempt to make herself less conspicuous.

The walk to the house seemed to take an eternity, and she constantly turned, checking for Marinowsky, his assistant or the police behind her. She was still very upset and a cold sweat ran down her body. At last, she reached the house and urgently rang the doorbell. After a few long moments, Malka opened the door.

"Hello, Sara! Where have you been?" she asked, while bundling her inside. "I've been worrying about you since finding your note."

As she noticed that Sara was looking around anxiously, she added:

"Don't worry, Gabriel is upstairs playing with his wooden wagon, but tell me, where did you go? Why did you suddenly leave the house without warning?"

"Because if I had told you where I was going, you wouldn't have let me leave."

5

Although Spring had officially begun, it still snowed, and it was very cold. Sara shivered in the makeshift hut in which she had taken shelter for the night. She placed Gabriel on the small suitcase where she kept their things. She had covered the boy's clothes with an old jacket that had belonged to Piotr, and which was far too big for his tiny body. In addition, she had wrapped him in a woollen blanket, inside which she had tucked his feet. The last rays of a wintery sun could be seen over the horizon and the darkness almost completely enveloped the shed. She had gathered a few logs to start a fire, but Sara knew that it would have to wait until dawn, when the cold would be more intense, to warm them and to prepare coffee in the metal bowl she carried.

It had been five days since she had fled Piotr's house, for Lublin, and she had barely halfway there. As was to be expected, Marinowsky had used his power and influence to get together a group of men in order to find her. For that reason, she had found herself forced to flee in the shadows of the night She had escaped into the shadows of the night, after Piotr had warned her that the prefect had denounced her to the Russian authorities and offered a substantial reward for her capture.

She was obliged to careful in order not to be found. As a result, she could not run the risk of renting a cart; so, she found herself walking down icy roads under darkness, and seeking refuge in abandoned sheds and barns during the day. More than once she had stumbled over rocks in the road, and by the end of the day her feet hurt as did her arms from carrying Gabriel for much of the journey in addition to their suitcase in her other hand.

During the day she remained hidden, to avoid being found by Marinowsky's henchmen or others seeking the bounty. This forced them to travel short distances by night, as long the temperature did not drop too much. Near Ploski, when she saw that it was snowing and that she was almost fainting, she took a risk to hail a cart going South. The labourer driving it agreed to take her to Bielsk Podlaski for six silver roubles. Although this felt like robbery, she had no choice but to accept.

She had tried to take the utmost care of the savings that Isaak had given her the day he was arrested, but the situation was unbearable, and she had to accept it.

The labourer, taking advantage that the woman was travelling unaccompanied, attempted to charge her even more. When Sara refused, he forced her to descend along with her son, driving off and leaving them in the middle of the road. Fortunately, it hadn't been necessary for her to give him all her money since she had carefully hidden it in three different places. She had stood there, in the middle of nowhere, weeping at her misfortune, but as the cold of night came, she took little Gabriel in her arms, picked up the suitcase and sought shelter.

On the seventh day, she arrived in Semiatycze, burning with fever, a strong chest pain, and a constant cough. She decided against sleeping out in the open risking the weather, as she couldn't risk getting a serious illness. Gabriel had no one else in the world, and her beloved son was all she had left, although she continued to hope she would see Jana and Aliza again. She decided to enter the town in search of an inn to spend the night.

The innkeeper looked at her dubiously. Sara, in her muddy coat, looked like a beggar, but her bearing and dignity shone through even her ragged appearance.

"Good evening, ma'am," said the innkeeper, "what can I do for you?"

"I need a room, and something to eat for myself and my son."

She coughed several times, the innkeeper continued to look at her strangely.

"I think you also need medicine, ma'am," he continued, "do you have money to pay for your accommodation?"

"Of course, I do," she exclaimed, before having another coughing fit.

She took out one of the little bags in which she kept the money and showed it to the innkeeper, who brought her a wooden bench and motioned for her to sit, as he left through the back door.

"Wait here a moment, please." He said, before leaving.

He returned a minute later accompanied by a woman, slightly overweight with a strong build. She approached Sara and placed a hand on her forehead.

"You're burning with fever, ma'am," then she said to the innkeeper, "Jacob, I think you should go to find the doctor."

Upon hearing the innkeeper's name, Sara asked:

"Are you Jews?"

The innkeeper and his wife looked at her, as if suspicious of her question. At last Jacob answered.

"Yes, madam, we are Jews."

"Thank you, Hashem," Sara said, then looked towards the sky and then fainted.

She spent six days between life and death; she had pneumonia which kept her bedridden in a semi-conscious state through most of that time. The innkeepers appeared to be heaven-set, not only caring for her attentively, following the doctor's instructions, but also looking after little Gabriel, who they kept apart from his mother. When she finally began to recover, she felt that, despite her hardships, God had not forgotten her. In her journey she had encountered the worst and the best of humanity. On the one hand, there were the Russians, who had led Isaak to the death camps, Marinowsky, and that cruel labourer. On the other, she had met Maretska, Piotr, Malka, and the innkeepers.

Indeed, Jacob and his wife were true angels to Sara and Gabriel. In addition to caring for them, they sent their son, a 17-year-old boy, to accompany them to Lublin in the family's own cart. Sara paid them for their services, as well as the doctor who had saved her life. She had very little money remaining, but those savings given to her by beloved husband before they left had kept her and Gabriel alive and made them ready for challenges ahead.

'*Oh Isaak, beloved husband*' she thought as the cart took her to her destination, '*you don't know how much I miss you, and how much we need you.*'

"Are you thinking about father?" asked Gabriel, who was sat next to her.

Sara winced and turned to her son, wondering if she had been thinking aloud.

"Did you hear me speak, son?"

"No, mother, but I had a strange feeling, something told me you were thinking of him."

She took the boy in her arms and held him tightly to her chest. Tears welled up in her eyes. She was surprised that at just five years old, Gabriel could express himself in such a way.

"I always think of him, my son. I will love him all my life, and never forget him."

"I don't forget him either, mother," Gabriel exclaimed. Sara wept.

At that precise moment, in the early spring of 1863, Isaak and 134 of the other Polish, Lithuanian, and Russian prisoners were entering a forced labour camp near Yakuts, in cold and distant Siberia. They had no reason to think they would make it out of there alive. The camp chief, a ruthless ex-military man who had lost an eye in the Crimean War, reminded them of that.

"Forget your past lives! You are dead to the world, your present and future will be labour, until the day you rot in the ground like the dogs you are. And from now on, you can forget any notions of leaving here. This'll be your final resting place!" he shouted, pointing with his whip towards a small hillock, covered in wooden crosses.

Isaak thought of his loved ones, as he looked towards the hill, wondering under which cross his bones would lie. A tragic end, for both innocent and guilty. Despite his strong character, two tears rolled down his cheeks, but he consoled himself that for some reason God had given this fate. Yes, he would die there, but he would live on through his beloved Gabriel, and his descendants. Some of them, maybe his grandchildren, of his grandchildren's grandchildren, would fulfil his dream of returning to Eretz Israel and look upon Mount Zion. '*Next year in Jerusalem.*'

Sara walked slowly, dragging the cart in which she carried loaves of bread. She felt satisfied; today was her first day delivering the bread that she had kneaded and baked herself in the modest bakery she had recently found. She hoped that, after so many trials and tribulations, she could finally achieve some stability for herself and Gabriel. He was all she had left, and she would work tirelessly to give him the best, so that he could be like his father: a good man and a good Jew. She looked up at the clear sky, dominated by the summer sun that reflected from some tin roofs, like sparks from a fire.

Behind her were the days when, newly arrived in Lublin she discovered that the Jewish shopkeeper, whom she had planned to seek work from, had closed the bakery and left for the city, closing the bakery. She had rented a miserable little room that, as spring advanced, filled with bedbugs, fleas, and cockroaches. Despite cleaning it thoroughly daily before morning prayers, by noon it had been filled with bugs from other parts of the house. After giving Gabriel a frugal breakfast, and sipping her weak coffee, she went out looking for work. Things continued that way, day after day. She searched the streets and squares to no avail; being Jewish was an obstacle. With that daily search, she always returned to the little room overwhelmed by disappointment and sadness at not finding anyone to employ her. The days passed and her meagre savings were running out, to the point that she ended going out to the market every afternoon, looking for food amidst the leftovers. In the evenings, once Gabriel had fallen asleep, she cried inconsolably. To see how her little one grew thinner day by day broke her heart.

These were hard times, plagued with sacrifice and struggle. Life in the city was terribly difficult; she was willing to work any trade, to feed her son, but it wasn't easy for a young widow to raise a child, especially as a Jew in the Congress Poland. Discriminatory anti-Jewish laws made it nearly impossible to find good work. She had just to show her documents stating her Jewish status, as required by law, for her to be denied job opportunities; failure to do so constituted a crime.

Furthermore, she suffered from what she called '*Sara's curse*'; she seemed to attract men who wanted to take advantage of her. Because of this, it had been difficult to get ahead in her trade: preparing and selling bread.

'*Why must these kinds of men always cross my path?*', she said to herself while pushing the cart.

In truth, she had come across a few decent men, although most tried to court her, thanks to her beauty and widowhood. She received many proposals, some earnest and other not so, but had rejected them all. She knew that some of her suitors had honest intentions, or at least appeared to; however, she was now so mistrustful of men that she resisted any approach. Inside, she knew it was not only a question of mistrust, but also that Isaak remained in her heart. That is which she turned a deaf ear to all kinds of advice, including that of Irenka, her only friend in the city, who repeatedly told her:

"Sara, I know how you feel, because I lived through a similar situation. For that reason, I tell you that you have every right to remake your life."

"It's not something that interests me right now, my friend."

"You should reconsider, you aren't lacking in suitors."

Irenka was a wealthy woman who had been married to a successful merchant. Once, when returning from business in Warsaw, he had suffered an accident when the axle of his carriage broke. He suffered a severe head injury that kept him in a coma for several days, until he finally died. This caused Irenka great pain, but also left her a small fortune. Not an extraordinary amount, but enough for her to live a comfortable life in a beautiful and spacious house. In her living room, she held various functions that were attended by characters from the city's social circles, including the Russian military and authorities. The group could have been called Lublin's high society, people with a lot of local influence. Nights at Irenka's lasted until early morning, regardless of season. She had a reputation as an excellent hostess, supported by a butler, four servants, a coachman, and three cooks. All of this was great luxury in a Poland which was not exactly prosperous, and whose peasantry were poor and sometimes suffered greatly.

Irenka was a Catholic, like her second husband, a lawyer who conducted business throughout Russian Poland. For that reason, he spent more time travelling than at home. However, while in Lublin, he took part in the gatherings and follies of his wife, participating in all the parties, walks, and treats that she organised. The pair, unlike most other citizens, did not hold the slightest prejudice against Jews.

Irenka met Sara one day, when she descended from her carriage outside her residence just as Sara was delivering bread to the butler. The housewife was struck by the imposing beauty of the woman, but also her bearing and distinction, despite the humble clothes she wore. She started a conversation with Sara and was even more surprised to hear her elegant way with which she spoke, immediately realising that she was more cultured than a simple deliverer of bread, and thus became curious to know more about this woman. She invited her inside, to continue, but Sara cordially excused herself; she had to finish her deliveries. However, she accepted an invitation for another day. Thus, in such an unusual way, a sincere friendship was born between these two women, which grew stronger when Irenka learned the Jewish widow's sad story.

Sara's permanent melancholy also caught her attention. Caused by the events of the beginning of the year, when in one day she had lost a husband and the two young girls who had become part of her life, together with her home, businesses, and savings. Her crime? Being a Jew. When they first met, Sara was living in the back room of an older man's shop, where she worked from sunrise to sunset to earn enough to put food on the table and support Gabriel.

After those hazardous days fruitlessly searching for work, she was left physically and mentally exhausted, with only a few coins to pay for her room. Eventually, she managed to find employment with the owner of a bakery, with the added advantage that he would allow her to live in the back of his premises, essentially in a corridor with a straw mattress on the floor. However, she did not have to worry about her rent. Her wardrobe and bedside table were the small suitcase that Malka had given her before leaving Bialystok.

The owner was a harsh man, who forced her to work almost without rest. She got up at four in the morning to knead the bread, then baked it, stocked the counters, and left at seven o'clock to delivered house to house. After a frugal lunch, she prepared and baked the afternoon batch, and then deliver to the rest of the city, returning at nightfall completely exhausted. In the afternoons Gabriel accompanied her, as he only went to Cheder in the mornings.

She arrived, weakened by fatigue, to prepare her son's dinner, tuck him up in a small bed which she had built herself from planks found in the street, and then collapsed onto the straw mattress. Despite the exhaustion, she struggled to fall asleep, as the shameless owner of the bakery, despite being elderly, had a habit of trying to get into bed with her. The poor thing, in addition to her cruel work, was forced to remain awake every night to protect herself from the advances of her employer. He was stubborn and, despite the rejections, did not abandon his disgusting attempts.

Sara was repulsed by him, and her dignity suffered greatly, to the extent that one day, when she could take no more abuse, she slept with a cane in hand. When the old man approached her, before he could touch her, she hit him, wounding on his forehead. The next day, she was thrown out on the street, with her belongings and son, wondering why she had always to suffer so greatly. The answer was obvious, it was easy for cruel and indecent men to try to take advantage of her: beautiful, helpless, and alone.

These painful events strengthened her conviction that Isaak was the only decent man on Earth, but he was dead. When she lost her work, she hadn't a penny to her name and her owner didn't pay the money he owed her. With nowhere to go, she went to Irenka's house, who, already knowing her past hardships, Sara felt could be trusted with her present ones. She went to the door and rang the bell. Irenka received her kindly and, upon learning the details of her situation, took pity on Sara and gave her and Gabriel a place to stay. During that time their friendship strengthened and, soon afterwards, Sara got a job at another bakery, which was for sale. Irenka, with her kind heart, loaned her the money to buy it and start her own business.

"What did you say to me?"

"What? How?" Sara asked, emerging from her thoughts.

"Were you daydreaming?"

"Sorry, Irenka. I was remembering how you took me in when I had nowhere to go and then lent me the money to set up my own bakery."

"Yes, yes, my dear friend, but you're changing the subject."

"I know, Irenka, but it has nothing to do with the number of suitors. I'm just not interested."

"Oh, my friend! Consider it, and think of Gabriel, you must offer him the opportunity to dream of a more secure and stable future."

"You know how I have worked so that he doesn't lack anything. If I must, I will work twenty-four hours a day. Do you know that my Gabriel also thinks of his father. We talk of him often."

"I know, Sara, it's important for you both to keep his memory alive. I'm not telling you to forget him, but to think of your future, and that of your child. You are extremely beautiful; any man would be lucky to have you as his wife. There is no lack of eligible bachelors in Lublin. What about Doctor Prichodny? He is a prestigious doctor, and he gets nervous whenever he sees you."

"Oh, Irenka. I would never marry a man who is not a Jew. But regardless, Jewish or Catholic, I will never remarry.

"You're very stubborn, but one day you will come to your senses."

But Sara remained in the world that she had created for herself, and from which she had no desire to leave. Not for one single day since arriving at Lublin did, she stop thinking of her late husband. She tortured herself by reliving in her mind the moments they shared. When she did, she transported herself into the past, when she was happy and with the best man in the world. However, when returning to reality, sadness and melancholy made her cry for his absence. In those moments, she said to herself:

'*In honour of your memory, my beloved, there will never be another man in my life.*'

The bakery bought with Irenka's loan was prospering. Sara began to innovate her recipes, remembering Jana and Aliza's legacy. Before long she ran the only bakery in the city that prepared different varieties of bread. She worked even harder than when she was with old Robovich, but she was now very satisfied, as each hour of work and all the sacrifice was for the benefit of her and Gabriel. She rose every day, except Saturday of course, at exactly half past three in the morning, prepared, kneaded, and baked the bread. Later she stood at the only counter of the small shop until nine in the morning, then went out to make deliveries. Then in the afternoon she repeated the same process.

However, Robovich, envious of Sara's success, decided to take revenge on her, and falsely accused her, claiming she had stolen some of his savings. Despite the weakness of his claim, and all the time that had passed since he had dismissed her, the Russian authorities detained her. Irenka came to her aid once again, and thanks to her influence managed obtain her release. As she knew from experience, Sara was at a disadvantage because she was Jewish. So, in order to get rid of the criminal proceedings she had to come to an arrangement with the old man, transferring ownership to him of her own bakery. Injustices continued to pursue her.

Despite all her misfortune, the only positive thing was that she had already repaid half of Irenka's loan and, through her well-known perseverance in saving every penny, had a small sum to pay to her friend. But, given the circumstances, this money would now allow her to survive, while she is deciding what to do. Irenka advised her to give up the small room in which she lived with Gabriel and to stay at hers, as she had done in the past, so that she would not have to pay for rent while planning the future. Her friend also advised her to stay in the baking business, as she knew it well, but not in Lublin. It was clear that Robovich would never leave her alone; as the old man was Russian rather than Polish, he had been born in Smolensk, and so had some influence with the authorities.

Sara was thinking about where she could move in order to start a new bakery. She was deeply disappointed to realise that she would have to start at the bottom again. She is brooding over this when she heard her friend arrive home.

'How kind Irenka is,' Sara thought.

She felt that she should tell her personally, and thank her for her friendship and generosity, so she went to the living room to meet her and express her gratitude. As usually, Irenka blustered in. As soon as she saw Sara, she approached and said:

"I have something important to tell you!"

"So do I." answered Sara.

"You too? So, you know?"

"Know what?" replied Sara, confused.

"Well, if it's not the news, then what it the important thing you want to tell me?"

"It may not be so important for you, but it is for me. I want you to know that you are a woman with a kind heart, and that I have no way of thanking you for your friendship and generosity."

"Ha! Oh, my dear friend, you're so sweet!"

"It is heart-felt. In my life, I only ever meet very cruel people, or very kind ones. Of course, you belong to the second group."

"Obviously that's not true, I don't mean that I am not from that second group, but what happens to everyone happens to you. We always remember those who change our lives, for better or worse, and we forget those tens or hundreds that bring us neither happiness nor sadness."

Sara considered that her life was filled with more sadness than joy.

"But anyway, I must give you the news. A surprise event has occurred that could change your situation!"

"Oh no, Irenka! Don't tell that you've found another suitor!"

"For God's sake, my friend! You don't need me to find you suitors, you have dozens of them."

"So, what's the news?"

"Old Robovich is dead!"

"How? What happened to that wretch?"

"You wouldn't believe it! The old man had hired a maid, a peasant barely 17 years old, and it turns out that the old man hadn't given up the tricks he pulled on you."

"Don't tell me he tried to get into this girl's bed!"

"Not only trying, apparently, he succeeded! The peasant was apparently more accommodating than you, and it turns out that last night the strain was too much for the old man. The effort gave him a heart attack, and he died in the act."

"Well, God forgive me, but it's well deserved."

"He really wasn't a good man, look at what he did to you. But anyway, in the face of this unexpected occurrence, I can see an opportunity for you to get your bakery back!"

"That would be wonderful! It's worth a try, right?"

Indeed, she was able to recover her premises, but it wasn't as easy as she and her friend had imagined. The old man's son, sole heir to his property, did not object to returning Sara's bakery, provided she paid for it in full. He was not at all interested in the business to which his father had dedicated his whole life and had decided it was in his interest to sell the inherited properties as soon as possible.

So, she had no choice but to pay for what was rightfully hers. However, at least she would not have to leave the city and start anew elsewhere. She could remain in Lublin where she already had clientele, as well as her wonderful friend Irenka, who came to her aid once again, as Sara's savings could not cover the price asked by the heir.

Meanwhile, Gabriel was progressing with his studies as he was a very conscientious and intelligent boy. His teachers had told Sara that he was ahead for his age, highlighting his curiosity, and desire to know more of his subjects than what he was taught in the Cheder. The Rabbi, who had lived in Constantinople and Thessaloniki for many years, had a fondness for the boy, so that in addition to studying the Torah and Judaism, he gained knowledge of the ancient Mediterranean civilisations. He learned about the peoples who lived in Asia Minor, and the lands of Palestine. Gabriel acquired this knowledge with ease, and thanks to his impressive memory, could fluently recite passages from the Torah and was particularly interested in the history of Israel.

He had a great desire to learn, and a special gift for mathematics as well, so his teachers introduced him to the world of numbers. Sara felt great pride for her son when she received reports of his progress. The boy was growing up, but kept his childlike face, framed by blonde hair the colour of wheat fields. His features were beautiful; his grey eyes and charming smile, like those of his mother, shone out from his face.

Strikingly, he had Isaak's strength of character, despite not yet having reached six years.

Like Sara, he missed his father, treasuring vivid memories of Isaak's affection and kindness. He always remembered that last meeting in the stable, surrounded by snow, which despite his young age, was a moment that he never would forget. Gabriel suffered in his absence in silence, especially when he saw other children sharing the moments of joy with their parents. It was the same tragic feeling that oppressed his mother's heart whenever she saw children playing with families in the park.

Of course, Sara was never happy. She rightly considered her existence to be grey and empty, the days passed like waves of melancholy, and she only felt joy at Gabriel's progress. Irenka, who had become her guardian angel, invited her to stay permanently in her home, which to Sara was like an oasis in the middle of the desert. While Gabriel played in the garden or a small adjoining room, the two friends would talk. Irenka commented the political or social developments in Lublin and, although Sara wasn't much interested in them, she loved to spend time with her friend.

However, in those conversations she felt there was little she could offer, aside from her hardships and, recently, how her small bakery was growing through hard work. Those beautiful grey eyes held a perpetual sadness and distance. Losing the love of her life was a blow that she would never recover from, as well she felt the disappearance of Jana and Aliza. Six months had passed since the last day she had seen then, and every day her hope to see them again grew fainter. The three and a half years of life they had shared had been filled with hard work, but also great joy.

'*Joy that will never return.*' Sara said to herself when she remembered those times.

Her friend always tried to cheer her up.

"You must not lose hope, my dear friend, according to what you have told me, the girls already fled Odessa once and were able to reach Poland."

"It's true, but it's been more than four months since the events in Bialystok no one has seen them since. I've already sent four messages to Piotr and the response is always the same, despite them searching constantly. You can't imagine how much it hurts me not to have my girls with me."

Irenka tried to comfort her, but to no avail; Sara's life had not been easy. She had lost her father as a child and, when, she was barely seven years old, her mother had died of cholera. Just two months later, her two older sisters had died from the same disease, leaving her in the care of an aunt. The woman was married, but the husband was a freeloader who didn't take life seriously. A heavy drinker and gambler, he chased any woman that met his eyes. He was fortunate to be the heir to a large inheritance left by his father, a Swiss merchant who had made large profits supplying cloth and leather for the Napoleonic armies. However, the son squandered the fortune within a few years and ended up abandoning his wife for a gypsy dancer who worked in a circus.

Their financial situation became precarious. Sara's aunt worked at embroidery and needlework to survive, but her clientele was small, because the woman suffered from arthritis that caused her semi-paralysis and severe pain. Sara had to work from the age of eight, performing all kinds of odd jobs: courier, street vendor, laundress, cleaner, kitchen assistant, newspaper deliverer. Her childhood was on the streets of Warsaw, filled with all kinds of menaces, insults and difficulties. In adolescence her extraordinary beauty complicated her life, so from a young age she learned how to get deal with bullies.

Poverty prevented her from enjoying her youth as she would have liked. The only positive thing was time spent with the Rabbi of her community, who discovered a great intellectual potential in her, and due to her ability and interest in learning. He ran a Cheder, and a few girls attended an annex of it, run by his wife. Of course, Sara's aunt could not afford to pay for her education, but both the Rabbi and his wife, noticing the girl's interest in study, accepted her in exchange for work cleaning the premises. Thanks to the couple's extensive library, the girl developed a fondness for reading; they loaned her countless books which she devoured by candlelight. Thus, she learned not only of her Jewish ancestors, but also classical thought, creating a strong cultural foundation.

Sara's ability and interest enabled her to absorb knowledge on a wide range of subjects. Therefore, she was able to educate herself in a range of scientific and cultural areas. Without a doubt, had she the opportunity to attend university, she would have excelled at whatever she chose. Furthermore, her aunt, although impoverished, came from a wealthy and traditional family in Warsaw. She instilled in her the language, behaviour, and manners of a lady. In fact, despite their poverty and isolation, Sara would not have been out of place in any high-class environment.

But the event that changed her life was when she met her future husband. She was sixteen, and he nineteen. Isaak's mother had commissioned Sara's aunt to make the dress that her daughter would wear to her Bat Mitzvah celebration. Isaak had gone to pick up the garment for his sister and Sara answered the door. The two of them stared at each other lost for words. He was struck by her natural beauty, and she could not hide her fascination with this boy's distinguished and handsome appearance.

"I think I fell in love with him the moment I saw him," she admitted to Irenka, "you can't imagine it, he looked so handsome in his black jacket, with bright dark eyes, and smile that captivated me."

"Love at first sight!" Her friend said, with a laugh.

"Yes, that it was. It was tenderness, but also strength and a sense of protection."

"Ha!" Irenka laughed, "and you nearly declared your love within seconds of meeting him!"

"It was truly magical," Sara remembered, smiling slightly, "the moments passed and neither of us moved. I couldn't take me eyes off him, nor he from me. Finally, he shook his head slightly and asked for my aunt. I led him into the office and offered for him a chair, but he remained standing until she arrived. I followed their conversation, looking at him out of the corner of my eye. Happily, I noticed from his clothes that he was a Jew, just like me."

"What happened next? Tell me everything," Irenka asked, excitedly.

Sara sighed deeply as she pictured the scene, her friend looking at her expectantly.

"My aunt told him that his sister's dress was ready, and when she went to fetch it, Isaak turned to me and presented himself cordially. It was clear that he was a real gentleman. I also introduced myself, I remember managing to tell him that I worked in the leather business. Then my aunt returned and handed him the dress wrapped in paper. He paid her, then politely said goodbye. I accompanied him to the exit, he bowed slightly and left. I watched him as he walked down the street, until he looked back. Embarrassed, I immediately went inside and closed the door, ran to the living room window and, through the curtain, caught a glimpse of him for a few more seconds."

"You fell in love with him."

"That's right. An hour later he returned and told my aunt that his mother wanted me to put ornament on the dress. She went to the sewing room to make the change, while we talked in the living room. I was enthralled with his conversation, his bearing, his manners, his elegance. I thought him so handsome, his features were almost perfect, his broad shoulders, his stature. In short, he was like a dream for me."

"Oh!" Irenka signed, "What a beautiful story. But tell me, what came next?"

"The next day he returned with the dress again, saying his mother wanted us to put ribbons on the sides; my aunt didn't object. Although our finances had improved, as by chance a bank account was found in Switzerland that had belonged to her dead husband, the freeloader, a few extra coins wouldn't hurt."

"Well, his mother's whims gave you a chance to see him again."

"Yes, of course. Although I later discovered that Isaak's mother never sent him to make any changes, he made it all up himself, while telling his mother that the dress wasn't yet ready."

Irenka laughed again, then exclaimed:

"And of course, it wasn't your aunt that he wanted to see again! What a nice story, dear friend."

"Yes, it was the beginning of the happiest days of my life. His courtship was the most beautiful and romantic than you can imagine. He was the most chivalrous man in the world. The day of our marriage is engraved onto my heart. When he lowered my veil and whispered to me:

'*my love is greater than your beauty, but your beauty is so great that they're almost equal.*"

"How beautiful, Sara!"

Irenka was glad to see her friend smile as she remembered those days, but the spell was broken when she returned to reality.

"My happiness lasted for the seven years I lived with Isaak. He was the most wonderful man, the greatest husband, and the best father."

Her friend rose from the chair, approached her and put a hand on her shoulder. Sara stood and the two women embraced each other.

Irenka tried to cheer her up in every way she knew how. She continuously invited Sara to her functions, but she always found an excuse. Very occasionally, she managed to convince her to attend a social gathering, and on those occasions the guests were fascinated with the woman, not only for her beauty, but also her culture, intelligence, manners, and conversation. One could talk with her about any topic, and, as she spoke Russian fluently, it was common for the Tsar's officers to try to sit with her to enjoy her company. Only Irenka knew how much of a sacrifice it was for her to attend these parties, she knew that her friend only did so to please her as thanks for all the help Irenka had given her.

As she had a true affection for her, she did not cease her efforts to present her with favourable candidates to win her heart. Whilst Sara paid them little attention, she knew that time healed all wounds. She was still a beautiful young woman, not without many other qualities. It was logical that her charms would not go unnoticed.

Sara worked hard, rising before dawn, and going to bed late at night. Always thrifty, she paid back Irenka's loan and would not accept the cancellation that her friend offered her. Before long, she once again making the most sought-after bread in the city and invested her profits in improving her premises. She managed to expand it by renting the connecting property and built an additional oven. Very soon, her number of clients increased, and she had hired a boy for deliveries. She also gained an assistant, a Jewish girl who had fled a remote town on the Black Sea, to escape the abusive couple with whom she had lived.

The girl was tender, and intelligent. She was not the classic image of a Russian girl, blonde hair, and blue eyes. On the contrary, her hair was jet black, very long and straight, reaching almost to her waist. Her eyes were brown and framed by beautiful, thick lashes. The girl was pretty, with a sweet character. Most importantly, she was dedicated, honest, and a responsible worker. Although, for obvious reasons, Sara had no love for the Russians, she was moved by the girl who, to her, was a Jew first and a Russian second. Now it was Tatiana who slept in the back of the bakery, although in better conditions than those Sara had endured, a few months ago, as she had a bed, a nightstand and a chest of drawers.

A letter brought news that Irenka's husband would be arriving home soon, providing the perfect opportunity for her to throw a large party. Of course, she invited Sara, who as usual, refused.

"I'm very grateful, but I'm not one for big parties. Besides, I have a lot of work."

"Alright, but the party is at night, and on a Saturday when Shabbat is over."

"You're very kind to invite me, but you know that Sunday is a busy day at the bakery."

You know perfectly well that Tatiana can take charge of the first batch for one day, come on, don't turn me down again."

"Oh, my dear friend! I don't even have a decent dress that's fit for one of your parties, which are usually very elegant."

"That's not a problem, I've already talked to my dressmaker, and she will make you a dress for the night, come on, accept. This is important for me, do it for your friend."

After all that she had done for her, it was difficult to reject the proposal. Irenka had not only helped her through the harshest times, but also been a source of sincere and genuine friendship.

"In that case, I will gladly accept and accompany you to your party!

"Ha! Thank you so much, princess Sara!" She said, embracing her, "Tomorrow at three my dressmaker will be here to take your measurements. She must work quickly, but for her it's no trouble. She is an extraordinary seamstress."

Indeed, the next day the dressmaker arrived punctually, with her work kit and a young assistant. She was a friendly and lively woman who hardly stopped talking, although her subjects were limited to fashion and city gossip.

"I have the perfect model for you," she said, producing a folder dress sketches, the titles and notes of which were in French.

"Very good, very good!" Irenka exclaimed as she looked at the designs, then looked at the dressmaker and said: "You must put your all into this dress, I want my friend to be the queen of the party."

Sara blushed a little, the last thing she wanted was to be the centre of attention. For her part, Irenka smiled to herself, her secret desire was to present a suitable suitor, hoping Sara would notice him. He was a very handsome officer in the Austrian navy, whose father, a career diplomat, had married a young Polish woman from Lublin during a mission to Warsaw, and had settled in the city after retiring from the service. Because of this, the sailor visited them every year. The officer, like Sara, had been widowed for a few years and had a young daughter who lived with her grandparents in Lublin. Irenka thought they could be the perfect couple.

The dressmaker had not finished her work when the butler announced the arrival of the shoe merchant, owner of Lublin's most exclusive shop, who brought with him a wooden trunk filled with various examples. Sara was overwhelmed, and Irenka chose a pair to match the colour of her dress, which she had already chosen for her friend.

The day after the arrival of Carl Kobielsky, her husband, Irenka sent for her friend to introduce them. He was a jovial man, with an obvious worldliness. He spoke with great ease and self-confidence and had the typical assuredness of one who has never gone to bed hungry. He was elegantly, yet modestly dressed, and often held a drink in one hand and a cigar in the other. Physically, he was unremarkable, medium height, normal build, short hair with grey streaks, and a well-groomed beard and moustache.

Sara liked him, particularly for the openness and sincerity of his behaviour. While he maintained his dignity, he could not conceal the impression that the beauty of his wife's friend had made on him.

"I am very delighted to meet you," he said, after being introduced, "my wife has not stopped speaking of you since my arrival. I am glad you have become such good friends. I think you provide her another excuse to organise parties and gatherings."

"Don't make fun of me," Irenka told him, tapping him on the shoulder with her Spanish fan that she always carried in the summer.

The two laughed, Sara could immediately see that this couple was united more by sympathy than love. They seemed less like a couple, and more like great friends.

"My wife tells me you are Jewish."

"Yes, I am."

"What is your last name?"

"Rothman."

"That's a name of Prussian origin, right?"

"Austrian. It's my husband's last name."

"Yes, of course," Carl said, "Irenka has told me of your husband's misfortune."

He noticed that Sara's eyes had turned sad and changed the subject at once.

"Several of my clients are Jewish businessmen from Warsaw and other Polish cities, I'm friends with some of them."

"I'm glad you have Jewish friends, the same cannot be said of all Christians."

Carl was thoughtful, and puffed at his cigar, remembering the problems he had had representing the interests of Jewish clients.

'It's not fair,' he thought, 'to discriminate and mistreat another person over the simple matter of faith or customs that harm no one. I have never known a single Jew to cause me a problem, in fact, the opposite.'

This thought occupied his mind. Obviously, there must be some Jews whose behaviour was not of the best. But personally, he could not recall any Jew behaving immorally or aggressively within the members of the community with which he had had dealings. It caused him great sadness that people did not think and act more humanely in this country.

6

The chandeliers were so numerous that the hall seemed illuminated by a bright sun; the sofas, chairs, tables and orchestra were perfectly arranged to receive guests. The movement in the kitchen was frantic, Irenka was an extraordinary hostess, supervising even the smallest detail. Carl, who knew what she was like when organising events, chose to visit friends. '*To not get in the way*', he said to himself.

Meanwhile Sara, in the guest room of the first floor, had finished adjusting her dress with the help of one of Irenka's servants, who tied the ribbons behind her back. She was glad to see her friend so enthusiastic for the party she was putting on but felt so no such excitement herself. It was not that she disliked parties, in fact, she greatly enjoyed them, but only at Isaak's side. And that was something she was no longer possible. The truth was, she was lonely and, at night, when Gabriel had fallen asleep, she found it difficult to sleep herself. Memories of happier times came to her mind, of when she was with her beloved husband and the two girls.

'*Oh, God*,' she thought, '*how could I have become so bitter?*'

She knew Irenka was doing everything she could to distract her, but the truth was that nothing excited her.

'*She's a great friend, she's not even a Jew, neither am I from her social class. She could easily dedicate the time she spends with me to other Lublin socialites. I hope that one day I can return everything she has given me.*'

At that moment there was a knock at the door, it was Irenka herself.

"Hello Sara, I see that you're ready! You look beautiful in that dress; I wasn't exaggerating when I said you would be the queen of the party. Even I pale in comparison, you are like an Empress!"

"Oh, my dear friend, you overwhelm me with your compliments!" Sara replied with a smile, blushing slightly. The servant finished adjusting the ribbons, Irenka approached and said:

"I made the right choice; it fits you perfectly. Turn around..."

Sara obeyed, turning slowly. She really did look beautiful, the light blue dress clung to her body, emphasising her figure and falling gracefully to the floor. Irenka watched, very pleased with the result of her efforts. Under the light of the chandeliers, Sara's grey eyes took on the same colour as the dress. Irenka indicated to the servant to put her shoes on, Sara felt a little uncomfortable, not only because of her garments' elegance, but also having someone to help to her dress.

"Excellent," said Irenka, "we are ready, my dear Sara. Gabriel is playing in the other room, I've already given instructions that he be given dinner and put to bed, so you can relax and enjoy the night."

Sara went to the door while Irenka and the servant girl remained admiring her, not just for her beauty, but for her elegance and demeanor. In any palace she would have passed for a real princess.

They went to the main hall, where Carl was talking to two men while smoking his customary cigar. Meanwhile, the orchestra tuned their instruments, and the servants were making the finishing touches. Irenka led Sara into the kitchen, showing her the delicious and extravagant meals that would be served later in the night.

'*Our entire house in Bialystok could fit in this kitchen*,' Sara thought, watching the cooks busily giving orders and carrying plates and trays hither and yon. In truth, she felt out of place, not because she disliked the beauty of the house, its furniture, and its decoration. Rather, it was all so different from her aunt's house, where she had spent her youth, and the modest houses she had shared with Isaak. These had been poor, but in contrast the one in Bialystok had been build and decorated with their own hands. What made her uncomfortable was the feeling that she did not belong in this world, to the social class to which she had been introduced, almost by force through Irenka. It was not that she felt lesser than the guests that were arriving, simply different.

Gradually, the house began to fill with Irenka and Carl's guests, some of whom Sara had already met at the gatherings Irenka periodically organised. She tried to maintain a little distance, but men and women observed her closely, causing her uneasiness. Many guests must have wondered who the beautiful blonde in the blue dress was. At last, the mistress of the house came to her rescue, taking her by the arm and leading her to a group that was conversing on the terrace. The cool summer night made this the most pleasant place in the house. Irenka

introduced her to the guests, emphasising a man in his 30s with a thick
moustache and round race who was jovially talking with Carl.

"Hello Sara!" Carl said to her, "come, come over here."

The man with the moustache was delighted to meet Sara when Carl
introduced them. He took her hand and kissed it.

"Enchanted, madam," he exclaimed, bowing, "you are doubtlessly the
most beautiful woman at this party."

"Thank you," she replied rather dryly, but with a strained smile.

"Sara," said Carl, "our friend is Henryk Wieniawski."

She widened her eyes and turned towards the guest, obviously the
name meant nothing to her.

"Excuse me, sir, I do not know you. You must be someone important
in this city."

"Ha!" Carl laughed, "Our guest is one of the most illustrious sons
of Lublin, a virtuoso at violin. He is recognised in the most prestigious
salons of Europe.

"It is an honour to meet you, sir," Sara said, slightly bowing her
shoulders.

"Henryk was born here in Lublin," Carl continued, "but he currently
resides in St. Petersburg where he is no less than the first violinist at the
court of Tsar Alexander."

Sara winced upon hearing the Tsar's name, it was for his sake that
Isaak had been taken to the death camp. However, she turned to the
musician and said:

"Allow me to congratulate you, sir, and I wish you many successes
with your art."

"Thank you very much, madam," replied Henryk, who clearly
wanted to continue conversing with this beautiful woman, but at that
moment Irenka arrived like a whirlwind. She took Sara by the arm and
dragged her away, saying to the two men:

"Excuse me, but I must deprive you of my friend's company."

Carl laughed heartily; he already knew his wife's impetuous ways
well. The musician, with disappointment in his eyes, followed Sara with
his gaze, as he would have wished to have prolonged the conversation.

Irenka took her to a far corner of the room, all men followed Sara with their eyes. Irenka noticed, and whispered to her:

"Oh, my dear Sara. You could have any man in Poland, I think there are many that would like to marry you."

"And of those many," Sara replied, "which would be willing to convert to Judaism?"

"Oh, don't spoil the moment, please! I want to show off as my friend, and the queen of the party."

Sara squeezed her arm in gratitude, then returned the compliment.

"The queen of the party is yourself, not only as the hostess, but for your elegance and beauty."

"Ha!" Irenka laughed out loud, "very kind and flattering words, but they are too generous coming from you, no one can equal your beauty."

Certainly, although a wonderful person, she did not compare to Sara with regards to beauty, although she eclipsed her in terms of joy and spontaneity. Irenka was not ugly and had her own charm. She had dark hair which matched her eyes, resembling a Greek woman. Despite being a little overweight, she a very striking woman, with a touch of sensuality that Sara lacked. In any case, they both shone like jewels.

At the far end of the room, Irenka stopped before an officer wearing the dark blue uniform of the Austrian navy. His epaulets and gold buttons gleamed by the light of the chandeliers. The naval officer was tall with an imposing bearing, dark haired with bushy eyebrows, a straight nose, and large blue eyes. He was a handsome man and demonstrated great self-assuredness in his gestures and expression.

"Captain Hoffman!" Irenka called.

The officer turned to face the woman.

"I wish to introduce my friend, Sara."

Hoffman fixed his gaze onto her, his eyes immediately lit up. He took her hand, bowed, and kissed it gently.

"Pleased to meet you, miss."

"Madam," Sara corrected, "it is a pleasure to meet you, Captain."

"Madam ..."

"Rothman, Captain"

"A Germanic name."

"Austrian, to be precise."

"Is your husband Austrian?"

"Polish, of Austrian origin, Captain" Irenka interrupted, "the poor man is dead, Sara is a widow." She continued, as if to say, "*My friend is available.*"

"I'm very sorry," replied to officer.

Irenka called one of waiters over. She took two glasses and handed them to Captain Hoffman and Sara, then took one for herself and raised it, exclaiming:

"Let us toast this pleasant meeting!"

The three glasses collided, then Irenka immediately made her exit, leaving Sara to the sailor's conversation. '*I've done my part; the rest is up to them.*' She thought as she left.

Captain Hoffman did not leave Sara's side for the entire night, in truth, their conversation was exhilarating. He was quite the gentleman with a captivating personality. She fascinated the officer with her expression and intelligence. The Captain was a cultured man, something he recognised in his beautiful companion, which impressed him deeply.

When the dance began, he monopolised her entirely, despite others wanting to dance with her. Then, later in the evening, he invited her to talk on the terrace. Although the breeze was somewhat cool, Sara was warmed by the wine and the Captain's company. His conversation was very pleasant, and he was always gentlemanly, which fascinated Sara, who was accustomed to attracting cruel men her 'curse'.

When Hoffman made his farewell, he said:

"This has been the best evening of my life, to spend time with such a charming lady would be worth more than a thousand trips from Vienna to Lublin."

"You flatter me, Captain, perhaps as a result of the champagne."

"You're wrong, it's not the wine, it's your beauty that has intoxicated me." He was silent for a moment, then continued, "and your intelligence, which was a delightful surprise."

"They say that intoxication changes one's perspective, I insist that the champagne is the culprit."

"Perhaps, but the only thing that has intoxicated me tonight is your charm and loveliness."

"Thank you, Captain, I see that your tongue always knows the right thing to say."

"It's not my tongue speaking, but my heart."

"If you were not a gentleman, I would think you were flirting with me."

"In which case, I beg your pardon, perhaps there are a few drops of brandy left on my tongue."

"I'm sorry to contradict you, Captain, it seems to me that it is sugar, rather than liquor, that you have on your tongue."

"You are charming," he said, laughing a little, "I see that I'm not the only one who always knows what to say."

"Maybe it's because I make sure that I'm never left with any drops of drink."

The Captain laughed at this intelligent observation, then raised his right hand to his chest and, with a slight bow, said:

"I thank you for such a wonderful evening."

"I am equally grateful for your company, Captain."

"I must go, I wish I could stop the ticking of the clock, but that's one thing I'm yet to learn in the navy."

This time it was Sara who smiled. "I think the drink is playing with your tongue again."

"That is not the case, enchanting Sara. I wish you a pleasant night, or rather a good morning, and I pray to God that you will allow me to see you again."

"You are very kind Captain."

Hoffman leaned down to kiss her hand, leaned a little too close. Sara felt a slight chill. The officer bowed, turned, and left. She could not help but follow him with her eyes, he really was a handsome and charming man, and a gentleman.

Irenka, who had been watching them the whole night, could not resist the urge to speak to Sara. As soon as she said goodnight to the officer at the door, she ran towards her friend.

"Well?" She asked her.

"Well, what?"

"Oh God, Sara! Don't do this!" she approached her, "What did you think?"

"He's quite the gentleman, that Captain."

"Is that all you have to say?"

"What more do you want me to say?"

"Oh, don't play dumb with me! Tell me, tell me, how did you like him?"

"Well, Irenka, he is a really special man, not like others. He is an excellent conversationalist, and his language is flattering."

"And what else?"

"What else?"

"Yes! What do you think of his physique? And his personality, do you like it?"

Sara thought for a few moments, Irenka looked at her questioningly.

"You want the truth?"

"Of course, I want the truth, Sara!"

"Ha ha ha!"

"Why are you laughing?"

Sara laughed again.

"What do you want me to say? He's very handsome, I'm sure all the Austrian women fall at his feet."

"And the Polish ones! It seems that you've charmed him, he was the one who fell for you."

"You exaggerate!"

"Do you know what he said to me as he left?"

"What did he tell you?"

"He said: 'Thank you for introducing me to the most beautiful woman in all of Poland.'"

"Lies!"

"No, Sara, that's what he told me, I swear!"

"Well, the truth is that I had a very pleasant evening, thanks to you, my dear friend."

"You have given me the pleasure of seeing you enjoy yourself. I achieved my aim."

"It seems to me that your aim was to introduce me to Captain Hoffman."

"Oh, no Sara! How could you think that?" she replied, widening her eyes in mock offense. Then quickly embracing her, flew to the door to bid farewell to the other guests, covering her laughter with her hand.

It was almost dawn when Sara finally lay down next to little Gabriel, who was sleeping peacefully. Irenka had invited him to stay in the guest room, as there was no time for him to return to the small rented apartment near the bakery. She rested her head on the pillow and thought on the night's events. The party had been very pleasant, she did not regret having attended; she had made her friend happy and had worn a most beautiful dress. She had enjoyed herself and had met a most handsome and charming man. Captain Hoffman truly was gallant; it was difficult for her to resist his charms. She replayed the evening in her mind until sleep overtook her.

A few hours later she woke; while she would have liked to remain in bed resting a little longer, duty called. So, she got up, woke Gabriel, dressed him and then went to the bakery. She did not say goodbye to her friends, as Irenka and Carl were sleeping peacefully.

She arrived flustered, as she was somewhat late to start work. However, Tatiana had got there at four-thirty in the morning and had everything up and running: cleaning the bakery, preparing and kneading the bread, and had already finished baking the morning the batch. She was already preparing the second batch. The baked loaves were ready to be distributed throughout the city, and the delivery boy was ready to set out on his round. When Sara arrived, the girl was attending to customers who had already come in.

She looked at the girl with pleasure. Tatiana had proved to be a really good worker, responsible and honest. Sara thanked her for what she had achieved that morning, then sat on a bench, took off her shoes, and massaged her right foot. The shoes she had worn to the party were beautiful, but they were tight and had left her with a small blister. Noticing the shoes that she had taken off; memories of Isaak came to her.

A few days later, Irenka invited her to have tea at her house. As soon as she arrived, the butler escorted her tot the terrace where her friend sat in a large armchair, resting her right leg on a cushion on a stool.

"What happened to you, my dear friend?" Sara asked her.

"Oh, Sara, a sprain! I stumbled down the stairs. But it's nothing serious, I just need some rest."

"That's something difficult for you, but I'm glad it's not serious, even if it's just after Carl left for Warsaw."

She sat next to her on the sofa, while Irenka poured a cup of tea.

"How are you feeling, Sara?"

"Very well. Why do you ask?"

"Just to know if you are now more satisfied with life here in Lublin."

"Generally speaking, well, you know that I have to work very hard, but I'm getting ahead."

"You work too hard! It's incredible how, in a few short weeks, you've grown your bakery. I'm glad you feel happy in Lublin."

"The best part of this city is having you at my side. You are so kind and very much my dear friend."

"It's true, the best thing that has happened to me has been meeting such a wonderful woman."

"You'll make me blush, but I'm not the only one you've met in Lublin."

Sara understood immediately what her friend meant. She turned her head and stared at her, but Irenka pretended not to notice, continuing:

"Is that not true?"

"Yes, I have met other people."

"Sure, some other people. But is there no one in particular?"

"Yes, your husband Carl. He is a very nice man and a good conversationalist."

"Oh, Sara! Stop joking!"

Sara laughed, but her expression turned serious as Irenka continued.

"It's a pity that he had to return to Vienna so soon after the party; however, he will return next week. I received a note from him today, it looks like you've bewitched him."

"I didn't slip a potion in his drink or anything, only danced and talked."

"And have you thought about it since that night?"

Sara felt as though Irenka had punched her in the stomach. She did not reply.

"Your silence is enough of an answer, my friend."

"Oh, Irenka!" Sara said, looking down at the floor.

"Tell me, what does that sigh mean?"

"It means you've confused me."

"That's a good thing."

"No, Irenka, it is not. Look, the Captain is a very special man, a very charming man. I would be lying if I said that I have not thought about him. Any woman would be by a man like him; he handsome, with a brilliant career, chivalrous, excellent at conversation, a great dancer, with noble intentions. In other words, he lacks for nothing and has plenty of qualities.

"You've described him perfectly; I knew you'd like him."

"Oh, my friend, I am so sorry to disappoint you! Yes, I really like the Captain! What woman wouldn't?"

"So, what's wrong?"

"Irenka, my friend! I could never love another man. Although I have lost him, I still love Isaak."

Irenka was taken aback, she could not believe what she had just heard. If Sara's husband were not dead, she could understand it, but she was a widow with an opportunity to restart a life with a man who was without a doubt, her best match in all of Austria and Poland. Meanwhile, Sara looked at her apprehensively.

"Oh, Sara! Why are you so stubborn? Look, I understand that you loved your husband with all you heart, but I assure you that he himself would have wanted for you to be happy again."

"I don't think I ever will be. No man could make me happy again."

"That's ridiculous, you should get that thought out of your head."

"No, Irenka, it's not ridiculous. Anyway, putting my feelings aside, there is one thing you're forgetting."

"What's that?"

"I am a Jew, Irenka! Have you forgotten?"

"No, of course I haven't forgotten."

"Well, even if there were something between Captain Hoffman and me, it could never be anything serious."

"But why not?"

"My friend, I could never marry a man who was not a Jew, it's prohibited by Jewish law."

Irenka felt dispirited. This was something she had not considered. Lublin had a high proportion of Jewish residents and, yes, they married amongst themselves, but she also knew of many cases of marriage between Jews and Christians. Obviously, in those cases, one had abandoned their religion and converted to that of their spouse.

"Well, one of you could convert to the other's religion," she said, naively. To her, not having strong beliefs, it didn't seem unrealistic. She looked at Sara, waiting for a response.

"My dear friend, you are deluded. You know me, do you really think I would abandon my faith?"

Irenka didn't know what to say, so she merely shrugged and fell silent.

"Well, I'll answer myself. I will never stop being a Jew! I was born a Jew, and I will die a Jew! What's more, Gabriel will grow up to be a good man and a good Jew, just as his father predicted the last, we saw him, before he left for Siberia."

Irenka continued to stare at her.

"But also, my dear Irenka," she went on, "Captain Hoffman is a Catholic, he told me himself, as are all Austrians. Do you really think he would renounce Catholicism to marry me? Can you imagine Captain Hoffman converting to Judaism? Can you really picture a high-ranking officer in the Austrian navy being a Jew?"

Irenka remained silent, she obviously had nothing to say in response to Sara's argument. She wasn't even interested any more as she felt terribly disappointed. She had imagined a fairy-tale meeting, without ever considering whether or not it were realistic. She had grown fond of Sara, which is why she wanted her to rebuild her life. But of course, she could never be with the handsome and elegant Austrian officer, nor with any Pole, unless he was a Jew. Still, she thought Sara too stubborn; it seemed the memory of her late husband would accompany her to the grave.

She was absorbed in thought when the butler arrived onto the terrace, bowed, and announced:

"Excuse me, madam, but the boy who works with Mrs. Rothman is here, he says he needs to talk to her."

"Tell him to come through," Irenka said.

"Madam, the boy is not properly dressed."

"I'll go to the door!" Sara said, getting up.

"No, no, what nonsense!" Irenka replied, then addressed the butler, "Tell the boy to come through."

Sara had stood up; she was surprised to see that her delivery boy had come to speak to her. The news couldn't be anything related to Gabriel, as he was with her in the house, in the kitchen, where the cooks spoiled him with treats. Had something happened at the bakery? She was about to make for the door, but Irenka stopped her.

"Calm down, the boy is coming here."

Indeed, Sara's delivery boy, not yet 15, came to the terrace accompanied by the butler. In his hands he clutched his small beret, which he fiddled with nervously. Sara sensed that something was wrong, and addressed the boy:

"Tell me! What has happened?"

"Mrs. Sara, Tatiana sent me. There are two men looking for you."

"Two men at the bakery?" Sara asked.

"Yes, ma'am."

"Do you know them? Have you ever seen them before?"

"No ma'am, they're strangers."

Sara was intrigued, she had no idea who they could be nor why they were looking for her, but something told her it wasn't good. She continued to question the boy.

"Did they ask for me by name? Or just for the owner of the bakery?"

"By your name, ma'am," replied the boy, "Sara Rothman, the Jewess, they said."

Sara was confused, who could they be?

"Did you say they were strangers?"

"Yes, ma'am. They aren't from Lublin; I think they come from Bialystok."

Sara heart skipped a beat. Bialystok was becoming an increasingly distant memory to her since arriving in Lublin. It had never occurred to her to return to the city, her only connection with it were the notes she exchanged with Piotr in the search for Jana and Aliza. Maretska, her kind neighbour, had disappeared off the face of the earth, and nothing had been heard of her. She thought for a moment, she was beginning to suspect something she did not like.

"The men sent you to look for me. Did they ask you where I was?"

"No, ma'am, it was Tatiana who sent me to let you know. But I think she noticed something strange about their visit, because she told them she didn't know where you were. While, of course, she knew you were here."

"Why do you say Tatiana noticed something strange?"

"Because the men said they would wait for you, she offered them a seat, then hurriedly packed the basket with loaves and ordered me to deliver it, even though it's not yet delivery time. I was confused, but she whispered in my ear so that they could not hear and told me to tell you, because it was very important. She told me to tell you not to come back to the bakery for any reason."

Irenka listened attentively to the conversation. At last, she exclaimed:

"This is very strange, what do you think these two men want?"

"I don't know, Irenka, but it can't be good. Tatiana is a very smart girl, if she sent Henrik to warn me not to return, she must have noticed or heard something disturbing. She also didn't tell them that I was here, at your house."

"We have to find out what it is," Irenka said.

"Alright, but I shouldn't go."

"Of course not! Wait," she took the bell from the table and rang for the butler. A moment later he arrived, Irenka said to him:

"Call one of the girls, tell her to prepare to leave immediately. I have a task for her."

Sara was still thinking, suspecting that this surprise visit did not bode well. When the girl appeared on the terrace, Irenka gave her precise instructions; to go to Sara's bakery and buy some bread, as an excuse to talk to Tatiana without anyone listening in. That way, they could find out who these individuals were and what they wanted. They should talk in the back room, under no circumstances should she have anything to do with the men, much less tell them where she worked or that Sara was at here house.

The girl left quickly, leaving Sara worried and Irenka curious. The wait for her to return seemed to last forever. When she finally returned, the two women nearly pounced on her.

"Tell us, tell us, girl!" Irenka said to her, "Are the men still in the bakery?"

"Yes, madam, there were two men sat on the bench, talking."

"Well, what did you find out?"

"Well, Madam. I spoke to Tatiana; she told me that the two men were from Bialystok."

"By God, girl! We already know that! What else did Tatiana tell you?"

"She heard the men talk about an arrest warrant or something."

"An arrest warrant?" Sara asked, her voice trembling a little.

"Well, that's what Tatiana told me."

"Anything else?"

"Yes, madam, she heard one of the men say that a Marsosky would be arriving soon."

"Marsosky?" Sara asked her, she was about to continue, but flushed, and gently let herself fall onto the sofa.

Irenka was distressed, "Sara, what's wrong with you?"

"I know who she means," she said, "it's not Marsosky, it must be Marinowsky."

"You mean the wretch who tried to take advantage of you?"

"Yes, the same one who stole Isaak's shoe shop."

"I think I understand, my dear, but an arrest warrant? Why?"

"Because he can, Irenka. That swine holds a lot of power in Bialystok and is a friend of the Russian authorities. He can easily get a warrant for any crime I haven't committed. He's a very vindictive man."

"Good God, what will we do now?"

"I don't know, I don't know what to do." Sara admitted.

"Well, what we do know is that under no circumstances should you go near the bakery. You must stay here."

7

The straw from the barn, and the insects that swarmed there irritated her skin. Despite trying to sooth her skin Sara's skin was becoming red. Beside her, on a threadbare blanket. Gabriel slept peacefully, oblivious to his mother's suffering. She said to herself:

'My God, what have I done to deserve this punishment?'

She immediately repented her thoughts, she realised she had no right to address Hashem in that way, and apologised for the expression, focussing on her situation. The truth was that since the tragic events at the beginning of that year, when she had lost Isaak and the girls, her life had been a whirlwind of constant anguish, with little relief.

Once again, she had been forced to flee. Obviously, she had not returned to the bakery, and had stayed at Irenka's house, while Robiak, her coachman, a responsible 19-year-old boy, patrolled the surroundings to keep them informed of any events. Thanks to his reports, they learned that a couple of hours later Marinowsky had arrived, accompanied by two thugs. His face wore the satisfaction of finally having found Sara. However, as she was nowhere to be found, he took out his frustration on poor Tatiana. One of his men left for a few minutes, then returned with two policemen, who then intimidated the girl. She was forced to give up the address of her employer's apartment. Two of Marinowsky's made their way there, and the landlady allowed them in after they showed her the arrest warrant. The old woman could not read, but upon seeing the official markings, she did not resist. Her few, modest belongings were thrown to the floor, as the cruel men rummaged through the drawers. The Menorah that Isaak had inherited from his grandfather ended up smashed on the floor; however, when one of the men realised it was silver, he stashed it in a pillowcase, along with two or three other items. He found what little there was of value, including the savings that Sara had hidden behind the wardrobe, which were revealed when one of the savages had smashed it. Sara, being a woman and a Jew, could not open a bank account, so she had hidden the few coins she had, saved in the hope of one day collecting enough to buy the place where she baked the bread.

Marinowsky began to interrogate Tatiana and threatening her into revealing Sara's location. The girl bravely refused to speak, despite the blows she received, until a trickle of blood flowed from her mouth. Marinowsky was frustrated at the girl's silence and ordered his henchman to rip off the top of her dress.

"Let's see if, after a few blows to her breasts, this bitch starts talking," she said, as his thug slipped her dress down to her waist.

At that moment Tatiana taking advantage of the fact that the brute's hands were occupied pulling down her dress, ran for the door of the bakery. In her flight she stumbled, falling flat outside, but she got up quickly, going out into the street where two policemen and Marinowsky's other man were. The man caught her, while the policemen were stunned by the girl's naked torso. Desperate, Tatiana yelled at them in Russian:

"I am a subject of His Majesty Tsar Alexander! These Polish men trying to rape me, I am Russian, you have no right!"

The officers were Poles, but their chief, the Police Commissioner was a Russian. They knew well that he firmly opposed anyone harassing an imperial subject, and they preferred to avoid any trouble.

"Release the girl!" one of them said to the man, who held her tightly by the arm.

Marinowsky watched the scene from the doorway and gestured for the man to release Tatiana. She immediately pulled up her dress to cover her torso and fled the place. One of Marinowsky's men tried to follow her, but he stopped him.

"Leave her, Lublin is not so big that one Jewess can hide from us. We're going to police station, with my position and these documents they will me with the job."

At that moment the two men from Sara's apartment returned, informing him that they had found nothing. One of them was hiding the silver Menorah under his shirt, the other had in his pocket a pair of earrings and a silver chain that Irenka had given her friend to wear at the party. Sara's savings had also been distributed among them.

Tatiana ran to her employer's apartment, finding it in a mess. Sara and Gabriel's clothes, and their few belongings and kitchen utensils were scattered on the floor. The smashed wardrobe lay against the broken bed. The landlady, still in shock, asked who would pay for her furniture. Tatiana took a ribbon she found on the bed, using it to tie the upper part of her torn dress, then made for the door. As she was leaving something caught her attention, a cloth bag that lay under a broken painting, in the farthest corner. She picked it up, inside were two leather pouches, containing a crucifix and a note. Of course, Tatiana had never seen them before, but deduced that they must be important to Sara, and hid them under her dress and hurried out, ignoring the landlady's wails.

Meanwhile Robiak, Irenka's coachman, who had witnessed the entire scene along with several other bystanders, felt revolted at Tatiana's mistreatment. He had seen her before on several occasions when he was sent to the bakery with a message or to buy bread, a job he had taken from the kitchen assistant. This was not his role, rather he did it only to have a chance to see the beautiful Russian girl, with whom he was secretly in love. Although, due to his shyness, he had never gone beyond a cordial greeting and furtive look. Obviously, Tatiana had noticed this, making her blush, as the Polish boy was handsome and well-mannered. She was not entirely indifferent to him either.

As soon as Marinowsky had left, Robiak ran to the house to inform them of what he had seen. Irenka and Sara received him with anguish and listened to his story.

"I must flee, immediately." Sara gasped.

"No, Sara!" Her friend replied, "Where would you go?"

"I have no idea," she continued, "all I know is that I must leave Lublin as soon as possible. You don't know Marinowsky, he's vengeful and has a lot of power. Keep in mind that your coachman overheard him saying he was going to the police station. He'll find me eventually. Also, I can't put you in this position, they could accuse you of harbouring a fugitive."

"You are not a fugitive; you haven't done anything."

"You and I both know that, but do the Lublin police know it?"

"I don't care, I won't let you run away like a criminal. You'll be safe in my house."

"No, Irenka. If Marinowsky has an arrest warrant against me, the authorities will come for me. Neither the police nor judges in Lublin know that I am innocent and that the warrant is a fraud. If I stay in your house, it could cause you serious trouble and I can't allow that."

"That may be so, Sara, but situations like this are opportunities to demonstrate true friendship."

"Oh, my dear friend! You have always shown strong and unconditional friendship, you've given me more than I deserve and because of that, I have no right to cause you the slightest harm, let alone with the Russian authorities."

"No, Sara! You have nowhere to go."

"I'll see. Don't you worry, we'll keep in touch."

Irenka refused to give in and insisted that she stay in her house. Finally, Sara prevailed with her arguments and promised that she would return after hiding for a while. Irenka ordered Robiak to ready the carriage immediately.

Sara knew she would not be able to return to the bakery or apartment, and she did not even have a change of clothes, nor the minimal toiletries, but there was no time to lose. Irenka gave her a bag with a few coins and a basket of food. Words were unnecessary, Sara looked at her, then took her by the hand, saying goodbye to her friend with an embrace. She took Gabriel's arm and ran to the carriage that Robiak had waiting out the front of the house.

As she had told her friend, she had no idea where she would go, all she knew was that she had get as far from Bialystok as possible. She told the driver to take the Krasnik road. Sara was considering her situation, working out her next step now that she had become a fugitive overnight. She had the money Irenka had given her before leaving, but was afraid to take shelter in an inn, as she could easily be tracked there. She planned to stay in the countryside, as she couldn't take any risks. She would avoid staying in any locals' houses, as any one of them could give her away for a reward.

She remembered her flight from Bialystok, now she had least had Irenka's carriage and the summer weather, meaning that the nights would be more bearable. She thought that if she managed to make it to Krasnik, she would have put enough distance between herself and Marinowsky. But once there, what would she do? Sara was tired of having to work hard to achieve stability, only to have to run away and start all over again. Her disillusionment was such that she wasn't sure what she should do.

As night approached, Robiak told her that they would have to find a place for Sara and Gabriel to spend the night, as he had to return to Lublin. Sara sighed and said to the man:

"Given the circumstances, I won't be able to ask for accommodation at any house, nor go to an inn. We'll have to seek refuge somewhere in the countryside."

"Near Niedrzwica there's an abandoned farm, I've seen it from a distance. I know nobody lives there if you want, Mrs. Sara, we could have a look."

"That seems good to me," Sara replied, "let's go there, and I'll see what I can do tomorrow."

When they arrived at the crossroads, the driver directed the carriage to right. Indeed, about four hundred metres away, there lay an abandoned house and barn. on arrival they got out of the carriage; the house was completely uninhabitable, the roof and three of its walls had collapsed, and the remained one was leaning precariously. Because of this, they headed for the barn, which was also in a state of disrepair, at least it retained part of its roof, and the loft was accessible by an old ladder.

"Well," Sara said, "at least we'll have a shelter in case it rains tonight."

"Yes," Robiak replied, "it would be worse to have to sleep outside. Mrs. Sara, I must go, it's already late to return to Lublin."

"Thank you for everything, Robiak, I hope to see you again under better circumstances."

"I hope so too, madam," the man said, taking out some crumpled sheets of paper and a pencil from his shirt pocket. Handing them to Sara, he said:

"Mrs. Sara, I know you won't be able to stay here forever, and you'll want to avoid contact with people around here. Because of this, I propose that we keep communication about your location. Whenever you reach a crossroads, leave a note telling me where you plan to go and which direction, you're heading in. Hide the note under a stone, branch, board, anything, on the right side of the road after crossing. Do you understand?

"Robiak, I see you're a very smart man. I'll do as you say."

"If, for some reason, it's not possible to leave a note, do so at the next intersection. That way, no matter which direction you've headed, I can check all possible intersections and cardinal points."

"Oh!" Sara said in amazement, "You think of everything. I thank you."

"Thank you, madam. And one more thing, I lived with my father for a few years in Kyiv, so I speak Russian, and I can also read and write. The peasants in this region only speak Polish and very few can read. To keep our messages confidential, write to me in Russian."

"I'm impressed, Robiak, I'll follow your instructions to the letter."

The young man got on the carriage, encouraged the horses, and trotted back towards to Lublin. Sara stared at him as he went for a few minutes. She felt a terrible sense of loneliness overcome her. Leaning back against a nearby log, she placed Gabriel on her lap and couldn't help but weep. She cried with bitter sadness, until night fall upon them, and then entered the barn before the darkness made it difficult to see. She thought it would be safer to spend the night on the top floor, and so motioned for Gabriel to go upstairs before following him. The staircase had several rotten steps, so they took great care with each step. At last, they reached the top. Sara reached for the basket of food, taking out two pieces of bread and cheese, and a bottle of water. The two ate in silence.

She couldn't fall asleep, the barn was full of bedbugs, fleas, and other insects. Sara took off her dress, using it as a sheet for Gabriel hoping it would protect him from the insects, then covered him with her petticoat. Being half dressed, Sara's bare skin made her vulnerable. The next day she was covered in bites, making her desperate not to spend another moment there. However, when she was preparing to wake Gabriel, she heard voices and laughter. She quietly stood, trying to work out where they were coming from; the voices seemed to be approaching. She peered through the cracks of the wooden wall, and saw three men heading towards the barn, apparently drunk. They laughed loudly and walked unsteadily, and one of them still clutched a bottle in his hand. His ragged appearance and coarse gestures worried Sara, who at that moment felt a terrible chill, and panicked when she remembered her almost total nudity. Three ignorant and drunk peasants were heading towards her while she was not fully dressed. Realising the danger, she quickly woke Gabriel, telling him not to make the slightest movement and keep quiet, as the noise would alert the men. She quickly pulled up the ladder and hid it under the straw. She then curled up next to her son, motionless.

Sara could feel her heart beating out of her chest and tried to make no noise with her breathing. The drunkards entered and sat in the stable's doorway. One of them exclaimed:

"Well, show us, where did you leave the bottles?"

"Right here, wait and see."

The woman stood still listening to everything, including their foul language.

"Ha ha ha! I told you, the three bottles I stole from the old man are safe here."

"Fine, but didn't you say there were five?"

"Yes, of course, but I wasn't going to leave them all in the same place! Do you think I'm stupid?"

"You're only stupid for being with your wife!"

"Say that again and I'll being your nose!"

The third man interrupted them.

"Stop arguing, where did you hide the other bottles?"

"Up in the loft," answered the first man, "I'll go up for them."

Sara felt a chill run through her body, she almost fainted from the panic.

"Well, I can't see the ladder, it looks like someone's taken it!"

"Well, let's leave it then. It's late, let's take these bottles and pick up the ones you left on the way back. Come on!"

Sara felt a tremendous sense of relief, but she remained motionless and barely breathed, until she heard the voices fade into the distance. Carefully, she got up and looked through the crack to check that the men were going away, then she sighed in relief.

She left the barn and headed for Krasnik, avoiding any passersby. Whenever she saw a cart or rider in the distance, she would get off of the road and hide. On two occasions she didn't manage to find cover, but there was no trouble as the travellers, despite staring, did not bother her beyond a greeting.

She reached Wilkolaz, which was only a cluster of eight houses on either side of the road. Sara had already decided that under no circumstances would she spend another night in a place like the barn; in addition to being unable to sleep, the insects had bitten at her all night long. The bites, especially on her legs, had turned into a real torture. She would ask to stay in a house and pay for the lodging, but first she wanted to pray for forgiveness from God, for ever having doubted him. She truly was thankful for be a Jew and had the conviction that He would never abandon her.

The moment she finished praying, she noticed something that warmed her heart. She couldn't be certain, but as she approached the second house on the left, all doubt left her mind. Next to the door was a *Mezuzah*.

"Oh, Hashem, thank you, thank you!" She exclaimed.

It was a Jewish home, and if anything defines that people, it would be their solidarity and kindness to those in need, particularly towards another Jew in a desperate situation. She did not hesitate before knocking at the door. A short while later a middle-aged woman opened it, staring at her strangely. Apparently, it was not common for strangers to call, as they usually passed through, headed for Krasnik.

"Shalom Alechem," Sara greeted her with a slight bow.

"Alechem Shalom," the housewife replied with a smile, then upon noticing Gabriel who clutched Sara's hand, invited her inside. Sara smiled gratefully, she hadn't even asked what she wanted, simply invited her inside.

'*What a joy to find a Jewish home.*' Sara said to herself.

She had spent two days at the Jewish couple's house in Wilkolaz; she had been welcomed like a daughter of the house. The wife, also named Sara, had treated her skin irritation with a special concoction made from camphor, and they had provided them hot food and a place to sleep. The house was modest and simple, but it had a large living room, dining room, and even a spare room, to which they were welcome. This was a blessing for Sara, her second night as a fugitive was totally different from that in the barn. The next day, very early, she left her usual note at the crossroads with about four hundred metres from the house. The hosts had told her that she could stay with them as long as necessary, until she recovered from her skin problems. Sara thanked them wholeheartedly and offered to pay for her stay, but the couple flatly refused.

On the second day she was sitting helping her hostess to prepare a meal, while telling her the story of her life, when there was a knock at the door. Sara was startled, got up and took Gabriel's hand, who was playing on the small sofa in the living room. The housewife opened the door and asked the stranger what she could do for him. When he answered, Sara immediately recognised Robiak's voice and ran to the door.

"Hello, Robiak! What a joy it is to see you!"

"Good morning, Mrs. Sara," replied the boy, "I have come to find where you are, on behalf of Mistress Irenka."

"Tell me, how is she? How are things in Lublin?"

The young man looked at the housewife again, but Sara reassured him:

"My hostess knows the whole story; you can speak with confidence."

"What I know is that the man who seeks you is still in Lublin, but my mistress wants to tell you the details directly."

"Alright, but I don't think I can return to Lublin."

"That won't be necessary, she asked me to locate you so that she could come to see you personally. Now that I know where you are, I can pass on the information to her."

"It would be wonderful to see her."

"Very well, Mrs. Sara. I will return to Lublin. I should arrive with my mistress tomorrow."

"I will delight to wait for you. Thank you, Robiak."

The next day, Irenka arrived as impetuously as always. Sara received her joyfully with an embrace. She introduced her to Sara, the housewife, indicating that they could speak freely in front of her and her husband, Tobias, who was yet to arrive.

"I see that you are well, my dear Sara. I am very relieved."

"It's thanks to my hosts, God placed them on my path. But tell me, how are things in Lublin?"

"Marinowsky is very stubborn and seems to have influence among the police. I have already had the displeasure of meeting him as he came to my house."

"He came to your home?"

"Indeed, he arrived with five or six policemen. He is a vile character."

"What did he do?"

"He behaved in a was rude and arrogant manner. He also tried to intimidate me for having received you into my house."

"How typical of that wretched man!"

"But you know that I am not a fool, I put him in his place at one. Among other things I told him that I was free to choose my friends and have whosoever I please in my house."

"You told him that?"

"Yes, of course, and that wasn't all. I also made it clear that I knew the true story of the events in Bialystok, and the fact that he had tried to abuse you."

"You are very daring, but I understand that he is still in Lublin. Has he not sent men to look for me in the surrounding area?"

"Ha! My dear Sara, I already told you, I am not stupid, and I also have contacts."

"What do you mean?"

"I took advantage of the fact that I have a friend with certain influence amongst the police. He has spread the rumour that you remain in the city."

"Oh, Irenka! You're amazing!"

"That's not all. I've sent a message to Carl for him to return to Lublin as soon as possible. You know that he is a lawyer, and he'll take care of this case. Marinowsky may have influence, but it's one thing to face a lone widow, and quite another to take on a prestigious lawyer."

"Irenka, you have been a true guardian angel to me," she turned to the housewife and said, "you see why I told you she is a very special person?"

"It's not like that, you know the love I have for you," Irenka replied with a mischievous grin, "and there's more."

"Something else? What do you mean?"

"The day you fled, I received a message from Captain Hoffman asking about you, expressing his desire to see you again."

Sara remembers the dashing officer. However, she had too many problems right now to devote any thought to the Austrian.

"That's very kind of him."

"It's much more than simple kindness, although he is, of course, a gentleman. I replied immediately telling him of the events you were facing, and the injustice of them."

"Oh no, Irenka! Why did you tell him?"

"Do you mind that he knows of the matter?"

"No, it's not that, only that I ashamed for him to find out. Although it's unfair, the police are looking for me to arrest me. That's nothing to be proud of."

"Well, I'm sorry but I'm sure it's already arrived. I sent my letter as quickly as possible, although in our country that doesn't mean much."

Sara changed the subject, instead asking her friend:

"What about my apartment? The landlady must be wondering why I have not returned. I hope everything is alright."

"Oh, my dear Sara! I'm sorry to tell you this, but Marinowsky's men ransacked your apartment."

"Oh, God! What other evils will this man bring upon me?"

"What's more, your bakery is closed, Sara. The police shut it down."

"What's happened to Tatiana?"

"I have not heard from her."

"What will become of her? She's a brave girl."

"Robiak is looking for her, but so far, he has found nothing. It's as though the earth has swallowed her."

"Poor girl," Sara said, "I have a great love for her, and I owe her a lot. May God grant that nothing happens to her."

"She also showed you an unquestioning loyalty, when the men looked for you at the bakery, she never revealed that you were at my house."

"Yes, and she acted intelligently by warning us. She must be hiding somewhere."

"Robiak will continue looking for her, I think his interest in finding her goes beyond simply following my orders."

Sara thought for a moment, there was nothing unusual about this. Tatiana was very attractive and had a sweet character. The young man was also intelligent and helpful, as well as attractive. They could make a wonderful couple.

'*Unfortunately, he's not a Jew, like Tatiana,*' Sara thought.

"Well, my dear friend, I must leave." Irenka said, interrupting her thoughts "I will come to see you the day after tomorrow, with better news, I hope."

Irenka got up, Sara accompanied her to the door, thanking her, not only for the visit, but also for everything she was doing for her in Lublin. Although her terrible situation was yet to be resolved, and prison for no crime was still a prospect, she felt strangely calm. Tobias and Sara had received her into their home as if they had always known her. She felt a special warmth there, although she could not say why. The house was so reassuring that she could almost forget her problems.

That night, once little Gabriel was asleep, she reflected on her sense of tranquillity, until she understood it. The reason was simple; for the first time in many months, she was in a Jewish home, with its customs, food, and respect for the simple but important things in life. Life there meant reading the Torah, and a daily prayer that Tobias never forgot with his Tefillin. At that moment she realised that if her apartment had been ransacked, Isaak's Tefillin, which she had treasured, must have been lost. Likewise, her savings would also be gone, but what she truly missed was the Tefillin. That and the silver Menorah were the only reminders he had of her beloved Isaak. She closed her eyes and wept silently.

The next day passed slowly and leisurely. Sara talked with her hostess a lot, telling her the whole story of her life, from when she was a child, to her misfortunes in Bialystok and now in Lublin. Tobias also spent the day at home, as the mill he owned was undergoing maintenance. The couple told Sara their own story. They had lived their entire lives in Lublin, and the last five years in this village. They had two children, both grown up and married. One lived in Warsaw and the other was much farther away, in Antwerp, where he had prospered in the diamond industry. Every year, the two children visited, either in the summer or for Hanukkah.

"They are our blessings."

"I can believe that I'm happy for you."

"Although we miss them, I'm happy that they have settled in big cities where they have been able to get ahead. In these ignorant and remote parts, they would never had made it."

"I think the same," said their mother, "I really need them, but I know that they are well, and the most important thing is that they are both married to good women; pious Jews who maintain beautiful homes."

"That is wonderful," said Sara, "it is important to maintain one's traditions. Besides, here you live peacefully."

"Indeed," exclaimed Tobias, "these are times of relative calm, not like those my father had to live through. He passed away last year, but I always remember him telling me that the world was in a permanent state of madness, because of men's ambition. He would sit with a glass of wine, and always say to me: 'Now one doesn't even know which nation one belongs to, my son. I was a Pole, then Napoleon's troops came, and we were French. Then we were Prussians, now we are Russian. What will we be tomorrow? Chinese?'

I would laugh, but I had to accept that my father was right. Eastern Europe has not had stability for centuries. We live in accordance to whims of tyrants and end up having to learn four or five languages. At least we Jews have been smart; we all speak Yiddish, even if we have to learn another additional language. It does not matter in which country we live; we always understand each other."

The hours passed pleasantly for Sara, as the couple's conversation was interesting and engaging. However, she could not stop thinking about how events were unfolding in Lublin, which would determine her future and that of Gabriel. She carried this anxiety within, though it only surfaced from time to time. She nervously waited for tomorrow to come, and for Irenka to bring her news.

Indeed, just as her friend had promised, she arrived at the village around eleven in the morning, with baskets overflowing with food for the couple, in return for their generosity in helping her friend. Everyday Sara was given more reasons to believe that God had sent this woman to her. The fact that when she visited, she made a detour to avoid being followed and thus not giving away Sara's location, was a sign of affection and friendship that Sara greatly valued.

Irenka's visit was a cause for joy in itself, but it brought no definitive news. Marinowsky had not abandoned his efforts to find her and continued searching Lublin inquiring about her location with the help of the police, which, Irenka affirmed, seemed to have nothing else to do.

Irenka puzzled over this. Why the obsession of Marinowsky to capture Sara? If she had committed some act against him, it would be understandable, but the opposite was the case. Did he really seek revenge for the beating she had given him inside the shop that he had stolen from her husband? Irenka couldn't believe, partly because on one else had seen it happen. She concluded that the only explanation could be his obsession with taking her to bed. Which had become his sick obsession. Certainly, Sara possessed an extraordinary and unusual beauty; so it was not strange for men to fall in love with her and seek to woo her, but to pursue her in such a way, using an arrest warrant to catch her, meant that she was already lost to him.

She had considered this during her trip and had come to tell Sara her conclusions. After listening to her, Sara agreed. She confessed that she had not noticed it, but upon analysing the events, it seemed to be his motive.

On the other hand, the only other news Irenka had for her was from Captain Hoffman; he had received the message and become very interested in the situation. He was not able to come to Lublin as he had orders to travel to Trieste, but he had contacted a family lawyer with instructions to take up the case alongside Carl. He wanted Sara to know that as soon as his mission in the Mediterranean was over, he would return to Poland to visit her. Sara passed on her thanks but did not like being so indebted to the Austrian officer.

"Well, my dear friend, I will visit you the day after tomorrow, or the next, depending on Carl's arrival."

"Thank you so much, I will wait attentively."

"I must go, I do not wish to arrive at Lublin too late."

Sara hugged her and walked her to the carriage, then followed her with her gaze as she drove down the dusty road.

'Well,' she consoled herself, '*in two or three days Irenka will return, I hope that this horrible situation will finally end.*'

However, it didn't take that long for Irenka to return. Barely five hours had passed before she arrived like a hurricane; she rushed down from the carriage and shouted for her friend, before even reaching the door.

"Sara, Sara! It's Irenka, open the door, quickly, open it!"

Her cries echoed throughout the village, Irenka seemed to have gone mad. Sara was startled by her screams; she went to Gabriel who was in the next room, to flee through the back door. She assumed that Marinowsky was coming for her, accompanied by who knows how many policemen.

Tobias opened the door and Irenka rushed into the house. Sara stood terrified on the far side of the room; her friend called to her desperately.

"Come, come, you won't believe it! You won't believe it!"

She took her hand and practically dragged her onto the street. Outside, her friend pointed towards another carriage. When she saw it, it was as if her heart jumped out of her chest, a violent shake ran through her body. She put her hands to her face and began to tremble, then opened her arms as the two girls ran towards her. Finally, she was able to utter a word:

"My girls! My girls!" She exclaimed through tears. Her words were interrupted by sobs.

The three of them embraced with such force that they could not breath. Sara did not stop crying, she tried to speak, but the words came out as a whimper. All she could say was:

"My girls, my girls, it's a miracle!"

Her cheeks were coated in tears, and she held Jana and Aliza so tightly that they were nearly suffocating. It was as if she thought that were she to let them go they would vanish. The two girls clung to Sara as though she were a lifejacket in the middle of a stormy sea. Irenka had taken out her handkerchief and dried her own face, which was also wet with tears.

More than two minutes had passed, and the women were still embracing. Sara did not stop crying and had buried her head between their shoulders. At last, though still weeping, she began to speak more normally.

"I thought I had lost you forever! I love you so much, my girls!"

Immediately, she started crying again; it was a moving sight. Tobias had not spoken a word to his wife as they watched the emotional scene, standing still. Irenka also remained motionless, and a boy who had also dismounted from the carriage and looked upon the women with evident joy. Meanwhile, some neighbours who had left their houses when Irenka had screamed, looked curiously on the events. They did not know these women but were moved to tears by the happy reunion.

Finally, Sara parted slightly from the girls and took their faces in her hands, first the oldest.

"My dear Jana, my beloved doll!" Sara said as she pressed Jana's head against her chest. She made the same gesture to the younger of the two, saying sweetly.

"My beautiful girl, my darling Aliza!"

She then took them by their arms and pressed them to her sides, looking at them with such tenderness and love that they could not resist pouncing on her again, and hugging her tightly. After a few moments, Irenka approached, Sara drew her in, and the four of them embraced.

The young girls remained at her side each taking Sara by an arm. She looked at them and exclaimed:

"I can't believe it, I spent so many nights in anguish, thinking about my girls, and now I have them back!" she looked up to the sky and exclaimed, "Thank you, Hashem! In the end, you do not forget your people! Thank you, thank you!"

Only then did she begin to breathe more evenly, trying to recover a little. Sara, her hostess, approached and gave her a hug, saying:

"I can't tell you how happy I am, this is such a beautiful scene."

Then she held each of the girls, saying:

"I have learned over the last few days of your sad disappearance, and today Hashem gives us the opportunity to witness a happy ending, I'm so overcome with joy."

Everybody was excited. Tobias had still not moved from the door, from where he told the neighbours what he knew of the story. They held hands, looking at Sara and the girls with expressions of joy. Finally, Tobias' wife said:

"Well, I think we all deserve some tea to celebrate this reunion. Come on, let me invite you inside."

Jana called the boy who stood next to the car where the girls had dismounted, indicating for him to come closer. She took him by the arm, led him to Sara, and said:

"I want to introduce Oizer to you. Thanks to him, we've made it here."

Somewhat intrigued, Sara looked at him gratefully, and greeted him kindly.

"It is a delight to meet you. I don't know the details, but thanks for bringing my girls to me."

Sara still had some tears in her eyes. Gabriel, who remained in the guest room, playing with a rocking horse that Tobias had given him, had not noticed the dramatic events. He came outside at that moment and shouted:

"Jana! Aliza!"

The boy ran towards the girls, and they knelt down to receive him. The three of them formed a tight hug, while everyone present smiled at them tenderly.

Sara was sitting on the living room sofa, between the two girls. Her face was radiant, and her charming smile did not leave her for a second. Irenka, meanwhile, looked at her with tenderness and joy. Gabriel was sat on Jana's lap, who stroked his hair. Their hostess was busy making tea, helped by her husband. The atmosphere was filled with happiness.

"I'm the happiest woman in the world!" Sara exclaimed, "I almost feel reborn having them by my side again!" They smiled and moved closer to her. Sara turned to her friend and exclaimed:

"You don't know how much I appreciate you forgiving me so much happiness, my dear Irenka," she continued, "But tell me, how did you find my girls?"

"I didn't find them," her friend replied, "they found me."

"What do you mean?"

"They came to my house looking for me, but as I was still returning from seeing you, the butler had them wait in the living room until I arrived. Of course, it was a wonderful surprise; so, I didn't waste a moment and I came straight back here with them."

Sara looked at Jana first, and then Aliza.

"But, my girls, how did you get to Irenka's house?"

"It's a very long story, mother," said Jana.

Sara had thought she had reached her limit for happiness that day, but to hear '*mother*' made her heart want to burst.

8

Upon hearing the screams of the crowd, Jana remembered a similar scene. Some years ago, in Odessa, she had encountered a similar scene and had heard anti-Jewish slogans being shouted. She took Aliza's hand, looked into her eyes, and realised that they were both thinking the same thing. They had both already suffered through a bitter experience and knew that they should not stay where they were a moment longer. As Maretska hid her daughters in the far room, Jana hastily packed a canvas sack with food from the kitchen: bread, cheese, chickpeas, a bottle of water from the cupboard, and said to her sister:

"Come on, Aliza! There's no time to lose!"

The two girls rushed out, circled the house, and ran down the side path. The crowd was less the one hundred metres away, and some were already attacking the home of another Jewish family on the same street, and others were heading directly toward Isaak's house. The two girls narrowly escaped notice by crouching down as they crept through the snow.

They moved cautiously, going around the rear of the houses on the outskirts of town. From there, they could see the parts of Bialystok where there were anti-Jewish riots, and to realise that they had to get away from the city as soon as possible. It was not the first time that the girls had come across this sort of situation, so they cut through fields looking for the route to Grodek. Once on the road they advanced at a quick pace, intent on putting as much distance between the city and themselves as possible, and on reaching Grodek before nightfall. Fortunately, they were both wrapped up warmly, but it would not be enough to endure a winter's night out in the open.

They continued walking at their fast pace, avoiding any passers-by, until there could see the first houses of the town in the distance, just before night fell. They knew that that it would not be wise to seek refuge in any of them, so they looked for a stable or barn. From prior experience, they that the latter would be preferable, as stables tended to be closer to peasant houses were dogs could alert the owners to a stranger's presence.

They wandered around but couldn't find any suitable place, until at last they noticed a small wooden building. It was half ruined, but at least there was some thatch, a roof, and four walls.

That night was terrible for the girls; they could not sleep because of the cold, and constantly had to move their arms and legs to avoid freezing as, although there was some dry wood, they had no way to start a fire. Despite holding each other close they could do nothing to fight off the cold; so, before dawn they resumed their march, realising that they had to keep moving to avoid freezing. As they walked, they ate some bread and cheese.

They walked as quickly as possible along the path. The cold was still unbearable, but at least they had warmed a little thanks to the exercise. They soon approached the next town, Pogranichnyy.

"We'll have to ask for help here," said Jana, "we can't survive another night outside."

"Alright," Aliza replied, "my feet are freezing."

"I'm also freezing, but that's not all. Look, it's starting to snow."

Sure enough, snowflakes began to fall, heavier and heavier. The girls quickened their pace to try and reach a farmhouse as soon as possible. About three hundred metres ahead they noticed something strange; a carriage had stopped. The girls continued along the road, getting closer. They saw a tall, stocky man supervising the work of two others who were struggling to replace one of the carriage's wheels. Next to him was a boy in a black coat and fur cap. When the man noticed their presence, he was surprised, looking down the road from where they had come, as if trying to spot a carriage or cart. It was very strange to see two girls walking down the road in these conditions. The man turned to the boy, giving him instructions. The boy trotted towards the girls, and asked them in Russian:

"Hello, do you speak Russian?"

"Yes, we can." Jana replied.

"Very well, my father wants to talk to you."

He pointed them towards the carriage, accompanying them as they approached. The man in the coat stood staring at them.

"It's unusual to see two girls walking through these parts in the middle of winter. Where do you come from?"

"Good afternoon, sir. We come from Bialystok," Jana answered, shivering with cold.

"And where are you headed?"

The two girls looked at each other, they weren't sure how to answer.

"Well, the truth is we don't know."

The man looked them, puzzled. He motioned to his men to hurry their repairs, then took the girls aside.

"This is very unusual; I don't quite understand. Where are you going? Why are you alone and without any means of transport?"

The two girls lowered their heads and did not reply, which only increased the man's curiosity.

"Why don't you answer?"

At last Jana raised her head, and said to him:

"We're going to Minsk."

"To Minsk? You're going to that city alone, on foot, in the middle of winter?" He came a little closer and said, "Come on, girls, tell me the truth."

"Well," said Jana, "the truth is we don't really know."

"You don't know?"

The man thought for a moment, then asked them:

"What are your names?"

"I am Jana, and this is my sister Aliza."

"Hmm" the man stared at them, then asked, "Are you Jews?"

The girls were a little startled, they turned to one another. At last Jana spoke, answering firmly:

"Yes sir, we are Jews!"

The two of them looked at him fearfully. The man raised his hat a little, then completely removed it. They could see that he was wearing a kippah. They were relieved, Jana released the breath she had been holding in and smiled.

The man understood that they were fleeing the persecution and riots that Jews were suffering in Bialystok. He was curious to know their story, but this was neither the place nor the time, they were both freezing standing in the middle of the road. He told them to get into the carriage while the repairs were finished, so that they could shelter from the cold. Inside there was a small stove that generated some comforting warmth. The sisters sat together, as close to the heat as they could.

A few minutes later the damage had been repaired, the two workers got on the driver's seat, and the man and boy entered the carriage, but not before shaking off the snow that had fallen on their heads and shoulders.

"Well, I see that you girls are coming round now," he said, taking out a thick blanket from under the seat to warm them even more.

"Thank you," they replied in unison.

"My name is Jared," he said, "Jared Czemerinsky, this is my son Oizer."

"Pleased to meet you, my name is Jana Rothman, this is my sister Aliza."

"Well, Jana and Aliza, now I'd like to hear your story."

The girls told him the details of their experiences in Bialystok during the last three days, and how they had to flee to save themselves, leaving at the precise moment that the mob had attacked their house where they had had to abandon all their belongings. Jared took pity on their situation, reassuring them that he would not abandon them in their hardship.

"A Jew never abandons another, when he is in danger," he said quietly.

Soon after sunset, they arrived in Vawkavysk, stopping at an inn where the owners knew Jared, cordially greeting him by name and attending to him promptly. Shortly, they were sitting at a long wooden table enjoying a hot and hearty Zurek, the typical and tasty Polish Soup. They were next to couple of diners whose eastern features indicated that they were beyond the Urals. Jared thought about what to do with the two girls; they were helpless and could not be left unprotected in such harsh conditions, but on the other hand, he could not delay his business trip, which had already dragged on too long for various reasons.

Jared was a timber merchant, running a logging company in the Pinsk area. From there, he transported logs to Brest Litovsk, where they were shipped down the western Bug river to Nowy Dwor, near Warsaw, where he owned a sawmill with some Polish and Prussian partners. The wooden planks were sold partly in Warsaw and partly in Prussia. It was a good business, but it required a lot of paperwork, good management, and transport, since the process had to start no later than a month after the start of spring, so that by the time the timber needed to by transported by water, the river had already begun to thaw.

Jared had been greatly affected by the instability of administrative regulations under imperial rule. Every time a new official arrived at one of the relevant ministries, the rules of the game changed. That year, Tsar Alexander had introduced new bureaucratic appointments, bringing with them a complex bureaucratisation of permits for the felling and transportation of timber whose sole purpose was to collect more in taxes. In addition, he also had to consider the bribes and supplements he was forced to pay, as a Jew, to be able to carry out his business extra demands from an anti-Jewish Russia.

Hence, the importance of his trip; he had to get to St. Petersburg as quickly as possible to obtain the necessary permits that would allow him to start logging in mid-April. These procedures took time and required many appointments and endless waiting rooms. As if that were not enough, this time he had to carry this out personally, having lost his connection in the imperial capital. Iván Borisov was the person who had made contacts between mid-ranking court members and officials who worked in the web of government offices.

Borisov could not have thought of a better way to fight of the cold and boredom of winter nights, than to spend them under the sheets with the wife of an official in the Central Tax Office. Unfortunately, the tax officer had returned to St. Petersburg early, having conducted some official errands in Moscow. Consequently, Ivan found himself leaping, naked, out of a window into a snow-covered street, trying to avoid a pistol shot that the man intended for him. In addition to enduring the laughter and mockery of passers-by, he also caught pneumonia from which he did not recover, dying a few days later.

These events, which were the talk of capital's society for a few days, had indirectly affected Jared. Not only had his business group to a halt in St. Petersburg, but he had the contacts. Delaying and making it more difficult for him to acquire all the necessary permits to start the process of felling and transporting wood.

He considered this while smoking a cigar and having a glass of vodka in front of the fireplace. At one side was his son Oizer. His sixteen-year-old son, Oizer was at his side, but was an avid reader, now absorbed in a book, taking advantage of the light from a lamp on a nearby table. On his other side, sharing the same chair and half-asleep, were Jana and Aliza. Jared looked at them, was moved remembering their story, and how helpless they had looked after the tragic events that they had suffered on two occasions. He thought again about what to do; he could not leave them there, but to take them with him would be absurd. He had too many responsibilities in the near future to take responsibility for two girls he had just met. He addressed Jana, who seemed to be the only one to speak.

"We must decide what will become of you. I must continue my journey early tomorrow morning, and my destination is quite far away."

"Don't worry, Mr. Czemerinsky, you have helped us a lot," said Jana, "I understand your situation. We will decide what to do tomorrow."

The boy, listening to their conversation, intervened.

"Father, we cannot abandon them."

"I am not suggesting that, but we have to decide what to do in these circumstances."

He thought for a moment, then continued,

"You cannot return to Bialystok," he said, turning to them, then added, "it would be too dangerous, hate has been stirred up against the Jews. So, we will do the following. You will remain here in the inn, Oizer will stay here with you. I will go to the city to look for your adoptive parents. I need you to give me the directions to your house, or what is left of it. Hopefully I will be able to talk to the neighbours; therefore, I need the names of people your parents knew. As for the city authorities, I will contact them if necessary."

Unfortunately, there was not much the girls could tell him, other than the names of some other residents in the neighbourhood. Despite Isaak and Sara being popular and appreciated in Bialystok, and their greeting people they met in the street, Jana and Aliza did not know their names nor where they lived. However, they gave Jared directions to find the Rabbi and Maretska, and the location of the shoe shop and bakery.

"Well," he said, "not to worry, with these names and the help of the authorities, I will surely be able to find them."

He rose from his chair exclaimed:

"Now, let us rest, it's been a very exhausting day."

Very early next morning, he left for Bialystok. Indeed, he found the city on edge, with an uncontrolled anger against Jewish people. Despite being one, he did not worry. He was a Russian citizen and wealthy merchant, as clearly demonstrated by his carriage and clothing.

He reached the ruins of what had been the Rothman's home, the snow almost completely covered the charred timbers. Some of the surrounding houses had also been burned or suffered extensive damage. He inquired of some of the neighbours; however, all he could learn was that the girls' adoptive mother had taken refuge in a neighbour's house before leaving for the city centre, accompanied by the neighbour's son, who had soon returned alone.

"Can I speak with their neighbour? What's her name?" Jared asked.

"Her name is Maretska, but she doesn't live here anymore," they replied.

Jared made his way to the city centre, passing Isaak's shoe shop, where he found men picking up debris and repairing the front door. They informed him that they were working under the orders of the prefect of police. Jared assumed that the police had taken this responsibility to prevent looting. From there, following Jana's directions, he went to Sara's bakery. At first, he couldn't find it, as practically all shops on that street had been destroy and some burned down. Someone pointed out to him where the business had once been. It was totally burnt out.

Finally, he spoke with the authorities, while his men visited the hospital and morgue. The only thing that was clear from his inquiry was that Isaak had been arrested and sent to Siberia. As for Sara, she had apparently fled the city. He was faced with no choice but to return to Vawkavysk to continue his journey, but what could he do with the girls? He pondered this, when he noticed a man walking down the street who had once been his agent in Brest. He remembered him as a good worker, efficient and honest, in charge of receiving logs and preparing them for shipping. He was a good man but had resigned after a family tragedy; his adolescent daughter had died of cholera. He could recall his name and called to him, while ordering his driver to stop.

"Hey, Piotr, Piotr Poniatowsky! How are you?"

Piotr turned his head and narrowed his eyes, trying to place the man who was speaking to him. When he finally recognised him, he took off his hat and approached the carriage.

"Good afternoon, Mr. Czemerinsky," he said, bowing slightly, "I'm glad to see you. What brings you to Bialystok?"

"Business, business, as always," Jared replied, noting the toy that Piotr was holding, a beautiful wooden stroller.

"Do you still practice woodwork as a hobby? Looking at that stroller, I see that you haven't lost your ability."

"No, Mr. Czemerinsky, I've left that hobby. I made this toy for a boy who came to visit me a couple of days ago".

He suddenly he fell silent, realising how unwise it was to talk about his guests, even with his former employer. After all, Sara and little Gabriel remained hidden, as the city was still in turmoil.

"Well, Piotr, I must be on my way, but I hope to see you in the near future. I often go through Bialystok, when I return, I will come visit. Where do you live?"

"Very close by, Mr. Czemerinsky, just around that corner, in the green house with the small front garden."

"I'll keep that in mind, my old friend, say hello to your wife, uh ... I can't quite remember her name ..."

"Malka, Mr. Czemerinsky."

"Yes, Malka, give her my regards."

They said a cordial farewell, and, as the carriage went through the streets in search of the road to Vawkavysk, Jared thought about what to do with the girls; he would have to take them with him, he could not abandon them to their fate.

Jana and Aliza cried inconsolably upon hearing the news from Bialystok: Isaak deported by the Russians, on his way to Siberia, Sara and Gabriel disappeared. The girls felt like the sky was falling, they felt they were reliving the tragedy they had experienced in Odessa. To be orphans again broke their hearts. Jared tried to comfort them:

"Girls, you will come with me. I will protect you and keep you in my care."

They looked at him gratefully but could not stop crying. Jared knew Isaak's fate was sealed but held out hope that Sara was still alive and that one day they could find her.

"I give you my word that I will do everything in my power to find your mother. Tomorrow we must continue the journey, but as soon as possible we will return and begin our search, I promise."

"Thank you so much, Mr. Czemerinsky," said Aliza.

Jana nodded, echoing her sister's words.

"Well, should rest, as we leave early tomorrow. I wish you a good night," he said, climbing the stairs to the second floor.

The girls were left in their sadness, sitting in front of the fireplace thinking over their misfortune. Oizer joined them, trying to comfort them.

"Don't worry, my father is a good person. He treats his workers well and always helps. He keeps his word and if he has promised to look for your mother, you can be sure that he will."

"Yes, Oizer, we can tell that he's a good man," Jana said, "can I ask you a question?"

"Of course, what is it?"

"Where are we going?"

"St. Petersburg."

"So far?" Jana said, widening her eyes.

"Oh no," said Aliza, "how can we look for our mother when we are so far from Bialystok?"

"My father has business in St. Petersburg, but don't worry. As soon as he finishes, we will return to Minsk, where my mother and brothers live."

The two girls disconcerted. A strip to St. Petersburg would take many days, and many more to return. By the time they were back in Bialystok it might be too late to try and find Sara.

That night a snowstorm began, making the roads impassable. To Jared's frustration, they had to spend three whole days in the town without leaving the inn. The girls took the opportunity to get to know Oizer better, with whom they got on very well as they were about the same age. He was a very mature, calm, and focussed boy. He had travelled with his father on various occasions, and was familiar not only with Warsaw, but cities as distant as Berlin and Budapest. Additionally, he had become well-versed in the ins and outs of the timber business; as his father wished, he was preparing to one day take over the reins of the company.

Finally, the weather began to improve, and the roads became passable again. They got in the carriage and left for Shcuchyn, arriving at nightfall. They spent the night there, and the next day continued on the road, arriving at Lida in the afternoon. Shortly before entering the town, at a crossroads, two soldiers on horseback forced them to stop the carriage. Leaning out of the window, Jared asked one of the soldiers:

"Good afternoon, gentlemen, is there a problem?"

"Good afternoon, please wait here while the wagons pass."

Jared, Oizer, and the girls looked to the left; indeed, several horse-drawn wagons were moving slowly, escorted by cavalrymen. Behind the rough, wooden railings were several dozen dirty, gaunt men, some with heads uncovered and all shivering with cold. It was obvious that they were prisoners, as their ankles were shackled. The scene was hard to watch; Jared asked the soldier closest to the carriage:

"Where are you taking those prisoners?"

"To Siberia, they'll arrive before summer."

The prisoners seemed interested in the carriage that stopped by the crossroads; they raised their eyes and stared at Jared and the girls. All but one, who kept his head down and seem to be praying. From his prayers in an almost inaudible voice: '*Hashem, if this is the destiny you chose for me, I will accept it with humility. I only ask you to protect my wife, my beloved son, and my precious girls.*' He then said to himself: '*I would give anything to be able to see you again, even for a moment.*'

At that moment, like the rest of the prisoners, he looked upwards towards the carriage that was being left behind. For some strange reason, he felt a shiver.

Jared strode into the living room, took off his coat and hung it on the rack, and, rubbing his hands, he headed for the fireplace. Even though spring had been with them for over fifteen days ago, it seemed like the St. Petersburg sky had not been informed, and snow still fell.

"Hello, girls," he greeted Jana and Aliza, "I have good news, I've finally been granted the necessary permits for my business this year. The wait has been long and the work arduous, but I've succeeded at last. We can prepare to return to Minsk."

They had been in the city for a month and a half, during which time the girls had taken advantage of being in the imperial capital, which was impressive and large. The palaces, museums, parks, avenues, and bridges seemed unreal to Jana and Aliza, everywhere they looked was impressive. However, their walks throughout the city did nothing for their grief, nor diminish their burning desire to return to Bialystok to find Sara. Jared saw that this was the reason for their sadness and understood it.

"Don't worry, as soon as we arrive in Minsk, we will start the search for your mother."

They both liked to hear Sara referred to as their mother, as, to them, she was. They had already lost one and did not want to lose a second. They could not hide their excitement to be starting the search.

During the trip to Minsk their excitement grew, perhaps because they felt that every verst, they travelled was bringing them closer to Sara, wherever she might be. The journey was long and difficult due to the poor condition of the roads; the thaw had turned some of them into impassable quagmire. On more than one occasion they had to dismount the carriage to free the wheels. Jana and Aliza had no problem getting off and pushing alongside the men, nor had they ignored the housework in the apartment that Jared had rented during their stay in St. Petersburg.

Finally, in mid-April, they arrived in Minsk. It seemed a bit cold to girls and lacking in charm. Of course, they had come from St. Petersburg. However, the city was much livelier than Bialystok and considerably larger in size. The Czemerinsky household was located near the river, in the heart of Ulitsa Zybiskaya. It was not very big, but did have a certain elegance and sophistication, the typical home of a man who doesn't have a fortune but does have the means to live comfortably. Anya, Jared's wife, already knew of the girls' arrival and was eager to meet them. As soon as they arrived, she ran down the stairs to hug her husband and Oizer, excited to see them after more than two months of absence. Two boys, nine-year-old twins, also came down the stairs and pounced on their father, who knelt down to greet them.

Meanwhile, the two girls lingered near the door, as the servants brought in the luggage. Anya turned to them and smiled broadly. As she approached.

"So, you are Jana and Aliza, which is which?"

"I am Jana," said the girl, bowing, "it's a pleasure to meet you, Mrs. Czemerinsky."

"And I'm Aliza, it's a pleasure to meet you too, madam."

"What well brought up girls, I'm pleased to meet you, but we can forget formalities. You can call me Anya."

She looked them over for a moment, "You are a very pretty and nice pair of girls, I think we'll have a lot to talk about." She smiled, putting her arms around them, then added, "Come with me, I've prepared a room for you. You'll see that it's very comfortable and well-lit."

"Thank you very much, Mrs. Anya," said Jana, "you are very kind."

"And you are very polite, Jana," she smiled again, "well, Irina will help you get settled, then she'll run a hot bath. Afterwards, we'll meet for a drink in the study, and have an early dinner as you must be tired from your trip."

Their reception was cordial and friendly, and life at the house was pleasant for the girls. Anya was a sweet woman with a gentle character, she treated them with great kindness and quickly grew fond of them. The girls also soon grew attached to the woman and often accompanied her on walks to the park and to go shopping. When the three of them went, out together with Irina, the maid, each of carried a basket while Anya decided what to buy.

Anya saw something in the girls that she could no longer have; the birth of her twins had been traumatic, making her unable to conceive again. Jana and Aliza felt at ease in the Czemerinsky household, living gratefully with the couple and Oizer, who cared for and protected them as an older brother. However, not a day went by without them feeling sadness and nostalgia for their lives with Isaak, Sara, and Gabriel. Despite this, they avoided mentioning it to anyone in the house.

During their first month in Minsk, they had not broached the subject of finding Sara and Gabriel, as Jared was terribly busy and spent little time at home, instead constantly travelling to Pinsk, where he had his logging business. The girls thought it wiser to wait a while, until he was less occupied. They had greater confidence in Oizer, to whom they had explained their feelings. Although the boy spent a lot of time accompanying his father on trips, he had promised to help them.

That was why it occurred to Oizer to ask his father for permission to start the search for Sara. Jared agreed that his son could stop joining him on his trips for a while, instead dedicating himself exclusively to organising the search, along with one of Jared's trusted workers. For that reason, the girls travelled with him to Bialystok and began their search. Between May and September, they had travelled seven times to the city and its surrounding towns. The spoke to dozens of people, placed notices everywhere, and even had a painter from Minks make a portrait of Sara, based on a description from the girls, to use in their inquiries. However, all of this was in vain.

Jana and Aliza found it painful to return to Bialystok. There, they had been happy with Isaak, Sara, and Gabriel. It was particularly difficult for them to return to the street where the bakery had been, the place where they had worked, to discover that it no longer existed, replaced by a cartwheel repair shop. They also found the old shoe shop, and that it was still in business, although closed. On their last visit to the city, they found it open and decided to speak to the assistant, asking about Sara. They showed him the portrait and did not notice that the man's countenance change when looking at it. He hid his face, but of course the two sisters were unaware about what had happened with Marinowsky. The clerk was friendly but made a note to tell his employer about the event.

As soon as Oizer and the girls had left, he closed the warehouse and ran to Marinowsky's office to tell what had happened. He knew very well that the prefect had not abandoned his search for Sara, and still offered a reward for information about her whereabouts.

"What are you doing here?" his employer asked as he saw the man enter.

"Good afternoon, boss. I must tell you about something that has just happened."

"Tell me, what is it?" he said, not putting down his newspaper.

"I think I recognised the two girls that used to work with Sara Rothman. They have just been to the shop."

"Go on!" Marinowsky said, setting aside the paper.

"They told me that they were looking for her, they even had a portrait."

"What did you tell them?"

"That I didn't know her, and I hadn't seen it."

"Perfect, you did the right thing. Do you know anything else? Did you find out where they were staying or where they had come from?"

"No, but they did say where they were going."

"Explain."

"The lad who was with them said, before they left the warehouse, that his father had suggested they speak to a man from Bialystok who could help in their search. When one of the girls asked his name, he said Piotr Poniatowsky."

"The owner of the sawmill?"

"He's the only Poniatowsky that I know of in the city, sir."

"Of course!" Marinowsky exclaimed, "I've been so stupid, he was one of Isaak Rothman's closest friends, that probably were Sara took refuge."

He clenched his fists, furious with himself. He turned to his employee, and said:

"We have to talk with this Poniatowsky," then he thought for a moment, "but not right now, those girls must be there. Do you know where he lives?"

"Of course, boss, it's five blocks from the warehouse."

"Very well, go immediately and keep watch. When the girls leave, come straight here, and let me know, without delay."

The girls indeed had gone to Piotr's house but found no one home. As it was getting late to begin their trip back to Minsk, Oizer recommended they return the following month. They got in the carriage and headed back. Marinowsky was also unable to find Piotr that day, as he and Malka were in Warsaw, visiting her mother in hospital.

Twenty days later, the Poniatowsky returned to Bialystok. Unfortunately, Malka's mother had not been able to overcome her illness and had died in hospital. As if their deep sadness at this was not enough, the next day the wretched Marinowsky appeared at their house, threatening to arrest Piotr for having harboured the wife of a Jew convicted for having risen against the Empire. Piotr was faced with the dilemma of confessing where his friend was or ending up in jail. Faced with such a difficult choice, he told Marinowsky that Sara had fled to Lublin, but that her whereabouts were unknown.

The prefect was satisfied, and immediately dispatched two men to Lublin to find the woman. He had ordered them not to arrest her, that he wanted to do himself. Meanwhile, Piotr hurriedly sent an urgent note, alerting her to the situation. That note arrived at Sara's apartment and was given to Tatiana by the landlady the day she found the place ransacked by Marinowsky's henchmen.

A week later, Oizer and the girls returned to Bialystok to continue their search. The first thing they did was visit Piotr's house. While he was not in at the time, when Malka opened the door, she gave a cry of joy upon recognising the girls. When they saw her, they remembered that on occasion they had seen Sara talking to her in bakery but had never learned her name. She invited them inside, saying:

"I can't believe you're here; my husband has been searching for you for months. Sara asked him to."

"What can you tell us about her?" Jana asked anxiously.

"She's in Lublin," she answered.

Jana and Aliza shouted and jumped for joy, hugging each other as tears ran down their cheeks. They then hugged Malka as well, Oizer also joined them.

"Thank you, thank you!" Jana said, unable to hide her emotion, "But is she alright?"

"She is well, Piotr, my husband, has been in correspondence with her, as she asked him to look for you two. He has been trying to find you throughout the last few months, travelling to every town within fifty versts."

"Thank you very much," Jana said again, "you have the best news of our lives."

"I am very happy, both for you and for Sara, for we love her very much."

"Let's go to Lublin, right now," Aliza said, let's not waste time.

"Wait, girls, I'm going to give you the address where you can find her."

She took out a piece of paper and, while writing the address, told them about the month Sara had spent in hiding at their home, and how she had had to flee. She then handed them the note, recommending that they leave immediately, as Marinowsky was also seeking them. The girls kissed and hugged her, hurriedly got in their carriage, and sped towards Lublin. When they arrived, they did not find Sara at the address Malka had given them, but the landlady gave them Irenka's address, who was known throughout city and was Sara's closest friend.

9

The visit to the cattle farm, near Las Palmas, had been very pleasing for Eitan. He had always loved animals and enjoyed seeing them in the countryside. It had also been good to leave the city, especially on such a warm spring day. To add to this was the charm of spending time with his family, his son, and grandchildren. His years did weight on him, so he entered Moshe's home somewhat tired; thankfully, Martha offered him a cup of coffee, serving it in the study. This was his favourite place, not just in the house but in all of Argentina. He loved to sit in the armchair, from where he could contemplate the beautiful views of the Río de La Plata estuary.

He was sitting, tasting the coffee that his daughter-in-law had given hem, when David entered.

"Hi grandpa, are you feeling tired?"

"A little, my lad, it's been a busy day for me."

"Oh, I'm sorry! I thought we could continue the story."

"Don't worry David, I'll never be too tired for that, take a seat."

"Thanks, grandpa, please carry on, I was so happy that the girls found Sara again. She must have suffered a lot."

"Yes, she went through some very hard times. Poland in those days was not an easy place to live, even less so for Jews. Despite being the majority in many cities, they still suffered from the antisemitism that dominated Russia. In the time that your ancestors were alive, Russia had annexed Poland."

"Please tell me more, grandpa, I am really interested."

"Very well, but first I want to tell you another aspect of the ancient Jewish people."

"Of course!" David exclaimed, giving the old man his full attention.

"Well, as you remember, we are the people with the oldest written history. This history, of course, is in our sacred texts and oral traditions, that is, the Torah and Talmud. Do you follow me?"

"Of course, yes."

"Very well, you also remember from our previous conversation that the Christian Bible is the history of the Jewish people, including the Gospels, as Jesus was a Jew."

The boy nodded and stared at Eitan, showing his interest. His grandfather continued:

"Well, the thing I wanted to tell you today is related to the Bible, as some detractors want to delegitimise our claim to the antiquity of the Jewish people, and often argue that the Bible is not so ancient."

"What do you mean, grandpa?"

Eitan smiled and said to him:

"Since ancient times, people have denied that the Jews are the people with the oldest written history, to this end, they say that the Bible was compiled in the Middle Ages, that is thousands of years after the birth of the Jewish people."

He leaned over to his grandson and exclaimed:

"But, my dear David, that's not the truth. There is evidence that the stories from our Torah and the Bible are authentic, and date from the times indicated."

"Really?"

"David, our people have always had two special characteristics. The first is an interest in history, and the second is a willingness to write it down."

The boy listened intently.

"As I've told you, the Jews were the great writers of antiquity. As you can see, there are more and more things of which you can be proud of as a Jew. No other nation on earth can say that their ancestors were the first to begin collecting their own history. They were historians, and, among the many texts that they wrote is the Bible; it's a historical book from start to finish."

Eitan took a deep breath, then continued.

"Around the same time that our state of Israel was founded, when I was a little younger than you are now, some scrolls were found near the Dead Sea. This extraordinary discovery is one of the proofs as to the authenticity of the Bible. Although there are several differences and inconsistencies, there are many more coincidences between these scrolls and the Bible and Torah, as we know them."

"Incredible."

"That's right, .and the other important thing about this subject is that many works from those ancient times, together with oral histories, prove that the Bible fits most of the historical framework of the events of those times. Do you understand me?"

"Of course, yes."

"I'm glad, you're learning a lot, not only to have arguments against those who criticise the Jews, but also to understand that you have an infinite number of reasons to be proud to belong to the Jewish people."

"Yes, grandpa, now I can see now that we belong to a people that has many special things."

"Your words make me happy, my boy. This means that you'll be able to easily understand something very important about which I'd like to talk to you about, later. I will give you several answers to the question that others have asked about the Jews throughout the centuries: *Why do people hate Jews so much?* You will see that the first reason is simple; envy.

"I think I know what you mean."

"Very well, now we will continue with the history of our family."

10

That night Sara slept embracing the two girls. A peaceful sleep did not come easily, due to the great joy that overwhelmed her. She was no longer worried about the whole Marinowsky affair nor her bakery nor what might come; she had recovered her girls and had them by her side. Everything else now seemed possible, she would take the next day as it came, and confront it.

Irenka, who had returned to Lublin in Oizer's carriage, returned the next day bringing more good news.

"Hello, my dear Sara!" she said, hugging her, "I have some news that will make you happy."

Sara thought that being reunited with her family, she already had enough reasons to be happy; however, she replied:

"Lately you have only been the bearer of good news, my dear Irenka, tell me, what can it be?"

"We have found Tatiana, and she is well!"

"Oh, how glad I am!" Sara said, putting a hand on her chest, "And where is she?"

"In my house, as a precaution she went into hiding for the last few days. Robiak searched all over the city and finally found her."

The mistress of the house made them tea and they all gathered in the living room. They discussed the steps they would take, bearing in mind Sara's situation. She had decided that she could not continue to abuse the hospitality of Tobias and his wife, they had already done enough for her and Gabriel. Oizer suggested:

"I think the best would be for you to come to my parents' house in Minsk."

"Oh, no, Oizer!" Sara said to him, "Your proposal is very kind, but I don't know your parents, I am a stranger to them."

"You will never be a stranger at my parents' house, Mrs. Rothman," said Oizer, "you are the mother of Jana and Aliza."

Sara smiled gratefully at the boy's words, both for the offer of hospitality and for treating her as the girls' mother.

"You are very kind, and your words are very generous, but although I am the mother of Jana and Aliza, I am still a stranger."

"Come on, mother," said Jana, "I disagree, there are several things you must know."

Sara turned to her, intrigued. Jana continued:

"Look, first of all, you cannot imagine how wonderful Oizer's parents are, they are a source pride for the Jewish people."

Jana knew that, in saying that she would immediately alter her mother's conviction.

"Yes, mother, they have very kind hearts, Aliza and I were welcomed as if we were family, and they have treated us as such throughout all these months."

"It's true, mother," Aliza interrupted, "they have been our protectors, given us all the love they could, and always supported us in our search for you."

"That's right," Jana continued, "look, mother, Oizer has been like a brother to us, and I can assure you that Jared and Anya will be as happy as he was that we have found you. They will be delighted to receive you into their home."

Sara looked at her girls, then at Oizer.

"I don't know what to say," she finally let out.

Irenka also agreed with Oizer's suggestion:

"The boy is right, Sara." she said, nodding, "As you know, Carl has prolonged his absence and it will take him a couple of weeks to return to Lublin, only then can he act in your defence against Marinowsky. As the police are still looking for you, it's not wise to stay here either. If they found you, that could affect Tobias and Sara too."

"I think you're right; this is a way of putting distance between Marinowsky and us for the time being. But I can assure you that I will return to Lublin and finish this once and for all, it's where I have my business, and I'm not willing to start all over again."

So, they left for Minsk. Sara said farewell to Tobias and his wife, thanking them deeply for all their care and promising to visit in the future, once her situation was under control. They left for Lublin, stopping at Irenka's house just long enough for Sara to see Tatiana.

During the trip they had agreed that the girl would enter Irenka's service until the bakery could be reopened, as it was now closed by the authorities, obviously at Marinowsky's request.

Sara was excited to see Tatiana, her loyal employee, and she thanked her for everything, assuring her that the bakery would soon reopen. Sara recommended that she serve her friend well, of which she had no doubt as she knew the girl's many qualities. Finally, she gave her a hug, did the same to Irenka, and mounted the carriage to leave. At that moment, Tatiana stopped her:

"Wait, Mrs. Sara," she begged, running back to servants' quarters.

She returned a few moments later, carrying a cloth bag which she handed over to her employer. Sara opened it and felt tears brimming in her eyes; inside were Isaak's Tefillin, Tallit, and the crucifix with Maretska's note. Overjoyed, she gave the girl another hug, in awe of all the happiness that God had given her lately. She got into the carriage once again and was driven off.

During the trip to Minsk, Sara fully enjoyed Jana and Aliza's company. It still seemed unreal to her, to have them by her side. She was a little apprehensive to be visiting the home of two strangers, but the girls told her how wonderful and caring Oizer's parents were. She knew that she would be slightly uncomfortable anyway, as she did not want to abuse their hospitality, especially as she felt so grateful to Jared and his wife already. They had rescued and cared for her girls, giving them a true home for several months.

Indeed, Sara was received at the Czemerinsky household with all the kindness and hospitality that the girls had predicted. In fact, Anya soon became a close friend of hers, as she filled the void left by the loss of Anya's only sister a few months prior. When she was told about life with this recently deceased sister, Sara could not help but remember that she too had lost sisters while still a child. For this reason, she supported Anya emotionally; almost unexpectedly, their bond became a great friendship. Sara liked her, feeling that lately, while she had been blessed with exceptional friends: Maretska, Malka, and Irenka, but they were all Catholic, while Anya was a Jew, like her, and they were united by a different bond.

The days were slow and peaceful. The girls attended private lessons, and Gabriel went to the Cheder, all paid for by Jared. Sara was grateful for this, but it made her feel helpless, thinking that it was her duty to pay for education of her own children. Jana and Aliza maintained their brotherly friendship with Oizer, and the boy continued to take care of them and protect them. Gabriel spent his time playing with the twins, the three of them filling the house with shouts and laughter. Meanwhile, Sara spent a lot to time with Anya; there was no shortage of afternoons with conversation shared over a cup of tea, or lively gatherings when the mistress of the house invited close friends over. Little by little, Sara and her children were integrating into Minsk society; they were happy there.

However, Sara was painfully aware that it was all temporary, sooner or later she would have to take back the reins of her family and her business. While it was true that the Czemerinskys and Rothmans had become very close, she could not abuse their hospitality forever. Also, she did not want to delay the resolution of her problems with Marinowsky. It was true that the wretch had a lot of power, but she belonged to a people who had never given up on fighting for their rights, even when their lives were at stake.

'No one had oppressed us forever. We faced all of them at the right moment; they may have won a thousand battles, but we were always victorious in the end. Marinowsky has beaten me many times, but the time for the final confrontation has come. I will face him for the honour of the Jewish people and in tribute to my husband', she said to herself.

Sara had already made up her mind, she knew that Jared and Anya would try to persuade her to stay longer in Minsk, but she did not want to drag this matter out any longer. She had maintained a regular correspondence with Irenka, thanks to whom she knew that Marinowsky was no longer in Lublin, although the police and others in his service continued to seek her out, obviously motivated by the tempting reward he had offered.

She finally decided to talk to them about the choice she had made, explaining the reasons behind it. Of course, Jared and Anya were in favour of her staying for longer, until things calmed down concerning Marinowsky, but Sara was certain in her conviction. She had spent eight months in Lublin, assuming that the matter was forgotten, when Marinowsky reappeared with an arrest warrant for who knows what crime which obviously she had not committed. Marinowsky had proven himself to be a spiteful and vindictive, in addition to the fact that he had not been able to overcome his obsession with her. She had to address this situation once and for all.

Her hosts understood that it was useless to cotinine insisting that she change her mind, so they resigned themselves to respecting her decision. However, they had a suggestion that for good reasons that she accepted. They suggested she travel alone to Lublin, leaving the girls and Gabriel in Minsk. Sara knew very well that they would safer and more protected there. In addition, it was important for her peace of mind to know that her children were cared for, giving her more freedom to face the situation that awaited her in Lublin, which would certainly not be easy.

"I will never be able to repay you for everything you have done to help me and my children," she said as she clasped Anya's hands.

"You don't have to mention that my dear Sara," replied Jared, "the true strength of the Jewish people comes from our unwavering love for God, the unity between us, and our charity for those who need it."

"It is so," Anya confirmed, then clarified, "we are also blessed to have enjoyed your company and that of your children; they have brought us joy and happiness."

Sara stood and embraced them with great emotion.

Two days later she left for Lublin; the farewell was emotional and filled with tears, and for Sara it was hard to part from the girls, and particularly from little Gabriel, despite knowing that they would be safe in the Czemerinsky household. Given the circumstances, the children would be much better off with them. Jared arranged for Oizer to accompany her to Lublin, to ensure that Sara arrived safely. Once settled in Irenka's home, he would return to Minsk.

As the carriage departed, Sara thought on what awaited her in Lublin. The carriage moved slowly along the roads that were sprinkled with snow. Hinting at a harsh winter to come. After two overnight stops, they were close to entering the city. She had sent a letter to her friend informing her of their trip, so that she would be aware of her arrival.

'*How lucky I am to have Irenka,*' she thought, '*were it not for her this unpleasant business could have taken a very different turn as I would have to face it all on my own.*'

In her pocket she had the few coins that Jared had given her, which she had only accepted as a loan; she already owed him enough after two months in his home. Sara was very proud and committed to what she considered her duty as a mother, which is why she had promised herself from the beginning that, once she had got her bakery back up and running again, she would pay Jared and Anya back for everything they had given her and her children.

Indeed, Irenka was already expecting her arrival, as soon as the butler informed her of the carriage's presence, she ran downstairs to the entrance to receive her friend.

"Sara, my dear! How delighted I am to see you again!"

"I feel the same way!" she answered, ging her an embrace.

"You look great," she spun her around and added, "and as dazzling as ever."

"You haven't changed, my dear Irenka, always so flattering."

"Ha! The truth is that I am happy to have your back, we should organise a party to celebrate."

"As I said, you haven't changed a bit."

They laughed and went into the living room. Irenka gave instructions to put Oizer and his coachman up, then the three of them sat down for dinner. Despite knowing that she was in Lublin to face Marinowsky's slander and persecution, Sara was calm and serene; she no longer had that melancholy look with which Irenka had become so familiar. Obviously, it was down to her recovery of Jana and Aliza, and the knowledge that both were safe and well in Minsk.

"I'm happy to see you calmer, my dear Sara," Irenka said, "even your eyes are brighter."

"Yes, my dear friend," she answered, "as you can imagine it's because I have my girls with me again."

Irenka looked at her and thought to herself '*the only thing you lack is a good husband*', but obviously she did not express this.

"And Tatiana? How is she?" Sara asked.

"Better than ever she was," she replied, then added "she's in love."

"In love? What do you mean?"

"Exactly that, she's madly in love with Robiak."

"The coachman?"

"Yes, he's been in love with Tatiana since she worked with you at the bakery."

"He's a nice and intelligent young man," Sara said, "but do you think their relationship is serious?"

"I would say that he is not only serious, but too serious!"

"Oh, God! But Tatiana is so young!"

"Yes, she is young, but she'll soon be fifteen years old."

"And Robiak is a Catholic, and you know that Tatiana is a Jew."

"Yes, of course I know. But I'm beginning to doubt the lad's Catholicism."

"What do you mean?"

"I've seen him talking with the Rabbi a lot lately."

Sara thought for a moment, Tatiana was a great girl and her happiness made her happy too. Her role with the girl had almost been that of a mother, she had tried to watch over her future with. She would talk to her.

Sara changed the subject.

"Well, my dear friend, any news from the bakery?"

"It's as I said in my letter, it has been appropriated by the authorities and remains closed."

"Well, at least Marinowsky has not stolen it from me, have you heard anything about him?"

"He was around again but has left leaving his men behind seeking the reward he offered. It seems to have become his greatest obsession."

"I am determined to face him once and for all, I can't live in fear of him for my whole life."

"In the next few days Carl will arrive and, with his advice, you put an end to this unpleasant saga."

"I hope so."

While they awaited Irenka's husband's arrival, Sara remained at her friend's house. She left only once, in disguise in the carriage, to visit

Tobias and Sara. She never forgot what they had done for her and Gabriel, and their place brought back joyful memories of being reunited with the girls. The couple were glad to see Sara and gratefully accepted the gifts she had brought them from Minsk.

She also used her time at Irenka's house to talk to Tatiana about her relationship with Robiak, which she in principle supported. She was pleased to hear that the boy was in the process of converting to Judaism, although she was slightly concerned that it less out of conviction, but rather love for the Russian girl. In any case, being a Jew had always been an uneasy and often dangerous in Poland; however, it brought with it a profound joy in the depths of her heart for that intangible something that sprang from 'the Jewish soul'.

"I don't have to rights over you, my dear Tatiana," she said to the girl one day, "but you know that I would never approve of you marrying a man who is not a Jew."

"You do have the right to guide me, Mrs. Sara, because you rescued me when I most needed help. I didn't have anything to eat, and you gave me an unconditional loving support."

Saying these words, the girl bowed her head and began to sob. Sara was so touched that she got up from her chair and approached the girl and gave her a hug. Tatiana had proved to be a very good girl, with a kind heart and excellent work ethic. Sara had instantly taken a liking to her, but not until that moment did she realise the true affection she had for the girl.

Tatiana's life had been no bed of roses, either. Born in a rural part of Mariupol, on the shores of the Azov Sea, to a family of Georgian origin, she had led a childhood full of hardships. Her mother was an illiterate peasant, widowed while Tatiana was still in her womb. They had survived by growing vegetables on a small plot and selling them at the city market. The girl had worked since she had been able, and they were so poor that they only wore shoes in the Winter. Her mother, despite her lack of education, had raised her according to the Jewish teachings, but never had the means to educate her daughter.

Her mother had contracted tuberculosis, and as the disease had progressed it became more difficult for her to work to provide for the two. Realising how much she was deteriorating, day by day, she desperately sought someone who could look after the girl before it was too late. After several weeks of searching, she managed to find an old Jewish woman who had been widowed a few years prior to adopt the girl, now eight years old. Two days after leaving home, Tatiana's poor mother passed away. The old woman welcomed her with affection, even hiring a woman to give her a Jewish education and teach her to read and write.

Despite this, life in her new house was a traumatic and disillusioning experience. In addition to the loss of her mother was the fact that due to elderly woman's age and ailments, the house was run by her nephew, who lived there with his wife and son, who was two years older than Tatiana. The man was proud and despotic, and he seemed to detest the girl. Although born into a Jewish family, he had converted to Russian Orthodox Christianity and had become, paradoxically, a fervent anti-Semite, making the girl's life a misery. His wife was also a cruel and inhumane woman, who took every opportunity to make the girl suffer. She was treated as a servant, constantly beaten, and threatening to throw her out of the house if she ever told the old woman. The son was a spoilt boy, who constantly tormented the girl, causing her great pain. Because of this, there was not a single night that Tatiana did not cry herself to sleep in the tiny basement room that had been allotted to her.

She felt despondent in that house. The owner was unaware of what was happening to Tatiana, and to the fact that her nephew and his wife were only waiting for her to die so that they could inherit, not only the house but also other assets in Mariupol and a fish-processing plant in Sevastopol. However, he seemingly took great care of his aunt; three times a day, his wife would provide the old woman with her medicine. Despite this, this did her little good, as her condition continued to deteriorate, until the poor lady suffered a stroke one day. When the doctor arrived, she had already left this world.

From that tragic moment, Tatiana's already painful life became hellish. The beatings from the new mistress became more frequent, now assisted by the boy who had moved from verbal abuse to physical assault. They also made her work from dawn to late night at various household chores.

In the end, Tatiana, now eleven years old, decided she could no longer bear her mistreatment, and fled the house. She had planned her escape, choosing the perfect day, as the evil family would be celebrating their son's birthday in an exclusive hall in the city, giving her the opportunity to sneak away. Once the cook had fallen asleep, she packed a bag with her few belongings and fled under the cover of night. This was not before compensating herself, at least in part, for the years of suffering she had endured there. Before leaving, she entered the master bedroom and took from a chest hidden behind a painting, a good handful of coins and jewellery, and then took the nephew's important documents from a briefcase in the study. Tatiana did not know exactly what kinds of papers were within, but as they were important to the cruel man, she took them. This would be her revenge.

Before leaving the city, she passed by the docks and threw the briefcase into the sea, still unaware of its contents. These were the property titles of the Sevastopol premises, some high-value bonds, and various debtor bills of exchange, the value of which exceeded a few thousand roubles. Tatiana watched as the briefcase sank, touching the pockets of her dress which held the coins and jewellery. She considered it payment for all the time she had worked, and especially for all the suffering she had endured.

She managed to escape, and for two years, wandered through dozens of villages, finding work in all kinds of trades. At first, she survived thanks to her stolen jewellery, but that soon ran out, especially as she did not know their real value and was cheated on more than one occasion whilst others were stolen. She wandered from town to town, taking work where she found it, from cleaning to tending over a tavern. She had developed a strong and determined character, forced to fight to survive, facing off many adversities and men who, as with Sara, tried to take advantage of her despite her young age.

On one occasion, while working as a barmaid's assistant in Lutsk, a drunk had dragged her to the back of the establishment and started to grope her. She had managed to wriggle free, went into the kitchen the kitchen and seized a knife, but the drunk, fat and as strong as a bear, was not intimidated. On the contrary, he forced her outside the tavern, threw himself on top of her and tried to take advantage of her. Tatiana did not hesitate; she plunged the knife into his chest and abdomen several times. She stood and fled, fearfully, from that town. She never found out whether that wretch had died, but if that were the case, it was no great loss, she thought.

Like Sara, she was fortunate to find kind people on occasion, who helped her or defended in when things were at their most dire. Despite this, she suffered a lot during this time, not only because she often lacked the wherewithal to look after herself but because she had no one to support her emotionally.

Her travels throughout the west of the empire eventually took her to Lublin, worn down by her hardships, malnourished, and recovering from typhus which she had acquired while worked as a kitchen assistant in a roadside inn, from which she was expelled as soon as they learned of her illness, without paying what they owed her. However, it was thanks to that illness that she avoided being raped by bandits who caught her in an alley of a nearby town, looking for food amongst the scraps. By the time she reached Lublin, she was so morally, physically, and emotionally drained that she had given up on life. With nothing to eat, she decided to go to the market to scavenge for any leftovers. She was wandering around, collecting fruit peels off the ground, when Sara came across her, while buying vegetables.

She was moved by the girl, who was obviously emaciated and hungry. She spoke to her in Polish, but Tatiana did not understand her, then she asked in Russian, to which Tatiana replied. She was so helpless that Sara could not help but remember her own hardships; she took her by the arm to a nearby restaurant and ordered vegetable soup with meat, which the girl devoured in an instant, before telling her tragic story. '*This life is too cruel for a thirteen-year-old girl*,' Sara thought. She regarding her compassionately, knowing in that instant that she could not abandon this little girl with black hair and sweet eyes.

"I have given you no more than what you deserved, my dear, you are a wonderful girl." Sara said, continuing to press her against her chest.

"Mrs. Sara, I have only tried to partially return all the kindness and love you have given me. Thanks to you, I stopped being an orphan and gained a mother."

Sara couldn't prevent a tear running down her cheek and held the girl even tighter.

-ooo-

Carl's arrival, as always, precipitated a flurry of events at Irenka's house; the visits and social gatherings grew tenfold, rooms were filled with smoke from pipes and cigars, the aroma of wine and vodka filled the house, and the kitchen was more frantic that ever. Laughter and conversation became perpetual fixtures of those endless evenings, which obviously made the hostess very happy. Of course, she involved her friend in all events, knowing that Sara's presence always graced the gatherings and gained her more renown as a hostess. Sara, always reluctant to attend, used her lack of a wardrobe as an excuse not to attend when the number of functions became overwhelming. Irenka solved this by making dresses and shoes or altering her own to suit Sara's measurements. So, Sara resigned herself to this social lifestyle, considering it a duty towards the friend who had helped her so much in the last year.

Sara's unease also stemmed from the fact that the days passed in one social occasion after another, but Carl showed no sign of beginning his defence against Marinowsky's case. She was careful not to insist too much as, after all, he was not charging for his services and would do it as a personal favour. However, on a few occasions, a little self-consciously, she had broached the subject with him. Carl always replied with his infectious smile:

"Do not worry, my dear Sara, your case will be child's play for me. I've already studied the details, once I begin you will be free of suspicion within minutes."

Sara was not completely reassured by Carl's words; he might see it as a simple matter, but it had already caused her great strife and suffering. Certainly, she really did not see the matter as child's play.

As usual with this explosive couple, once the lawyer finally took charge of Sara's case, it was like a volcanic eruption! After a particularly lively night of socialising, Sara had gone to bed very tired. Early the next day, Irenka burst into her room.

"Come on, my dear! You must get ready to go to the police station with Carl! He's almost ready to leave."

She got up and fixed herself up at full speed; when she finally made to the carriage, there was the lawyer, elegantly dressed and smoking a cigar. As soon as Sara arrived, he doffed his hat in greeting and invited her into the carriage. She was still a little sleepy by the time they arrived at the station.

"Come, my dear Sara," Carl said, offering a hand to help her get down.

As he did so she looked up and noticed the yellow and white flag of the empire flying in front of the building next to the red and white of Poland. She disliked seeing the Russian standard; it had always been associated with the loss of Isaak. As soon as she entered the building, she felt a chill, that developed into genuine fear by the time they reached the secretary of the police commissioner's office. Carl looked relaxed, but she was terrified, thinking he might leave her there.

'Of course, he's not the one with a warrant for his arrest,' Sara thought.

There were several people in the office, among them an elegant gentleman with a moustache and a refined manner, carrying a leather briefcase under his arm. As he saw them enter, he got up from his chair and addressed them.

"Good morning, my dear friend."

"Good morning, Gustav," Carl replied, then indicated towards Sara, "I present to you, Mrs. Sara Rothman."

"Delighted to meet you, Mrs. Rothman," he said, bowing slightly, "it is a real pleasure to meet you."

"Likewise, sir."

"Gustav is a lawyer, and an old friend, my dear Sara," said Carl, "he is also the attorney for the Hoffman family."

Sara tilted her head a little, now remembering what Irenka had told her about Captain Hoffman's interest in her case.

"Well, my dear Gustav," Carl began, "let's settle this matter once and for all; shall we proceed?"

"Very well," replied the lawyer, approaching the secretary's desk.

The man stood and knocked on the office door, entered, then emerged a few minutes later, indicating to the visitors that they could enter. Sara's sense of foreboding grew; she was anxious at not knowing what was about to happen, and Carl's presence did little to calm her.

The commissioner was an intimidating man, a gigantic Russian man who inspired fear, not only due of his tall height and great build, but because of the thick, dark beard that covered half of his face. His eyes were fierce, and his lips thin. When he spoke, Sara felt her fear increasing; his booming voice seemed to shake the windowpanes.

In smaller towns, prefects and sub-prefects were Poles, but in some cities those offices were held by Russian officials. Lublin was one such city. Sara took this as a bad omen, and was even more frightened, especially noticing his rude and insensitive gestures. The closest he came to courtesy was to tell them:

"You can sit down, if you want," pointing to some chairs against the wall.

"Thank you," Carl replied, inviting Sara to do the same.

"The lawyer for the plaintiff is coming, this matter is his domain. We know this Jewish woman's case well, this meeting will not take long," he said, dismissively, without even looking at Sara.

He then sat in his chair behind the desk, his large body making the wood creak. Sara felt her heart beat furiously. At that moment the police lawyer, another large, unpleasant-looking man, entered, accompanied by the plaintiff's lawyer. Unlike the others, he was a short, thin man. The commissioner said:

"Let's begin!"

The lawyer began to read the file, going over Marinowsky's lawsuit. He had accused Sara and her husband Isaak of illegally setting up businesses in Bialystok, without meeting the requirements demanded of Jews. He also accused her of attempted murder and causing him physical injury, by assaulting him with a blunt instrument. Finally, he was charging her with theft from his shoe shop in Bialystok, to the sum of 500 roubles in bills and silver coins.

Sara's eyes widened in total disbelief. She turned towards Carl, but both he and Gustav seemed undaunted. Marinowsky's lawyer continued reading, indicating the documents and witnesses that supported his case. When he had finally finished, the commissioner took the floor, stating explicitly that in light of such compelling evidence, he would proceed to carry out the arrest issued by the police prefecture of Bialystok. Sara broke down, but at that moment Carl raised his hand, asking for the floor. With evident disgust, the commissioner granted his request, telling him he only had one minute to speak.

"I don't need that long, commissioner," Carl said, then continued, "I oppose your decision to enforce this arrest warrant."

"On what grounds?!" the commissioner asked.

"On the grounds that it is an illegal order."

"How can you make such a claim?"

"It's very simple, it's based on the laws that regulate criminal and police procedures throughout the empire; laws which, by the way, also govern you, Mr. commissioner."

"How dare you?! Are you trying to intimidate me?" he yelled, enraged.

Carl remained impassive before the Russian's screams; he was well-versed in legal matters, but more so in the political, legal, and judicial bureaucracy that had developed in Russian Poland. For this reason, nothing worried him.

"Of course not, commissioner, it was just a small reminder."

"And to which law are you referring to, exactly."

"To be exact, I'm referring to the first paragraph of article 23 of law 08985.06, ordered and signed by His Majesty Tsar Alexander. This does not legitimise an arrest warrant issued by the plaintiff, as it has been in this case. Therefore, this warrant is illegal and whoever executes it would be violating a law issued by the Tsar."

"Well, the Tsar is a long way from Lublin, and I hold power here!" the Russian roared, then continued, "nobody else decides on the application of law in my jurisdiction."

"I fully agree with you, commissioner," Carl said slowly and calmly, "you decide how laws are applied, that is your duty. It is also your duty to understand that, while you apply them, you do not define them. That has already been done by the Tsar, who presumably does so with conviction that all his officials, without exemption, will comply with and will enforce them."

"Who are you to tell me how to carry out my duties?"

"I'm sorry, but I'm nobody important, nor need I be. As I've said, it's the Tsar who decides what your duties are. Incidentally, it is also he who decides on sanctions against those officials who do not fulfil their obligations to him."

"Are you threatening me?!"

"Of course not, commissioner, I would never dare do such a thing," Carl said, his tone now slightly mocking, which did not go unnoticed, "I know that you are well acquainted with your obligations and duties."

The commissioner turned red with anger. *How dare a simple Polish lawyer speak to him in this way?* However, he felt disarmed by him; without knowing what to say, he turned to the prosecuting attorney, as if asking for support. Carl quickly intervened to stop the man from speaking.

"The attorney for the plaintiff will not be able to advise you, commissioner, as doing so would immediately delegitimise any decision you make, based on obvious collusion with one of the parties involved."

"Who do you think you are?" cried the exasperated Russian, "And who do you think you're talking to? I am the commissioner, and I know my powers."

"I am pleased to hear you say that commissioner, as it gives me certainty that, knowing the scope of your powers, you will not issue an arrest knowing full well that it is illegal."

The Russian became even angrier, his eyes glinted, and his breathing became laboured. What infuriated him most was Carl's mocking tone. At last, he exploded:

"You can do whatever you want with your codes, laws, articles, and subsections as you like! I am the authority here, and the decision according to my criteria!" he boomed, the sound echoing throughout the room, whilst slamming his knuckles on his desk.

"That's fine with me, commissioner, as long as your criteria are in accordance with the legal codes and procedures. On the other hand, I am pleased that you reaffirm your authority, as you implicitly acknowledge your duty to defend and apply the law. Thus, you ensure that the people of Lublin comply with the laws. If you did not, your power would lose all official legitimacy, or am I wrong?"

Sara listened carefully to Carl's words. He spoke so confidently that she couldn't believe it; however, she remained terrified of the conversation's outcome. The Russian shouted again, this time louder:

"You are a pedant! I could have you detained immediately!"

"On what charges, commissioner?"

"I define the charges!" he cried, letting himself be carried away by his anger.

"I'm sorry, sir," Carl replied calmly, "I must inform you that you do not define them. Charges are defined by the law."

"Here, I am the law!"

"I'm sorry to contradict you, but you are the authority but not the law," Carl challenged him with utmost calm, speaking slowly, and pointing at him his index finger, then he continued "and as the authority, your first duty is to meet and enforce the imperial regulations."

"You have crossed a line, and you'll pay for that! You don't know who you're messing with, I'll have you arrested!"

"The one who has crossed a line is you, commissioner," Carl said, raising his voice for the first time, "overstepping your authority and disobeying the Tsar's orders!"

Meanwhile, Sara was stunned, listening to the conversation, and she could not believe that Carl had gone so far as to raise his voice to the Russian.

"Secretary!" the commissioner shouted.

The little man who acted as secretary scuttled in, standing motionless in front of the commissioner, who had risen from his seat.

"Tell the prefect to come immediately, with two men!"

"Yes, sir!" he replied, then ran off at full speed.

Sara sank into her chair, feeling totally defeated. If they arrested Carl, she was certain to be in jail by the end of the day.

"Now you'll learn who you've been dealing with and see where you'll spend the night." The Russian said to Carl.

"I already know you, Mr. commissioner, and I can see that you exceed your duties and do not comply with the law. However, I'm pleased to inform you that you'll be meeting a certain person tomorrow."

No one understood exactly what Carl was trying to say, Sara was still shocked that he had the audacity to directly accuse the commissioner of violating the law. The Russian was equally confused, and asked him:

"To whom do you refer?"

"To my good friend, General Sokolov, I assume you've heard the name," Carl replied, reverted to his slow, theatrical tone, this time accompanied by some mocking gestures.

"Oh?"

"If so, you will know that he is the delegate of His Imperial Majesty, Tsar Alexander, for the police force of the western provinces."

"Are you trying to intimidate me? Of course, I know who General Sokolov is, but mentioning his name will not free you from punishment for your disrespectful behaviour towards a police commissioner!"

Sara followed the conversation completely stunned and limited herself to turning her face from one to the other of the two men.

"As you wish, commissioner," Carl said, slowly rising from his seat and taking a piece of paper from his jacket pocket. He approached the desk, and continued:

"You may be interested in reading this handwritten note, written by the General himself and adorned with his personal seal. He is very nearby and will be my guest in Lublin from tomorrow. Of course, I hope that I will be able to host him at home rather than in a cell, although I know Ivan so well that I'm sure he wouldn't hesitate to come visit me at the police station.

Sara noticed how the General had been referred to by his first name, demonstrating Carl's familiarity. This was not lost on the commissioner either; he took the note from Carl's hand and read it, turning livid. He reread it; this time, his hands trembled slightly. He was thoughtful for a moment and, refusing to concede, asked Carl in a much softer voice:

"What assurance do I have that this note is genuine?"

"You have none, commissioner, but I can assure you that he will confirm it tomorrow."

"You know, I doubt your words. Do you really think that if General Sokolov come on an official visit to Lublin, my superiors would not have informed me?"

"You are absolutely right, commissioner. Surely your superior, Captain Wasilewski, who, by the way, is also a close friend, would have informed you. But it just so happens that the General's visit is not official. He is travelling to Minsk and has decided to deviate from his route in order to visit me."

"And you continue to insist that he is such a great friend, so much so that he comes to Lublin exclusively to talk to you?"

"Well, I am pleased to inform you, Commissioner, that this is precisely the case. We greatly enjoy talking. In fact, I can remember the last time we spoke, he told me that His Imperial Majesty was in need of a Police Commissioner to send to Vladivostok."

This finally exhausted the commissioner's patience and resistance. He sat back in his chair, snorted, and exclaimed:

"Well, enough is enough. This meeting is over, you can all retire."

"I thank you, Commissioner," Carl said, "but before I leave, there are two documents I require."

"Require? What documents? Are you giving me more orders?"

"I assure you, no. It's only part of your duty."

"Well, what is it?"

"I need documentation that you have annulled the arrest warrant against my client as illegal, and proof that, in the view of the accusations against her, you authorise the case be settled in a hearing presided over by a judge or other competent authority in the jurisdiction of Bialystok, it was there that the complaint was filed. That is all."

"Alright, we will proceed in that way. Is there anything else, Mr. Lawyer?"

"Yes, with your permission, Commissioner, I believe that it is no longer necessary to keep my client's bakery closed, don't you think?"

The Commissioner signed, exasperated. However, he reluctantly replied:

"I'll order them to lift it today. Have you finished, or do you have another request?"

"No, that is all. Although I would appreciate it if the documentation be sent to my house," he put his hands to his chin, allowing a moment to pass, then added, "although, on second thoughts, I can come again tomorrow to collect them. Perhaps Ivan will accompany, so you can greet him."

The Russian regarded him with venom.

"Do not worry, they will be taken to your house this afternoon."

"Thank you very much, have an excellent day, Commissioner."

Robiak could not understand why the three passengers were laughing so hard. He had noticed them beaming as they boarded the carriage, which had made him happy, as he obviously understood that Sara's case must have gone well. He had great sympathy for her, knowing that she had rescued Tatiana, provided her with a more dignified life. The girl thought of her as a mother, so to him, she was as a mother-in-law.

"Did you see his face when you mentioned the General?" Gustav was saying.

"Ha! What about when he read that note three times?" Carl laughed, "his hands shaking."

"That's nothing," Sara said, "when you said 'Vladivostok', his eyes widened so much they almost rolled into the back of his head!"

"But how about when you told him you were a friend of the Captain?"

"Well, we've passed the first obstacle," Carl said with great satisfaction, "we calmly move onto the next. For now, Sara, you can stop worrying about the warrant and your bakery."

"Thank you, thank you, Carl. You really surprised me, I swear, I almost fainted when you raised your voice to the Commissioner like that."

"It's no less than what these arrogant individuals deserve," he said.

"Now I understand why you postponed the hearing for so long, you were waiting to have such an ace up your sleeve, right?"

"Ha!" Carl laughed, pleased with himself, "Of course, Sara, I invited Ivan over a month ago when he told me he was coming to Poland, I first needed to have his answer in hand confirming that he was coming to Lublin."

"In any case, I'll never be able to repay you for what you did, Carl, and you, Gustav. Thank you so much."

"You can so very simply, Sara, give me a kiss," he said, daintily tapping his cheek with his forefinger several times.

Sara laughed and, without hesitating, gave him a loud kiss on the cheek.

"Oh, God! I have never been kissed by such a beautiful lady!"

"I'll tell Irenka that!"

All three laughed heartily.

That afternoon, there was a party at Carl and Irenka's house, and this time Sara was delighted to attend. They sent Robiak to notify several friends and began to organise the celebratory event. Sara told Tatiana the good news as soon as she arrived home. The girl was overjoyed and rushed to hug, her but suddenly stopped, a little embarrassed at the impulse. Sara smiled tenderly and said:

"My daughter, my girl, you can hug me whenever you want."

Tatiana began to weep with emotion upon hearing those words, and they held each other in a tight embrace. Meanwhile, Irenka began giving instructions to prepare for the night's gathering. Carl and Gustav enjoyed a cigar and a glass of wine on the terrace, as a maid prepared the guest room for the next day's visitor.

Sara went up to her room to write a letter to the Czemerinsky and the children, telling them the good news. She was about to finish when Tatiana knocked on the door. She entered, and Sara indicated for her to wait for a few moments as she finished writing. When she had, she reread her letter, folded it, and put it in an envelope, on which she wrote the Minsk address. Then, she turned to Tatiana.

"Tell me, my girl, what is it?"

"I wanted to show you something, moth..."

"What were you going to say?"

"No, nothing, nothing."

"Say it."

"Well, I was going to say ... mother."

Sara's eyes moistened, she looked at the girl tenderly, and said:

"I like hearing you say that, please, I'd like you to call me that from now on."

"Thank you, I will … mother."

"Come here," Sara said, opening her arms.

She kissed and hugged her, then tenderly stroked her face, saying:

"You know, I'm so grateful to God. He has given me a beautiful son and three beautiful daughters."

Tatiana was so moved to hear those words that she could not resist the urge to hug her again as her eyes watered.

"Well, what did you want to show me?"

The girl took her by the hand and led her into the next room. Irenka had arranged for Tatiana to sleep there from now on, so that she would no longer have to use the service rooms. Sara was so grateful, what a great friend God had brought her.

"Oh, my dear girl!" she said, "life has been so good to me lately, I'm scared that my luck will run out…" she then added "…and I wish my Isaak could be here to share this moment with me, I miss him so much Tatiana. With him by my side, my happiness would be complete."

The girl came over and held her hands, Sara wiped away a tear.

11

Indeed, everything was going well for Sara; she began to look to the future more optimistically. In her sky the sun was shining, the one cloud was the Isaak's absence. On several occasions, she thought that she could get accustomed to life without him, and that time would heal her wound. However, she knew that she was deceiving herself, not a day went by without the memory of her husband coming to mind. Despite this, she knew that life must go, and that there was work to be done. After all, she no longer had one child to take care of, but four.

With many of her problems solved, she had to start working again. It was true that she had escaped prison, and that the bakery could be reopened; however, her trial for Marinowsky's allegations was still pending. Although they were false, the case was still not fully resolved. Of course, she felt more at ease having Carl and Gustav at her side, as Marinowsky's greatest strength, his position and influence, were beginning to fade in the face of Irenka's husband's connections, knowledge, experience, and, above, his great legal ability.

Indeed, she was so impressed by his skills and cunning, for which she expressed her profound gratitude. Car thanked her and reiterated that she could rest easy about the trial that they would face. Together with Gustav he was preparing her defence. In fact, Sara was much calmer than before the hearing with the Lublin commissioner, Carl had a proven command of these issues, and this generated a lot of confidence.

On the other hand, she was grateful to Irenka, but could not allow herself to abuse her friend's hospitality any longer; it was time to regain her independence. With the lifting of the bakery's closure, she could begin to regain the means with which to live with her children again, as she missed Gabriel and the girls very much. However, Irenka always found some excuse to keep her for longer in her house: first using the visit of General Sokolov, who turned out to be a kind and friendly individual. Sara had an understandable reticence towards the Russians, but the officer had great wit and charisma, as well as being an excellent conversationalist.

Then came Irenka's birthday party, so she couldn't return to Minsk for her children until after the party. Finally, her attendance was required at a customary charity banquet that was held in the city every year, organised by socialites and the Catholic Church. Thus, the days passed, and she remained in Lublin. Of course, she wasted no time, working on putting the bakery back into operation. This was no easy task, as when she returned to her establishment, she found it had been looted and left in a terrible state of neglect. As usual, Irenka loaned her the funds to begin again. With the help of Tatiana and Robiak, they were putting the place to rights again.

The young man worked hard and was a great help in repairing the bakery. Of course, he was only too happy to do so, not only to be close to Tatiana, but also to ingratiate himself with Sara. She was amused to watch the young couple's closeness; it reminded her of her own courtship with Isaak. The lad was quite handsome, and certainly had an amiable personality. Meanwhile, Tatiana was becoming more beautiful by the day; her black hair now flowed down to her waist, and her face was symmetrical and very pretty. She was a graceful girl, who attracted attention for an exotic and unusual beauty in those parts of the Empire.

Her beauty was enhanced by her stature and shapely body, as well as her expressive eyes which were framed by long, curved eyelashes. But undoubtedly, her greatest asset was her hair: deep black, straight, and long. When she walked the streets with Sara, no man could avoid glancing at them; the contrast between the blonde and dark-haired women was extraordinarily striking.

Sara enjoyed seeing how Robiak was captivated by Tatiana, he stood before her as if hypnotised. It was obvious that he could not resist looking at her and admiring her. Even more amusing was how the youth became jealous and infuriated whenever men looked at or flirted with his girlfriend. She would laugh and say:

"Calm down, Robiak. men may admire her, but only one man has her heart."

Sara was eager to have to bakery running by the beginning of December at the latest, so that she would be able to rent a small house to bring Gabriel and the girls to Lublin. However, she didn't have enough time, as she had to regain her clients, which would not happen overnight. Because of this, following Irenka's advice, when the bakery was about to reopen, she left Tatiana in charge, along with the delivery boy who had worked with her previously. She travelled to Minsk to spend Hanukkah with her children at the Czemerinsky household. She would return at the beginning of the year to start life anew, with her whole family in the city.

Saying farewell in Minsk was hard; the Czemerinsky family had already become very accustomed to having Gabriel and girls around. Anya missed Sara, and their usual afternoons of tea and sewing when they would converse for hours. They promised to keep in touch and visit often.

"Do not worry, my love," Jared said to his wife, "this year we will move to Pinsk, as I must be more involved with business in that area. We'll be closer to Lublin, so you'll be able to see each often. I also will have to travel to Brest periodically, which is just a day's journey from Lublin. "

When they returned, they stayed at Irenka's house while Sara bought the furniture needed for the little house they would rent. The servants were glad to see Gabriel again, as he was the darling of the maids and cooks; they were all fascinated by his beautiful little grey-eyes blonde. '*They spoil him,*' Sara thought, but she smiled with satisfaction when she saw her beloved son surrounded by those who doted on him. Meanwhile, Jana and Aliza met Tatiana, with whom they got on with well. The truth was that all three girls had very kind hearts, so it was not unexpected that they would become friends. Also, Tatiana and Jana were exactly the same age, so they became not only sisters, but close and intimate friends.

The Russian girl, with her extraordinary diligence and sense of purpose, already had the bakery up and running, and had managed to significantly increase the number of orders. Of course, she continued to live in Irenka's house although no longer as one of the servants, but as the daughter of the housewife's great friend and head of the bakery. However, thanks to her kind nature, she never had any difficulties with her former workmates, and treated them with the same deference and friendship as she had before. She never allowed them to call her Miss Tatiana, but insisted they continue to use her first name. She often ate with them in the service dining room, and they talked about work, gossip, and of course, her relationship with Robiak.

The bakery began to find its place itself in the city once again; thanks to the hard work of the three girls, it made bread in great quantities and, as usual in Sara's establishments, in a wide variety. Soon they began to make not only bread, but biscuits, cookies and cakes to order for all kinds of events. The four women worked tirelessly, but one could see the fruits of their labour. By spring, they had bought two carts, one small and one large. In the first, they delivered bread twice a day throughout the city, and with the second the delivered to the surrounding villages.

Little by little, Sara was paying back the loan Irenka had given her and was now able to pay for Gabriel's studies at the Cheder. The girls also visited the Rabbi's wife twice a week, to receive an education. While they were out, they were replaced by two temporary workers whom Sara had hired and taught how to make bread. Neither was particularly young, but they were very dedicated. One was a spinster, who worked to support her sister who could not earn a living because of a disability incurred in an accident several years ago.

The other was a single mother with two children, who told Sara how, when the boys' father was going to marry, he had died in a street fight., leaving them in her sole care. Sara was pleased to be able to support these two women, who proved to be quick learners and hard workers. On the other hand, they were Catholic; so, they took charge of running the bakery during Shabbat.

By May of that year, 1864, the trial against Sara took place, thanks to Marinowsky's pressure. Despite learning of the results from the hearing a few months earlier at the police station, he had maintained his unhealthy obsession with the woman. Sara already knew of Carl's skills and experience, and fully trusted both him and Gustav. Despite this, of course, she could not stop worrying and feeling anxious about the process. Of course, when she had to travel to Bialystok, she did not take the girls with her, as she had nowhere to lodge them, and they had responsibilities in the bakery. Despite their youth, they had already taken charge of the entire process of making and distributing the products. Irenka, once again proving herself a true friend, had instructed her to butler to check in daily to see if the girls ever required support. She travelled with Carl to Bialystok to take part in the trial.

Sara stayed Malka and Piotr's house, her dear friends, who gave her a hand when she needed it most. It was very nice to meet them again, especially in much more favourable circumstances than those they had experienced the previous year. The couple had decided to adopt a little orphan who had lost her parents to smallpox, now they were happy with the girl who was seven years old. That pleased Sara because the girl had brought new hope to that home.

The trial was to be carried out in a city courtroom, chaired by a single judge. The man in question was said to be very close with Marinowsky, so the outcome seemed predictable. However, Carl did not appear concerned in the slightest. Moreover, all of Bialystok had heard of the plaintiff's defeat at the Lublin police station hearing. The man was despised throughout the city, especially amongst the Jewish community, as they had not forgotten how he had promoted rioting against Jewish merchants the year before.

The benches for the public were filled to bursting; many did not want to miss the spectacle as the trial promised to be an interesting one. The Prefect of Police himself was involved, as was a beautiful Jewish lady, who everyone knew had been the real victim. Within the audience, of course, were Irenka, Piotr, and Malka. Finally, those involved began to arrive. First came Marinowsky with his lawyer, who sat on the left side of the courtroom. Sounds of disapproval could be heard from the spectators. About five minutes later, Sara, Carl, and Gustav, this time greeted by applause and cheers.

Sara, at Carl's recommendation, was not wearing her usual scarf, under which she usually kept her hair. On the contrary, she wore her hair down, topped with an understated hat that matched her simple but beautiful green dress. Irenka had given it her for that occasion, and it greatly enhanced her figure. Everyone in the room noticed Sara's presence, which made her somewhat uncomfortable.

The Judge arrived, immediately heading to his place; all those involved headed to their respective places. The Judge was an older man, his hair was completely grey. He had been born sixty-eight years ago in

Warsaw, and as a young boy had entered the service of Count Anastase Colonna-Walewsky, husband of Maria Walewska, whom he served for several years. For this reason, it was said that he knew many secrets about the Countess' relationship with Napoleon, and was a close friend of Alexander Colonna, son of the French Emperor and the Polish noblewoman. Thanks to this friendship he had had the opportunity to study law at the Imperial University of Warsaw.

Traditionally, before the trial began, both accuser and accused must stand with their attorneys before the authority, to be given their corresponding instructions. Carl intentionally stood Sara next to Marinowsky; it made her uncomfortable, but she now understood why Carl had asked her to wear the striking green dress and her hair down. What the lawyer sought was to juxtapose the two; a man, of short stature, somewhat stunted with a malicious face, who's most outstanding characteristics were a very thin moustache and aquiline nose. At his side the defendant: at least two inches taller, with a beautiful face, imposing figure, and a kindly expression.

"We start winning" Carl whispered to Gustav.

The Judge began the case. As is usual, the accusing lawyer stood and read from the complaints filed against Sara. Once he had read them, he proceeded to argue each point, starting with the charge that she had unlawfully opened businesses. By not complying with the registry, both the shoe shop and bakery were forfeit to the competent authorities. Without a doubt, this was just a ruse to justify the usurpation of Isaak's warehouse and workshop. This first allegation being used by Marinowsky's lawyer to, as he put it: 'demonstrate the illegal behaviour of the Jewish couple'. Of course, all of Isaak's records that he had kept and deposited in the city's mercantile office had been made to disappear.

Without these records, Sara would have no proof that she and her husband had acted in accordance with the law; therefore, she would have no evidence with which to recover her shoe shop that Marinowsky had stolen. The lawyer, with great decorum, took a sheet of paper from his desk and presented it to the Judge, saying in a loud voice:

"Your Honour, this document has been issued by the Mercantile Office of Bialystok, stating that nowhere in their records do the names of Isaak Rothman or Sara Rothman appear. Therefore, these two Jews carried out commercial enterprise illegally in this jurisdiction." The Judge took the document and looked it for a few moments. Then he turned to the lawyer.

"Are you going to call witnesses?"

"No, Your Honour.

"Do you have anything else to add, Mr. Poliansky?"

"No, Sir, I consider this document more than enough evidence to support the accusation against this Jewish woman," he said, uttering the last words with contempt.

"Please, Sir, show the lady more respect and refer to her by name."

A murmur could be heard amongst the attendees on the benches. Sara was surprised, but even more Carl, who whispered to Gustav:

"Didn't you say he was close with Marinowsky? I think that this gentleman will turn out to be more impartial than we had expected, good news for us."

The murmur of approval continued from the benches, where most of the attendees were Jewish.

"I give the floor to the defence lawyer," said the Judge.

"Thank you very much, Mr. Judge," Carl said, standing.

He walked to the centre of the room and began his defence.

"The document presented by Mr. Poliansky indicates that there is no record on file in the mercantile office in my client's name, but this does not mean that one could not have existed in the past."

"Explain," said the Judge.

"Want I mean, Your Honour, is the possibility that the aforementioned records existed, but have been removed, cannot be ruled out."

"Are you suggesting that someone has stolen these records? On what basis do you make that claim? Do you have any proof?"

"Not specifically, Mr. Judge, but I do have a document from the same office which states that there are two gaps in the consecutive record. In other words, the numbering is skipped twice, coinciding with the time that Isaak and Sara Rothman opened their businesses."

"That doesn't prove anything," said Poliansky.

"Agreed, my colleague, but it does prove that two records are missing, which could be precisely the ones I'm referring to. I'm sure it would be very convenient for certain parties is those records disappeared.

"Are you insinuating that I, or my client, have taken those records?" Poliansky asked sternly.

"No, of course I'm not insinuating that. On the contrary, I'm sure that you would both be incapable of doing such a thing. You as a lawyer and Mr. Marinowsky in his capacity as Prefect would both know perfectly well that such a thing would be a very serious crime, even more so if your intention were to deceive an Imperial Judge."

"Well, then you must withdraw your words."

"Excuse me, Sir, but I see no reason to withdraw them. I have only said that two records are missing and wondered who benefit by their disappearance."

"You are making direct insinuations; anyone could see that."

"I think what anyone can see is that you seem to be taking things for granted."

"You insult me!"

At that moment the Judge intervened.

"Very well, gentlemen, we are not here to discuss allusions nor coincidences," he continued, "tell me, Mr Kobielsky, where are you taking this?"

"To a very simple conclusion, Your Honour: that the two missing records are precisely the ones belonging to the Rothmans. I can't tell you who took them, unfortunately I can't imagine who would, nor, do I suppose, can anyone in this room."

"You're playing a dangerous game, Mr. Lawyer. This is a trial, not a festival; you must be more specific and get to the point. How can you be so certain that these missing files are those submitted by the accused?"

"I beg your pardon, Mr. Judge. But I make my statement based on the fact that I have evidence that proves it."

Marinowsky and his lawyer looked at each other anxiously, a motion that did not go unnoticed by the room.

"And what is this proof?"

"It turns out, Mr. Judge, that according to Imperial Law No. 02543 from June 1860, all commercial records in towns with more than 5000 inhabitants must be registered in a file, which must be sent, in turn, to the capital of each province, for inclusion in the archives of the Department of Finance, Taxes, and Statistics."

The Judge stared at him; it was obvious where Carl was going. Marinowsky was evidently confused, but his lawyer appeared to show concern.

"It turns out, Your Honour, that my faithful colleague Gustav Ivanovich, here by my side, visited Warsaw some days ago. He took a walk through the city centre, admiring the beautiful architecture. It was while doing so that a particular building caught his eye: the imposing structure of the Department of Finance of our capital."

It was evident that Carl's circumlocution served no purpose other than to infuriate his legal counterpart, but he was also exhausting the Judge's patience.

"Please, sir, be more specific and direct. This is not a theatre."

"A thousand apologies, Mr. Judge," he cleared his throat, then continued, "as I was saying, my colleague entered the Department and, curious, he leafed through the files concerning commercial business here in Bialystok. To his surprise, he came across two files under the names of Isaak and Sara Rothman, which correspond precisely with the consecutive numbers which are strangely missing from the commercial office in this city."

Then he headed for the table where Gustav handed him a piece of paper, then returned to the Judge, saying:

"This document was issued by the Warsaw Department of the Treasury; it certifies what I have told you. You will be able to verify, Mr. Judge, that this is the letterhead, signature, and seal of the Secretary General.

He handed the paper to the Judge, who examined it carefully. Meanwhile Marinowsky's lawyer sank into his chair. The audience was stunned, all that could be heard were exclamations of astonishment and satisfaction. Irenka rose from her chair and, approaching Sara, squeezed her shoulder joyfully, directing her eyes towards Carl with obvious admiration and respect.

Of course, the Judge did not need long to come to his decision. He declared the allegation filed by Marinowsky to be reckless and inadmissible, thus exempting Sara from all responsibility. The audience applauded and cheered; Sara sighed deeply, then stood from her chair and hugged Carl, then Gustav, she turned and did the same to Irenka with evident relief.

After issuing his decision, the Judge ordered a recess before continuing with the case, which would address Marinowsky's accusation that Sara had attempted murder. Of course, this allegation was far more severe, however Carl remained composed and serene.

The trial resumed, and Poliansky began.

"Your Honour, my client filed a lawsuit against this lady since she attempted to kill him. She repeatedly and violently hit him on the head and other parts of his body. When Mr. Marinowsky was lying on the ground, the defendant fled Bialystok and went into hiding in Lublin, in an attempt to avoid justice.

"What evidence do you have to support these claims?" asked the Judge.

"I have three witnesses, Your Honour, in addition to the victim's statement."

Sara could not believe it, not only were there no witnesses to the event, but the blows she had inflicted on Marinowsky were not capable of seriously injuring him, much less kill him.

Of course, it was all a lie, the lawyer called Marinowsky to testify first.

"Mr. Marinowsky, please tell us the facts," Poliansky asked to him.

"Mr. Judge, I was inside the shoe shop that I own, calmly minding my own business, when suddenly this angry Jewess arrived and, without saying a word, attacked me with a cane. She caused me many injuries, which left me unconscious, then immediately fled, leaving me there to die."

"Where did she hit you?" Asked his lawyer.

"Everywhere, but especially on my head, which knocked me unconscious."

"Did she attack you in any other way?"

"Yes, she punched and kicked me."

"Where on your body?"

"All over, but most dangerous ones were to my face. But that was not enough for her, as she made to leave the shop, she turned and tried to hit my private parts, but I curled up and used my knees to protect myself. The pain in those made it difficult to stand later."

"Do you think that the lady's intent was to murder you?"

"Without a doubt, due to the violence of her attack."

"Why do you think the lady wanted to kill you?"

"Because she blames me for the arrest and deportation of her husband, a Jew who participated in the January revolt."

"Do you know why she blames you?"

"Perhaps someone told her I was close by when the Russian soldiers detained him."

"And were you close to the Jew during his detention?"

"Indeed, but I had nothing to do with his capture. The soldiers were simply doing their duty, as the Jew was one of the organisers of the revolt."

"Thank you very much," said the lawyer, "I have no further questions."

Sara could not hide her tears as she heard the wretch describe Isaak as he did, telling so many lies without so much as flinching. She could not believe that a man could be so cruel.

"Attorney for the defence," said the Judge.

"With your permission, Your Honour, I'll reserve my questions for later."

"Very well, that is your right. Bring forth the second witness."

The shoe shop clerk who had been with Marinowsky came forward. Poliansky asked him to tell his version of the events.

"Well, I was with the boss when the lady came in and assaulted him with a cane, leaving him lying on the floor."

"Did she only hit him with the cane?"

"No, she also punched and kicked him."

"Do you believe that the lady's intent was to murder your employer?"

"Yes, because she acted very aggressively."

"What did you do during this event?"

"After the lady had finished and left, I quickly went to call the police."

"I arrived with the police officer, finding the boss holding his head in pain. I then accompanied him to the doctor's to be examined."

"Thank you, Mr. Judge, I have no further questions."

Again, Carl requested to question the witness later, as he did when the doctor was called up as a witness. This man stated that he had treated Marinowsky that morning, finding a traumatic head injury that could have cost him his life. He had prescribed treatment then sent him home to rest. Next, a police officer declared that he had arrived at the shoe shop and the clerk's behest, finding Marinowsky almost dying on the floor. When he had been told what had happened, he went out immediately to track down the assailant, but was unable to find her.

The witnesses fully supported Marinowsky's version of events; the clerk, doctor, and policeman. Therefore, the lawyer considered them sufficient to prove his allegation of attempted murder. Carl, however, considered that the context of the testimonies was not strong enough, they had several weaknesses. Obviously, it had been agreed beforehand; it was evident that the men had coordinated their statements. However, to the lawyer's mind, there were several loose ends that would surely unravel in Sara's favour. But first, he had to follow a few leads to confirm his suspicions, so he decided to request a postponement of the trial. The Judge, in compliance with the law, granted it for until the following day.

The following morning all involved arrived punctually, the benches were full again and a good number of people had gathered outside the building. Sara arrived wearing a different dress, and new woven straw hat. In addition, she wore her hair braids, giving her a youthful, almost childlike look. Again, this was in accordance with Carl's suggestion, who seemed an insight into human psychology.

The Judge gave Carl the floor, who called Sara as a witness.

"Mrs. Rothman," Carl began, in a sombre tone, "could you tell us how you first met Prefect Marinowsky?"

"I first met him around two years ago, when the Prefect's son suffered a severe accident and was on the brink of death. My husband, Isaak, upon learning of this and, knowing that Marinowsky did not have the financial means, paid for the boy to be taken to Warsaw and for life-saving surgery."

"A generous humanitarian gesture. And tell me, did the Prefect ever reimburse your husband back?"

"No, he never returned a single rouble."

"But surely, he appreciated your husband's noble gesture?"

"Yes, his gratitude was appropriating my husband's shop."

"I request an intervention," blurted out Marinowsky's lawyer, "my client did not appropriate the shoe shop. It was confiscated by the authorities, then later assigned to him."

"Mr. Kobielsky, please limit yourself to the matter at hand."

"My apologies, Your Honour. However, my questions are relevant, as you'll soon see." He then asked Sara:

"Tell me, Mrs. Rothman, why did you visit the shoe shop on the day of these events?"

"Because I wanted to complain to the Prefect, because he had appropriated my husband's business."

"And did you arrive cane in hand, prepared to assault him?"

"Of course not! I don't walk with a cane, and my intention was never to hit him. I just wanted to tell him to his face that he was a heartless, ungrateful man."

"Very well, madam," Carl continued, "and did you hit him?"

"Yes, I hit him."

"And why did you do so, if that was not your intention upon entering the establishment?"

"Because he was disrespectful and made advances to me."

"Could you please go into detail? What do you mean when you say 'advances'?"

"He made unseemly proposals tome, which are not made to a lady."

"What type?"

"He proposed that I become his mistress, arguing that I was a poor Jewish widow and that he could support me, together with my son."

A disapproving murmur and an occasional whistle rose from the benches, forcing the judge to reprimand the public once more. Carl continued:

"You stated that you had also gone too far, could you explain to us what happened?"

He cornered me against the counter and then, forcibly and against my will, placed his hands on different parts of my body.

"What do you believe were the Prefect's intentions?"

"They were simple, he intended to rape me."

A great deal of murmuring and whispers could be heard from the benches.

"Silence please," said the Judge, "I demand order."

"Why do you believe those were his intentions?"

"Firstly, from the violent way he touched my body, but also because he made his assistant leave, then went to the door and bolted it."

"And after he had locked the door, what did Mr. Marinowsky do?"

"He turned around and leapt at me, starting to touch me and trying to kiss me by force."

At that moment Marinowsky stood up and yelled.

"That's a lie! That Jew is lying!"

"I order you to behave, Mr. Prefect," replied the Judge, "you must respect the proceedings, you will have the opportunity to speak again, if you wish, at the appropriate time. Please, continue, Mr. Kobielsky."

Carl went on:

"I apologise, madam, for what I am about to ask you. I understand that it is somewhat embarrassing question, but it is necessary. Of course, you may refuse to answer if you wish. Could you tell us where he groped you?"

"Yes, it is embarrassing for any decent woman, but I will tell you. He touched my breasts and behind, below the waist."

More murmurs could be heard from the benches, and the Judge frowned. However, Carl continued with his questioning.

"How did you manage to escape and avoid the Prefect's advances?"

"He grasped me firmly with both hands, against the counter. I was struggling to free myself but could not. At that moment my scarf fell from my head, causing my hair to slip down my shoulders. While he was distracted by that I took the opportunity to hit him in the face with my fist."

Laughter came from the benches. The Judge said nothing, but a slight smile momentarily played on his face before he regained his composure. Carl did not wait for him to speak.

"My goodness, Madam, I would never advocate violence, but I congratulate you. You defended your honour very well. Tell me, what happened next?"

"The Prefect began bleeding from his nose, and I saw that he was about to retaliate, I kneed him between the legs."

The spectators winced at the image.

"In other words, you acted legitimately in self-defence, firstly as a woman defending your honour, then in defence of your safety when you saw he would attack."

"Your Honour, I protest!" said the lawyer for the accused, "the defence is directing the responses of his witness."

"You're correct, please change your question and refrain from influencing the witness' answers," said the Judge.

"My apologies, Your Honour, I will do so," then Carl addressed Sara, "Could you tell us why you acted as you did?"

"Because I was acting in self-defence, first of my honour as a woman, then for my safety when I saw that he was about to strike me."

Irenka, Piotr, and the entire audience laughed out loud.

"Silence!" ordered the Judge, "if you do not compose yourselves, I will have to order you to leave the courtroom."

Everybody fell silent, but muted chuckling could be heard.

"Well, what happened next?" Carl asked.

"The Prefect fell to the floor, and I kicked him in the face."

"So, you accept that you struck him in the face?"

"Yes, I accept it, I kicked on the nose."

"And then you left the premises?"

"I went to the door and removed the latch, but I noticed that he was trying to stand, so I took his own cane and struck twice at his legs."

"In other words, the witnesses spoke the truth when they said that you hit the Prefect with a cane, punched, and kicked him."

"Yes, that is correct."

"I reiterate, is everything they said true?"

"No, not all of it."

"How so? What is true and what is not?"

"Of all that they have claimed, the only truth is that I hit the Prefect, everything else is a lie."

A fresh bout of quiet laughter came from the benches, Carl had clearly instructed Sara very well.

"So, you assert that the other witnesses have lied?"

"Yes, they have all lied."

Lawyer Poliansky stood and exclaimed:

"Mr. Judge, how can you allow this Jewish woman to say this?"

"Mr. Lawyer," the Judge said fiercely, "I understand your concern, but what I cannot allow is for you to address me in that manner. Behave, or I will expel you from the courtroom. And I repeat, if you do not agree with the statement, you will have the opportunity to question the witness," he then turned to Carl, "please, continue."

"Tell us, Mrs. Rothman, did you intend to murder Prefect Marinowsky?"

"Of course not. What's more, if he had not messed with me, I would never have done so."

"But when you did hit him, did you consider that doing so could cause his death?"

"I'm sorry, Mr. Lawyer, but that's absurd. The blows I gave him were not particularly serious nor forceful, how much strength can a woman have? I was merely lucky that my fist struck his nose, making him bleed."

"Why do you say 'lucky'?"

"Because had I not done so, he would have raped me."

Murmuring filled the room once again, but this time the Judge did not react. He was increasingly fascinated by this questioning; he could not tell whether the lawyer or witness was more intelligent. Then came three more questions, undoubtedly prepared in order to give Sara an opportunity for a little revenge.

"Do you not think, madam, that he was incapacitated by your blows?"

"No, the wound to his nose was very slight, the only real damage was to his pride."

The audience laughed once again.

"And you weren't afraid that he might hit you in retaliation, hurting you?"

"Well, he had already hurt my honour and dignity. For a woman, it is greatly damaging that any man touches her forcibly. As for a physical assault, yes, I felt some fear, although perhaps this was unfounded."

"Why do you say that madam?"

"Because he never behaved like a real man might have done, though I must admit that his being shorter than me was to my advantage."

This time the benches howled in laughter, reacting to Sara's words with loud applause and shouts of approval. Two insults in one answer, calling him short and a lesser man. The Judge lowered his head and put a hand to his brow, no doubt impressed by the extraordinary woman and the lawyer's skill. The moment he removed his hand and raised his head, the benches fell silent. To avoid the Judge having to reprimand the spectators, Carl hurried onto the next question, thinking that having public support was in his interest.

"A final question, Mrs. Rothman. Do you regret hitting the Prefect?"

"Of course not."

"Why not?"

"Because he stole my husband's shoe shop."

This time the prosecuting attorney remained silent.

"So, would you hit him again?"

"Of course, but not in the same way."

"What do you mean?"

"This time, I would hit him harder."

Hearing this, the spectators leapt to their feet, cheering and applauding; they no longer cared what the Judge would say. In response, he stood from his chair and ordered a half hour break. What the man really wanted was to retreat into his office to laugh alone without anyone noticing.

After the break, Carl requested that Marinowsky's clerk take the stand. He then began his examination.

"Can you tell me how old you are?"

"I'm 22 years old."

"Very well, and what is your height?"

"About two and a half Arshin (1.8 metres)."

"I see that you're very strong, it looks like you exercise to stay in shape. Do you do a lot of sport?"

"Yes, sir. I like to run and swim."

"Congratulations."

No one understood Carl's line of questioning, but Sara, although confused, was certain that Carl would surprise her again.

"Tell me, are you loyal to your employer, Prefect Marinowsky?"

"Of course, I am."

"Very well, I congratulate you again," Carl slowly returned to his desk, took a sip of water, then returned.

"You witnessed the events that are being dealt today; could you tell me the colour of the cane with which Mrs. Rothman entered the shoe shop?"

The boy was surprised, not knowing what to say. At last, he replied:

"The cane?"

"Yes, the cane."

"Which cane?"

"You said in your statement yesterday that you were in the shoe shop with your employer when Mrs Rothman arrived and immediately assaulted him with a cane. Can you remember its colour? What type of cane was it? Did it have a handle?"

The boy stuttered, searching for an answer. After a few moments, he finally spoke.

"I can't remember."

"Well, you can't remember the colour of the cane, but you're certain that the lady entered with a cane in hand, correct?"

"Yes, that's right."

"And do you remember whether she hit him with the cane first, or was it with her fists?"

"I think it was with her fists."

"The lady entered the establishment, approached the Prefect, and began to punch him?"

"Yes, exactly."

"How many times did she punch him?"

"I don't know, many times."

"How many is many? Five? Ten?"

"I would say ten.

"All on his nose?"

"The nose?"

"Yes, were all these punches to his nose?"

"Yes, on his nose and the rest of his face?"

"And after punching him, did she hit him with the cane?"

"Yes, she did."

"And how many times did she hit him with the cane after hitting him with her fists?"

"I don't know, I can't remember very well."

"Do you consider yourself a calm person?"

Again, the boy was puzzled at this question. However, he answered truthfully.

"Yes, I don't cause any trouble."

"But you're not always behave like that, do you?"

"I don't understand, why do you say that?"

"Because a couple of weeks ago you were in a fight outside a bar remember?"

"Yes, of course."

"And you beat a coachman, knocking him out, am I mistaken?"

"Well, that's true, but it was because the man had beaten a boy who had accidentally knocked over his glass of beer."

"Well, in that case you were in the right, as the man had committed an injustice, correct?"

"Yes, I was."

"I'll repeat myself, you are a calm, reasonable person, but under the right circumstances, you react when necessary. By the way, this coachman was a strong, young boy like yourself, correct?"

"Yes, I think so. I didn't know him before that night."

"Can you see Mrs. Rothman here?"

"Of course, I can see her."

"Who would you say she is stronger than the coachman?"

"What? Stronger?"

"Yes, you heard me correctly, would you regard her to be stronger than the coachman?"

"Of course not."

"Then I'd like you to address a question I have; if Mrs. Rothman is weaker than this coachman you knocked out, and you are as loyal to Prefect Marinowsky as you say, why did you not defend him as she attacked him aggressively, as you described?"

A fresh wave of murmurs came from the benches. The boy was lost, unsure of what to say.

"Shall I ask you again?" Carl said, staring at him, "Why, if you were present the entire time, did you not help your employer? Why did you allow her to hit him?"

The boy was silent.

"Oh, and one more thing. Why did you affirm that the lady entered and started attacking with the cane, only to say today that she immediately attacked the Prefect with her fists?"

"What?"

"Which version is the truth?"

"I don't know, I don't remember."

"You don't remember?"

"No, I'm confused."

"Well, before you get further confused, tell me: why did you not defend your employer?"

"Because ... well ... I don't remember very clearly, I was ..."

"According to your statement yesterday, you were present throughout and witnessed the events. I'll remind you of your exact words: 'After the lady had finished and left, I quickly went to call the police.' In other words, the lady was gone by the time you went to the police."

The man remained silent.

"Then I ask you again, if you were present the whole time, why didn't you help the Prefect?"

"I don't know, I..."

"I know why, could it be because you were not present and did not witness the scene?"

The boy looked frightened. Carl looked at him questioningly, then said in a fatherly tone:

"Look, young man, you lied yesterday, and have lied again today. It's time for you to tell the truth. This trial is presided over by a Judge of the Empire, and it's a very serious crime to conceal the truth, you could go to prison."

The man hung his head, completely stunned.

"Tell me the truth, were you in the shoe shop when the events occurred?"

"No, I wasn't."

"But you were there when Mrs. Rothman arrived, correct?"

"Yes, I was there at that time."

"And did she enter aggressively, with a cane in hand?"

"No."

"And after she entered, why didn't you remain in the shop?"

"Because the boss ordered me to leave, and I did so."

"And did you see what he did once you had left?"

"Yes, he went to the door and bolted it."

"I have no further questions, Your Honour."

This time the spectators didn't utter a word; everything had been said. Lawyer Poliansky was floored. Marinowsky looked confused and lost. Carl seized the advantage, not waiting for the Prefect to recover from the blow.

"I request, your Honour, that Mr. Prefect Marinowsky takes the stand."

Marinowsky looked like a scolded child as he approached the stand, his downcast demeanour an obvious admission that his house of cards was collapsing. Carl walked towards him, then said:

"Mr. Prefect, I give you my word that this questioning will not take longer than a minute; so, I'll get straight to the point. You affirmed

yesterday in your statement that, as a result of the blows that Mrs.
Rothman gave you, you were left lying unconscious on the floor, is this
correct?"

"That's exactly how it happened."

"You also stated that when she was about to leave, she turned from
the door and tried to hit your upper parts. But you curled up your legs
and she hit your knees making it difficult for you to stand up afterwards.
Am I correct?"

"Exactly."

"Could you please explain to me how, if you were left unconscious,
you were able to curl into a ball to protect yourself from her blows?"

Marinowsky's mouth hung open, and he looked at his lawyer. The
room was so silent you would have heard a pin drop.

"No more questions, Your Honour," Carl said, returning to his seat
next to Gustav. Under his breath he told him:

"Your ability to write quickly has been a great help, there would have
been no other way to have to exact statements of the witnesses!" He then
chuckled with satisfaction.

The Judge came to Marinowsky's rescue, although seemingly more
out of pity than supposed friendship; he ordered a half-hour recess. In
any case, had the Judge not ordered it, Carl was considering requesting it,
as it gave an opportunity for Gustav's persuasiveness to come into play.
As soon as the break began, he contacted the doctor who had testified
the day before, asking for a quick word outside the courthouse.

"Doctor, I'll go straight to the point. You were a witness yesterday
and today, according to order of the proceedings, you will be the next
who is called to the stand, do you agree?

"I suppose so."

"Well, you have already seen how the events are unfolding; it is
obvious that the whole thing was a set up."

The Doctor did not answer, nor did Gustav give him the
opportunity to do so.

"I can assure you that the Judge is already certain that both the
Prefect and his clerk lied yesterday, wouldn't it be unfortunate if he
found out that you had done the same?"

"What do you mean?"

"You and I both know that, given your position, it would be very harmful to your reputation."

"Your implication is deeply insulting!"

"Doctor, please don't prolong this any further than necessary. I will be more specific. While it is true that you attending to Marinowsky on the day of these events, your diagnosis was not head trauma, but a severe bruise to the nose and nothing else."

"How can you say that? Are you a doctor, or were you there?"

"Of course not, Doctor, but I do know that, by the time you saw the Prefect, several hours had passed since the event. In that time, he carried out various actions, at his residence, at the bank, and at the Police Prefecture. There are numerous witnesses, documents proving a bank transaction, and the police guard's minute books that prove what I'm saying. Do you really believe a person with head trauma could have carried out such activities? Wouldn't one's natural reaction be to see a doctor first? I can assure you that the defence attorney will ask similar questions of you."

The doctor bowed his head slightly, as if trying to collect his thoughts. Gustav continued.

"I don't know the nature of your relationship with the Prefect, nor your motive for testifying yesterday, but I think you should consider whether that man is worth risking your reputation and career for."

Upon hearing these words, the doctor realised he was trapped, and that he had been making a terrible mistake.

"What do you propose I do, Lawyer?"

"It's very simple; talk with Marinowsky and his lawyer, Poliansky. Make them understand that their game has been exposed, and that it would be worse for them if they continued with this charade."

"I doubt that he will give up because of my advice, he is a stubborn and malicious man.

"You don't match the prefect's malice, but he does not match your intelligence."

"I don't follow."

"That he may be very cunning, but he lacks your sharp reasoning."

"I am still a bit confused, Lawyer."

"I will explain. There are two remaining witnesses, you, and the policeman. The latter's evidence will not contribute much of relevance as he arrived on the scene after the events took place. However, your questioning will be of greater importance to the judge and the public. Doubtlessly, you have seen how Lawyer Kobielsky handles questioning witnesses. Do you really believe that you will emerge unscathed from the defence lawyer's questioning?"

The doctor was silent and rubbed his hands together nervously. It was not necessary for him to answer; his body language was very eloquent. However, he still couldn't make up his mind.

"I fully agree with all of your assessments, but honestly I am concerned about how that gentleman will retaliate if I fail to comply with the favour that he has requested of me."

"If you have paid attention to this trial, you will have already confirmed that knowing how to be grateful for favours received is not one of Marinowsky's qualities."

"Well, I think you're absolutely right, I'll talk to him."

"I congratulate you doctor, it's the most sensible thing to do. On the other hand, you can count on my total discretion, you have my word."

"Thank you."

Once the hearing had resumed, Marinowsky's lawyer requested the floor, stating that his client was withdrawing his lawsuit against Sara, for attempted murder. The Judge accepted the proposal, but not before admonishing the plaintiff. Jubilation broke out in the chamber, people applauded from the benches. Irenka and Sara embraced, then Sara also hugged Carl, Gustav, Malka, and Piotr. She felt as though a great weight had been lifted from her shoulders. She smiled with satisfaction; justice was finally being done.

The case for alleged robbery was still pending, however, given the humiliation Marinowsky had already suffered throughout the trial, his lawyer advised him to also withdraw that charge. Sara was greatly pleased by this, and Irenka radiated joy, laughing contagiously.

"This calls for a celebration," she said, "as soon as we return to Lublin, we will have a great party!"

"Yes," Carl added, "and we've already invited Marinowsky and the Lublin Commissioner!"

Everyone laughed heartily, then went over to Piotr and Malka's home to toast their success. Sara felt calmer and could now go ahead with her plans.

"You must be careful, Sara," Carl said, "Marinowsky is a dangerous and spiteful man, the fight is not over, now you must recover your husband's shoe shop."

The memory of her husband was the only thing that clouded Sara's happiness. She reflected on all her recent good fortune: she had recovered Jana and Aliza, Gabriel was progressing in his studies, her friendship with Irenka was strengthening by the day, she had met a wonderful family in the Czemerinskys, Tatiana had become a daughter to her, her bakery was proving a success, and her anguish over the Marinowsky affair lessened. However, she felt her husband's absence. Malka looked at her, guessing her thoughts.

"That is life, my dear Sara," she said, taking her by the hand, "it gives and takes away, we must adapt to all circumstances."

"Oh, Malka! You are as wise as ever. I am happy with how things are going now, I cannot be ungrateful to God for all that he has given me, but I have a void that cannot be filled. I wish I could share this happiness with my Isaak."

A few tears came to her eyes. Malka took her hand again, saying:

"It's hard to lose loved ones, Sara, but you must know that time heals all wounds."

"But the scar remains."

"Yes, but we must learn to live with those scars."

"Oh, God! Mine pierces my heart!"

12

The carriage drove along dusty roads under a hot sun. The heat was overpowering, to the extent that Sara and the three girls had taken off their shawls in an attempt to of the refreshing breeze that managed to get inside. The entered a wooded area, where the trees reached skyward blocking the sun's rays, providing a brief respite within their compartment.

"You'll see what nice people the Czemerinskys are." Jana said to Tatiana.

"I feel like I already know them, from the amount that you and Aliza talk about them."

"I'm so happy to see them again," Aliza interrupted, then she turned to Gabriel and said:

"You're happy too, aren't you, Gabrielin?"

"Of course, and I want to play with the twins!"

"Ha! You'll have fun with them soon, my son," Sara said, looking at him tenderly.

Gabriel was increasingly demonstrating his intelligence and ability to assimilate knowledge. He had a deductive mind that surprised both his family and strangers, especially considering his young age. He also had an impressive memory, speaking Polish as his mother tongue, Russian as the language of his three sisters, and some Yiddish as taught by his mother and the Rabbi, which was used in the Cheder. At home he was spoiled, his sisters indulged all his whims and mischief. Sara was the one who imposed rules and discipline. However, the boy had developed a mature personality despite barely being eight years old, increasingly showing signs of his strong and determined character. Sara was proud of him, as well as of her three daughters.

The girls were also growing up; Jana had just turned 17, and was already a woman, beautiful and tender, which enhanced her attractiveness. She was very organised and took responsibility for all her tasks, both at home and in the bakery that she ran; she was responsible for the first branch of main bakery. This catered mainly to peripheral neighbourhoods and nearby villages, which were serviced by three carts, supervised by Robiak, Tatiana's partner. He no longer working as a coachman for Irenka and, thanks to Sara's support, had formed his own transport company. With great effort and savings, he had already managed to pay in full for two of the three carts, which worked not only to deliver bread, but also were hired for various other services. Sara was fond of the young man, because of his education, work-ethic, and manners.

He was a good man, hopelessly in love with Tatiana, which he was unable to hide, causing Jana and Aliza to tease him, as they already considered Tatiana their lifelong sister. Indeed, her sweetness and candour had a similar effect on most people; all found her charming. She got on very well with the other girls and, although they sometimes argued, that was to be expected of sisters. They had become inseparable, recognised throughout Lublin as they always walked in each other's presence. Wherever they went, whether to the synagogue, market, or to festivals, they always aroused the attention of the local boys, who wooed and complimented them.

When Sara was unable to go with them, they were always accompanied by Robiak, who, it turned out, was jealous not only over his girlfriend, but also her sisters. He was like a scarecrow when walking with the girls, furtively warding off any conversation, to the point that the girls preferred Sara's company when walking; despite her being strict with her 'girls', as a woman she understood their situation, finding it amusing. The problem was that when it was just the four of them, Sara did not appear to be the chaperone. After all, she was not an old woman, she had just turned 27 and still maintained a youthful freshness, which is why some thought her their older sister.

The shyest of the three was Aliza, who was always thought of as the little girl who required protection. At this, she protested, and not without good reason; she was only two years younger than the others. She had a certain complex over being less short than her mother and sisters, but Sara soon fixed this without difficulty. She was the one who chose the girls' footwear, and, of course, Aliza's shoes always had a slightly higher heel.

In short, they were all excellent workers who helped to run the bakery very well, including expanding into another branch. Regarding their education, Sara spared no effort in that her daughters could fulfil their religious devotions and strict adherence to the rules of Judaism. She also instilled in them models of etiquette and behaviour, as well as a love of reading and general culture. Jana was in love with a boy whose greatest aspiration in life was to become a Rabbi, which did not displease her mother at all.

Aliza had no suitor, at least none that were serious, but she had secretly fallen in love with a young Austrian. The young man periodically came to Lublin to visit his parents. Aliza dreamed of the young man, although she could not tell her mother, as he was a Catholic. The young man was a dashing second lieutenant in the Austrian Imperial Army, nephew of the naval captain who travelled to Lublin frequently, almost exclusively to woo Sara, with whom he was in love. But, to his regret, she always maintained a dignified distance between them. Tatiana could not understand her rejection of him and would like to have seen her mother with a man as important and handsome and Captain Hoffman. More than once, she urged her to pay him a little more attention. She knew that all the ladies of Lublin yearned for the officer, yet the only one that interested him, continued to reject him.

Sara looked at her daughters as the carriage continued through the endless forest. She was immensely satisfied and proud, she loved them as if she was their biological mother. Her thoughts drifted to the tragedies they had overcome to reach this point. Now, they not only had each other's company, but were also great support both in the bakery and at home. It had been three months since they had moved into their new house; their profits and savings had allowed them to afford a higher rent, so they had moved from their modest initial two roomed dwelling to a simple, but more spacious house. It had three rooms, one for Sara, one for the girls, and a small one for little Gabriel. It also had a small hall and dining room attached to the kitchen together with a garden and patio. It was not a luxurious place, but it was comfortable; Sara and the girls had decorated it in very good taste, and they felt the warmth of a home when they entered.

The new house permitted them to receive visits from Irenka, Sara, and Tobias, who had been so kind to them at their lowest moments. They even welcomed Jared, who stopped by one day in the company of Oizer. In this new home, they had set aside a special shelf where they kept Isaak's Tefillin from Israel and the silver Menorah which, by an incredible turn of fate, they had managed to rescue from an antique dealer in Bialystok, although they had to pay three times its value. On another shelf were Maretska's crucifix and note, of whom nothing had been heard. The only thing they had learned was that she had emigrated to America, but they had lost track of her after that. despite this, Sara continued to treasure her gifts.

Sara emerged from her thoughts and regarded the girls with affection; they had become beautiful young ladies.

"My girls, how I love you."

"Mother," said Jana, "we love you very much as well."

"I know, my dear daughter," she then addressed all three of them, "you and Gabriel are my life, the greatest gift God has given me."

The three girls rushed to embrace her, shaking the carriage, and nearly making it slip. They all laughed while Gabriel watched them in amazement. At that moment the driver shouted from his seat.

"Ivanana in sight, ladies! This is the last stop of our trip; we'll eat here so that the horses can drink and rest for a couple of hours."

Sara leaned over to the window and poked her head outside.

"Very well, how far are we from Pinsk?"

"About four hours, Mrs. Rothman. We'll arrive around eight this evening."

"Perfect, thank you very much," she then addressed the girls, "let's take this opportunity to stretch our legs and have something to drink."

Their arrival in Pinsk was quite an event for the two families. Although Sara had already visited them with Gabriel, and Jared had been to Lublin, this was the first time they would all be meeting, now including Tatiana. Anya was overflowing with joy to see her friend, not to mention the children. The Rothmans arrived laden with gifts for them all, Sara had not forgotten what Jared and Anya had done for them. If there is one thing that can be said of the Jewish people, it is that they never forget a favour and are forever grateful. Pinsk was much smaller and quieter than Minsk, but the two families were most interested in spending the time with each other and walking in the countryside together.

Fortunately, Jared's business was going well and Oizer had definitely become his right-hand man. The boy was very responsible in his work and was quickly learning the details of the timber trade. He was the pride of his father, who saw in his son the potential to continue his company. Anya had been a little sick but had now fully recovered and was able to take part in all the families' activities.

These were fifteen days of rest and joy for all, but it was soon necessary for them to return to their duties in Lublin. They arranged their trip home, but not before planning to meet again to celebrate Hanukkah together. For this, the Czemerinsky would return the visit. The journey home was smooth, but Gabriel felt slightly unwell, with a fever and occasional cough. Once they had arrived home, Sara visited a pharmacy for a syrup to soothe the boy's throat.

The following two months were hard work for all of them; they were determined to diversify their business by learning how to prepare desserts and sweets, based on recipes taught to them by an expert. This was a Swiss confectioner who knew the secrets of Oriental desserts, having lived in Constantinople for several years. Sara had met her at Irenka's house during one of her usual gatherings, as her husband was a colleague of Carl, and they were handling some cases together in Prussia. The couple enjoyed a few days off at the Kobielsky'.

The addition of her various exotic desserts in the two bakeries was a complete success, to the extent that Sara had the idea to hold a festival of desserts. This event was so popular that the City Council asked her to hold it every year, as a way of promoting the city. Sara's bakeries were gaining more and more prestige, and her sales were increasing, generating significant profits for her family which she carefully saved. Her aim was to buy a house nearby Irenka's that was for sale; it was smaller and less sumptuous that that of her friend, but it was beautiful and, more importantly, would be her own.

The Czemerinskys visited for Hanukkah. Settling happily in the Rothman home despite the house's small size and the cold of the Winter of '65. When Sara took them to see the changes, she had made to the bakery they were taken aback; gone was the old wooden room and green-framed windows, it had been transformed now looked like one of the finest bakeries in Warsaw.

"It looks just like the ones in Vienna and Paris" Jared complimented her.

"What a beautiful sign you have put up, my dear," Anya commented, "it shines like gold. But tell me, what does your bakery's name mean?"

"The name does not symbolise anything, but it has a special meaning to me."

"Please, explain it to us," her friend said, reading the sign: '*ISROTH*'

"It's the name, Isaak Rothman, in honour of my husband, the love of my life."

"How lovely," was all Anya could think of saying, thinking on how difficult it must be a widow, especially when one has loved so intensely.

Without a doubt, things were going well for the entire family. However, certain dark clouds began to appear on their horizon. Gabriel's sore throat and persistent cough increasingly recurred. His mother took him to a doctor, who recommended that he inhale eucalyptus vapours, and to massage his chest and throat with warm pine oil. Sara complied with his instructions, treating the boy daily, as instructed by the doctor. Initially, she saw some improvement, however he later relapsed; his cough was more and more frequent, and Gabriel lost his appetite.

His distressed mother took him back to the doctor, who examined the boy carefully. In addition to the cough, he had a constant fever. The doctor analysed the symptoms, then said to the mother:

"Continue with your treatment and give him plenty of fluids. To lower his fever, place clothes dampened with cold water on his forehead."

"Understood, doctor, I will continue to follow your instructions. But tell me, what do you think his condition is?"

"It's too early to be able to give a diagnosis, this may be the result of a cold. If so, this treatment should work. However, we must keep him under observation to see how it develops. Return in two days, or sooner if he worsens.

Of course, due to the deterioration of Gabriel's health, Sara stopped working in the bakery, instead staying at home to take care of him. Tatiana took charge of business at the main bakery, with the support of Aliza, while Jana continued to manage the branch and directed all affairs related to deliveries. The girls, as expected, fully carried out their responsibilities and business ran smoothly.

Gabriel did not improve, his health continued to deteriorate rapidly. Sara spent many sleepless nights with the boy. The girls offered to take her place, but she never accepted. Every half hour she placed a damp cloth on his forehead, but the fever did not subside. She decided to take him back to the doctor, who meticulously analysed his condition. He checked his temperature and, placing his ear to the boy's chest, listened to his heartbeat and breathing. After doing so, he was still for a long time, his clenched fist held against his jaw. He turned to Sara and said:

"I'm sorry, madam, the symptoms indicate that your son has contracted the white plague."

"How? The what?"

"The so-called white plague, ma'am, tuberculosis."

A chill ran through Sara's and her head span, the mere mention of the disease made her shudder.

"Doctor, are you sure?"

"No, but it's what the symptoms indicate."

"Oh, God! What can be done?"

"There really isn't much, you must keep him in a place with clean air, away from the winter cold, as the low temperature will affect his lungs even more. Continue giving him fluids and try to lower his fever with a damp cloth."

"Oh God! My little one!"

"At the very least he isn't coughing up bloody sputum, which is a good sign. Other than that, he must rest and, although he may not want it, he has to eat something, even a light soup would do."

"But doctor, will my boy be cured?"

"I cannot say, madam. It's in God's hands, we will do all we can, but it's up to nature. He is a strong and healthy boy, and his youth is the greatest strength he has, that should give you hope."

While Sara heard all the doctor's words, they didn't register with her.

"I understand your pain and concern, madam. We must pray for a speedy recovery."

"Is there anything else you can do, doctor?"

"There's not much, madam, except keep an eye on the boy's condition, which of course I will."

Sara tried not to break into tears, the doctor tried to comfort her, but he spoke his mind directly.

"The disease is very serious, but I repeat, the boy is strong. Try to maintain a hygienic environment, as ventilated and pleasant as possible. That should help too."

"Yes doctor, I will."

"And there's one more thing, madam. I met a French colleague last year in Vienna, his name is Villemín; he holds the belief that the disease is contagious, and I share this theory, as does another Frenchman, the researcher Louis Pasteur."

Through her daze, Sara recognised the name Pasteur, although she did not understand what the doctor was implying.

"What does that mean for me, doctor?"

"That the disease is contagious, thus it is essential that the boy remain completely isolated. No one should approach him nor have any contact with his personal items, such as his sheets, utensils and so on."

"Absolutely no one?"

"No one, except yourself, who is taking care of him."

"I will follow your instructions, doctor."

Unfortunately, despite the doctor's care and advice, Gabriel's health continued to decline. His coughing did not stop, neither did his fever subside; the boy quickly lost weight, had no appetite, and developed a pale complexion. In his weak voice, he complained about his aching throat and chest. Sara fell to pieces along with her son, she practically never slept, and the little food she ate was only at the insistence of her daughters. She was becoming became pale and thin.

She placed her bed next to Gabriel's, and refused anyone entry to the room, except the doctor, who came every day to see his patient. The look on his face when he left was not reassuring, but he still insisted that the fact the boy had not coughed up blood was positive.

Sara's friends proved their worth; Irenka visited daily to comfort her, Jared and Anya travelled from Pinsk to keep her company for a few days, as did Piotr and Malka, Lublin's Jewish community also showed their solidarity; including many people that Sara did not even know who stopped by her house offering help in whatever she might need. Most did not disturb her, but rather left messages of support, letting her know that they prayed for the boy's recovery.

Spring came, and still Gabriel showed no sign of recovery; the doctor was increasingly concerned from his daily visits, and Sara felt that her beloved sone was slipping away. She had run out of tears and was overcome by melancholy. She prayed daily and begged that God would not take her little son from her. She did so with such faith and fervour that even the rabbi was moved to the depths of his heart, and he felt that he no longer had any words with which to comfort her.

The three young women were also very affected by the deterioration of their beloved brother's health. Tatiana in particular felt an additional concern and sadness, because she could not but remember that she had lost her biological mother, through the same illness.

One night early in April the boy had a violent coughing fit. Tatiana put a coat on over her pyjamas and ran for the doctor. Sara held her son closely and tried to rest him against the pillows, terrified that the boy was suffocating. Gabriel coughed and trembled so greatly that he spasmed in his bed. Jana and Aliza screamed desperately, while Sara pressed him against her chest. When the doctor arrived, she gave way to allow him through; in that moment she saw with terror that her dress was stained red with blood. In that instant she collapsed, shaking all over.

Jana and Aliza picked her up and sat her on a chair, then held smelling salts below her nose. Meanwhile, the doctor laid Gabriel back against the pillows, also holding a bottle in front of his nose. The boy had lost consciousness, Sara, who had come to, raised her head, and let out a piercing scream. The doctor took the boy's pulse and pressed his ear against the boy's chest, then said to the girls:

"Get your mother out."

Sara feared the worst, her daughters struggled to take her into the living room and sit her in an armchair. She was in tatters, between sobs she gasped:

"My God, I beg you, do not take my son from me, I beg you, Lord, do not take him away. I could not bear it!"

The girls held her tightly, but she freed herself from their grip and ran into the room just as the doctor was emerging. His face said everything.

"I'm very sorry, there's nothing I can do."

"No!!" Sara screamed, "Not my son, God!"

She rushed in and threw herself at the foot of the bed. At that moment, Gabriel had a fresh bout of coughing, but this time his shakes were much weaker.

"Make your mother some tea," the doctor said to Jana, as he returned to the boy's room and obliging Sara to leave again. He closed the door behind him. The girls held tightly to Sara, who tried to break free and re-enter the bedroom. They managed to sit her down. Shortly, the doctor returned.

"Calm down. I can't say that the danger has passed, but his pulse is better, and I think his coughing has dropped a little. I think he may be leaving the worst behind him."

Sara put her hands to her chest, breathing deeply, although a little calmer.

The rest of the night was terrible for everyone; the doctor remained at the boy's side until dawn. He made him to drink a concoction that he himself prepared in the kitchen. Strangely, Gabriel fell into a deep sleep and, although his cough continued, it was less frequent and violent.

"I'm going to change and rest a little," said the doctor, standing and addressing the girls, "I'll be back before noon, try to get your mother to rest as well."

Throughout the day Gabriel's cough persisted, but he was no longer bringing up bloody sputum. The little food he was given did not agree with him. That night felt eternal for Sara again. There was no new crisis, but the boy looked so weak that his desperate mother did not want to leave his side for a single moment. The doctor made her withdraw around ten that night, and he remained at the patient's side until dawn again. The girls, who were also unable to sleep, heard him speak to the boy occasionally through the door.

"Hold on, boy. You're strong, you'll get through this. Come on, I know you can."

Aliza, who had the last shift before sunrise, managed to get Sara lay her head on her lap so that she could sleep, at least for a few minutes. As the girl gently stroked her mother's hair, she heard the doctor speak to the boy, calling him by name.

"Come on, Gabriel, you will recover, you are not going to give up."

Aliza was touched by the doctor's words, although she was certain that the boy would not hear him because of his high fever and general weakness. However, she was surprised to hear the doctor say to him:

"Courage, boy, you will get through this. There is a lot you must do in life; you must fulfil your father's dream. You will be a good Jew and one day you will look upon Jerusalem."

Aliza almost jumped out of her seat, nearly waking Sara who's anguished head she cradled. How could the doctor, being a Catholic, say that to Gabriel, she wondered? How did he know Isaak's dream?

"What's happening, my girl?" Sara asked, worried to see her so agitated.

"Nothing, nothing, mother. Rest some more."

Of course, she did not pay attention. She got up and went into the boy's room.

The doctor followed his same routine the next day, retiring at sunrise and returning around eleven in the morning. When he arrived, he found Irenka, Carl, and Tobias in the living room. The doctor made them leave.

"Wait outside, please. Too many people will not be good for the boy."

They all went out into the street. As he entered the room, Sara stood from Gabriel's side, giving way to him.

"I see that he is still sleeping," said the doctor, approaching the boy, "has he awakened since I left?"

"No, doctor, and his coughing fits have declined."

"Has he coughed blood again?"

"No, thank God."

The doctor looked at him, before something caught his attention. He frowned, scaring Sara, then brought face closer to the patient and, in his usual fashion, held his chin in his left hand. Sara couldn't bear it anymore, and asked:

"What's the matter, doctor?"

"It's strange," he replied, taking out his handkerchief and wiping sweat from the boy's forehead.

"What? What is, doctor?" Sara insisted, holding her breath.

"With this disease, it's normal to have night sweats, but not so during the day. Do you see these little droplets on the boy's forehead?"

Sara knelt down, then answered.

"Yes, doctor. I see them."

The doctor felt Gabriel's neck and wiped the sweat again. He then bent down and placed an ear to his chest, before raising his head and turning to Sara.

"Do you see that droplets of sweat have formed on his head again?"

"Yes, doctor, is it a good sign?"

"It is the best of signs, madam."

Sara felt a shudder run through her body.

"His fever has decreased for the first time in over a month."

Sara put a hand to her mouth, her eyes dripped with tears.

"Also, his breathing is steadier," added the doctor, "and not only that, throughout the time I've been here he has only coughed once, lightly."

Sara wanted to reply but the words would not come. She breathed heavily and put her hands to her face, looking expectantly at the doctor. He had knelt again to put his ear against Gabriel's chest. He raised his head and said:

"His fever has almost completely disappeared, and his breathing indicates that his lungs are working much better."

He looked at the wall for a moment and narrowed his eyes, then, make his usual gesture of holding his chin. He then looked at the boy again and smiled, nodding his head up and down as if to affirm his words. Sara understood the meaning of his gestures and look of satisfaction. She

turned towards her son again and gave in to her urge to cry. The door
opened and Jana and Tatiana entered, looking anguished. The doctor
hurried to tell them the news.

"Calm down, everything indicates that the boy is recovering."

The two girls looked at Gabriel then hugged their mother.

"Please, all three of you must leave for a moment," said the doctor,
while lifting the covers and laying Gabriel against the pillows.

Aliza greeted them in the living room, and Jana immediately passed
on what they had been told. They all embraced and wept, before running
to inform their visitors who were still gathered outside on the street.
They could not contain their joy; Sara was still unable to speak. At that
moment the house was filled with happiness. A few minutes later the
doctor entered the living room, he had a serious expression, but his eyes
had a triumphant look. Everyone stared at him expectantly, as though
their lives depended on his words.

"Well," he finally said, "my knowledge and experience indicate that,
without a doubt, the boy has overcome the most critical stage in his
illness. He is no longer in danger."

"Thank God!" said Tobias.

"However, we must still be very careful," continued the doctor, "we
must continue to provide care in order to avoid the risk of a relapse."

"Doctor, we will do everything to look after him," Sara told him, "it
has been a miracle."

"Yes, madam, that is right. I confess that I have never seen such a
sudden recovery from a patient with this disease."

"We must thank God greatly," Aliza interrupted, "but also you,
doctor. Not only did you treat him, but you poured out your faith to
him."

The doctor turned in surprise at the girl's words, but did not have
time to consider them, as everyone surrounded him to shake his hand
and embrace him. Amidst the praise and thanks, Aliza took her mother
aside and repeated the words that the doctor had spoken to Gabriel
the night before. Sara's jaw dropped, she looked at the doctor still
surrounded by her friends, then looked to the sky and exclaimed:

"Thank you, Hashem!" and then, weeping, she added, "And thank you, my beloved husband. Your son will fulfil your dream, '*next year in Jerusalem*'."

13

As soon as the doctor had left, leaving his instructions, Sara went to the synagogue to share the good news with the Rabbi and his wife, and to pray and thank God. Neighbours and acquaintances, regardless of religion, came and greeted them, sharing in her happiness. The Rothmans were highly respected in Lublin, and many of the city's poor were thankful for their generosity. They were genuinely pleased at the boy's recovery.

Little by little, Gabriel recovered his health. With each passing day his recovery became more certain; he regained his appetite and the colour returned to his cheeks. The girls also came to terms with their overwhelming experience. As for their mother, she had lost a lot of weight and looked quite emaciated, but her peace of mind, smile, and lost weight soon returned to her.

In the middle of their efforts to deal with Gabriel's illness, the bakery had dramatically reduced its production as the girls' main concern was with supporting their family. Of course, none were especially concerned about their work as all their efforted were directed toward Gabriel's health. Once the situation had been overcome, the four resumed their work diligently, motivated by the knowledge that, in the end, everything had turned out well.

At the beginning of May, when the flowers blossomed in all their splendour, filling the gardens and parks of Lublin with pleasant fragrances, Sara left the synagogue where she had gone to prey and thank God for her son's recovery. She decided to walk through the park before heading to the bakery and returning home with Gabriel. Tatiana accompanied her, holding her arm.

"Come on, daughter, let's walk by the lake. It's especially warm for this time of day and the sun is shining in the sky. What do you say?"

"Of course, mother," answered the girl, "and we can try the ice creams sold at the kiosk there."

"Let's go."

They were dressed simply, Sara in a light grey suit that matched the colour of her eyes, and a straw hat with a blue bow, under which her hair was tied up. Tatiana wore a light blue dress and small hat, with her jet-black hair loose, the colour of which contrasted brilliantly with the lightness of her clothes. The girl drew attention from boys as they passed. Her mother smiled, looking at her with pride.

They bought the ice creams and sat on a bench to taste them, pigeons and other birds fluttering in the sky. They were both very happy after the fateful days that they had endured. They stayed seated for about twenty minutes, until Sara thought it time to leave for the bakery, and then home. She did not want to be away from her son's side for too long, although obviously at that moment Aliza was watching over him.

They stood and made for the bakery, arm in arm, talking about how beautiful spring was in Lublin, when they heard a male voice shout from behind them. They turned and saw a man running in their direction. After a moment, they recognised him as Piotr. The pair stopped, intrigued, why was he calling to them so desperately? At last, he reached them.

"Sara, I've spent the last hour looking for you. I've been to your house, the synagogue, and to the bakery!"

"What's wrong, Piotr? Has something happened to Malka?" She asked in a worried voice.

"No, Sara, it's something very important. You must come with me!"

"Gabriel?" she said, her eyes widening with fear.

"No, no, neither Gabriel nor the girls. Everything is fine! It's urgent, you must come!"

He grabbed her arm, almost dragging her behind him. Sara allowed herself to be led away, but still didn't understand.

"Please, Piotr, tell me what this is about."

"Come on, I can't tell you here on the street! Let's go quickly, we're almost there!"

They turned the corner and, still leading Sara by the arm, Piotr entered an old abandoned building that had served as a grain warehouse. Sara was surprised to see Malka in the entrance; she went to greet her, but Piotr tugged on her arm, prompting her to look further within the building.

Sara felt as though she had been struck by lightning, she began to shake.

"Ohhh!" Her cry echoed throughout the building.

His hair was disheveled, and he looked rather thin, but this was the same man she had fallen in love with at first sight. Not knowing how to react, she was paralysed and began to weep uncontrollably.

"It can't be, it can't be, my God! Am I dreaming?"

"Sara..." he murmured, almost imperceptibly.

"Isaak? Is it really you?"

"Yes, my love, I'm here."

At that moment, crying with of joy, she ran to embrace her husband with such force that she almost knocked him over. Through sobs, she repeated his name.

"Isaak, Isaak, my beloved, I can't believe it!"

She was crying profusely and holding him tightly; she could no longer stand up and sank to the ground. Isaak also fell to his knees; they joined in a salty kiss through their tears, then hugged each other once again, as he stoked her hair. Sara held his face in tenderness and disbelief.

"I can't believe it! It's a miracle! Tell me that you are not a dream, my beloved Isaak."

Finally, got up, Sara moaned, cried, and shouted with joy, raising her face to the heavens in thanks to God. She looked at him again and held him tightly. She was ecstatic, a whirlwind of happiness.

"It's been so long ... so long without you!"

"I've missed you every day, my love! God has given us a chance to start again in this second life."

"This is ... this is incredible," Sara exclaimed, "my love is here for me, oh God what happiness! This is a miracle, a miracle!"

Meanwhile, Piotr and Malka had kept a certain distance; she was crying and wiping her tears away with a handkerchief. Piotr could not contain his own tears and laughed with joy. Beside them, Tatiana, who was at first was motionless in surprise, realised what was happening and big tears rolled down her cheeks. She would have liked to join the embrace but held back. Isaak did not know her, but that was not why: it was the couple's moment.

They still held each other; Sara sighed and leaned her head against her husband's shoulder. At last Isaak asked:

"What of Gabriel?"

"He is well, my love," Sara said, still moaning, "for him this will also be a second life. He has missed you greatly and suffered in your absence."

"And the girls, are they alright?"

"Yes, my love, they will also be extraordinarily happy."

At that moment she remembered that Tatiana was with her and called her over.

"Come here."

Isaak watched, bewildered, as Sara motioned for her to come closer. She turned to her husband and explained.

"This is Tatiana, your new daughter."

Isaak looked at her and smiled, asking no questions. When Tatiana reached them, the three embraced. The girl was also immensely moved, she shared in her mother's happiness and understood that this was, indeed, a dream come true; it was a miracle. She was Russian and knew very well that those condemned to the camps of Siberia never returned. Then Piotr and Malka approached. There was no need for words, the five held each other gratefully.

14

Lying on the pallets of the crude wooden beds, they tried to fight off those tiny yet implacable foes that tormented them every night, interrupting their sleep, and the little sleep they could enjoy. That army of fleas, ticks, and lice attacked them mercilessly. From experience, they knew that after the death of some unfortunate person, the number of the creatures increased as they escaped from the corpse and pallet, hurriedly seeking a new starving host.

That day, five of their luckless companions had died, so hundreds of arthropods were settling on the bodies of those who still endured the hardships of confinement, malnutrition, and forced labour. In that way, the blood that flowed through their veins was shared amongst thousands of tiny creatures, shortening the miserable existences of the men.

They did not have the right to be illness, as there were no doctors nor treatments. From dental decay to fracture or muscle injury, they must heal themselves or resign themselves to the consequences. Although there was an infirmary, it lacked the minimum of equipment and medicines needed for the nurse to fulfil his role. He was a prisoner and had been exempted from work in the mines in order to care for those suffering an injury or accident. His knowledge was not of much use; although he had studied the profession in Vilnius, it was difficult for him to exercise his skills due to the lack of supplies. The prisoners all knew that the infirmary was essential the antechamber of the cemetery on the hill.

Every day, at dawn, they were woken by the expletives and then lashes of their jailers. The convicts then went to the canteen of tables and wooden benches to take their watery gruel, before heading directly to work in the mines. On their return they did not have the energy for anything, other dropping onto their pallets and trying to asleep, shivering through the perpetual cold most of the year or enduring disease in the summer. Their will to live was long forgotten, and suicides became a common event.

They were no longer human, rather, machines. The only interruption to their monotonous existence was the arrival of new group of prisoners. Their dull, sunken eyes watched the newcomers without the slightest trace of feeling, knowing that within a few weeks they would be like them, senseless walking corpses without willpower. Daily, they woke, dug into the bowels of the earth, extracted its minerals, returned to camp, ate a potato broth with a crust of stale bread, and then returned to the shed in which they slept.

The winter was unbearable because of the extreme cold. They were wrapped in rags, mostly snatched from the corpses of those who had been unable to endure; as night approached, they tried in vain to share their warmth. Despite the cold and few hours of sunlight, they often preferred to work through the semi-darkness, as movement at least somewhat mitigated the bite of the cold.

As the cruel Camp Commander always told the newcomers, the world had forgotten them, and this place was forsaken by God. Their graves would be there, and no one would ever know of their fate. They resigned themselves to this. At first, they longed to escape, but as the weeks passed, bodies and minds weakened and the prospect of ever leaving their icy prison grew ever more distant. Within a short time, those condemned souls succumbed to the endless cycle of rising, eating, working, and sleeping; repeating the cycle tomorrow, and the day after that, and forever until they died.

Life expectancy in the camp were brief, even the strongest did not survive longer than a few years. Death there was common event. Although the human body desires to live more than one can imagine, it seemed that the men lived more out of habit than out of a true desire to remain in this world. Their souls were first to die; the minds of those poor wretches ended up abandoning all emotion and memory, then finally even their gods.

But there were two prisoners who, despite suffering as harshly as the rest, were exceptions to this rule. They had not lost faith in their beliefs. One answered to the name of Jacob, a Ukrainian Jew who had, impulsively, struck a police officer who had disrespected his wife at a festival in their hometown of Korosten. The other, also a Jew, whose crime had been owning a successful shoe shop, and marrying a beautiful woman who was desired by a heartless man with some power. They had both been in the camp for seven months and, unlike the vast majority, they still retained hope that they might one day escape. In fact, that conviction had been held by Isaak since before completing his first twenty-four hours of captivity.

With an innate intelligence, he determined that to plan an escape would take several months. He understood that the more time that passed, the more his strength and health would deteriorate. In exchange for the weakening of his strength, he would use this time to plan his escape in detail, minimising the risk and increasing his chances of success. In a region so inhospitable and remote from civilisation, there were two fundamental necessities: to provide yourself with enough food, and decide the precise time to undertake the flight, taking into account the unforgiving temperatures in that part of the world.

Isaak began the process with great caution, first ensuring that he did not discuss his plan with anybody. He knew that he could be betrayed to the guards for as little as a crust of bread and would then subject to cruel punishment to discourage other prisoners that also intended to escape. In fact, the guards themselves were more concerned with maintaining the mine's production rather than preventing escape. Their attitude was justified; the barrenness of the region, frigid cold throughout most of the year, rewards for denunciation, and severe punishments for helping a fugitive, left them little cause to be concerned about escape attempts.

In his planning, he considered even the smallest detail, planning every possible step, as though they were pieces of a puzzle that had to fit perfectly together. Firstly, he always behaved strictly in accordance with the camp's rules, so as not to attract any attention or risk punishment that would have diminished his physical abilities. Secondly, he remained silent and distanced himself from the other prisoners, to avoid friction or even fight, which occurred more often than the Camp Commander would have liked. His intention was to go as unnoticed if possible.

He noted in his mind the steps he would have to carry out, weighing factors he would have to take into account. He concluded that there were five of importance: food, clothing, knowledge of the terrain, tools for survival, and natural medicines. Once these parameters were established, he began his second stage, the gathering of knowledge and equipment necessary for his plan.

He developed a great capacity for observation and analysis of all his surroundings, of anything that could further his escape plan. No detail escaped Isaak, whether in conversations overheard between prisoners or the guards and their routines, or in any other activity that could be useful for his purposes. Thus, he became familiar with aspects of the region's geography. On the other hand, the only prisoner he interacted with, other than Jacob, was the Lithuanian nurse, as he was interested in learning the best methods for treating injuries and ailments.

This was of great importance for Isaak for several reasons; first, he gained experience of first aid techniques and how to improvise medical supplies from materials common in the region. Secondly, he was appointed assistant nurse, thus gaining an exemption from the heavy minework, at least on Saturdays and Sundays. This meant a brief respite for his body and allowed him to conserve his strength. Third, a chance event allowed him access to information essential to his aim. One Sunday, when the nurse had to go to the mines to deal with an accident, he was alone in the infirmary when a guard arrived.

"Where is the nurse?" he asked.

"He left for the mines, there was an accident."

"Hey, what a coincidence!" the guard complained, "So today two nurses are absent."

He was referring to the nurse from the emergency room, who was far less knowledgeable than the Lithuanian but was better supplied with equipment and medicine.

"Well, come with me, if there's no one else."

He led Isaak to the field commander's office, a man with the eye patch. He was bare chested with blood flowing from his back from near his right shoulder blade. He had suffered an accident in the camp smithy, resulting in a deep cut.

"Where's the nurse?" he asked in a biting voice.

"He's in the mine, Commander, there was an accident."

"Is today the day of accidents?" he said, loudly, "Ours in Yakuts and that of the workers in the mine, but who is this?"

"He's the Lithuanian's assistant, Commander."

"Ha, what a waste! The workers have become helpers." He stared at Isaak for a moment, then continued, "Well, don't just stand there like an idiot, can't you see I'm bleeding? Do something before this wound gets infected."

Isaak was unsure; with the limited equipment he had brought with him, he did not know how to proceed. The Commander broke him out of his embarrassment, ordering the guard:

"Go with him to the infirmary, take whatever you need."

The man pushed him over to the building. Although his knowledge was limited, he was surprised by the extent of available equipment and at its organisation, bottles, bandages, creams, scissors, plates, and lighters. Isaak took the items he thought necessary, suddenly noticing a map of Russia on the side wall, along with two smaller maps. Realising that the lighter was on that side, he said to the guard:

"I must boil water to treat him."

The man, visibly bored, simply nodded.

He placed a pot with water to boil, as it heated, he carefully studied the maps, taking care that his interest in them was not noticed. He then carried out his treatment to the best of his ability and, although the Commander kicked him out for causing him pain during the procedure, he was satisfied with the information obtained. He knew they were near Yakuts but did not know the precise location of the camp and inhabitants. The map had enabled him to determine the best escape route.

Any item that Isaak considered potentially useful for his plan, he hoarded with great care. On one occasion, the cook threw a knife with a broken handle into the waste. Isaak surreptitiously picked it up it and buried it behind one of the barracks. He did the same with a small metal jug that had been discarded by one of the guards. On rare occasions the prisoners were given fish to be cooked over makeshift campfires. Isaak was the only one who would not consume the viscera, but rather extract the oil and fat, and then bottle it in leftover medicine vials. After sealing them up, he would also bury them beneath the snow.

Only Jacob knew of his plans, having gained his trust as a devout Jew. Although he was worried, Isaak knew that a solitary fugitive had little chance of successfully escaping, even two would be insufficient as he required at least four to fulfil the roles that his risky plan required. This was why he and Jacob set about selected two other prisoners to join in their flight. After two months of weighing the options. The decided on another Pole, who had been a lumberjack. He was a huge and well-built man, who, despite the hardships of camp, had kept his strength almost intact. Although not very intelligent, his physical strength could be of great help. The fourth man ended up being the Lithuanian. Although they were reluctant to leave the prisoners without a nurse, the man simply said:

"What difference does it make, if there are no medicines or supplies anyway?"

His words were true, and he had the added benefit of already having their trust. Isaak instructed the three men so that, with great caution, they gathered various items that could be of use: clothes, medicines, and tools of any kind.

They decided that their escape would take place in the April of the following year, at the beginning of the Spring of 1865, but before the thaw. This was because the guards tended to be more vigilant during the summer, considering it to be the logical time for escape attempts.

"We must flee before the guards expect it," Isaak pointed out, "but we cannot escape if the winter is still harsh, as we would not survive several days out in the open in such low temperatures."

He had already decided that they would take the route to the east, heading for the sea, as the journey south was too long and dotted with Russian towns, increasing the danger of recapture. His plan was to reach the Sea of Okhotsk, then head down the coast to Vladivostok. Being a larger city and a port, it would be easier for them to go unnoticed. This would not be a simple trek, as it meant a journey of almost 2,500 kilometres through inhospitable and wild lands, with temperatures often several degrees below zero, with no map to guide them. When he informed his companions of the route, they were stunned.

"I know it seems crazy, and it is, but the alternative is death here. I don't know about you, but I'd prefer to perish in the attempt rather than abandon hope of gaining freedom and seeing my family again."

The others nodded, faced with such a choice, there was little they had to consider.

Winter had already begun, and they waited patiently for the new year to arrive and the season to progress. The awaited month of April arrived, and, within a few days, they convened for the last time to decide of a definitive date. They would leave in two days' time, at nightfall, which meant four in the afternoon. They carefully collected their equipment and gathered behind the barrack closest to the edge of camp. Isaak, Jacob, and Idris, the nurse, all arrived on time. Only Andrzej, the Polish lumberjack was missing. Just when they thought he had abandoned the plan, he arrived with a partner. Isaak took him aside.

"Who is this man?"

"His name is Henrik; he is Polish like you and I. He wants to join us."

"Why did you tell him about our plans?"

"Because I know him well, he is from my hometown, and has lived for many years in the North of Russia working as a hunter, he'll be useful to us."

"Fine, there's nothing that can be done now," said Isaak, "come on."

They stealthily made their way along a predetermined route that they had already traversed several times, until they could recognise it in the dim light. They walked as fast as the snow would allow, gradually distancing themselves from the camp. Around thirty minutes later they realised someone was following them. Terrified, they hid behind the trees, observing two men, one tall with broad shoulders, the other thinner but also of a high stature. Isaak watched them, realising that they were not guards, but prisoners. When they were close by, the stockier man called out to them.

"Comrades, we want to come with you!"

"Who are you?"

"My name is Igor, I am Russian and my partner, Malkov, is also a subject of the Tsar."

"How did you know about our escape?"

"You don't need to be that smart to notice that you were up to something, Jew."

"Do you know me? How did you know I am a Jew?"

"You are intellectual and meticulous, as Jews usually are."

'*Well*,' Isaak thought, '*at least we have a good reputation within the camp.*'

As hard as he had tried to go unnoticed, so that no one would know of his plans, the others seemed to be more perceptive than he had imagined.

"Alright, there's no going back now, so let's go," he said to the Russians, then moved on.

Walking helped them warm up a bit to withstand the cold. They travelled all night, coming to a rest shortly before dawn. They constructed a rough shelter from branches and small logs to shelter from the snow. Exhausted, they slept hoping to recover their strength. It soon began to snow again, which would aid them by covered their tracks.

Isaak know that conserving their energy was far more important than distancing themselves from the camp. He was convinced that they would be pursued, but also that the guards would not be too persistent. They themselves would not like to spend several nights out in the open, nor wear themselves out chasing starving prisoners. After all, they would be assumed to have died within a week, and their replacements would arrive within that period. Indeed, the Camp Commander was never held to account for the health, well-being or condition of his prisoners; so, for him, it would be as though seven more had died that day, and it was not uncommon for such a number to perish in just one working day. His only concern was meeting the production quotas for the mine, so if it became necessary to force the prisoners to work harder, it would be done. As the escapees' chances were practically zero, the other prisoners would be informed that they had perished, thereby discouraging other potential fugitives.

Isaak, as the undisputed leader of the group, decided that they would
advance at an ordinary pace and only during daylight hours.

"Two things are essential," he stressed to his companions on the run,
"finding food, and taking refuge from the cold."

"What if a beast appears?" asked Jacob.

"That won't be a problem," said Henrik, the hunter, "if that were to
happen, we will form circle around it, shouting. We will act as a larger,
more threatening creature, scaring it away."

The other men accepted Isaak's leadership without question, as he
had proven himself to be the shrewdest and most intelligent, the man
who had planned everything in detail. Under his direction they had
gathered what he called survival tools. They were simple objects which,
in a city, would have been insignificant; out here they could mean the
difference between life and death. These included: the knife that Isaak
had picked and skilfully made a wooden handle for, two hooks that
could be used for fishing, a bone needle and a spool of woollen thread,
various items of clothing and fabrics, the metal jug, and a small iron pot.
The two most important tools were a hatchet that Andrzej had stolen
from one of the guards, thereby bringing punishment upon the entire
camp, and Idris' contribution: flint and pyrite to light a fire.

Progress was slow and the nights were unbearable due to the cold.
Every day at sunset, they built a small palisade of timbers to protect
themselves from the icy wind, although no one could sleep longer than
an hour without needing to move to stave off hypothermia. They all took
regular shifts at guard duty, not out of fear at being discovered, but rather
to ensure that no one stayed still for too long. On the sixth day of their
march, the few provisions that they had brought with them ran out;
hunger and weakness began to take their toll on the fugitives. Three full
days passed without a bite to eat, and their strength was leaving them. At
one point Idris, who was struggling to walk because of a torn ligament,
leaned against a tree and said:

"Go on, my companions, I can't take another step."

Isaak, who was leading the way, turned and said:

"We are a group, and as such we will advance or die together. We
leave no man behind, if you cannot walk, I will carry you."

The others remained silent. Henrik finally stepped forward and said: "If so, we will all carry you, taking turns."

The others said nothing; the gesture was commendable, but they were hardly strong enough to walk, much less carry someone else.

The situation soon became worse. Two more days passed, and their physical and mental resilience deteriorated rapidly. They reached a small river and plunged in their hooks using the only thing they had left as bait: a piece of bone soaked in the fish oil that Isaak had prepared. They stood there for two more hours without being able to catch anything. Despair soon spread amongst them, especially in Idris, who also had a fever and began to rave madly. He endlessly repeated to himself that they had made a mistake and should return to the camp.

"At least there we had a daily crust of bread and a place to sleep in the barracks," he lamented.

The others tried to cheer him up, but the truth was that they didn't have to strength to keep their own spirits up either.

Idris' health and mental strength continued to decline. Isaak was convinced that he would not last long, and indeed it was so. On the fourteenth day after leaving camp, they awoke to find the Lithuanian dead. It was a difficult moment for all of them; using the knife and hatchet they dug into the earth beneath the snow and covered his body as best they could. They forded a stream and continued without saying a word to each other, despair could be seen on all their faces. They sensed that Idris' death was a harbinger of what would happen to them; in such dire circumstances, anyone could be next. Isaak was not exempt from such fears, he had been fond of Idris, as he had been the one to teach him the rudiments of nursing and had always been generous and jovial. From a practical perspective, it was also inconvenient to have lost the nurse as he could have been invaluable later. Isaak thought on the woman and two little girls in Vilnius, waiting for their husband and father to one day return from exile.

When hope had all but disappeared from the group, Henrik proved his value in the group by managing to capture a deer. It was a huge relief for the six men. With great effort, due to the wood's dampness, they managed to light a fire and ate until they were satisfied, and then lay down on some the logs that Andrzej had cut and rested for the rest of the day and night. The next morning, they distributed parts of the meat amongst themselves, without wasting anything, and then continued eastwards, guided by the sun.

Conditions improved and Henrik continued to show his value, catching several other smaller animals; they also began to have some success at fishing. The weather was becoming milder, and the thaw began in May. As summer arrived there would be more daylight hours, making both night and day less cold. However, their weariness at walking through such an inhospitable region took its toll on the men.

One afternoon they came to a river, far wider and larger than any they stream they had come across so far. The waters carried large chunks of ice downstream. This was the Aldán river and, although Isaak did not know it by name, he could remember having seen it on the map in the camp infirmary. He excitedly told his companions:

"I can remember this perfectly on the map that I saw. This river is halfway between Yakuts and the sea. We have already completed the most difficult part, my friends, the second half will be shorter, and this is proof that we have followed the correct route."

The others reacted to Isaak's words with obvious satisfaction, as he clenched his fists with great emotion.

"But now we must work out how to cross, the river is wide and strong."

"We can cross on pieces of ice," said Igor.

"But how will we direct them to the opposite shore? Asked Jacob, "the current will carry us away."

"We will use branches," Andrzej intervened, "we can split them in two so that they have a flat side."

They did as he had suggested, cutting thick branches in half. The problem was that most of the ice passed through the centre of the river, far from the bank. Malkov was forced to jump into the water and swim to a piece of floating ice. With great difficulty he climbed on it and began to paddle it towards the shore, but the current carried him downriver, forcing everyone to chase after it along the bank. At last, the Russian got closer to his companions and Andrzej climbed on, laying on it.

"This piece will not support us all," Malkov said, "come, Andrzej, let's find a bigger one."

They tried to do so, and with difficulty brought a second chunk back to the group. Malkov went for a third, but, when he tried to steer it, the ice broke. The man fell into the water, struggling to swim back to the ice, but the current, being stronger, dragging him away. The others followed along the shore as Malkov tried to swim towards the shore, but it proved useless. His companions urged him on as he struggled to get out of the icy water. But finally submerged beneath the icy water and was not seen again.

Everyone mourned Malkov's loss. Throughout the journey he had presented himself as shy and reserved, but was deeply supportive of the others, he never complains about anything. For a while they sat on some logs without saying a word. None knew anything of Malkov's family, not even Igor. They did not know where he was born, nor why he had been taken prisoner to the camp. All they knew was that, within the month and a half they had shared with him, he had proven himself to be a noble man.

Finally, they succeeded in crossing the river and continued their journey. As Isaak had predicted, their march became easier; the sun shone more frequently, food was easier to obtain thanks to Henrik, who seemed to have a sixth sense for finding game that allowed them to continue. The nights were no longer torture from low temperatures and, although they still had to bundle themselves up tightly and build palisades as shelter, they no longer needed to press their bodies together to preserve body heat.

At the beginning of June, they began their ascent of a low-lying mountain range, which they managed to cross within three days. A week later they finally spotted the sea, which filled them with great happiness. Against all odds, they had managed to cross almost a thousand kilometres of inhospitable terrain, surviving it in relatively good health, with the exception of Andrzej, who, while crossing the mountain range, had slopped down a cliff causing him and open wound from hitting sharp rocks. Isaak had bandaged and cleaned his wound as best he could, but it became inflamed and began to turn purple. The injury forced him to use a branch as a cane, and his difficulty in walking slowed the group down. Everyone took turns at helping him move, but he was very tired through supporting himself with one leg.

Isaak's plan was, after reaching the coast, to skirt south along it. The greatest advantage of having reached the sea was that they no longer had to fear getting lost; they could begin their journey by following the coast from the top of the cliffs, skirting a large bay at the end of which a peninsula could be seen. That night they camped in a sort of cave that opened up in the rock, using dry branches to make a bonfire with which they could warm themselves and cook what little meat they still had.

Andrzej's wound still refused to heal, on the contrary, he began to worsen, and everyone feared that he didn't have long left, especially as he began to have a high fever. That night, the woodcutter was delusional, babbling incoherently in Polish, which only Isaak and Henrik could understand. He muttered about his hometown, saying he wanted to become a priest. The others passed the night taking turns looking after him. By dawn, his health had weakened further. His wound was oozing, and his leg had taken on a deep blueish-purple colour.

"His leg is lost," Isaak said to his other companions.

"What can be done?" Igor asked.

"The only option is to amputate, but we don't have the knowledge or the medical instruments to do it."

"His fever is consuming him."

"Yes, his fever is severe, I think we will soon lose him."

Indeed, it was so. Around noon, with glassy eyes and a voice barely above a whisper, he called to his companions, who gathered around him.

"Henrik, I beg you when you return to our homeland, go to Plock. Once there, ask for the blacksmith, his daughter is my wife-"he fell silent for a moment, struggling for breath, "-please talk to her, her name is Ana, tell her that I love her, and my children,"

Tears rolled down his cheeks and his companions were deeply moved.

"Give me your hand, Henrik," Andrzej said, and once he had taken it, he continued, "promise me you will."

"I swear to God that I will give this message to your wife and children."

"Thank you, my friend. I hope that you all return to your homes."

He began to cry like a child until, little by little, his sobs faded. They buried him in a small flat area about five hundred metres from the edge of the cliff. Henrik cut two branches and tied them together with vines, forming a makeshift cross.

At the end of the bay, they saw a town. They did not know then, but it was Aylan, a fishing village. This was the first time they had seen any vestiges of civilisation since they had left camp, but they preferred to avoid it for fear of being betrayed to the authorities, wasting the superhuman effort they had already made, costing the lives of three companions. The surviving four continued their progress south. Game became increasingly scarce, and their supplies were running out; however, Henrik, with his innate abilities, would always catch something that maintained their strength for the long march. Thanks to the cliffs, they were able to move faster; there were even days when they managed to cover over twenty kilometres.

They kept going avoiding small towns that they came across along the shore, subsisting on hunting and fishing. Thus, guided by the sea and taking advantage of the improving weather, they continued south. They passed June in this way; however, by the end of July the group was unfortunately further reduced. Jacob, the oldest, could not endure the physical effort and poor diet. He began complaining of severe abdominal pain, then became exhausted and lost his appetite. He wasted away until his weakness was such that he could no longer stand. He died one night in Isaak's arms, as he recited verses from the Torah to him.

A few days later, Henrik began to feel ill too. They were deeply worried as his symptoms resembled those suffered by Jacob, that is, intestinal problems. However, although they were forced to slow their pace, they did not stop. Henrik made a supreme effort and did not surrender to the pain. The sun was setting later and later in the day, and they took advantage of it by walking for a few extra hours, making up for their reduced speed.

With the coming of August, the temperatures rise, and they were able to remove some of their rags. One morning they arrived at the mouth of a wide river, in front of which they glimpsed a large settlement, at least in comparison to those they had seen so far. Isaak, Igor, and Henrik continued their way, preparing to enter the town, as they did not want to suffer the same fate as their deceased travelling companions. They also assumed that having travelled a great distance from Yakuts, they could risk making contact with the locals. They walked along the bank of the river to a point where it was possible to ford it to the opposite bank. They approached the town cautiously, nearing a wooden house with smoke rising from a chimney. There was a yard with chickens and a couple of goats.

They spent an hour amongst the trees, watching for any movement. At last, they spotted a man coming from town and heading towards the cabin. Isaak ventured out and called to him, the man froze, as if he had seen a ghost. The peasant raised his arms motioning for Isaak to stop.

"Good morning, sir," Isaak said to him.

"Who are you? Where do you come from?"

"Excuse me, sir, my name is Isaak Rothman. I come from the north, and I need your help, my friend has been ill for several days."

The man was extremely suspicious. Upon hearing unfamiliar voices, his wife peered out of the door, putting her hands to her chest when she saw Isaak's figure.

"Who is this man, Yury?" she asked her husband.

"I don't know, he seems strange, and I have never seen him before in Imperatorskaya."

"Excuse me, gentleman, and gentle lady, it was not my intention to bother you, but I must beg for your help. I am accompanied by two friends who are there in the forest, one of them is very sick."

The peasant and his wife glanced at each other, perhaps Isaak's polite manner convinced them to let him come a little closer.

He noticed the apprehensive way in which they regarded him, realising that his appearance must be strange and perhaps unpleasant, with his beard and hair uncut for several months and dressed in rags. He decided that there was no point in hiding his identity and origin, informing them that he came from the western reaches of the Empire in Europe, and that he had been unfairly taken to a labour camp in Yakuts, from which he had escaped with his companions. At first, they did not believe him.

"No one can escape the Siberian mining camps," said the man, "Yakuts is thousands of kilometres from here, and you say that you came by foot? That can't be true."

"Although it may seem incredible, what I say is true. It has not been easy, but we made it."

The couple turned out to be very kind, offering the fugitives a variety of food that to them seemed exquisite, not only because of the kind of food that they had had at the camp, but also because they had eaten only meat and fish for four months. The only exception had been a few berries which, following Henrik's advice, they only ate if the observes some animal was also eating them.

Later they washed themselves and put on clean clothes that the wife gave them, her husband had got from the town. Poor Igor, due to his large stature and build, was far too big for them. Isaak and Henrik laughed heartily at this, something they had not done in eighteen months. The farmer also lent them scissors and razor with which they could cut their hair and shave. They felt refreshed, and the couple could hardly recognise them. They were emaciated and very thin, but at least they looked like human beings again.

Imperatorskaya was a village that was based on fishing and timber. In the winter, they sent frozen fish to Vladivostok, using large blocks of ice that they took from the river. In the summer they cut fish into fillets and dried it in the sun, before sending it to the great port to the south. They cut timber between April and September. As it was difficult to find enough labour in such a cold, distant, and inhospitable place, the three men quickly found work in the town. The very couple that had welcomed them were currently in the process of drying the summer's fish, and the wife's brother ran the logging business. Henrik stayed to work with the peasants, while Isaak and Igor became sawyers.

The work was strenuous, but after what they had endured in the mines, it seemed a light task, with the bonus that they were now being paid. With their first wages they repaid the peasants for all the help they had been given, and for food and lodging, as the wife cooked for them and accommodated them in the barn. They also appreciated their discretion about their true origin, and the couple kept them safe until a ship docked from Vladivostok. When the boat set sail, they posed as workers who had arrived on it. Imperatorskaya had a floating population in the summer, as it greatly increased by temporary workers, so it was not difficult to justify their story. Although they had no papers, to say that they had been lost than to explain where they came from. As the farmer had noted, no one would believe that they had walked from Yakuts; however, they still preferred to avoid the authorities.

By the first days of October, once the season of dried fish and timber was at an end, they decided it was time to leave Imperatorskaya. They had no wish to spend the winter there, they had stayed only to regain their strength and earn enough money for the journey home. So, they said goodbye to their hosts. The wife cried, having grown accustomed to the three foreigners, as she called them, having a great fondness for them.

"We will never forget everything you have done for us." Isaak told them.

"And we will always remember you, God be with you," said the lady, wiping away her tears with her apron.

The boat took them to Vladivostok. During the journey Isaak, leaning on the rail, looked along the coast and remembered how difficult his walk along the cliffs had been. Once they arrived at the main Russian port on the Pacific, they discovered that the city was exactly that; a port and nothing else. Everything revolved around the commerce from the docks. They were also surprised to find that most of the population was Chinese. Their intention had been to continue the journey as soon as possible, but even Isaak was unsure as to the best route to follow to return to Europe.

The farmer had given them a note with the details of a contact of his; a Chinese merchant who bought the dried fish that he sent to the port. So, as soon as they arrived, Isaak and his companions set out in search of Mr Zhao. It did not take long to locate him as he was one of the better-known merchants in town. Fortunately, the man spoke Russian, so they were able to understand each other without any difficulty. He was kind and cordial to his visitors; Isaak explained their reason for seeking him out, that they sought advice on how best to return to Europe.

"It's not often I'm asked for that kind of thing," he said with a wide smile, "we are on the other side of the world."

"We know, Mr Zhao, but we've been told that there is not better man in Vladivostok for this kind of advice."

Zhao's smile widened even further as he exclaimed:

"It seems that whoever told you that, also taught you flattery."

"That's what we were told, sir."

"And how eager are you to reach Europe? There are two routes, each with different characteristics."

"We would like to reach it as soon as possible, to see our families."

"And which country is your destination?"

"Any, so long as it is in Europe. From wherever we arrive, we can travel towards our homes."

"And where might your homes be, gentlemen?"

Isaak thought that the Chinese man was asking too many questions, but he was the only one who could help, so he answered.

"We are from Russia; we all live in the Empire. Henrik and I are from Poland, and Igor is from Novgorod."

"Well, you have two options. The first is to make the journey by land; various caravans go to Irkutsk and from there you can continue your journey, although the roads are terrible and mostly impassable in winter. I would certainly not recommend this route, and especially with the snows approaching."

The thought of travelling a path infested with Russian authorities did not appeal to Isaak, nor did passing through Irkutsk, a city of unpleasant memories from their trip to Yakuts.

"What would be the other option, Mr. Zhao."

"Through my country, China," he replied with a broad smile, "but don't worry, I'm not referring to the Silk Road. It may be ancient and fascinating, but it is also dangerous, long, and exhausting."

"Then where?" Isaak asked.

"The best option is Hong Kong."

"Hong Kong? But Hong Kong is British."

"I am sorry to contradict you, my dear friend, but Hong Kong has always been and will always be Chinese, the British hold it only temporarily."

The truth was that Isaak could not care less who held Hong Kong, what he understood was that Zhao was right: the city was a British colony, meaning that it would have ships leaving for Britain. It was the perfect route, and their best chance of avoiding the Russian authorities.

"I think that we were wise to consult you, Mr. Zhao, that seems like the best option."

"I am immensely pleased that you have accepted my humble suggestions," he formed another of his smiles, then continued, "however, you know that advice alone is not enough, you must also know how to carry it out."

"I agree, sir. What do you recommend we do?"

He smiled once again.

"I can tell you the steps you must take to reach Hong Kong."

"You are very kind, Mr. Zhao, I would be very interested to know the way."

But the Chinese man, despite his smiles and friendly manner, was a merchant first and advisor second; he showed his well-cared for teeth and said:

"You must understand that advice is free, but reaching Hong Kong will have a cost."

Isaak understood this, of course.

"I would be very grateful if you could inform me of the costs of reaching Hong Kong."

"Well, you must first go to Shanghai, as no ship travels directly from Vladivostok. I could get you a place on a freighter, depending on the type of accommodation you would like."

They couldn't afford any comforts on the ship, so they negotiated for the cheapest ticket. Zhao could only guarantee their arrival in Shanghai; however, with a smile, he promised that, for a small fee, he would give them the details of a contact in the Chinese city who spoke Russian. He would accept silver roubles and assist them in their aim to reach Hong Kong.

'*Surely, he will do so through a hundred smiles*' Isaak thought.

There was also the issue of their lack of documents, without which they would not be able to leave Vladivostok. Perhaps Zhao could assist them with that matter as well?

"There is another matter of utmost importance: we do not have our identification documents."

"If you don't have them, I can make copies for a small fee."

"Thank you, Mr. Zhao, although we do not need copies, rather new documents. Obviously with our real information, not false."

The Chinese man understood, looking at him with a mischievous smile while playing with his hands.

"I understand, they have been lost *permanently*. But there is nothing to worry about, I have contacts who can deal with cases like these; however, you must understand that this will cost something more."

"And what would this 'something' be?"

"Well, you're in luck. I pride myself on my good relations with the Head of the local Town Hall, although my reputation is strengthened by my great friendship with the man who appointed him to his position, Count Nikolai Muriavov, the Governor General of Eastern Siberia."

"I hope that such esteemed friendships do not make the acquisition of documents too expensive."

"Oh no, on the contrary. Thanks to my privileged contacts you will receive a substantial discount."

"That would be of great help to us, Mr. Zhao, as we are short on money."

"You can rest easy; I give you my word that the Head of the City Council will be sympathetic to you."

"It is a relief to hear you say that."

"Although, of course, I cannot speak for any middlemen."

Until then, Isaak had been flooded with relief, but he had no way of knowing how many middlemen he would have to go through, including Zhao himself, of course.

The documents proved to be more expensive than the passage to Shanghai, although one had to admit that Zhao's contacts were efficient. When they called on them, they asked no questions about their origins, intentions, nor presence in the city, and simply requested they fill out a form. To be truthful, it was Isaak who filled out the forms as he was the only one of three that knew how to read and write. He recorded all their information onto the form, the truth of which was not questioned. Isaak signed his card, Igor and Henrik marked theirs; finally, they went to celebrate with some beers. What they had accomplished since leaving the camp had been extraordinary, and they were two days away from completing their adventure: leaving Siberia with 'authentic' documents.

Their journey to Shanghai proved eventful; a terrible storm forced a stop at Busan, a Korean port belonging to China. During the storm they were forcibly restrain Igor, as the gigantic man who was such a beast on land, once on the high seas, fell prey to his fear of sailing. He had previously shown this during their journey from Imperatorskaya to Vladivostok, although on that occasion he had been calm aside from some dizziness, causing no trouble. This time, they had to tie him up after he was gripped by a frenzied terror. Isaak and Henrik laughed at this behaviour, more befitting of a scared child. Their laughter increased when the Captain warned Igor that he would not tolerate another such scene; he must control himself or, in keeping with the law of the sea, he would be thrown overboard.

During their forced stay in Busan, as repairs were being made to the ship, Igor quickly recovered from his maritime fear and seasickness. When they were about to set sail, Isaak and Henrik searched for him all over the port, finding him with minutes left before the ship was going to cast off, practically dragging him out of the room of a Korean girl. She was beautiful, but there was no doubting her profession. Isaak was furious with his companion, strongly rebuking him for his irresponsibility.

"How could you do such a stupid thing?" he said as they resumed their journey to Shanghai, "you could have been left at Busan, or worse, you could have made Henrik and I miss the ship's departure."

"I swear, that was not my intention."

"It's not enough for you to say that! You were irresponsible, nor do you understand how important it is for us to return home. Even more unforgivably, knowing how little money we have, you waste it on women!"

"It's not my fault that I'm irresistible to women!"

"Don't be an idiot, Igor! Your money is what's irresistible! The Siberian cold must have frozen your brain."

"I'm sorry..."

"I don't care if you're sorry! Give me your silver coins, lest the girls in Shanghai find you irresistible as well!"

Sitting beside them, Henrik was amused by his companions' argument. In truth, despite Igor's size, beard, and deep voice, he was more like a child in his attitudes and naivety.

Shanghai seemed exotic to them; it was vastly different from any city they had ever known. Not one of three could really be considered a traveller, in fact, the first time that Isaak and Henrik had left the so-called Zone of Settlement was when they had been when deported to Siberia. They were surprised by some Chinese customs, especially by the men's clothing. Many wore silk robes, with trousers only being reserved for the poorest. Another ubiquitous custom were the men's queues or ponytails, which, to Igor, seemed ridiculous. They were also surprised at the lack of carriages, with passengers being carried by small carts pulled by men instead. However, what surprised them most about the city was the tiny size of the women's feet.

Shanghai was the commercial capital of China, this was noticeable everywhere: the city had a frenetic energy, both at the docks and in the districts, which were dedicated to many different businesses and merchants. Many foreigners, particularly Europeans, could be seen in the streets. Despite this, they felt out of place in this bustling and disorderly city. The language became an issue for them, as despite the instructions that Zhao had given them in Vladivostok, it was very difficult to find his contact who could help them gain passage to Hong Kong. The note they had been given was written in both in Russian and with Chinese characters, however, when they asked people on the street, the reply would in a dialect that incomprehensible to them. Finally, they found a European and, although he did not know Russian, he knew of Zhao's merchant friend, and indicated how to reach his office, which was nearby, close to the docks, a place they had passed by at least three times.

Indeed, they were able to obtain passage to Hong Kong on a sailboat which, luckily, would sail in just three days' time; they would not have to linger for too long in a city which none of the three liked. After paying for their tickets, they had but a few coins left, barely enough to feed them during the voyage. Despite having bought the cheapest tickets, they were forced to sleep on bags of merchandise by the docks. They were not too uncomfortable, especially considering all that they had endured over the last two years.

Finally, they embarked for Hong Kong. Their ship sailed under a British flag, carrying both cargo and passengers. The section designated for the latter had both first- and second-class accommodation, each with its own cabins, lounge, and dining room. The deck, however, was communal, so all travellers could socialise there. Isaak, Igor, and Henrik's tickets could be called third class; they technically did not exist. In order to save their few remaining coins, they had for their arrival, they chose to travel without paying for accommodation, although they had access to the second-class dining room and the deck.

On their fourth day at sea, Isaak and Henrik were conversing, leaning against the railings, when the former noticed a pair speaking in Yiddish. They were two boys, aged about eight and ten. Immediately the image of his own son came to mind, who would now be about their age. He approached the boys, partly out of curiosity, partly out of a desire to hear more of his mother tongue. The children were playing with a spinning top and a pair of ropes; one threw the toy with a little too much force, bouncing it off the deck and into the air. The other pounced on it, unaware that he was leaping toward a gap in the railing, which was only protected by two ropes.

A sailor cried out when he realised that the boy was in danger of tripping and falling overboard. Isaak, who had moved closer to the boys to hear their conversation, was close enough to react. In a split second he rushed towards the boy and managed to grab him as he fell onto the ropes, which were the only barrier between him and the emptiness towards the sea. The chances of the boy bouncing off and falling on the deck were indeed greater, but Isaak's quick actions still caused quite a stir on the ship. Two sailors quickly arrived, responding to a passenger's call for help and the other boy's screams, a distraught woman came with them. She was the mother, who arrived to see the boy lying on the deck alongside Isaak, who was still holding and who him. She dropped to her knees beside him.

"What happened?" the woman asked in English, "are you alright, my son?"

"Yes, mother!" the boy replied, "nothing has happened, this man saved me from falling."

The lady regarded Isaak again, who had not yet stood.

"Thank you very much, Sir."

He did not understand, merely looking at her while getting up. At that moment a man arrived who was clearly the boys' father and who helped his wife and the boy up. The newcomer spoke to the lady, then turned to Isaak to thank him for his actions. Of course, he could still not understand, but remembering that the boys spoke in Yiddish, he assumed that their father would also be able to, so he replied in that language.

"There is no need to thank me, Sir, I did nothing extraordinary."

The man was surprised to hear him speak and replied in the same language.

"You are wrong, you have saved my son, I express my thanks once again. I am also pleased to discover that you are Jewish, we are not common in these parts of the world.

"The pleasure and honour are all mine, Sir. I only did what any other person would have done, it was truly nothing."

"Your modesty is praiseworthy. Yes, anyone could have helped my son, but you were the one to do so. I would appreciate it if you would do me the honour of sharing a drink with me."

"You are very kind, but you have truly no reason to feel indebted to me."

"Please, you are a Jew like me and, if you have children, you will understand that this is not out of obligation."

Isaak thought of Gabriel once again, imagining what he would do for a person that had saved his life. He abandoned his reluctance.

"Very well, Sir, I will gladly accept your invitation."

"Thank you" he said, bowing his head ceremoniously. He then held out his hand to introduce himself, "Israel Moore, at your service."

"Nice to meet you, Isaak Rothman."

"I'm American, are you Prussian?"

"Polish. My grandparents were Austrian."

The event had been a simple matter of luck, but the child's parents exaggerated the real danger of the situation and the importance of Isaak's actions. Nonetheless, they felt great gratitude towards him, which they expressed by inviting him to dinners and for drinks, over which they had lively conversations. Isaak's general knowledge of culture was not especially profound, but the education and manners that his parents had instilled in him, and which were reinforced by Sara, provided him with the means to hold a pleasant conversation.

The American businessman got along very well with him, and their meetings became a daily occurrence. He told Isaak that he worked for the Russian American Company, but also carried out some private business, for which reason he had established residence in Hong Kong. Isaak, however, preferred not to reveal the truth of his situation. After all, there were many Russian merchants in those parts, in fact two were travelling on the ship. He limited himself to mentioning his work with timber, and that he hoped to soon return home and be reunited with his wife and children. Israel told him of the United States, how the nation was formed, about the recent Civil War and conquest of the Western territories. Isaak, in turn, recounted his life in Russian Poland, and how difficult life was for Jews there.

He was also interested in English, considering it a pleasant-sounding language, so Israel offered to teach it to him. Even more so, as he had noticed Isaak's incredible ease with which he assimilated the new language. His progress was remarkable, thanks in part to his dedication, prodigious memory, and capacity for understanding. The American's wife and boys also took part in his teaching, so Isaak received language classes almost constantly. By the time he arrived at Hong Kong, he was able to defend himself quite well in Shakespeare's tongue.

"You've become an intellectual and have forgotten your friends," Henrik teased him.

"Yes!" Igor agreed, "You are now the star student of the Far East!"

"Mock me all you will, my friends, but remember that English is spoken in Hong Kong. There we must find work and earn enough money to return home. Have you thought about that?"

Now they both understood why.

Hong Kong shared some similarities with Shanghai, but it was more developed and civilised. Although most of the population was Chinese, there was little doubt that it was the Europeans, especially the English, who governed the city's destiny. There were districts in which entire streets and buildings were identical to those of many European cities. Furthermore, it was noticeably wealthier and more organised than Shanghai. They found it a more pleasant place, especially because of the mild climate, despite the oncoming winter.

Their main priority was to find work that would allow them to gather the necessary funds for their purposes. Key to this, were the support and contacts of Israel, who was very sympathetic towards Isaa. Thanks to him, Igor and Henrik were able to work together. The first as a watchman and odd-job-man in the mansion of a Russian businessman who lived in Victoria Peak, the most exclusive part of the city. While Henrik worked in a sawmill owned by a timber merchant, also Russian, with whom could communicate as well as with the foreman and manager.

"As your bosses are Russian, be careful not to mention our adventure to anyone," Isaak warned them, "especially you, Igor, as you tend to overly talkative."

Isaak began work directly for Israel, as his most important business in Hong Kong was a tannery. It was fortunate that this was the very trade which Isaak had mastered since he was a boy. As such, he had the opportunity to demonstrate his skills at work that he like and knew best. Israel quickly noticed the Pole's great knowledge of leather processing and promoted him to supervisor, directing overall production in the tannery. He did not come to regret this decision as, in addition to performing his duties perfectly, he began to innovate based on his previous knowledge and experience in Poland, substantially improving the manufacturing and the quality of the final product.

His contribution proved even more beneficial; after a month of working in the tannery, he proposed to Israel that he take advantage of the leftover pieces of leather to make footwear. His initiative and creativity so impressed the businessman, that he accepted Isaak's proposal without hesitation. Before long, they were making footwear with the leather that had previously been discarded. Such was the success of this project that Israel decided to establish a small workshop which, within six weeks, was already supplying the two most important shoe shops in Hong Kong. Meanwhile, he authorised Isaak to use a small space in the back room as a shoe repair workshop, thereby using another of his skills. He worked there in the evenings, after completing his other responsibilities, managing to earn a few extra pounds.

Israel was pleasantly surprised at Isaak's abilities, so he proposed that he partner with him to expand the leather business to Macao and other Chinese cities. He had never met anyone with such a capacity for work and business acumen; however, but Isaak could not accept his proposal. Although tempted, his goal was to return to Poland to be reunited with his family.

"Consider it, together we could build an empire in these parts."

"I'm sorry, Mr. Israel, believe me that under any other circumstances I would accept your proposal."

"What are these circumstances?"

"I'll be honest with you, Mr. Israel, as you have been kind to me, and I owe you, my loyalty."

He then told him the whole truth of how, unjustly, he had been detained for participating in a rebellion in which, not only did he play no part, but he had publicly disagreed with. How he had been deported to Siberia and sentenced to forced labour three years ago, and for that reason his priority was to return to Poland. Israel listened intently, noticing the contrast between a lot of Jews in the United States and their Eastern counterparts. When Isaak finished his story, he could only say:

"I fully understand your situation, I would have the same desire as you to return home, without a doubt, you should leave as soon as you can."

"Thank you for understanding, Mr. Israel, I knew that a man like yourself would know how I feel."

"However, do not forget my proposal; you could return to Hong Kong and settle here with your family. Together we could achieve great things."

"Of course, I will keep it in mind. It would be an honour to return to work for you."

"It would not be for me, but with me."

"You honour me, but I think you overestimate my abilities."

"Of course, I'm not overrating them! You have worked with me for a mere three months, and within that time you have strengthened my business and started a new and quite successful one. Aside from being a visionary, you are a loyal worker and an intelligent man."

"You continue to assign me qualities I do not possess. It is a matter of effort, rather than intelligence."

"I have proof that my words are not empty."

"What do you mean?"

"Have you noticed which language we are speaking in?"

Isaak was surprised, Israel had made him realise that they were communicating in English. Their conversation had flowed naturally.

"Do you see now? Not just anyone could express themself so well in a foreign language after only three months.

"I don't know what to say, Mr. Israel."

"Go, Isaak. Go and find your family. But don't forget that you could have a good future here, for yourself, your wife, and your children. You know where to find me."

"Thank you, I'll keep that in mind."

Isaak continued working hard to save for his trip to Europe. He knew that the best route to England would mean passing through Singapore, Bombay, and Cape Town. It would be a long and expensive journey, but far less gruelling than travelling by land. Anyway, by now he had experience of sailing on the high seas.

Isaak maintained his contacts with Igor and Henrik; they met regularly to talk and share their experiences over a few beers. Of the three, Henrik had the hardest work. Sawing wood was a strenuous and underpaid task at the best of times, made worse as he was competing with Chinese workers paid just a few shillings every day. However, Henrik, consumed by his desire to return to Poland, worked overtime and guarded every penny earned.

Igor's trade was relatively simple and comfortable and less demanding, working in the wealthy Russian's mansion. He lived in the servant's quarters and ate with the other employees, so his living expenses were minimal. Of course, with his reckless disposition, he more than once squandered his savings in the bars in the port, involving himself in fights defending some drunk or prostitute.

Isaak and Henrik constantly berated him for his dissolute life and for spending money rather than saving it for the journey home, but he did not seem to care too much nor share their great desire to return to Europe. Of the three, he was the only bachelor with no wife or children waiting for him. Here, he proved himself an excellent worker at the mansion; his boss was very satisfied with his performance. With his fierce demeanour, he intimidated any marauder who approached the house by his mere presence. He had already become famous amongst the Eastern petty thieves, who preferred to avoid confrontation with him.

At the beginning of January, at one of their regular meetings, his friends noticed a change in him. He appeared more serious and less untidy, they also found out he was no longer visiting the same sordid neighbourhoods of the city. They were surprised at the sudden change in character of their friend, initially thinking that he had re-evaluated his wastefulness, choosing to save his wages; the opposite turned out to be true. It seemed that of the seven men who had escaped from Yakuts, only Isaak and Henrik would fulfil the dream of returning home.

Igor would not join them, but for different reasons than the other four that had been left on the road. The burly Russian had fallen in love. His girlfriend was a Chinese girl who had come work at the mansion. Since laying eyes upon her, he had been taken with the young woman, although she had not paid any attention to his presence, partly because of the language barrier. Although Igor knew some Mandarin, it was not enough to win her heart. However, love proved itself irrational, and an unlikely romance began between the girl and the Russian. In addition to the cultural and religious difference was their obvious contrast in stature. But their feelings overcame these obstacles; when Igor introduced her to his companions the girl spoke a little Russian, and he a little more Chinese.

Thus, the trio of fugitives became a duo. Isaak and Henrik attended the ceremony held to unite the couple. Truthfully, they never knew whether it was a wedding or if it held some other significance, but that seemed unimportant as the pair were clearly very happy. Igor wore his usual smile, with a vaguely rough appearance, whereas the girl appeared shy and demure. She had beautiful features and a sweet character, and they could understand. why Igor had fallen madly in love with her.

January came to an end and Henrik and Isaak purchased their tickets to London on a ship carrying tea. They had been advised to postpone their return until June, when the weather was more favourable, as the monsoons made sailing dangerous at certain times of the year. Although waiting until summer or autumn would have been safer, they did not want to wait any longer, taking advantage of the fact that this Captain would be leaving soon.

The farewell between Isaak and Israel was more emotional than either could have imagined. The American held a true esteem for his employee, admiring his professional skill and personal qualities. On his side, Isaak was deeply grateful for the friendship and support that the businessman had given him.

Igor was filled with nostalgia; he would always keep his friends with him in his heart. After all, they had faced much adversity together, risking their lives on many occasions.

"I will never forget you, my friends!"

"We will keep in touch, Igor," Isaak told him, "I will write to you."

"I don't know how to write, but I'll find some way to answer," the giant said, laughing.

"Ask your wife to teach you," interrupted Henrik, "she seems to be very intelligent; I see that she's already learning Russian."

"Thankfully," Igor smiled, "if not, how would we raise a child when we have one? Mandarin is very difficult."

Everyone laughed and embraced each other. When the two travellers boarded their ship, Igor couldn't stop his eyes from watering.

They found the journey tedious at times, endless days were spent gazing at the sky, whereas others were hectic and dangerous, with storms and rain showers, thanks to the monsoons that are so characteristic of the Indian Ocean. Their stopover at Singapore was brief as the Captain seemed to have an obsessive desire to proceed as quickly as possible in order to reach England with his valuable cargo of tea. The timing of their trip was unusual, and they were faced with a decision between avoiding the adverse winds that could blow them greatly off course, or, on the contrary, taking advantage of those same monsoons for the sailing ship to reach high speeds. Fortunately, and to everyone's relief, the latter occurred. Although they had to repair several torn sails, on certain days the ship reached up to twenty-one knots.

The voyage turned out to be long and monotonous. Isaak took the opportunity to improve his English further, thanks to a new friendship with a young lieutenant of the Royal Marines, who had served for three years in the Far East and was returning to England for a promotion and new position in the capital. He was an officer with a keen interest in general science and was a passionate reader who possessed and unusual awareness for a man of just twenty-four. He had a great fondness for learning new things, as well as passing on his knowledge to others; so, it was understandable that he would try to learn Russian and converse with Isaak. They decided to teach each other their respective languages and practice daily.

The young officer answered to the name of Andrew Cronin, the son of a respected and wealthy lawyer who moved in the highest circles of English nobility. The lawyer had wanted his eldest son to follow in his footsteps, but the boy had other interests. Influenced by his maternal grandfather, a retired Naval Officer who had served under Nelson, he eagerly entered Her Majesty's service. He chose the Royal Marines and, once graduating the Naval College, asked to serve in the Far East. Most of his colleagues attempted to avoid such remote placements, but

Andrew was aware that service far from home in inhospitable and dangerous conditions was a good way to launch one's career.

"And it is better, my dear friend," he explained to Isaak, "to embark on such missions when you are still young."

"An intelligent observation, especially if it works out."

"I agree, my intention, if you want to know, is one day to become a General."

"Well, you are ambitious and determined, my friend. Although I suppose it may take years, I'm sure that you meet the criteria."

"I'll work on it."

"I hope that by the time you become General, you will have learned Russian."

"By the time I become General? I hope to God not! When I am promoted to Captain, I must already speak it fluently. As I expect my promotion to take place shortly after I arrive in England, I cannot waste time! Come on, let's continue with the lessons."

The men laughed for a few seconds, before continuing with their mutual language lessons.

Thanks to these chats and impromptu classes, not only did the trip become more bearable, but they also improved their knowledge of each other's languages; Isaak also learned of many subjects with which he was not familiar, and that the lieutenant had already mastered. They spent hours in study and conversation, although, to tell the truth, the latter largely consisted of a monologue from the officer, interrupted occasionally by Isaak's questions. However, aside from a mere exchange of knowledge, a true and sincere friendship developed between the two men. Henrik, on the other hand, hardly ever participated in these conversations, given his poor command of English. He also preferred to sleep for the majority of the time to combat his seasickness, which, despite his many days at sea, still plagued him from time to time.

Although he had not told him, Andrew immediately noticed that his new companion was Jewish. He broached the subject once, and Isaak was surprised at the extensive knowledge the Officer demonstrated about the history and customs of his people. One day he asked the man how he could know so much about Judaism, from its festivals, customs, and diet.

"I must confess, my friend, that my origins are Jewish."

Isaak was surprised, not so much because he had found an English officer of Jewish origin, but because he knew that Andrew was an Anglican.

"The story is as follows," the Lieutenant continued, "my maternal grandmother was Jewish, from an Austrian family."

"What a coincidence," Isaak interrupted, "my ancestors are also Austrian."

"For the sake of convenience, they converted to Protestantism and settled, first in Prussia and then in England. However, my grandmother never really abandoned her Jewish faith or customs and educated my mother as such. To the wider world, she is an Anglican, but I know that in her soul she still feels Jewish.

By the end of March, they arrived in Cape Town, but the Dutch authorities would not allow personnel to disembark as the port was under quarantine, due to an outbreak of cholera. They remained anchored while the crew stocked up on fresh water and fresh food. For the travellers it was a great disappointment as they had hoped to get to know a new city and walk on dry land. They longed for a respite from the sea, and the saltiness with which they had lived for over a month and a half.

"We must resign ourselves to staying on the ship," Isaak said to Henrik, "we only must resign ourselves to idleness, which is nothing in comparison to the hardships we endured on our journey from Yakuts to Imperatorskaya.

"Agreed, besides we are about to start the last leg of our trip, we are getting closer to Poland."

Isaak remembered his home and his family, first Sara, the love of his life, his beloved son, and the two girls that God had sent him. In his mind he revisited those times, dwelling on certain memories of each of them. When he thought of Gabriel, he felt a shudder. At that precise moment, then thousand kilometres away, the boy was entering the worst stage of his illness, and, in his fever and delirium, he felt the presence of his father.

They set sail, the ship heading north, skirting the African coast. The winds were favourable, so they advanced at a good speed, but after fourteen days at sea they were hit by a terrible tropical storm which destroyed part of the masts, forcing them hove to while repairs were carried out. Henrik was very frightened by the storm, which was surprising to Isaak as, despite his seasickness, he was by now a veteran of several voyages, and this was not the first storm they had faced.

"I'm anxious that something will happen to us now that we are so close to reaching our goal," was Henrik's answer.

After this setback, their voyage continued without any further incidents, until one morning. Henrik shook Isaak awake, who was startled and jumped to his feet, although he did not notice anything to cause worry. There was no showers, and the ship was advancing calm and steadily.

"What's happening, Henrik?" he asked, intrigued.

"Come with me, I want you to see something."

Isaak followed his friend to the starboard side. Henrik stretched out his arm, pointing with his finger. Isaak tried to peer through the early morning mists but could not make out what his friend was trying to show him. He rubbed his eyes and looked again but still could see nothing.

"I can't tell what you're trying to show me."

"Look carefully, into the distance."

Isaak tried again, fixing his gaze on the horizon until he could perceive a contour of hills set against the clouds. He continued staring and he finally made out a coastline.

"I see it, the coast."

"Yes," said Henrik, "but it's not just any coast, as sailor told me that it is called Cabo da Roca. It is Portugal."

Isaak was caught off guard, he looked back into the distance, then turned to his friend. He could not hold in his tears as he repeated, excitedly:

"Europe, Henrik! It's Europe! We've done it!"

The two friends hugged each other, after so many hardships, having endured the hellish camp, having travelled thousands of kilometres, and losing four companions, finally, they were close to home.

A few days later, sailing through the Bay of Biscay, they were surprised in by and even greater storm than the ones in the Indian Ocean or off the African coast. It was off such magnitude and duration that the two friends were really scared. However, the crew demonstrated their expertise in controlling the boat and weathering the storm. When they finally managed to regain control of the situation, and once the storm had subsided, they realised that the damage was considerable and that they had been close to being shipwrecked.

The Captain was distraught at the loss of part of their valuable cargo of tea, in addition to the serious damage to the hull, rudder, and rigging. Their arrival in Southampton would be delayed by several days as they made port to carry out the necessary repairs.

The only passengers thankful for this were Isaak and Henrik, as the Captain headed for the port of La Rochelle, in France, thereby shortening a little what had been a dramatic voyage for the two friends. Therefore, as soon as the ship entered the bay and was permitted to anchor by the port inspector, they bade farewell to their companions and boarded the boat which was taking the first mate ashore to coordinate the supplied necessary to start the repair of the ship.

Before disembarking Isaak said goodbye to Lieutenant Cronin.

"It has been an honour to share these days with you, Lieutenant."

"A mutual honour, my dear friend, I hope that we will see each other again someday."

"As do I, I wish you the best of luck in your endeavours. One day I shall have the pleasure of seeing you in your General's uniform."

"You shall, Isaak! Unless the Lord calls for me beforehand."

They exchanged their addresses for correspondence. Isaak, for reasons of security given his legal status, wrote down his sister in Warsaw. They parted with a hug.

Despite their worst fears, the port authorities stamped their documents and allowed them entry into France without any problems, after which they immediately arranged transport to Paris. Four days later, they entered the city of light. They were dazzled by the beauty, majesty, and turmoil of the metropolis; however, their tour of the French capital was hardly a priority, as they longed to return home and they only had a few coins between them.

Finally, they arrived in Poland, having completed the last part of their journey on foot. This was partly because their money ran out, but also because neither wanted any kind of interaction with border police or any kind of Russian authorities; they were, after all, fugitives from a forced labour camp. They entered Warsaw one night in late April and headed for Isaak's sister's house. Ruth was overjoyed because she, like Sara, had assumed that she would never see her brother again. She and Isaak were the sole survivors of their family of seven, their father, mother, and three brothers had been murdered during the anti-Jewish riots of '56 in Warsaw.

They spent the night there, and all went to the synagogue the next day to thank God for their return to their homeland. Isaak's brother-in-law lent them a few silver roubles so that they could afford transport for Henrik to head to Kielce, and Isaak to Bialystok. In Ruth's home, the two friends said farewell. They had spent three years of hardship together, but there had also been good times, especially in Hong Kong. They were aware that they had achieved a tremendous feat and that several of their companions had not. The truth was they had strengthened a friendship that would last a lifetime.

"Take care, my friend!" he said to Henrik while embracing him.

"Thank you for all your support, I will never forget everything we have been through together."

"Be careful not be caught by the Russian authorities."

"I know, my friend, I plan to emigrate to another part of the country or the Empire."

"Well, we will keep in touch. If, for any reason, we lose contact, we can use Ruth as a means to find each other again. Give your family my regards."

"Thank you, the same goes for yours. By the way, we must not stop writing to Igor."

"Of course, I won't forget."

They hugged each other once again, and each set off on his own journey.

The next day Isaak arrived in Bialystok, entering the city under the cover of night to avoid attracting too much attention. He headed for place where his house had once stood, only to find a deserted patch of land. He noticed that his neighbour Maretska's house was also in ruins. He was filled with anguish, and rushed to Piotr's home, his best friend in Bialystok. He arrived desperate, drenched in sweat. He rang the bell and after a few seconds a female voice answered from inside.

"Who is it?"

Isaak recognised the voice immediately.

"Malka."

When she heard her name spoken, she opened the door, and, once she realised who it was, she backed away in disbelief.

"Isaak, it can't be!"

She hugged him emotionally, then ushered him inside. He immediately asked her:

"What do you know of Sara?"

"She's fine, don't worry."

He sighed in relief, placing his hand over his heart.

"And Gabriel?"

"He is also perfectly well."

Isaak smiled with joy.

"Jana and Aliza?"

"All of them are well."

He felt reborn. Isaak put his palms together and prayed:

'Thank you, Hashem, I owe you everything.'

He took another deep breath and this time it was he who embraced Malka with emotion.

"But tell me, where are they?"

"They are living in Lublin."

"In Lublin? What are they doing there?"

"It's a long story, but the important thing is that you are well, my dear Isaak. I think that Sara will faint from happiness once she sees you, as will Gabriel and the girls."

Isaak then asked:

"And what about Piotr?"

"He has not arrived home yet, but he will be in for a big surprise when he does," she then added, "please, sit down, I will make you a cup of tea."

She made for the kitchen, but at that moment they heard the sound of a key being inserted in the lock. She ran to the entrance and announced to her husband:

"You won't believe who's here!"

Piotr was intrigued, then entered the room to see Isaak. He was visibly startled, then ran to his friend and hugged him.

"My dear friend, it can't be! How could you come back?"

"Making a superhuman sacrifice, Piotr, but I am here now!"

They decided that they would leave for Lublin on the next day before dawn. In part, for safety because they did not want anyone to recognise Isaak, but also because he was overcome with anticipation and could not wait to see his family again. Malka wanted to accompany them, but Piotr reminded her that she should stay, as the girl had lessoned the next day. However, his wife looked at him, saying:

"Well, I'll take her to my sister's, she can take care of her, or she can miss school tomorrow. I would not miss this reunion for all the world, even if it I have to divorce you to see it!"

Piotr and Isaak smiled.

"What a joy it is to have you here, my dear friend!" Piotr stressed, "your family has missed you greatly, this will be the best surprise of their lives!"

15

Eitan really liked walking through the parks near the Plaza de la Shoá, admiring the ponds and gardens, and then ending his tour at the Jewish Holocaust Memorial. Despite his age and his leg injury, he tended to complete this walk in just over two hours. As usual during his grandson's vacation, he accompanied him on the walk.

"I'm so glad that Isaak's adventure ended well, grandpa!"

"It was much more than an adventure, my son. Successfully escaping the Siberian forced labour camps was almost impossible."

"The important thing is that, after so much suffering, everything ended well."

"That's it, David. Well, as I promised you, today on this pleasant walk I will tell you the reason that our people have been persecuted so much throughout history."

"I'm very interested to know why."

"Very well. You know that, beyond being the chosen people, we Jews have kept our beliefs and convictions firmly throughout the ages. This makes us different, not necessarily better, or worse, than others. Many civilisations have fallen, others have merged foreign powers, adapting their customs and culture, effectively meaning their end and disappearance. We Jews have never done so, we have never allowed others to impose their practices on us, nor suppress our traditions. Do you follow me?"

"Of course."

"From time immemorial, the Jews have stood out as a highly intellectually advanced people, fully aware of their role on earth. They have strong religious convictions, to the extent that we have never been afraid to sacrifice their lives for the sake of their beliefs. We have never recognised other deities, that is other gods. Therein lay our spiritual strength, which no other people throughout history have been able to surpass. And do you know where proof of that lies, my dear David?

"Where grandpa?"

"All the great empires, both those that persecuted us and those that did not, have disappeared, but we Jews are still here. In other words, we have been successful, however, success creates a big problem. Do you know what that is?"

"I don't know."

"It leads to envy. Before the modern era, the intellectual capacity of our ancestors, as well as our strong convictions and the monolithic nature of our religion, caused other peoples to look upon us with suspicion, and want to destroy us. More recently, the capacity for work and production of the Jewish people has attracted the envy of those who want our property."

"I understand what you mean."

"Son, those who have little have always coveted what others have, but they do not realise that such prosperity is the result of immense effort. We Jews work tirelessly to for our well-being, but those who persecute and envy us never consider what we have sacrificed to obtain it. Do you understand?"

"Perfectly?"

"Why do they do this? Because their only desire is to take it from us."

"Of course, grandfather, because they have not worked hard."

"Exactly, David, they do not imitate our good work ethic, they have no desire to make sacrifices. It is easier for them to criticise and take away the fruits of others' labour, than to work hard themselves. You see, they envy us because we obtain wealth and, in turn, they envy our ability to achieve it and to overcome all adversities. Do you still understand me?"

"Of course."

"So, the next time you are mocked for the Jews' success in business, when they tell you contemptuously that we are bankers and owners of multinational companies, ask them if those Jewish bankers or businessmen were given their property, or whether it is the result of their hard work."

"Yes, I will."

"That's not all, David. When they reproach you that Jews only think of making money, you must answer them with another question: '*If you are not interested in money, if you won't sacrifice anything to earn it, why do you care if Jews want to get it?'"*

"Perfect, grandpa! What a good way to shut them up!"

At that moment they arrived right in front of the monument. The fresh sea breeze caressed their faces on that beautiful summer afternoon in Buenos Aires. Cars sped by on the avenue as Eitan gazed at the Holocaust memorial.

"Now, let's return to our family story."

"Yes, grandpa, I really want to know what happens next."

"It was a time of indescribable happiness for everyone. Sara had recovered her husband, Gabriel his father, and the orphan girls the man who had become theirs. Very well, let's continue."

16

Sara was no longer crying, she now laughed with joy and disbelief, she could not stop caressing her husband's face. She then wrapped her arms around him, kissing him with all the love she had kept for the last three years.

"I never stopped thinking about you, not once on any of the days we were apart."

"I've also always had you in my mind and heart," he replied.

She could not leave him for a moment, so, without releasing him, she said:

"Let's go home, Gabriel will jump with excitement. He's still a little weak, but I'm sure that this will make him forget his exhaustion."

"What's happened?"

"Oh, my love! He suffered badly from tuberculosis, but he's already making a full recovery. Don't worry, his joy at seeing you will help him."

Isaak was a little reluctant to leave the cellar in broad daylight, but Sara reassured him:

"Don't worry, my love, things have changed. Besides, we are no longer in Bialystok."

They went home very happy, Sara on Isaak's arm and Tatiana on hers. All the while, Sara told her husband how that young woman had joined their family, and how similar her story was to that of herself, Jana and Aliza.

"What a joy," he said, smiling as he looked to Tatiana, "now I have one more daughter. Come, take my arm."

The girl smiled tenderly, while she thought that in just a few minutes she sees the truth in what Sara had always told her: Isaak was a kind and very special human being.

Their arrival at the house was somewhat impressive, Sara rang the doorbell while she called to Aliza, who was looking after Gabriel. When the girl opened the door, she was frozen for a moment in shock, then she screamed and threw herself into Isaak's arms.

"How is this possible, father? I can't believe you're here."

"Yes, my girl," he answered, holding her tightly to his chest, that beautiful word still sounding in his ear. Although, before his deportation, he already considered himself their father, Aliza had never addressed him as such. Perhaps her nostalgia throughout their separation had led her to remember him in that way.

Aliza began to weep with joy, saying through sobs:

"Dad, I love you so much! What a joy it is to have you here again!"

Those phrases moved him so greatly that he could only say:

"My daughter, I missed you more than I can say."

Gabriel, who lay on his bed, stood when he heard noises from the entrance. He went to the door, seeing his sister embracing a man. Aliza blocked his view, so he could not see that it was his father, but at that moment Sara turned to boy and called out to him.

"Gabriel!"

Isaak turned instantly and saw him. He slipped out of Aliza's grip, running towards Gabriel at the precise moment the boy recognised him.

"Father, father! It's you!"

"My son, son of my soul!" he exclaimed with all the strength his heart could muster.

Isaak could not contain his tears, he stood up with Gabriel in his arms, repeatedly kissing the boy on his cheek. The boy screamed with joy.

"I love you daddy, I love you, I'm so happy to see you again!" Meanwhile he could not stop kissing his father.

For a moment he remembered that cold winter's day, when Isaak entered the barn, and he thought it would be the last time he would see his father. He innocently said:

"Now I can tell my classmates that I also have a father, a real father!"

"Oh, my son!" he murmured sweetly, "How happy I am to hold you in my arms. Of course, you have a father, one who loves you with all his heart."

He looked to Sara and Aliza, gesturing for them to come closer. He then remembered Tatiana and called to her too:

"Come, daughter."

They all embraced, overwhelmed with joy. Not least Tatiana, who, despite being the only who had not shared her life with Isaak, she was overwhelmed with the happiness of her mother and siblings, as well as those simple words: '*Come, daughter*'. She knew that she had just gained a father, the one that she had never had.

Sara ushered everyone into the house, not wanting Isaak to attract too much attention. She asked Piotr to find Jana at the bakery and bring her home as soon as possible.

"Please do not tell her, let it be a surprise for my girl. But reassure her so that she does not worry but tell her to come quickly as we have very good news for her.

When Jana arrived the same scenes of happiness were repeated, everyone laughed with joy when the girl crossed the threshold, as Sara had been waiting outside with a wide smile to tell her:

"You will find something at home that will make you very happy."

"What is it, mother, I'm curious."

"Come inside and you'll see."

She exclaimed in amazement, and both father and daughter cried tears of joy while running to hug each other.

"My sweet, little girl!" Isaak said to her, "How I've missed you, how I've missed you all."

"Father, father, we thought we'd lost you!"

Isaak knew that, as with Aliza, he truly was Jana's father. He hugged her tightly with a feeling of genuine happiness.

On the walk home with Jana, Piotr had bought two bottles of wine to celebrate the reunion. After so much suffering and separation, a feeling of indescribable feeling of joy overcame them, their chests could not contain their happiness.

Isaak's return became quite and event in Lublin. This unnerved him; he preferred to go unnoticed as he feared the Russian authorities, on hearing his story, would recapture him. He could easily be sentenced to death, the most common punishment for those who escaped labour camp. However, Sara reassured him. She was more confident since defeating Marinowsky in court, and she also had Carl to rely upon.

The first-person Sara wanted to tell of Isaak's return was Irenka, not only to share her happiness, but also as an act of loyalty to her friend. As Aliza prepared a bath for her father, Sara hurried to her friend's house.

This time it was the usually reserved Sara who rushed in like a whirlwind. She descended from the carriage, sprinting up the steps to ring the bell. The butler opened the door and Sara barely acknowledged him, running into the house.

"Good morning, Karius, where's Irenka?"

"In her chambers, Madam. Allow me to invite you into the lounge, and I will announce your presence to her."

But Sara was in no mood for protocols, she almost pushed the butler out of the way, as she rushed across the threshold desperately calling her friend.

"Irenka, Irenka!" she said, raising her voice.

Her friend hurried out of her room, stopping by the banister.

"What's going on, Sara? What happened."

"I have great news for you, you won't believe it!"

"Tell me, what is it?" she asked as she went down the stairs.

Sara waited until her friend had reached her, then cried out:

"Isaak! Isaak has returned!"

Irenka stood motionless, as though trying to comprehend her friend's words. She finally reacted.

"Isaak? Your husband? Who was sent to Siberia?"

"Yes, Irenka, he has returned!"

"It can't be! Is he in Lublin?"

"Yes, he's back!"

"That's incredible!" she said, immediately hugging her friend.

Irenka then laughed with joy.

"But that is extraordinary news. You must be so happy!"

"I've never been so happy in my life! I've got him back!"

"I share in your happiness. We must celebrate. We'll have a party!"

"Oh, Irenka, you never change."

They held each other once more, laughing with happiness. Then Sara returned home to a festive atmosphere; the women had gone shopping and were cooking various dishes that spread a delicious aroma now filled the room. They dined gratefully, thanking God, before sitting down to talk. There was so much to say about their three years apart; there had been so many adventures and experiences, some positive, others less so. But the most important thing was that everything had ended well.

At one point, Sara stood and retrieved the Isaak's Tallit and Tefillin from the shelf on the wall. He gazed upon them, smiling excitedly. He took them in his hands, kissed his wife, then left the room to pray. When he returned, Sara explained:

"We nearly lost them twice, first when our house was burned down in Bialystok. Maretska's son, our neighbour, managed to salvage them. The second time was when my room was looted here in Lublin, which is an event that I must tell you about. That time, Tatiana rescued them.

Isaak, of course, was unaware of these events, but he turned to Tatiana and said:

"Thank you, daughter, you don't know how much these mean to me."

He reached out and took Tatiana's hand, who couldn't hide her emotion.

That night Isaak and Sara barely slept, happiness had replaced sleep and exhaustion. They held each other for a long time, discussing their experiences throughout his absence. Both thanked God in their thoughts. Sara, despite had managed to remain strong, overcoming her adversities, looking after her four children. Isaak had managed to complete an almost impossible feat in his escape from the Siberian labour camp, returning home alive and in good health. They really had a lot to thank God for.

Little by little, Isaak adjusted to life in Lublin. The most significant event was that Carl managed to resolve his legal situation, allowing him to return to a peaceful life again, without the fear of capture by the Russian authorities as a fugitive from the Empire's labour camps. Carl's endeavour depended upon, once again, the good offices of General Sokolov, but it also required that Isaak renounce his claim to the shoe shop that Marinowsky had appropriated. This was under the condition that that wretch imposed for the charges be retracted, and to declare that Isaak was innocent of any participation in the Bialystok riots of 1863.

This was difficult for Sara to accept as she had intended to force the wretch to restore all that rightfully belonged to them; however, in exchange for Isaak's safety, she considered it a low cost. After all, Isaak could always start a new shoemaker's workshop, but if he were arrested, she would never see him again.

Of course, the Rothmans did not want to return to Bialystok; not only did it bring back bitter memories, but Sara had established herself and had a loyal clientele in Lublin. She was highly regarded in the city, as were her daughters. Isaak was also more comfortable there. Logically, he decided to venture into the trade he knew and had mastered: footwear.

Their interest in remaining in the city was not limited to business, all members of the family had their own powerful reasons to stay. For Sara, this was her great friend Irenka, as well as her closeness with Tobías and Sara, and the Czemerinskys who periodically visited. Tatiana because of Robiak, with whom she was deeply in love. Jana because she felt fulfilled managing the bakery branch, especially as her mother had announced that it would be hers within a few years. Moreover, she was seeing a law student who had his heart set on becoming a Rabbi.

Aliza, through her work at the bakery, had found a circle of friends that she greatly valued. Also, of course, there was the second lieutenant in the Austrian army who frequently visited her family, often stopping by the bakery. This was to the girl's happiness and torment, as every time she saw him, she felt faint. Gabriel because he already had a group of friends with whom he shared many happy hours playing, and even more so now that his father was at home. Isaak saw his family's happiness in the city and had also developed close a friendship with Carl and Tobias.

Of course, he did not remain inactive, and began the process of resuming his craft. He found a small place in which to in which to set up his shoe repair shop, then travelled to Warsaw to purchase the necessary materials and tools. He split his time between developing his business and supporting Sara in her latest project: a cafeteria and chocolate shop. Coffee was a popular drink in Poland, but chocolate was little known, and its consumption had not yet become popular. It was a risky idea, but worth a try, if the chocolate did not sell, there would always be coffee.

Additionally, they now found the small house that Sara had rented to be too crowded. She had some savings intended to buy her dream home, near Irenka's mansion. She was still far from the required sum, only having half the total price. Without a bank account, she was unable to access any type of credit, so Sara offered him the money to set up his shoe shop, but he refused. They had to find some way to buy the house, whether through a loan or otherwise.

"I think we should buy it," he said one night," I liked it too; it is comfortable, attractive, and in a good location. Also, I won't accept the savings you have worked so hard to build up, dreaming of buying a better home."

"My love, that money belongs to both of us."

"Maybe, but I will establish my workshop without forfeiting your dream, we'll find some other way."

In the end, they managed to convince the sellers to allow them to buy the house on credit, paying nine thousand roubles on signing the contract, and the rest in twenty-four instalments. This allowed them two years to cover the debt. They still needed six thousand roubles to pay for the first instalment, but Carl and Irenka came to their aid once again, lending them the money to complete their purchase.

They were so happy when they arrived at their new home; it was really beautiful. It had a separate hall, study, living room, dining room, and large kitchen. There was even a small terrace adjoined with a patio, next to a back garden in which grew apple and pear trees. Upstairs there were three rooms, and an attic with a smaller bedroom. For the first time, Jana would have her own room, and Gabriel would be able to enjoy his own private space in the attic. The house was not luxurious, but it was spacious, and it marked the first time that the Rothmans would not live in a wooden home.

Tatiana and Robiak wanted to marry, but the boy was yet to receive the Rabbi's permission to complete his conversion to Judaism. But if the Rabbi was hard to persuade, Isaak was firmer still.

"If you do not convince me that you are a Jew at heart, I will not give you permission to marry my daughter," Isaak warned him.

Upon hearing this, Robiak was confused. After all, Isaak was not Tatiana's true father, but as he had adopted her and she considered him as such, she would never have dared to contradict him. The truth was that Isaak had taken a liking to the boy and considered him a good match for his daughter; he was judicious, hard-working, and had noble intentions, yet he still put pressure on his conversion to Judaism. His hope was that, in the future home of his daughter and son-in-law they would pass on the traditions of the chosen people to a new generation.

Isaak had grown fond of Tatiana, for her sweetness and great qualities, and also for the sincere love that she showed towards her new siblings. The three Rothman girls were all beautiful, but it was undoubtedly Tatiana who attracted the most attention when walking in the street. This was to Robiak's despair, as he was overwhelmed with jealously whenever someone expressed a compliment or gave her an admiring look. Isaak and Sara were greatly amused by the situation.

For the winter holidays, the Czemerinskys visited them from Pinsk, so that the two families might celebrate Hanukkah together. It was at that time that Isaak met them and developed a very good relationship with Jared and Anya. Oizer also seemed to him to be an intelligent and kind-hearted boy, and he was pleased to see how well he got on with his daughters. When greeting them, he thanked them for everything they had done for his family.

"I is something that I will never know how to repay you."

"We are Jews like you," replied Jared, "we have never abandoned any of our people, and I am sure that you would have done the same for us."

"I know that perfectly well," said Isaak, "but that won't stop me from thanking you for the rest of my life."

Isaak did not yet know it, but he owed them another favour. It was Jared who, at Sara's request, had lent them the money with which he finally able to set up his shoe repair shop Lublin. She knew that Isaak would never have accepted it, so she hid the truth by telling him that it was a sum that was owed to her, of which she had never spoken as she was unsure as to whether it would be returned.

That was the first winter they spent together as a family, one which had grown thanks to Tatiana's presence. Isaak recalled the terrible winters he had spent in the camp and felt immensely happy his turn in his fortune; this one would be spent in the warmth of his home, in the company of his loved ones. Sitting by the fireside drinking a vodka with Jared, he watched his wife and children chatting with the Czemerinskys, their voices and laughter were heavenly music to him. He realised that there was no greater happiness than the well-being of those you love.

"Your health, Jared. Tell me what plans you have for the spring with your timber business?"

17

Irenka's mansion was decorated with many white ribbons and bouquets of flowers. Such was her happiness to celebrate the marriage there that anyone would have thought she was the mother of the bride. It had been difficult to convince the Rabbi to perform the ceremony in a Catholic home, but he was finally persuaded. The Rothmans owed a lot to their hosts, and the least they could do was grant them the privilege of hosting the event, especially as both bride and groom had worked there.

That summer of 1867 a splendid sun shone above Lublin; a warm breeze floated through the terrace as the afternoon progressed. Irenka and Sara had finished preparing Tatiana, who looked extraordinarily beautiful in her white dress. The house was already filled with guests, including Piotr and Malka with their little daughter, the entire Czemerinsky family, Tobias and Sara, together with various other members of the city's Jewish community, as well as many Catholics who shared friendships with the Rothman family.

Amongst the guests were a couple only known to Sara and Isaak. A month earlier, she had taken her husband to Semiatycze, on the road to Bialystok, staying at the village inn. The innkeeper recognised her the moment she arrived; she greeted him with great pleasure.

"How are you and your wife, Jacob?"

"Very well, I'm glad to see you again!"

"As am I."

At that moment the innkeeper's wife arrived, Sara greeted her with a hug, then turned to Isaak.

"My love, I present to you Jacob and Miriam. They saved my life and cared for Gabriel with love, when I was on the brink of death."

Isaak approached the couple and expressed his gratitude. Sara then retrieved two gifts from her bag, while the innkeeper offered them coffee before sitting down to talk. As they were saying farewell, Sara asked them:

"Jacob, Miriam, would you do us the honour of attending our daughter's wedding next month?"

"It would be a privilege for us."

Robiak felt very nervous waiting for Tatiana to come down. When she did so the voices that had filled the rooms and terrace died down to a whisper, everyone was captivated by the bride's beauty as she descended the stairs. Her jet-black hair shone beneath a white veil, her spontaneous smile, the one that Robiak fell in love with, lit up the room. The sweetness of her gaze left everyone captivated.

Tradition dictated that the bride be accompanied by her and the groom's mother, but Robiak was an orphan, the role of parent had been filled by Irenka, so Tatiana was accompanied by Sara and their hostess. In that moment, Tatiana remembered her biological mother and a tear rolled down her cheek as she thought about how happy she would have been to accompany her. Her sadness soon dissipated thanks to the guests' applause.

By tradition, the groom is also accompanied by his parents, but given Robiak's situation, Isaak and Carl assumed that role. The former said to him:

"You are now a Jew; you know your responsibilities and the commitment you have to your wife. If you forget, I will personally come to your house to remind you."

"Yes, sir," replied the young man, who was more nervous about the ceremony than the words of his future father-in-law.

At last radiant Tatiana arrived at the groom's side. The Rabbi blessed the wine, Robiak gave the ring to his future wife, and she gave him the Tallit. Wearing it, as the husband's responsibilities to his wife were being read aloud, Isaak look sidelong at Robiak with a sly smile; he could tell that Robiak was a good man and would be a devoted husband.

At the moment that Robiak broke the glass, Sara was reminded of her own wedding, and she felt her eyes water with emotion. She looked at her beloved Tatiana and smiled with both sadness and joy. She was glad to see her daughter happy, but sad that she would be leaving home.

"I may leave home, but I will always be in your life, my beloved mother," Tatiana had told her a few minutes earlier, before going down to the living room.

Sara became aware of the passing of time, especially in relation to her three daughters: there had been so little time when they could be a family together. After all, she was only ten years older than Tatiana, and she adopted her just four years ago.

The following year Tatiana announced that she was pregnant, which was a great joy for everyone. Isaak and Sara realised that they would become grandparents when he was only thirty-three and she was not yet thirty.

"When we walk with our grandson, people will be convinced we are his parents," Isaak laughed.

"Or our granddaughter," Sara replied, "we can't know yet."

The two continued working diligently and enthusiastically, as they had make the monthly payment for their home, which was very high. However, their small shoe workshop was beginning to make a name for itself in the city, to the extent that on many occasions it became necessary for Isaak to work late into the night. Sara also grew her business; although her cafeteria had taken a while to get started, it had begun to make a profit. Aliza, now seventeen, was working as the manager of the shop, while her sister Jana took charge of the bakery's branch. Robiak and Tatiana had also managed to build up their transport company, which still delivered products from both bakeries.

Gabriel was already ten years old and continued to demonstrate great intellectual abilities. He had a firm and determined character; when he set out to achieve something, he did so with great perseverance. He also had excellent deductive skills, for which his father believed he could become a scientist or researcher. In short, the family was happy and continued to prosper; the days of suffering were left behind them. They all worked hard and strictly observed Jewish customs.

Sara was immensely happy, every day she thanked God for the return of her beloved husband. She recalled that beautiful moment that they were reunited in that abandoned cellar, which she had revisited several times, simply to relive that unforgettable experience. On some occasions Tatiana had accompanied her to share her joy. Isaak felt the same the same, understanding that God had given him an opportunity often denied to men who had gone through what he had had to face.

He continued to maintain a close relationship with the people that had been a part of his incredible adventure. Unsurprisingly, the only person he had seen since was Henrik. Unfortunately for him, his story had not ended as blissfully as Isaak's. Upon returning home he found that his wife was living with another man. He had been able to recover his children, who were unhappy living under the same roof as their stepfather and moved to Warsaw with them. They were glad to be with their father again, and to start a new life in a better place. Isaak had the opportunity to support his great friend by finding him a good job in a sawmill of Jared's associates.

Correspondence with Igor was not smooth because of the distance, but they nevertheless remained in contact. He had done very well for himself; his Chinese wife proved to be an incredible woman. She was talented and highly intelligent, having learned Russian perfectly, then taught her husband to read and write. The letters he sent to Isaak were in his own hand, although his penmanship was like that of a small child. He still worked at the Russian merchant's mansion but had been promoted to head of security and now handled some administrative affairs for the businessman's companies.

Israel, for his part, always insisted that Isaak return to Hong Kong so that they might start a business together. Isaak avoided the proposal, remaining firm in his decision to stay in Poland, which was his homeland and where he had his family, especially now that Tatiana was married and expecting his grandson. Also, he knew that Jana and Aliza had no desire to leave Lublin, much less to a city on the far side of the world with such a strange an exotic culture.

He also maintained a regular correspondence with Andrew. He was already a Captain and had been assigned command of a Marine Corps company, embarking as a prize crew on a Royal Navy ship in the West Indies. He informed him that he would soon return to England to assume a position in London, and he wanted to invite Isaak and Sara to spend a few days in the English capital. Isaak was tempted by the proposal but knew that he must first finish paying off his debts.

In short, everything was going well. They lived better than they ever had in Bialystok, aside from the gastric pain that recurrently afflicted

Isaak. This was apparently a consequence of his poor diet during his time in Siberia and his flight.

18

There was a great commotion in the Rothman household over preparations for Gabriel's Bar Mitzvah. While Sara, Jana, and Aliza worked on the final details, Isaak spoke in the main room with his son. Ensuring he understood the great importance of the ceremony, especially its spiritual significance. The boy listened intently, although his father's words had already been repeatedly emphasised by the Rabbi. It snowed heavily outside, but the weather could not dim everyone's mood on this special day.

At the appointed time, they left for synagogue where they found Robiak and Tatiana, who held her little daughter, Sara, by the hand. The girl was excited to see her grandparents arrive; Isaak bent down and picked up his little granddaughter. She had become his darling, he played with her for hours and, unbeknownst to his wife and Tatiana, brought her sweets and treats that he bought on his way home and hid in his coat pockets. He held her against his chest, swung her in the air and kissed her tenderly while she laughed. Sara approached and reprimanded them.

"We are in the synagogue! Behave yourself."

They went to meet the Rabbi and his wife as the guests arrived; these were old friends who were like family. Irenka was there, unaccompanied because Carl was travelling, as were Tobias and Sara, Piotr and Malka with their daughter Martha, Jared and Anya, Oizer and his wife Rachel, who was a close friend of the Rothman daughters. Saúl was also present, Jana's fiancé who had also won over the hearts of her parents. He had now finished his law degree and was well on his way to becoming a Rabbi.

Throughout the ceremony, no one was prouder than Isaak. He was so excited that he made a mistake while reciting the blessing, saying *"the blessings of this boy,"* rather than *"the acts of this boy"*. The Catholics present were unaware of the error, but the Jews noticed. Jared couldn't hold in a slight smile until the Rabbi glared at him. Later during the reception, Isaak was made fun of for his mistake.

Gabriel looked very elegant, already showing a very manly bearing, and it was obvious that he would be at least as tall as his father. His hair was a brilliant gold that shimmered and framed the grey eyes that he had inherited from his mother. He already had more than one secret admirer, and his sisters fawned over him, saying he was the most handsome boy in Lublin and would be the most handsome man in Poland. They liked to walk the parks and boulevards with their brother, showing him off in front of the local girls.

But if everything suggested that Gabriel would be the masculine version of Sara's imposing beauty, his intelligence was not far behind. He was already a true autodidact and a compulsive reader. He had become the pride of his Rabbi of his community, and of the city's Chief Rabbi. He demonstrated this on that special day with his poise and confidence in reading the Haftarah, but especially during the traditional speech when recounting a part of the Torah, which he did with such mastery and with such profound reflections that he surprised everyone, both Jews and Christians.

There had never been such proud parents. Isaak was convinced that his son would follow in his Jewish heritage with genuine devotion. Sara, who of course shared in her daughters' appreciation of his appearance, wiped away tears of pride at the admiration her son inspired.

The reception held in their house was a great party, a bit over the top for the Rabbi's taste, but such was the hosts' joy that they were permitted some excess. Halfway through the party, Sara took the floor to say a few words, then, as tradition dictated, gave her son a gift. In a beautiful case she had made herself, she handed him an elegant ebony fountain pen, saying to him:

"My dear son, this gift has been made by Jewish hands far from here, in North America. I hope that you will treasure it for many years and that it will be of great use to you."

"Thank you, mother, it will be one of my most treasured objects."

The most emotional moment was when Isaak came forward to give his son his own Tefillin, saying to him.

"Beloved son, from today onwards you will assume all your responsibilities as a Jew. You are heir to traditions that have existed for more than four thousand years. You must always honour your ancestors, from Abraham onwards. One of your new duties will be to pray daily using the Tefillin. I give you mine, which I received from my father, and he from his father. I hope that you will wear them always, like a good Jew."

"Thank you, father," replied the boy, "you have my word that I will honour my ancestors, people, and faith every day of my life. I will never forget your teachings and those of our Rabbi, and I will always carry Eretz Israel in my heart."

Isaak couldn't contain his tears, and everyone present was moved by Gabriel's words. Irenka turned to Oizer and Rachel who stood next to her, and said:

"Hearing him speak like that … it's hard to believe that he's barely thirteen years old, don't you think?"

"When I met him, he was a five-year-old boy," Oizer said, "and you could already tell that he would be someone very special."

In the spring of that year Jana and Saúl were married. The joyous events seemingly never ceased for the family, while their financial situation continued to improve. They had already fully paid for their house and repaid their loans to Carl and Jared. Sara was still in charge of the pastry shop, she had transferred the branch to Jana, and the café was run by Aliza. Meanwhile, Isaak had opened his shoe shop. It had not yet matched the size or elegance of what he had had in Bialystok, but he was already working in three areas: production, repair, and sales.

Sara felt that the house looked more and more empty; however, as Tatiana and Jana continued living in Lublin, she had the opportunity to see them regularly which tempered her loss of the girls. They still celebrated all the Jewish holidays together and cultivated their other friendships, especially with Carl and Irenka in Lublin and the Czemerinskys in Pinsk, who now went by the name of Weizmann.

That summer they decided to spend a few days of their holidays in Anya and Jared's home, who explained that this change was due to circumstances related to business, and his ties with his German partners. Because of this he had abandoned the very Russian name of Czemerinsky and adopted a more Germanic one: Weizmann. In those days changing one's surname was common.

"It's much more Prussian – well more *German*, as we must now say – don't you think, Isaak?" he asked, raising his chin a little.

"I like it," laughed Isaak, "it's more like mine. Although your previous name could pass as Polish, it sounded too Russian. I'm pleased to call you Jared Weizmann."

During these holidays the two families reunited in their entirety, and the sound of children's voices that echoed throughout the house showed just how quickly time was passing. This was an opportunity for Tatiana's girl, Jana's baby, and Oizer's two little children to meet. They were the next generation, and both their parents and grandparents expected that the Hebrew tradition would continue through them, hopefully in better times for the Jewish people.

That time together was very pleasant, thanks to the great affection between the families. Isaak had become great friends with Jared, while Sara adored Anya, with whom she got on wonderfully. She would never forget how she had taken in her daughters when they were homeless, then welcomed herself and Gabriel as though they were family. Jana, Tatiana, and Aliza had a special love for Oizer, and they thought of Rachel like a sister. Gabriel, despite being much more mature than the twins, enjoyed their company very much.

The days were filled with walks to the countryside and surrounding forests, as well as along the banks of the Pripiat river. They went to see the house that Oizer was building in Motal, a town half a day's ride away. It had no charm in itself but was surrounded by lush forests and several beautiful lakes. While Oizer's future home was not yet fully finished, he arranged for visitors to settle in for one night and go rowing on the lakes the next day. It was a very pleasant country experience for all.

This was the last holiday they spent together, which is why it became such an unforgettable experience. However, they never lost contact and mutual visits continued. Isaak and Sara travelled periodically to see the Weizmann, in Pinsk and Motal, and received them many times in Lublin.

19

Upon returning to Lublin, storm clouds began to darken on the family's horizon, due to Isaak's deteriorating health. His stomach pains became sharper and more frequent. He ate less and less, and he would wake with a burning pain in his stomach at night. Despite the medications he was prescribed and careful diet, Isaak could feel his condition worsening. Obsessively, he dedicated himself to his work, pursuing his dream of opening an elegant shoe shop that would surpass the one he had left in Bialystok. He also focussed on his many other occupations to distract himself from the pain.

Of course, as the months went by, his health deteriorated. His diet was strict, but neither that, nor his medication, could dull the pain. Eventually, he found it hard to swallow and felt severe pain in his chest and abdomen. Isaak was deeply affected and concerned by his condition. One night, after noticing traces of blood on throwing up, he decided to take more drastic measures. He did not want to tell Sara so as not to worry her but opted to consult the doctor the very next morning.

So, it was that in the Spring of 1872, overwhelmed by pain, he went to the doctor.

"I have to be honest," the doctor told him, "To the best of my knowledge, you are doing all you can to alleviate your ailments, but this may not eliminate them."

"I understand, doctor. You mean to say that there is hope, but no certainty."

"Essentially, yes. But may I suggest there is a doctor and researcher who has made great advances in this field, residing in Vienna. I know him personally; I assure you he is the best gastrologist in the world."

"The best what?"

"Don't worry about the term. Medicine is quickly advancing these days, especially in Austria and the new German empire. So-called generalist doctors, such as I, no longer suffice. One needs specialisation. One such specialisation, that deals precisely with injuries and diseases to the digestive system is called gastro."

"I understand: you mean to say that there is an Austrian doctor who is an expert in cases like mine?"

"Precisely, if there is anyone in the world who might be able to treat you, it is Doctor Frizmann, of that I have no doubt."

"But do you really believe that I can be cured?" Isaak asked.

"I don't know, but I'll reiterate that medical science has progressed much in recent years, particularly in Berlin and Vienna where they have specialised in several areas."

That evening, Isaak told his wife about his conversation with the doctor, and the suggestion to go to see Doctor Frizmann in the Austrian capital.

"My love, nothing is more important than your health," she said, "and if the cure to your sickness can be found in Vienna, then we must go."

"Yes, I am seriously considering it. If there's a chance that this could alleviate my pain, we must try. My condition is no longer an annoyance: last night I brought up blood."

"What? You didn't tell me!"

"I didn't want to worry you."

"Well, there's nothing more to be said. Tomorrow we will prepare to go to Vienna."

The next day, over breakfast, they spoke with Gabriel and Aliza about their decision to see the specialist in Vienna. The pair agreed that it was the right thing to do.

Isaak went directly to the doctor's office to tell him that they planned to travel as soon as possible. Sara, before going to the bakery, stopped to explain the situation to Jana and then went to Tatiana's home for the same reason. Gabriel went to school convinced that the trip would be for the best; he had witnessed his father's daily suffering. Aliza thought the same way. If the cure for her father's disease was in Vienna, then that was where they should go.

Another thought also played on the girl's mind. Austria and Vienna held an additional importance for her: Karl Joseph Radetz, the dashing Austrian army lieutenant with whom she had been in love for more than four years. Sara suspected her daughter's feelings, but did not give them much weight, since their love seemed impossible. The foreign officer lived in Vienna and travelled only twice a year to Lublin to visit his widowed mother, who was Polish and lived in the city with his sister.

Furthermore, thought Sara, true love could not develop from letters. Therefore, she considered her daughter's feelings a passing fancy. Most decisively, the young officer was a Catholic, making marriage inconceivable. Both Isaak and Sara could never accept it, having already ceded enough in accepting the marriage of Tatiana and Robiak, although the latter had shown himself to be a good, respectful, and observant Jew.

Sara, worried about Aliza's infatuation, had once colluded with Irenka to introduce potential suitors but to the girl, to no avail. Aliza had attended parties and social events in the company of her parents, sisters, and friends. She had laughed, danced, and conversed with ease, but there was no doubt that her thoughts were elsewhere. Her mother was concerned that, at twenty-two, the girl showed no interest in marriage.

She had already discussed this with Irenka on several occasions. One day, shortly before Isaak first saw the doctor, her friend had said to her:

"I understand your concern, but you should worry less about Aliza's reluctance to marry, and more about the reason for it."

"What do you mean?"

"You know what I mean! Aliza's heart belongs to that young man, the Austrian."

"That's absurd! We both know those feelings are hopeless."

"Hopeless or not, for whatever reason, it reminds me of a friend of mine."

"I don't understand."

"I remember how I would seek a suitor to win your heart, or have you forgotten?"

"Of course not!"

"You knew then, as I know now, that your heart belonged to one man, another impossible love, since all though Isaak dead."

"You confuse me."

"Perhaps, but one thing is clear: back then you wouldn't listen to me, you listened to your heart. Do you regret that?"

"No."

"Well, I think Aliza must follow her heart."

Sara thought in silence. Of course, she wanted her daughter to be happy, but she could never allow her to marry a man who was not a Jew. As for Isaak, the thought would be inconceivable. Besides, how could she know that the Austrian officer truly loved her daughter? They only met two or three times a year. She left her friend's home confused, but the deterioration Isaak's health refocussed her thoughts.

What Sara didn't know was that Aliza had confided in Irenka, asking her to prepare the ground with her mother. The girl really did love Karl Radetz, and, from his words, he felt the same way. Her mind was made up: she would marry him and no one else.

Irenka understood the girl's struggle. Aliza's parents would never allow her to marry a Catholic. To make matters worse, Irenka knew Karl's mother to be a bad person; she had spoken against the Jewish people. Finally, she was an ardent Catholic, one who would never allow her son to marry outside their religion, particularly to a Jew. Nor was a conversion, as with Robiak, possible: an Austrian officer in the service of the empire could never convert to Judaism.

'She must be realistic,' Irenka thought, 'the boy's military career would be over.'

Of course, she said none of this to Aliza, who had wept on her lap like a child. Her love, although reciprocated, could never be. Despite this, Irenka promised to do everything in her power to win over Aliza's mother.

That afternoon Aliza hastily closed the cafeteria an hour earlier than usual. She rushed to her mother's bakery, hoping to talk to her while walking home. Sara, although surprised, was glad to see her.

"Hello, mother! I've come to walk you home. It's a beautiful afternoon."

"Of course, let me finish these accounts and we'll head out."

"Perfect! I'll wait here. There's something I want to tell you."

"What's going on?"

"Nothing important, mother. We'll talk about it soon."

Sara counted the day's earnings, passed on some instructions to the workers, and said goodbye, leaving arm-in-arm with her daughter. They walked leisurely through the streets. Sara was already thirty-four, but her beauty and health were undiminished. She could have been her daughter's elder sister.

"Mother," Aliza said, "I want to ask you a favour."

"What is it?"

"I want to go with you and father to Vienna."

Sara stopped abruptly. She looked into her daughter's eyes.

"To Vienna? Why do you wish to join us?"

"Because... well, I would like to go with you and to be by my father's side. It's important that he feels supported. And, because..."

"Yes, tell me, why else?"

"Because I've always wanted to see Vienna."

The true reason for her request was obvious.

"You've always wanted to see Vienna? Or for the last four years?"

"Of course, mother, for a few years now. I know that you know the reason for my interest! Please don't make it more difficult for me to ask."

"Oh, my daughter..." Sara sighed deeply, "I don't know what to do with you."

"Let me come with you!"

"You know it's not that simple..."

"Oh mother, please!"

Sara remembered Irenka's words: *Aliza must follow her heart.*

"I don't know what to say..."

"It's easy, mother, just say yes! I've been learning German. I can't speak it perfectly, but it's good enough. I'll be useful once we're in Vienna."

"When we're in Vienna? Are you so sure you're coming with us?"

"Of course, mother!"

"And why is that?"

"Because you and father love me very much and want to see me happy."

Sara couldn't help but laugh.

"Oh, my girl! It's true, I love you! I see you now as you came to me in Bialystok, like a helpless kitten. From that moment, you instantly won my heart."

"And you mine, mother."

"I'll think about your request."

"Thank you!"

Aliza squeezed her arm once again, then kissed her on the cheek.

"Have you thought about it yet?"

"Aliza, for God's sake!"

"Oh mother, just don't leave me waiting!"

Sara looked at her with tenderness. Although sweet and a little childish, she was already a woman. Sara could no longer treat her like a little girl.

"We'll, I'll raise it with your father tonight."

"Thank you, mother! Thank you!" Aliza squeezed her arm again and kissed her.

Sara pondered for a moment and realised why her daughter had studied German. She had wanted to learn the native language of the man she had fallen in love with. When Isaak arrived home, she mentioned the girl's request to him. Contrary to her fears, he had no objection to Aliza accompanying them. In fact, he was pleased and only asked who would oversee the café.

"The shop assistant will take charge, father," Aliza said. "And Tatiana can go every day to check and supervise the details. She knows the business perfectly."

She hadn't spoken to Tatiana, but she knew with certainty that she would support her in these matters.

Isaak had some notion of his daughter's feelings for the officer, but he assumed that they were youthful illusions. When she asked to travel with them, it never occurred to him that it was for something other than getting to know the Austrian capital and supporting her parents.

Isaak was right in thinking that Aliza wanted to support him. However, the trip presented a perfect opportunity to see Karl. That very night, she wrote him a letter, which she sent early the next day by express mail. The letter informed him that she would be in Vienna and contained suggestions on how they might meet. She then went to Jana's bakery, which she had had as the return address, to ask her sister to tell her immediately upon receiving a reply.

Meanwhile, preparations for the trip began. The doctor had sent a report to his colleague in Vienna, explaining Isaak's case and requesting an appointment. Aliza couldn't sleep because of her excitement at seeing Karl. She awoke early each day, and going to the café, would stop by Jana's in the hope that Karl's reply had arrived. Her sister would lean out of the bakery's second-floor window, where she and Saúl had established a beautiful little home, and with a sympathetic look confirm that nothing had arrived.

Aliza was consumed by anticipation. She would pass by Jana's bakery twice each day, at noon and in the afternoon, before returning home. As the days passed without a response, she began to despair. She feared that Karl had not received her letter or had forgotten her. She imagined him, married to someone else, or perhaps enlisted in the British army and sent to India. Frantic and absurd ideas flooded her mind as she walked the streets yet again towards her sister's bakery. Turning the corner, she spotted Jana leaning out towards the street. Aliza's heart skipped a beat: Jana did not usually wait at the window. Her sister was holding a string from which an envelope dangled. Aliza sprinted towards the bakery. As she neared, Jana raised the rope.

"If you can jump high enough to reach it, it's yours! Otherwise, come back tomorrow!"

"Jana, I'll break your door down!"

Her sister laughed and let go of the rope. Aliza seized the envelope and opened it immediately. The letter, written in Polish, expressed great joy that Aliza would be visiting Vienna. After reading these first lines, Aliza kissed the letter repeatedly, pressing it against her chest while her sister and brother-in-law laughed from above.

"Stop teasing!" She scolded, then continued to read.

Karl's letter reaffirmed his love for her and expressed his excitement at seeing her. He confirmed that he was indeed in Vienna and asked her to inform him, as soon as she could, where they would be staying in the capital. If she couldn't do so before their trip, he instructed her to leave a note on the bulletin board near the post office at the West Station. Finally, he provided directions to the barracks where he was stationed in case, they couldn't establish contact through any other means.

As Aliza read, Jana descended the stairs and opened the door, pulling her sister inside.

"Well, what did he say?" Jana asked.

"He gave me instructions on how we can meet in Vienna."

"Wonderful," Jana replied, taking her hand. "So, he is there, and you will be able to see each other. How happy I am for you, little sister."

"Oh Jana, I'm so happy. See how he ends his letter!"

She passed it to her sister, who read aloud:

> *Ever since learning that I would see you again, my heart beats stronger; it will only be calm by your presence. The clock is now my enemy, the hours will consume me until the moment comes when I can behold you. At that precise instant, time will stop and belong only to us.*

"My God!" Jana exclaimed. "He's not just a soldier; he's a poet!"

The sisters embraced, then bid farewell. As Aliza was leaving, Jana called out to her.

"Tatiana was here last night and needs to talk to you. Go to her house at noon."

"I will, thank you."

She blew a kiss with her hand and walked joyfully along the street, clutching the envelope against her chest once again.

During lunchtime, she made her way to Tatiana's house.

"Hello, you wanted to speak to me?"

"Yes, come in."

"Karl finally replied. I'm so happy that we can see each other," Aliza shared.

"You have no idea how glad I am for you, little sister," Tatiana said, then continued, "Actually, there's something I wanted to talk to you about regarding your trip to Vienna."

"What is it?"

"There may be something you haven't considered."

"Tell me, I'm listening."

"You're going to accompany our parents in everything related to the medical consultation, but also to see your young man. That's great but think about how difficult it will be to tell mother and father that you'll have a private meeting with Karl. It wouldn't be convenient for them to accompany you either. Can you imagine talking to Karl in front of our parents?"

"Oh, no, God, I hadn't considered that."

"That's what I was telling you."

"You're right, Tatiana."

"Furthermore, it's possible that father will be admitted for observation or given medication that requires someone to be by his side to take care of him. Mother could do that, but if that's the case, you also couldn't go alone to see Karl."

"That's true, what am I going to do?"

Don't worry, little sister, because I already have the solution."

"You already have it? What is it?"

"Very simple. I will go with you. I will propose it to our parents this very afternoon."

Aliza became excited.

"Of course, it's perfect! Thank you, Tatiushka, I adore you. But tell me, have you talked to Robiak?"

"Of course, I already spoke to him, and not only did he approve, but he offered to stay at home and take care of the little girl during my absence. You know he's an angel."

"Oh, sister, you have no idea how happy you're making me! I love you so much."

Tatiana looked at her with tenderness, feeling great happiness at the thought of having wonderful parents and siblings. It didn't matter that they didn't share the same blood in their veins because, in exchange, they shared the essence of their souls.

The journey was particularly exciting for Aliza. Every kilometre they covered increased her happiness. The weather was marvellous, and the setting sun sparkled. On the second day, they arrived in Krakow, in what was known as Austrian Poland, a Polish city that now belonged to the Austro-Hungarian Empire. They stayed in a hotel near the central railway station. The following morning, they took the train to Vienna. It was a new experience for all four of them, as they had never used that mode of transport before. Isaak had seen trains in France, and Aliza in St. Petersburg, but neither of them had ever travelled by train.

Everyone was amazed by this extraordinary invention. It seemed almost unreal to them, not only the smoothness and comfort of transportation but also the incredible speed it reached, far superior to that of carriages. Isaak, with an air of self-satisfaction, picked up one of the newspapers provided and began to read, occasionally glancing out the window. Meanwhile, the three women enjoyed the experience and the scenery.

The train sped through the fields of Bohemia, and by mid-afternoon, it arrived in Vienna. The station was quite modern and bustling with activity. The noise and the abundance of tobacco kiosks, cafés, and pastry shops caught their attention, as they were novel and impressive sights for them. The station itself reflected the grand city they had finally reached, after all, it was the capital of an empire.

As soon as they descended from the train, Aliza quickly slipped away with Tatiana under the pretence of needing to use the bathroom. They sought out the post office. On either side of it, bulletin boards were filled with various notes left by people. Aliza had her own note prepared, so she promptly placed it on the board. It specified the name of the place where they would be staying Imperial Hotel.

They took a carriage that took them to the hotel; the journey was even more impressive for everyone, including Aliza, who was already familiar with St. Petersburg. Undoubtedly, Vienna was even more beautiful than the Russian capital, or perhaps she saw it that way because it was associated with her love. Although Isaak had briefly seen Paris, he found Vienna to be more harmonious. Sara and Tatiana were impressed by the beauty and grandeur of the buildings. At one point, Sara leaned towards Tatiana and whispered:

"My dear, we definitely live in a remote village."

"This is absolutely stunning, mother. I never imagined that cities like this existed."

And it was no wonder. Vienna was the third largest city in Europe after Paris and London, with over a million inhabitants at that time. It was also the capital of entertainment, with music festivals, dances, and numerous public and private events that infused it with an unmatched vitality.

The carriage passed through the Ring Strasse, and they were able to appreciate some of Vienna's most iconic architectural landmarks, such as the Opera House, City Hall, and Parliament. Aliza felt like a princess about to be conquered by her Prince Charming. She was euphoric and clung tightly to Tatiana's arm, brimming with excitement. Her mother looked at her and understood her feelings; she seemed like a young girl. Despite the circumstances, she couldn't help but give a tender smile while observing her daughter's joy.

They arrived at the hotel, which was extremely luxurious. As soon as Isaak stepped out of the carriage, he turned in astonishment towards his wife, while a valet extended his hand to help her alight. His questioning gaze elicited a smile from Sara. She had personally taken care of reserving the hotel in the city and had chosen the most beautiful one. She approached her husband and whispered:

"My love, we have worked hard all our lives. It's time for you to enjoy what you deserve, just this once."

"But this hotel must cost a fortune."

"Relax, we're not going to buy it. We'll only stay here for a few nights."

"It's too much, Sara."

"Remember the times when you had to sleep in dreadful places. Now it's only fair that you enjoy something different for a few days."

Once again, she brought to his memory the terrifying nights they endured when they escaped from Bialystok with their little one.

The young women couldn't believe their eyes; the facade alone was majestic—a seven-story building with marble columns and ochre walls.

"It looks like a palace," Aliza said to Tatiana.

"Well, your charming prince will come to fetch you from this palace,"
her sister joked, smiling.

"It's like a dream."

The reception area truly resembled a palace, and the staff's
attentiveness made them feel like authentic queens. Everything was
incredibly elegant, with exquisite decor. Beautiful music, the famous
Viennese waltzes, wafted from the back of the hall, enchanting them
with their melody. The three women felt as though they were in a
fairytale. Isaak, on the other hand, thought the hotel was beautiful but
must have been quite costly.

When they made their way to their rooms, they used an elevator for
the first time. When the elevator doors opened, the elevator attendant
smiled, trying to reassure them:

"Don't worry; it's perfectly safe. You can step inside."

They all remained silent and motionless, feeling unsure of how to
proceed. Aliza's German skills came in handy, as they had heard of such
contraptions but had never ridden one before and felt a certain
apprehension. However, they also didn't move from where they stood
because they didn't understand what the young man had said. Aliza, who
had understood, told them:

"Come on, he says it's safe."

And she entered to reassure them.

If everything in the hotel had seemed splendid to them, the rooms
left them dumbfounded. They were opulent with elegant beds, soft
carpets, high-quality tapestries, and curtains framed by pastel blue walls
and exquisite furniture. Undoubtedly, everything was worthy of a royal
castle. When the bellboy left the suitcases and closed the door behind
him, Tatiana and Aliza, like little girls, ran and threw themselves onto
their beds. Then they sat up and started bouncing on the mattresses,
laughing.

That night, they dined in the hotel restaurant, illuminated by
numerous chandeliers, and accompanied by the magical sound of violins.
They were amazed, although Isaak ate something very modest due to
the strict diet he was following. The next day, they had an appointment
with Doctor Frizmann, so they retired to their rooms early. Just over an

hour later, there was a knock-on Tatiana and Aliza's door, and a bellboy brought a note from Karl.

"Oh, Tatiushka, it's him! He's downstairs in the salon! What do I do now?" Aliza exclaimed, feeling anxious.

"What do you do? Didn't you come to Vienna, among other reasons, to see him?" Tatiana responded.

"Yes, but..."

"No 'buts'. Prepare yourself nicely. I'll do the same, and let's go to the salon!"

They quickly freshened up, and as they descended, Aliza was filled with anticipation. The salon was a spectacle, resembling a festive event. Ladies and gentlemen mingled in different areas of the hotel. Some gentlemen smoked in a small adjacent room, several couples conversed animatedly in another section, and in the background, an orchestra played waltzes. There were various military officers in different uniforms in the room. Aliza searched the entire salon, looking among them for Karl but couldn't find him.

After a few seconds, she saw him walking towards her. He looked incredibly handsome and elegant in his blue uniform adorned with buttons and decorations. His smile was spontaneous, and his eyes sparkled with joy. He approached them solemnly, heels together, and made a small bow.

"Good evening, enchanting ladies. This salon was already illuminated, but now it shines with two beautiful suns."

The two young women smiled, flattered by his words. Then Karl turned to Aliza and, kissing her hand, said, "Thank you, my dear friend, for brightening my heart tonight."

"I'm the one who should thank you, Lieutenant," Aliza replied.

The officer turned to Tatiana, taking her hand to kiss it, and added, "And thank you, kind companion. You look so beautiful that I would be delighted to invite you to dance all evening."

"Karl, stop joking!" Aliza exclaimed, "Besides, you're offending Tatiana. You know she's a married woman."

The lieutenant laughed heartily and, breaking the protocol he had initially started with, he embraced Aliza and kissed her cheek. Then, he

lightly took Tatiana's arm and said, "Thank you, Tatiana, for being here. I
know you've come to support us."

"You guess correctly, my dear Karl. I'm very pleased to see you both
so happy," Tatiana replied.

He then offered his arm to both of them, and they made their way
to a table. They ordered wine and began conversing in the midst of
the pleasant and elegant ambiance. Aliza felt like she was in paradise,
enthralled as she gazed at Karl while he laughed and conversed with
grace and charisma. Eventually, he invited her to dance. Aliza was a bit
hesitant, as she wasn't an experienced dancer and was considered, at least
in Lublin, to lack the rhythm of a lady and a dancer. Aliza expressed this
to her companion, but he insisted without hesitation:

"Come on, don't be shy. Cavalry officers have a saying that goes, 'You
learn to ride by riding,' and we infantrymen maintain that 'You learn to
dance by dancing.' And as for the latter, don't worry, we're in Vienna, the
city of the waltz."

Tatiana watched them with great satisfaction, noticing her sister's
extreme happiness. Aliza appeared so enamoured that it seemed she
breathed through Karl. It was evident that he, too, was completely
captivated by Aliza, as his gaze lingered on her with ecstasy and love
reflected in his eyes.

When they finished dancing, they returned to the table, still holding
hands. They looked joyous and bantered with each other like children.
In Karl's opinion, Tatiana shouldn't feel like a chaperone, so he invited
her to dance as well. She politely declined, but Aliza insisted. Now it
was Aliza who observed her sister with gratitude and immense affection.
Upon their return, another officer approached their table, and with a
slight bow, he greeted them:

"Lieutenant Radetz, I see you're captivating the most beautiful
women in the salon."

Karl lifted his gaze, immediately stood up, assuming a firm posture,
and inclined himself slightly as he responded:

"Good evening, Colonel. It's a pleasure to see you. Allow me to
introduce my companions."

He pointed to Aliza.

"Miss Aliza Rothman, my fiancée."

Aliza felt a slight tremor as the sweet words "my fiancée" echoed in her ears. She was still lost in her thoughts when she extended her arm for the colonel to kiss her hand. Then she looked at Karl as he said to his superior:

"And this is Mrs. Tatiana Krikoviak, her sister."

"Pleased to meet you, madam," the colonel said, also kissing her hand. Then he continued, "May I join you for a moment?"

"Of course, Colonel," Karl replied.

He didn't particularly appreciate his superior joining them, but there was no remedy. The Colonel commented, "I didn't know about your fiancée, Lieutenant. Congratulations, she is a beautiful woman."

"Thank you very much, my Colonel. And please excuse me, but they are Polish. Aliza speaks German, but her sister does not."

"I'm sorry, my Polish is very basic. Which part of the former Poland are they from?"

"They're from Lublin."

"Ah, I see. Then I assume they speak Russian," the Colonel said in that language, which Tatiana understood.

"That's correct, sir."

"I lived in St. Petersburg for three years as part of the Austrian military mission to the czar's court."

"It's a city I don't know, but I've heard it is very beautiful, Colonel," Tatiana said. "However, I'm sure it's not as beautiful as Vienna."

"You are right, charming lady."

At that moment, Aliza intervened, addressing the officer, "Excuse me, Colonel. The Lieutenant asked me for the next dance. Would you excuse us?"

"Of course, miss," the officer said, rising from his seat.

Aliza nearly dragged Karl onto the dance floor. Once there, she placed her hands on his shoulders, looked deeply into his eyes, and asked, "Why did you introduce me to the Colonel as your fiancée?"

"Because I was going to propose to you during this very dance, but our superior interrupted us."

"Are you joking?"

"Of course not. I believe this is the perfect setting to ask you. The most exclusive and luxurious hotel in Vienna, beautiful music, excellent wine, and the most stunning woman in the world."

"So, you're serious?"

"Very serious, and thoroughly considered. You are the sweetest and most fascinating woman in existence, but above all, you have something very special that perhaps you haven't noticed."

"What is it?"

"You made me fall madly in love with you."

"Oh, Karl! You know I love you with all my heart."

"Intoxicating words," Karl said, "so I must seal this conversation with a golden clasp by asking you a question. Will you marry me?"

Aliza felt herself fading, so she clung to him. "Can you say it again?" she asked. "I want to hear it once more to convince myself that I'm not dreaming."

"Will you marry me?" Karl repeated.

Aliza didn't respond. Karl was about to say something, but she placed her index finger on his lips, took his hand, and led him to a corner of the salon near the elevator. She brought her face close to his, whispering softly, "Yes, a thousand times, yes."

Then she kissed him. He was a little taken aback, but she kissed him again. He responded with the same love and tenderness. After a moment, they separated and gazed into each other's eyes. She said, "I love you, Karl. I love you with all my heart."

"And I love you, my beautiful fiancée."

Then he took her hand and whispered, "We can still catch the end of this piece."

They went back to the dance floor and waltzed to a recently composed piece that was all the rage in the salons of the Austrian capital, "Tales from the Vienna Woods." Aliza wished that melody would never end.

When they returned, the Colonel was engaged in animated conversation with Tatiana. It was evident that he was captivated by her, as he looked at her intently and with a hint of audacity, perhaps fuelled by a few extra drinks. Truth be told, she looked radiant and extraordinarily beautiful. Her black hair and oriental eyes were uncommon in Vienna, which added to her allure. The Colonel increasingly praised her beauty, until it made everyone uncomfortable—Tatiana due to the disrespect, being a married woman; Karl, because it was his superior; and Aliza, because she wanted to be left alone to fully enjoy the unforgettable moment and share it with her sister.

Finally, Aliza decided to free Tatiana from the flatterer's clutches. "Excuse us, Colonel. I need to go the powder-room, and I would like my sister to accompany me."

"Of course, miss," he said, rising from his seat.

Tatiana promptly got up, without waiting for the officer to pull out her chair. Aliza took her aside and asked, "What do you think?"

"What, that colonel?"

"Don't be silly, it's what Karl said when he introduced me!"

"I didn't understand what he said, he spoke in German!"

"Oh no! I'm the silly one, Tatiushka, forgive me, he introduced me as his fiancée."

"What? That's how he introduced you?"

"And that's not all, when we went out to dance, he proposed to me."

"Aliza!" Tatiana almost shouted and embraced her, "It can't be true, how exciting."

"I feel like I'm in a dream, I'm the happiest woman in the world!"

"And I'm happy for you, it's beautiful, it's..."

At that moment, she fell silent, and Aliza understood immediately.

"Yes, I know what you're thinking, but I won't worry about that now. Tonight, I want to enjoy such an unforgettable moment. We'll see later what to do."

"You're right, little sister. Let's go back to the hall, we have to celebrate with a glass of wine."

To Tatiana's relief, when they returned to the table, the colonel was no longer there. Karl was talking to another officer, who appeared to be a comrade based on his age. As soon as he saw the two women approaching, Karl introduced them. When Tatiana asked him what had happened with the colonel and how he managed to get rid of him, he laughed and replied:

"He's getting a taste of his own medicine. The general called him over to his table and kept him there, probably telling him his usual barracks anecdotes."

The other officer, who also spoke Russian, laughed along with Karl, and then congratulated him. The girls looked at them puzzled, so he noted:

"Hasn't my colleague told you? We were just informed of our promotion. We'll be captains next month."

"What great news!" Aliza said. "Why didn't you tell us?"

"I didn't know until now. We were on the list, but it hadn't been confirmed. Supposedly, the selected ones would be decided next week."

"Well, Karl and I made the cut. I read the resolution a few minutes ago, signed by the Minister of War."

"Then that calls for a toast," Tatiana said, raising a glass.

Everyone raised their glasses and toasted. As if the evening had just begun, they ordered more wine. Karl's companion, quite different from the colonel, turned out to be very friendly and engaging in conversation. He treated Tatiana with utmost chivalry and respect as a married woman, without imprudently flattering her beauty. So, the four of them conversed, talked, and danced until almost dawn. Aliza was overwhelmed with happiness, as was Tatiana, seeing her sister's joy, although she knew that what lay ahead would not be a bed of roses, but likely a path full of thorns.

They practically didn't sleep, having had very little time to rest. At nine, they left with their parents to attend the medical appointment. The excuse was that Aliza had felt unwell after dinner, preventing her from falling asleep, and Tatiana had stayed awake taking care of her. For some reason, Sara wasn't entirely convinced, but she remained silent. The important thing at that moment was to focus on attending to Isaak.

They arrived at Doctor Frizmann's consulting room, who, despite being a true authority and renowned throughout Europe, turned out to be a very affable and unassuming person. He didn't speak Polish or Russian, but he spoke English perfectly, having lived in both England and the United States. He received Isaak with great kindness, asking him dozens of questions and examining him meticulousness. He focused on the abdomen, of course, but he showed interest in the entire body. Furthermore, his inquiries covered practically every aspect of the patient's life, including preferences, illnesses, ailments, habits, and even moods. After the consultation, Isaak confessed to his wife that answering the questions had exhausted him more than the multiple and detailed physical examinations.

The doctor focused his attention on the abdomen and back, occasionally applying pressure that caused Isaak intense pain, as he let the physician know. Apologizing, the doctor explained that it was absolutely necessary to verify the accuracy of the diagnosis. In the end, he handed Isaak his shirt to get dressed and approached the desk to jot down some notes, while Isaak and Sara sat in front of him. He continued with the notes, getting up twice to consult one of the books resting on a bookcase behind him, and other times doing the same with notebooks and manuscripts extracted from drawers. This process took about fifteen minutes, which felt like an eternity for Isaak and Sara. Finally, he removed his glasses, looked at them intently, and said:

"In my opinion, my friend, what you're suffering from is a hiatal hernia."

Isaak looked at him with a bewildered expression.

"Could you explain it a bit better, doctor?"

"Of course."

He took a book and opened it to a page he had marked with a paper, turning it towards the couple. He proceeded to explain, pointing to a drawing that depicted a man with his chest and abdomen open, revealing the internal organs.

"This is the oesophagus, and here is the stomach. There's a muscle that separates the thoracic cavity from the abdomen, which you can see here," he said, indicating with his fountain pen. "This muscle, so to speak, has a cavity through which the oesophagus passes before joining the stomach. At that exact point, we have what we call the hiatus. It's like a valve that prevents food from refluxing from the stomach. In a hernia, there's an enlargement in that area, and part of the stomach tends to protrude through that opening into the thorax. That's what causes all the discomfort you're experiencing."

Isaak translated for Sara, then the doctor closed the book and continued.

"The acidity, reflux, burning sensation in the stomach, and even vomiting are all symptoms of this enlargement we call a hernia."

"Well, doctor, what would be the treatment then?"

"It varies depending on the severity of the hernia. In your case, I'm concerned that you've experienced vomiting with blood."

"Although it was only once."

"That's a good sign. However, I'm almost certain it will happen again, sooner rather than later."

"And what can be done, doctor?"

"The first thing is to follow an even stricter diet than you've been following so far. The second is to take the medications and special preparations that I'm going to prescribe for you. And the third is to attend regular check-up appointments so that we can monitor your condition and determine the best course of action in your particular case. In my opinion, it's very likely that more specific measures will be necessary."

"What do you mean, doctor?"

"An operation, I mean surgery."

"Oh God!" Sara exclaimed, understanding the meaning of the word due to its similarity to Russian.

"That would be the last resort, madam. First, we need to see how your husband responds to the treatments that he will be following."

Isaak acted as the translator, allowing Sara to gradually understand.

"And how long will this process take?" Isaak asked.

"It depends on your body's response. It could be a few days or several months."

"Several months?"

"Yes, we'll start today. Since I know you've come from Russian Poland, I'll provide you with the diet and medications for a five-day phase. Based on the results of this initial phase, we'll make decisions. For now, let's schedule a follow-up appointment for next week."

"Very well, doctor."

"You must strictly follow the diet and take the medications consistently."

"I will do so."

"In the meantime, remain calm, avoid getting worked up about anything, and try to rest. I don't mean you should stay in bed all day. On the contrary, take some leisurely walks. Vienna has lovely parks and avenues to explore."

"Note taken, doctor. I'll follow your instructions."

"Lastly, two things are completely prohibited: tobacco and alcohol."

"Don't worry, I don't smoke, and I drink very occasionally."

"Well, for now, not even a glass."

"Agreed."

"Very well, I'll see you next week."

"Thank you very much, have a good day."

Upon leaving the doctor's office, Tatiana and Aliza were nearly dozing off in the waiting room.

"Come on, girls," Sara said to them. "It seems like you're the ones who are ill, not your father."

They returned to the hotel and agreed to meet for lunch. Both took the opportunity to get some sleep until noon. They couldn't rejoice or worry about the consultation results yet, as there was still nothing definitive. What did excite Aliza was knowing they would stay in Vienna until the following week.

"I'll be to see him for a longer, Tatiushka, don't you think?"

"Yes, but we must be more cautious. If our parents find out, their anger would be terrible. Besides, the lack of sleep last night was already enough. I wouldn't be able to sustain such a pace."

"Don't worry, there probably won't be parties and gatherings every night, and Karl said he can be free in the afternoons, so we could go for a stroll instead. I'll leave him a note at the reception as we agreed."

"Keep in mind that we also have to support mother and father."

"Yes, of course, I'll be right back."

The following days were a whirlwind for Aliza and Tatiana. The former had her rendezvous with Karl, while the latter played the role of chaperone. Walks or simple conversations had to fit into the shared time with their parents. Although Aliza had assured that they wouldn't, they still met Karl in the hotel lounge every night. Isaak and Sara always retired early because, seemingly, the diet and medication worsened the situation rather than improving it. On one occasion, Sara went to their room to find them but couldn't locate them, so she worriedly descended to search for them.

Fortunately, luck was on the daughters' side. That night, coincidentally, the commanding general of the division to which Karl belonged was present and invited them to join him, his wife, and his sister-in-law at the table. They were seated on the terrace instead of the ballroom. When Sara saw them, Karl had got up to attend to a message from a messenger at the hotel's entrance, so she spotted her two daughters conversing on the terrace with a high-ranking military officer and two older ladies. Sara decided not to approach them. Tatiana excused herself for a moment and went to talk to her mother, explaining that they had gone downstairs to have a drink.

When they returned to their room that night, Tatiana reproached Aliza, saying, "We look like two mischievous teenagers. It's been enough; we shouldn't continue behaving like this. I am a married woman with a daughter, and you're already an adult. Tomorrow, no more late-night meetings. Tell your fiancé that we'll only go for an afternoon stroll."

"Agreed," Aliza replied, laughing. "I'll never forget what you've done for me here in Vienna. I adore you."

She leaned over and kissed Tatiana on the cheek.

Isaak was not feeling any improvement with the new diet. After completing the scheduled five days, he returned to the doctor, who examined him again, asked some additional questions, and scheduled another appointment for the following day.

"I wish to consult with some colleagues of mine, I'll be expecting you tomorrow."

"Thank you very much, Doctor. We'll be here punctually."

Upon arriving for the appointment, Doctor Frizmann was accompanied by two other physicians, whom he pointed out, emphasizing their expertise in their respective fields. Introducing the first one, he said, "This doctor has worked with none other than Skoda and

Rokitansky." Neither Isaak nor Sara had the faintest idea who the two mentioned figures were, but they remained silent.

Then, pointing to the second one, he said, "And here, my colleague was a student and devoted follower of Ignaz Semmelweis' theories. Undoubtedly, his results are astonishing, but the underlying importance of asepsis remains unexplained."

Isaak exclaimed, "Excuse me, Doctor, but I'm not a doctor or scientist. I am unfamiliar with the gentlemen you mentioned, and I haven't understood anything you've just said."

"I apologize to you. I simply want to assure you that you'll be in the best hands if you decide to accept the recommendation, I'm about to give you."

"Thank you very much, Doctor. Please, go ahead. I'm listening."

"Well, as I mentioned last week, your condition is due to a hernia located at the entrance of the stomach. It's not something that would lead to a fatal outcome, at least not for many years, but it does cause a great deal of discomfort, affecting your quality of life and daily well-being."

Isaak translated for Sara and then addressed the doctor, "Please, continue."

"We have a dilemma. On the one hand, it would be advisable to further modify your diet and continue with medication on a permanent basis."

"Doctor, if I keep modifying my diet, I'll end up eating less than a bird."

"I agree with you, and I assure you that as the years go by, it will need to be even stricter. Well, the second alternative is to undergo surgery."

Isaak remained silent, and Sara looked at him, awaiting the translation, but he held her back, raising his hand.

"Tell me, how risky is the operation?"

"The surgery itself is not complex, and although it carries certain risks, normally it shouldn't lead to any complications. However, the postoperative period does require special care due to the possibility of infection."

"So, the greatest danger comes after the surgery?"

"Exactly, due to the possibility of infection spreading."

Sara was growing increasingly impatient, sensing that they were discussing surgery. Isaak translated, and her face turned pale.

"Well," Isaak continued, "what would you recommend?"

"I believe the best solution is surgery to definitively address your ailments, but I am not the patient. The decision must be yours, weighing the discomfort and pain you experience against the possibility of overcoming it, albeit with some risk."

"I understand, the risk of infection and death."

"The word sounds harsh, but that's precisely it."

Meanwhile, the two colleagues nodded in agreement with Doctor Frizmann's assessments.

"Thank you, doctor. And if I decide to proceed with the operation, when could it be scheduled?"

"It would be best to do it as soon as possible since the hernia appears to be progressive, but it doesn't mean it's urgent. It will depend on your wishes and availability."

"Thank you very much. Allow me to discuss it with my family, and I would like an appointment this afternoon to communicate my decision."

"Alright, I'll be expecting you at four."

They bid a polite goodbye to the three doctors and headed back to the hotel, where they held a family meeting to weigh the situation. Sara couldn't hold back her tears, and the two daughters were equally emotional upon hearing the doctor's verdict. Aliza felt that all the joy she had experienced during those days crumbled at the prospect of her father undergoing surgery. They spent over an hour analysing the advantages and disadvantages, but it was an exercise in futility as Isaak had made up his mind even before leaving the doctor's office, and he made it known.

"Sara, girls, we won't postpone this any longer. I have decided to undergo the surgical procedure. I would rather take the risk than live the rest of my days in this torment every time I swallow food. I believe it's the best course of action."

None of the three women dared to say anything. They feared the dangers that surgery entailed. However, they could see in Isaak's eyes that he was truly convinced and wouldn't change his mind. They all stood up and embraced each other.

That afternoon, they returned and informed Doctor Frizmann of their decision. This time, all four of them entered the consultation room and listened as he expressed his agreement, followed by:

"I will be very clear with you. You must be fully aware of the positive and negative aspects of the surgery. Let me begin with the latter."

Isaak translated, and the four of them stared at the doctor without even blinking. He continued:

"Every surgery, no matter how minor, carries a risk. There may be bleeding, or the surgeon may encounter unforeseen problems while making incisions and opening the tissues. Most importantly, there is the possibility of infection in the hours or days following the surgical intervention."

After the translation, no one said anything, but anxiety and fear were evident on their faces.

"But there are also many positive aspects. In Vienna, medicine is highly advanced, perhaps more so than anywhere else in the world. Our doctors are among the most prestigious in Europe, and we have extensive experience in performing surgical operations. Trust me, you couldn't be in a better place. Furthermore, the operation will likely be carried out by two of the finest surgeons in the entire Empire, with excellent instruments at their disposal."

He took a deep breath and continued:

"The recovery from this type of surgery is usually very rapid. You will have to adhere to an even stricter diet than before, but as the incisions heal, you will be able to consume larger portions and tolerate different types of food. Isaak will receive the best care during the postoperative period and his convalescence. Lastly, the procedure will not be painful as we will use chloroform."

"Thank you very much for the information, doctor. I would like to know when the earliest possible date for the surgery is."

"Now that you have made your decision and have the necessary time, it could be scheduled for next week, perhaps on Wednesday."

"That sounds good to me. One final question, what will be the cost of the operation?"

"I will need to consider all the details, and I can provide you with that information tomorrow."

"Very well, doctor. Thank you very much, and let it be so."

They decided it was the best course of action to definitively resolve the situation. The operation would cost a substantial amount of florins, so the first measure they took was to change their accommodation. They couldn't continue staying in such an expensive hotel, so they moved to a more modest but comfortable and pleasant one, close to St. Stephen's Cathedral.

Meanwhile, Tatiana and Aliza returned to Lublin to inform the rest of the family and friends about the details of the medical visit to Vienna and the decision to undergo surgery. Another reason was to gather enough money to cover the expenses associated with the operation.

Isaak's surgery astonished relatives and acquaintances. Jana and Gabriel decided to travel to Vienna to accompany their father. As soon as Irenka found out, she joined the others to be close to Sara. Meanwhile, Tatiana and Jana took care of the financial matters regarding the cost of the operation and the stay in Vienna.

The entire family group travelled by the same route, carriage to Krakow and from there by train to Vienna. This time, it was Gabriel who was amazed by all those new things: the train, the station, the bustling city. Jana was also fascinated by the Austrian capital, which she found beautiful and vibrant, although she remembered the grandeur of St. Petersburg.

They gathered at the new hotel, and it brought great joy to Isaak to have all his children by his side during those moments. If it weren't for the medical circumstances, it would have felt like a family vacation in one of the most beautiful cities in the world. He greeted each one of them warmly, and Gabriel and the girls expressed their full support and love. He appeared strong, but deep inside, he felt some fear.

Aliza had the opportunity to see Karl again, but their meeting remained brief. She chose to be much more discreet, considering that these would be the most inauspicious days for her parents to find out about their encounters. Besides, all attention needed to be focused on the upcoming events related to her father's operation.

The day before the surgical intervention, the family went to a nearby synagogue to pray. It was a magical moment for everyone, but especially for Isaak. His close encounter with God and his private conversation with the rabbi brought him such tranquillity of spirit that he emerged calm, almost healed, as he told Sara.

"Now I know that everything will go well tomorrow," he said to his wife, taking her arm.

"I'm so glad to hear you speak like this. I feel more at ease too," she replied.

"You know that every time I enter the synagogue, my spirit calms down."

"Oh, my love! And you know that the synagogue is a piece of Israel, so every time you enter, you fulfil a portion of your dream."

He squeezed her hand and, with a spirit that they hadn't seen in him for many days. He addressed his children, "Come on, girls, Gabriel, let's head to Stephan Platz. They sell delicious peanut and chocolate ice creams there, and I'll treat you all."

Isaak hugged and kissed his wife, each of his children, and Irenka, the unwavering friend. Then he entered the operating room accompanied by a nurse, but not before reassuring them with utmost confidence, "Don't worry about me. I managed to return safe and sound from a place from which very few can come back. So, this time, I won't stay either. God doesn't abandon me, and He will allow me to fulfil my dream: next year in Jerusalem."

Almost immediately, Doctor Frizmann arrived, along with two colleagues and the assisting nurse. They were all dressed in white gowns, with matching caps covering their heads. Before heading to the operating room, they stopped to greet the family and tried to reassure them, seeing their anxious faces.

"Don't worry, Isaak is in the best hands," affirmed Frizmann in German. "By my side, I have the most skilled experts."

Aliza translated, and the doctor continued, "There is no better abdominal surgeon in all of Vienna than my colleague, Doctor

Streichmann, here present," he said, pointing to the doctor beside him. "And his most promising student is Doctor Weizz, a faithful disciple of Semmelweis's techniques."

Aliza didn't fully understand and asked what Semmelweis's techniques were. The doctor smiled and explained, "It's not the name of any procedure, but that of a colleague we worked with here in Vienna a few years ago. He implemented rigorous cleaning methods, which, although we don't fully agree with, we must acknowledge have yielded excellent results. Our dear Doctor Weizz is such a fanatic of those techniques that he makes us wash not only our hands but also all the surgical equipment and even soak the sheets in calcium hypochlorite."

Aliza still couldn't comprehend how certain cleaning methods were related to her father's surgery. And she became even more confused by the mention of calcium hypochlorite; she had never heard of such a substance. She didn't know what to translate until Doctor Weizz stepped in to help her.

"Miss, I know you're confused, but don't worry. Tell your family that the best surgeons will operate on your father, and we will use the most advanced techniques, including high levels of cleanliness to prevent complications and aid in the patient's recovery after the surgery."

The doctors entered the operating room, leaving the family, as is customary in such cases, worried. Sara exclaimed, "It's always easy to say, 'don't worry' when it's not a loved one being operated on."

Two agonizing hours passed, everyone silent and wearing stern expressions. Even Irenka, who usually couldn't go a minute without speaking, remained quiet, holding Sara's hand. The breathing of those present could be heard—the three sisters sitting in adjacent chairs, and Gabriel anxiously pacing back and forth.

Suddenly, the door leading to the operating room opened, and young Doctor Weizz appeared, accompanied by one of the nurses. Everyone's hearts skipped a beat as they looked at him expectantly, but he didn't need to say a word. His spontaneous and natural smile conveyed everything. Sara took a deep breath, and everyone released their tension by exhaling the held breath. At that moment, the doctor exclaimed, "Everything's perfect!"

"Wszystko idealne!" Aliza repeated in Polish.

The women couldn't hold back their tears. Sara and Irenka embraced, and the sisters stood up, hugging each other, overcome with emotion. Gabriel approached the doctor and extended his hand in gratitude, doing the same with the nurse. At that moment, Doctor Frizmann entered, his gown stained with blood, which struck them, but what he said next made them forget about that fact.

"Everything went very well. He is a strong man, and he will surely recover quickly."

"Thank you, doctor. You have no idea what your words mean to us," Aliza replied, speaking on behalf of everyone. She quickly translated what the doctor had said.

"The greatest thanks should go to my colleague," Frizmann said, pointing to Streichmann, who was entering at that moment. "He is an excellent surgeon."

"Thank you, thank you, doctor," Aliza repeated.

Her German was not very good, but it was understandable. Besides, in any language, the doctors would have perfectly understood the sentiment.

"Well," Frizmann said, "half of the process has gone very well. Now we have the other half, which is the recovery. We hope there won't be any complications."

"There won't be," Doctor Weizz interrupted. "You will see that no infectious processes will develop, thanks to Doctor Semmelweis's technique."

Frizmann smiled and addressed his colleague, "I knew and worked with Ignaz Semmelweis. I greatly appreciated him, and although I'm still not entirely convinced of his technique, I am sure he would be very flattered to know that he left behind the greatest follower of his theories in Vienna."

"You will see, Doctor. With time, it will be proven that he was right, and justice will be done."

Except for Aliza, no one in the room understood the conversation. The young girl leaned towards her mother and sisters, explaining, "They are talking about a special cleaning technique. From what I understand, thanks to it, our father will recover very well."

Aliza and Doctor Weizz were right, but above all, it was Doctor Ignaz Semmelweis who had the ultimate truth. History would indeed recognize the value of his contribution. The entire medical and scientific community, as well as the millions of human beings who have since then been saved thanks to the Hungarian doctor's breakthrough, would acknowledge it. This included Isaak, who, thanks to the perfect asepsis, did not develop any infectious processes. His recovery was quite rapid and without any complications. Naturally, he had to follow a strict diet for a few weeks, but just two days after the operation, his countenance and mood had significantly improved. The doctors visited him twice a day and left very satisfied.

On the fourth day, he was able to return to the hotel, where he would stay in bed but in a more pleasant environment surrounded by his loved ones, who were relieved to see his quick recovery. Those extraordinary days in Vienna were filled with celebration. Each morning, Isaak woke up with increasing enthusiasm. A week later, he started taking walks with his family through the streets and parks near the hotel. The weather was also favourable, spring blooming with flowers and fragrances while the sun shone brilliantly.

Everyone was happy and enjoying the events in the grand capital, including Sara and Isaak, who felt content with their regained health and the opportunity to spend time with their children in such a delightful atmosphere. Gabriel explored the city's monuments and admired the beautiful architecture, while his sisters strolled along the boulevards and the famous Maria Hilfer Strasse, marvelling at the fashionable clothes displayed in shop windows.

Gabriel accompanied his sisters on some occasions, causing more than one sigh among the young ladies they encountered. At nearly fifteen years old, he was close to reaching his father's height. His physique already indicated that he would be a robust and distinguished man. His hair, firm chin, and striking grey eyes captivated the attention not only of teenage girls but of women of all ages.

His sisters laughed and vied for his attention, taking hold of his arm, much to Gabriel's annoyance. They would trap him and pester him with the gesture they had made since he was a child—pinching his cheeks.

"Gabriel is going to be a Casanova," Jana teased. "We'll have to keep a close eye on him."

"Agreed. We can't let him go out alone," Tatiana mocked, pinching one of his cheeks and squeezing his chin, a gesture that deeply displeased the young lad, causing him to quickly turn his head.

Karl would join the group when the four of them went out without their parents. Aliza was immensely happy, especially because her two sisters and Gabriel got along well with the young lieutenant, soon to be a captain. However, her expression saddened when she thought about having to keep their relationship hidden from her mother and especially her father. One day, she decided that she could no longer postpone the situation. She felt disloyal to her mother and understood that she would eventually have to reveal the truth.

One night, she finally approached Sara, taking advantage of the fact that Isaak was peacefully asleep after a busy day. They had all gone to Prater, Vienna's most famous park, enjoying a beautiful spring day as they walked through the meadows along the Danube Canal and even danced on the esplanade, precisely to the popular waltz "The Blue Danube."

"Mother, I need to talk to you," Aliza said.

"Tell me, my child."

"It's something very personal, and you need to know."

"Of course, tell me."

"Mother, I'm deeply in love."

Sara stared at her for a moment and then said, "I know."

Aliza was surprised, not only by the response but also by the calmness with which it was delivered.

"You know?"

"Yes, my child, of course."

"But... how, why?"

Sara smiled gently, softly caressing Aliza's beautiful light brown hair, and said, "Because I am your mother."

"Oh, mother, I don't know what to say!"

"His name is Karl, isn't it?"

Sara recalled meeting Karl in Lublin, but Aliza didn't know how to continue the conversation.

"Yes, mother, he has been to Lublin several times."

"And when did you last see him? Yesterday?"

Aliza lowered her gaze. Could it be that her mother knew everything? Had Tatiana or Jana been indiscreet? She couldn't find the right words to confess everything to her mother.

"I don't know how to say it, but what I do know is that I must," Aliza finally said. "The thing is, I'm not sure where to start."

"Perhaps from the beginning, my child," Sara responded tenderly. "What you want to tell me is that you have seen him several times here in Vienna. Isn't that right?"

"Yes, that's right. But how did you know? Tatiana or Jana..."

Sara smiled and wisely emphasized, "Like I said, I am your mother. Your sisters haven't mentioned anything to me. They may be meddlers, but they aren't indiscreet."

"Oh, mother, forgive me."

"Aliza, besides being your mother, I am also a woman. Forgive you for being in love? There is nothing to forgive," Sara said.

"I have behaved with decorum," Aliza replied.

"I have no doubt about that," Sara assured her.

"But if no one has told you about Karl, how did you know?" Aliza asked.

"Intuition, my child. A mother's intuition is worth more. I suspected it from the moment you showed so much interest in coming to Vienna with us, and I confirmed it when Tatiana decided to join us. Then I was certain that you two would meet here, which led me to deduce that you've been exchanging letters for a long time."

Aliza was surprised. Her mother could have been a perfect detective.

"How could you reach that conclusion?"

"Simple deduction."

"Even regarding the fact that we write to each other?"

"Yes, of course. If you were going to meet here, you must have had a way to let him know you were coming to Vienna."

"Oh, mother, I'm sorry I didn't tell you earlier!"

"My dear daughter, you know that I love you with all my heart. I only want your happiness. It's a very complex situation. But tell me, do you feel that your love is reciprocated as it should be?"

"Yes, mother! I know he loves me; he shows it to me completely."

Aliza didn't dare confess that he had already proposed marriage. Sara took her hands and pulled her closer, embracing her.

"It's so complicated. You know that a relationship like this is not feasible, right?" Sara said, and Aliza nodded in agreement. Meanwhile, Sara regretted that out of the many Jewish young men in Europe, her daughter had fallen in love with a Catholic.

"We will talk about it in Lublin, my love. For now, let's continue enjoying these warm days in Vienna while your father fully recovers."

"Thank you, mother. I had to tell you because I felt I wasn't being honest with you."

Aliza felt a great weight lifted off her shoulders. She knew her mother didn't approve of her relationship, but at least she hadn't explicitly said so. With her last words, Aliza felt that her mother tacitly authorized her to continue seeing Karl since they were both in Vienna.

The two friends were savouring a chocolate, seated by the window of the Demel confectionery. Of course, they were accompanied by two slices of the famous Sacher torte. Sara wore a dainty hat, and her loose hair cascaded to one side. In contrast, Irenka had her hair up and played with a delicate and very feminine parasol she had bought that morning. The place was completely packed, and the buzz of conversations filled the air.

"I don't know what to do, Irenka. I swear I find myself at a crossroads," Sara confessed.

"I understand, dear. It's not an easy situation," Irenka sympathized.

"It's much more than a difficult situation. Adversities can be faced head-on, but this is entirely different. It's a terrible dilemma," Sara replied, her voice laden with concern.

"Yes, it's very complicated," Irenka acknowledged.

"It means choosing between the love for a daughter or the love for God, even more, it's about customs and one's inner self," Sara explained, her voice filled with anguish.

"Something must be done. It was wise to recommend Aliza to speak back in Lublin. For now, let them enjoy the remaining days here. Besides, the most important thing at the moment is that Isaak is improving day by day," Irenka suggested.

"You're right. The doctors are very pleased. They will see him again next Monday, and everything indicates that they will permit him to return home," Sara shared, a glimmer of hope in her voice.

"That's great news. Vienna is welcoming and enchanting. We have shared wonderful days here, but I suppose you can't leave the business to the assistants for too long," Irenka pointed out.

"Fortunately, both Saul and Robiak are overseeing things. But as you understand, they have their own occupations," Sara replied.

"Yes, and no matter how well-intentioned they are, they don't possess the art of bread-making or shoemaking," Irenka remarked.

Sara chuckled. "That's true, my dear friend. In any case, Tatiana and Gabriel travelled back yesterday. Gabriel can't afford to miss more classes, and Tatiana missed her little one too much."

"That's understandable. We will make the most of our remaining days in Vienna. For now, I'll finish my drink while I continue to amuse myself watching that gentleman in the blue waistcoat who spilled his chocolate because he got distracted staring at you," Irenka teased mischievously.

"Please, don't start!" Sara blushed.

20

"Mother, I am no longer a child, and due to my age, they even say I'll become an old maid, which I don't mind. Gossip holds no sway over me. But I must warn you, I would rather remain unmarried than marry a man I do not love."

"My daughter, you must understand that love between men and women can change at any moment but love of God is unmovable."

"Mother, I have never stopped, nor will I ever stop loving God, but I will not cease to love Karl either."

"It is not just about God, it is about your essence, your traditions, your being. You are Jewish!"

"I am, mother, and I am proud of it. But my love for Karl surpasses even my own essence."

"For God's sake, do not say such things! It is blasphemy, it is unacceptable."

"But that's how it is, mother."

"Well, it cannot be like that, daughter. You know your father would never allow you to marry a man who is not Jewish. Look at Robiak's case, how long did it take for him to finally accept him as Jewish?"

"But mother..."

"Is Karl willing to convert to Judaism?"

"He cannot do that; he is an officer of the Austrian emperor."

"Then it is pointless to continue thinking about that relationship."

"Understand me, my love for my fiancé is above all else."

"Do not call him your fiancé; I forbid you to use that term!"

"But he is, despite everything."

"Do you not understand that it would break your father's heart? What his illness did not do, you would."

"Please, mother, do not say that. You know how much I love my father."

"If that is the case, you will not contradict him."

"But..."

"That's enough, let us speak no more of this matter. You must forget about it, period."

Aliza stood up, crying, and went to her room.

The events surrounding Aliza's relationship with the Austrian captain became overwhelming, and it was impossible to keep them hidden from Isaak any longer. By autumn, Karl travelled to Lublin with the intention of informing his mother that he had made the decision to marry Aliza. The lady nearly fainted.

"Have you gone mad?"

"No, mother, I have been in love with Aliza for several years."

"But she's a Jew!"

"What does that matter? She is the finest woman in the world."

"What do you mean, 'what does that matter'? I already told you, she belongs to that group."

"I know you don't like Jews, and I'm sorry, but personally, I have nothing against them. But that's not the point. I love Aliza, and I don't care if she's Jewish, Protestant, or Muslim."

"You are blaspheming! You are a Catholic! And not only that, you are an officer of the Austrian Empire."

"I am Catholic, I am an army officer, and I am a man in love with an exceptional woman."

"I repeat, you don't know what you're saying. Your father must be turning in his grave."

For a moment, Karl directed his gaze towards a large painting at the back of the hall. The figure of a stern-faced military man shone, wearing the white coat of the imperial army, adorned with golden epaulettes and general's insignia. The military tradition spanned several generations, and the officer in the portrait, Karl's grandfather, had also risen to the highest rank, distinguishing himself at the head of the imperial troops in Marengo, Austerlitz, Leipzig, and Waterloo. Karl continued to look at the painting for a brief moment, then turned to his mother.

"I apologize, but I believe my father would be turning in his grave for more significant matters, like our defeat in Sadowa a few years ago."

"More significant than the fact that his son, an officer like him, wants to marry a common Jew?"

"I beg you, mother, not to speak of my fiancée in such a way. She is a true lady."

"You seem to not understand. She's Jewish, and no matter how much you desire it, that marriage cannot happen."

"Well, we will do something about it because she will be my wife."

"Son, it's not just that. Have you thought about your career? Do you think the imperial Army will accept one of its officers marrying a Jew?"

"Of course, I have thought about it, mother. And Aliza has too. There is a solution; she can convert to Catholicism."

"More madness! She will still be Jewish!" She emphasized the word contemptuously, which greatly irritated Karl.

"I beg you not to treat her with such disdain. She will be your daughter-in-law."

"That will be the death of me!"

"It won't be like that. When you meet her, you will see that she is a remarkable woman."

"I never want to see her!"

"Mother, you will change your mind. I will not argue with you anymore. You know it, and it's a decision made. Tomorrow, I will go to speak with her parents."

The next day, when Sara arrived at the bakery, Karl's mother and aunt were already waiting for her. Immediately, the former spoke to Sara with great rudeness.

"You must know, madam!" she exclaimed, raising her voice in front of the employees without even greeting her, "that my son will never marry a Jew."

"Please, madam, I request that you calm down. We can go and talk in the back room."

"I have nothing to discuss with you, especially not in the back room of Jews. I only came to warn you that I will not allow my son to commit such stupidity. A Jew will never be part of my family."

"For the second time, I ask you to calm down. We can handle this in a civilized way."

"Nothing civilized can be discussed with a Jew."

"As you wish, but I ask you to respect me, especially in my own establishment and in front of my employees. Your words are offensive."

"How dare you?"

"As far as I understand, good Catholics do not go around insulting others for not being like them. And you have offended my daughter."

"She's just an opportunist who wants to ensnare my son. That insignificant Jew only seeks to climb the social ladder, but she will not succeed. I will prevent it even if I have to go to Vienna to speak with the emperor personally."

Sara could no longer bear the insults.

"Leave, madam, go speak to whoever you please. And if you insult my daughter again, you will get what you deserve!"

"Are you threatening me? Don't think you intimidate me. I repeat, my son will never marry a Jewish bitch."

Sara took a step towards the lady and delivered such a slap that, despite her excess weight, she stumbled and nearly fell to the ground. The sister rushed to her aid, gripping her shoulders.

"Get out of here!" Sara shouted, approaching her again. The sister dragged her towards the exit. The lady, touching her stinging cheek, retorted:

"Well, tell your daughter that converting to Catholicism will be of no use, and she still won't marry my son, you cursed Jews! Why don't you all leave our city?"

With that, still assisted by her sister, she hurriedly left the establishment, fearing another attack from Sara. It was unnecessary; Sara remained completely still upon hearing the lady's final words. She whispered to herself in a low voice:

"Aliza converting to Catholicism? Oh my God, it can't be."

She had to steady herself against the counter as she felt faint. One of the employees came to her aid, bringing a chair.

"Mrs. Sara, please have a seat. I'll fetch you a glass of water."

Sara sank into the chair and stared at the floor. The employee offered her the water, and Sara took a sip, trying to regain her composure. She took a deep breath, stood up, and without saying a word, left the bakery.

The girl wanted to accompany her, but Sara stopped her with a gesture, indicating that she preferred to go alone.

"I'm heading to the chocolate shop. Thank you."

She arrived at the shop, where Aliza was deeply shaken as Karl had left just a minute before. He had told her about the argument with his mother and his firm intention to speak with Isaak and Sara that evening. Before leaving, he asked her:

"Would you be willing to convert to Catholicism to marry me?"

Aliza took short, uneven breaths for a few seconds, then replied:

"I would do whatever it takes to never be separated from you."

Karl turned back, took her in his arms, and tenderly kissed her.

Sara had a heated argument with her daughter. When Aliza confirmed that she was willing to convert to Catholicism in order to not lose the man she loved, Sara replied that there was no power on Earth that would allow her to accept that. Aliza started crying and ran out of the establishment. Sara was bewildered, unsure of which path to take, so she decided to see her friend. Irenka welcomed her and became concerned upon seeing her in such a distraught state. She invited Sara to the terrace, offered her tea, and listened to her friend's troubles. When she finished recounting the events, Irenka said:

"First and foremost, I'm glad you gave that arrogant woman what she deserved, someone who has always felt superior in this city just because she was married to an Austrian general."

"Oh please, that's beside the point!"

"Let's take it step by step. You slapped her because she insulted your daughter, didn't you?"

"Of course."

"Alright, because honour, happiness, and the feelings of Aliza come first."

"Don't try to confuse me. In any case, she insulted her, and I wasn't going to allow it. It wasn't about her feelings."

"Of course not, it was about yours."

"What are you saying? You're trying to confuse me."

"I'm saying it was about your feelings because you couldn't bear to see such words spoken about a woman you deeply love, isn't that right?"

"Well, of course I love her! She's my daughter."

"Naturally, and you want her happiness."

"I know where you're going with this. Do you think you can convince me with that?"

"I don't have to convince you of anything. Remember when I told you that Aliza listens to her heart?"

"I remember, and I know that already, but this is much more serious than following one's heart. Don't you understand? Do you think I could bear to see her convert to Catholicism?"

"Yes."

"What are you saying?"

"It may sound absurd, but above religion, customs, ways of life, and everything else, there are loved ones."

Sara hesitated, trying to connect her thoughts but resisting it; it was something beyond her understanding. Irenka continued:

"Remember when you told me about the day you met Isaak?"

"Yes, of course. What does that have to do with anything?"

"It has a lot to do with it."

"Why?"

"Because I remember you telling me how deeply affected you were just by seeing him, that you were certain that from that moment on, you fell in love. Do you remember?"

Sara softened her expression for a moment and replied, "How could I forget?"

"You told me he was a dream of a man, that you realized you never wanted to be apart from him, that you felt the desire to be protected by him. I assume you still feel the same way."

"Of course, I do."

"In that case, I'm going to ask you a question. If when you met him, he hadn't been Jewish but Catholic, would that have changed your impression or feelings?"

"You're exaggerating and making absurd assumptions."

"Just answer me."

"Logically, I wouldn't have married him."

"Are you sure?"

"I'm telling you again, you're talking about unreal events, just hypotheses."

"You're avoiding the answer, so I'll rephrase the question. It's still based on assumptions but answer me honestly. You lost Isaak, and by some miracle that rarely happens in life, you got him back, but obviously, you didn't know it would turn out that way. Do you understand?"

"Mmm, I think so, go on. And let's discuss how I'm going to face this situation better."

"Alright, here's the question. If, when you didn't know he would return, someone had told you that if you converted to Catholicism, you would see him again, what would you have answered?"

"You're complicating things with so many conjectures."

"Answer honestly."

"I haven't fully understood."

"Yes, you understood. Don't pretend with me, I know how intelligent you are."

It's just that you're using hypothetical situations, conditional phrases."

"Do you see? You are intelligent indeed. You know how to find a way to evade answers."

"Isaak has nothing to do with this."

"Allow me to contradict you. Yes, he has a lot to do with it. The characters don't matter here because the true protagonist is love. I'll ask you one more direct question, and this time, you won't evade the answer. If you were to come home now and Isaak told you that he had decided to convert to Catholicism, would you turn around and abandon him forever?"

Sara fell silent, seeming absent, as if she hadn't fully absorbed what she had just heard. Her eyes moistened, and she stood up, embracing her friend in silence. Irenka's gaze shimmered with a triumphant gleam. There was nothing more to add, except for one word: "Find her!"

Sara kissed Irenka on the cheek and hurriedly left. When she arrived at the chocolate shop, she didn't find her daughter there. The shop assistant informed her that Aliza usually went to the pond in the park. Aliza enjoyed sitting on a bench and feeding the ducks.

Sara ran towards that place, every step feeling endless. She arrived at the park and frantically searched the benches. She saw her daughter sitting on one of them. For some strange reason, the moment when Isaak entered the house in Bialystok with two desperate girls abandoned by fate flashed in her mind. She hurried towards the bench.

Aliza hadn't noticed her presence. During those last steps, another memory came to her mind—the sight of two girls running into her arms in front of Tobias' house. When she reached her daughter, Aliza was already crying profusely.

Aliza turned abruptly and could only say, "Mother!" She stood up at the exact moment Sara embraced her with such strength that it almost took her breath away.

"My darling girl, my beloved daughter! I love you so much," she said, tears streaming down her cheeks.

"Mama, Mama, I love you too!" Aliza replied, also crying.

"My daughter, my daughter!" Sara repeated, holding her tightly.

Finally, she let go and took Aliza's face in her hands, stroking her hair and saying, "If Karl is the man you love, if he will make you happy, you have my blessing. You will marry him."

"Oh, Mother!" Aliza began to cry as well. "Oh, Mother, thank you, I adore you."

And now, it was Aliza who tightly embraced Sara. When they managed to calm their emotions, they sat down on the bench, and her mother advised her, "Now find a way to communicate with Karl. You must warn him not to come to our house tonight. I will handle the matter with your father, but I need to find the best way and the right moment."

"Yes, mother, and thank you again. You've made me so happy."

"My darling, your happiness is the most important thing to me."

They got up and headed towards the chocolate shop, while Sara thought, "Oh, how much I owe to Irenka. Thank you, my God, for giving me such an exceptional confidante."

For Aliza, the sun in Lublin had never shone so brightly, nor had the streets looked so radiant. It seemed to her that everyone she passed was the kindest person in the world, and she wanted to stop them and share her happiness with them. She arrived at the café and immediately wrote a note to Karl. She sent the shop assistant with strict instructions that it could only be delivered to him personally. The message consisted of just two simple lines: "Mother approves of our marriage and my conversion. Don't come to my house for now. I love you, Aliza."

When Karl read the note, he was filled with joy. He was aware that for Aliza, renouncing her faith to marry him was a great sacrifice. This fact alone made him fall even more in love and convinced him that his future wife was an incomparable woman.

Sara didn't want to postpone the matter, and although she preferred not to speak with Isaak that same night, she did so the next morning, very early. It was a devastating blow for him. He couldn't fathom that his daughter was willing to abandon Judaism. It was not only an affront to his beliefs but to his essence and, in fact, to himself. There was no argument; he simply stated that he would never consent to such foolishness, and Aliza would have to forget about that inconceivable whim. He immediately went to the synagogue to speak with the rabbi and seek his advice on avoiding such a grave offense.

From her room, Aliza heard her father's shouts and didn't dare to come out. When he left the house, she went to meet her mother. Sara took her hands and reassured her.

"Do you know what Irenka told me when I insisted that I couldn't bear for you to convert to Catholicism?"

"What, mother?"

"She simply said, 'Yes, you will.' And she was absolutely right because above all else, love is paramount. I've already accepted it because I love you with all my heart. Your father adores you, so he will eventually approve as well, and love will ultimately prevail."

"Thank you, mother."

"We just need to be patient. I will continue insisting, and you will prepare for your wedding."

Aliza smiled as she looked at Sara, reflecting all the devotion she felt for her. She hugged her and said, "You're the best mother in the world. I'm going to work, but before that, I'll go see Irenka because I want to thank her."

"You're doing the right thing, my darling. Give my regards to her and tell her I'll visit her this afternoon."

Aliza's decision deeply affected the family dynamic. Isaak vehemently refused to accept his daughter's conversion and stopped speaking to her. There were no violent arguments or altercations, but the harmony and family unity were disturbed. Tatiana and Jana deeply regretted the path their younger sister had chosen but supported her unconditionally. Both Saúl and Robiak, their two brothers-in-law, firmly shared Isaak's position, considering it a true outrage that their sister-in-law would abandon the Jewish community. Gabriel, perhaps, was the most neutral. He disagreed with his sister's decision, but he never criticized or reproached her.

Obviously, the most affected were Sara and Aliza themselves. The former was caught in a rather uncomfortable situation. As a good Jewish wife, she was obliged to support her husband, especially in such a delicate matter. She also bore the burden of knowing that in Jewish culture, the stability and well-being of the home rest on the woman, so she considered herself responsible for the prevailing emotional imbalance. Isaak never blamed her for anything, but she knew perfectly well that he must have thought more than once that she had failed. Aliza felt suffocated in such an environment, facing the worst possible dilemma, where family unity, love for Karl, and her religion became a tense and overwhelming cocktail for the young woman. Under that pressure, she chose to leave her parents' house. Both Tatiana and Jana offered her to live with them, but Aliza preferred to stay at Irenka's house, who had also invited her. She had a great affection for Irenka, and besides, she didn't want to disturb the family dynamics of either of her sisters, especially when she knew that both her brothers-in-law completely disapproved of her decision. Irenka was happy because she not only had a special affection for Aliza but also, due to not having children herself and Carl's constant travels, she sometimes felt very lonely.

The Kobielsky house was very pleasant and cozy, and it held a special significance for the Rothmans. After all, Sara, Gabriel, and Tatiana had lived there in the past. It was also the place where Tatiana had got married. Not to mention that Irenka was, by far, Sara's best friend and someone who had greatly influenced her life, offering a helping hand on several occasions. Aliza found some solace in the days she spent in that house. It couldn't be said that she was happy, as Isaak's attitude broke her heart, not to mention the pain she felt knowing that her mother suffered greatly because of her.

However, if the atmosphere was already noticeably tense for the girl, it worsened when the situation extended beyond the family circle. Karl's mother spread rumours in the town that discredited Aliza. She claimed that Aliza was not her son's fiancée but his lover. She also insinuated that during her time in Vienna, Aliza led a licentious life, engaging in various romances. These slanderous accusations hurt both Sara and Aliza deeply.

Enraged by these insults, Isaak reported Karl's mother to the authorities for defaming his daughter's honour. Naturally, he was deeply resentful of Aliza's decision, but that didn't mean he didn't love her deeply or remain indifferent when she was insulted. Unfortunately, the lawsuit did not prosper, and there was no retraction from the woman. After all, it was a dispute between a Jew and one of the prominent ladies of the city.

However, Irenka took matters into her own hands with better results. She intercepted the woman on the street and reproached her in front of several passersby for spreading falsehoods. She then threatened her, warning that if she continued with her malicious practices, she would personally inform the people of Lublin about the woman's escapades and nocturnal adventures when she lived in Vienna while her husband was stationed elsewhere in the Empire.

"Oh my, Irenka!" exclaimed Aliza that night when she heard about the incident. "Did you really know about the woman's escapades in Vienna? How did you find out?"

"I didn't know anything, I simply gave her a taste of her own medicine," Irenka replied.

"I can't believe you had the audacity to do that! You're quite bold. In any case, thank you."

However, the disturbing situation for Aliza in the city was not solely the result of her future mother-in-law's gossip; the Jewish community also rejected her. It was inconceivable to maintain any kind of contact with a Jewish woman who had voluntarily renounced her religion. The chocolate shop was the first to suffer, as it began to be boycotted by Jewish customers, who comprised the majority. The business started incurring losses to the point where it couldn't generate enough income to pay the rent and the employees. Faced with this possibility, Aliza understood that she couldn't harm the family business, so she decided to speak with her mother and resigned from managing the establishment, temporarily leaving it in Tatiana's hands.

As a result, life became increasingly untenable for the young woman in the city. In addition to that, the conversion to Catholicism was impossible in Lublin. Aliza's case was widely known, and it was no secret that she was doing it not out of conviction but to marry Karl. No Catholic authority would facilitate the process in Lublin, and most likely not in other cities in Poland either. The girl suggested going to Vienna to expedite the process, but Sara vehemently opposed it. She didn't want her daughter to be alone in that city, precisely where her fiancé lived, as it would give rise to rumours worse than those spread by Karl's mother.

The solution came unexpectedly but very opportunely, and from someone who had once rescued Aliza. Jared and Anya arrived in Lublin around that time, accompanied by Oizer, Rachel, and their two young grandchildren. They were in route to Berlin, to the home of one of the German partners in their lumber business, who had invited them to spend some time there. As usual, their stop in the city was to greet the Rothmans, and where they learned of the situation. Anya comforted Sara, reiterating what Irenka had told her: the most important thing was their daughter's happiness. Jared seemed to be much more liberal than Isaak, perhaps that's why he had changed his surname from Czemerinsky to Weizmann without any hesitation. He simply told his friend that it was sad that Aliza had decided to convert, but it wasn't the end of the world. Isaak glared at him, and Jared fell silent, quickly changing the subject.

Oizer loved the Rothman girls as if they were his own sisters, but he had always felt a special affection for the youngest. Therefore, despite not sharing her decision, he fully supported her, just like Rachel did. The couple already had two beautiful children and were living in the house they had built in Motal, while Jared, Anya, and the twins remained in Pinsk. Oizer and his wife visited Aliza at Irenka's house and engaged in lively conversation.

"And how are the twins?" Aliza asked.

"They're doing well, sister. They're in St. Petersburg, enjoying some time at my uncle's house," Oizer replied.

"That's great. Do you remember when we were there?"

"Of course. You and Jana wanted to go for walks every day, but the housekeeper Dad had in the apartment wouldn't let you out." He turned to Rachel and continued, "Imagine, my love, they asked the housekeeper to leave a door unlocked that led to the stables, and those two mischievous girls would escape from her and wander around the parks and avenues of the city."

"Yes, we were quite restless," Aliza laughed. "I remember that whenever Father Jared, came back, she would complain to him, but to her frustration, he would reply, 'Birds shouldn't be kept in cages.'"

"That's right. Then my father would tell me, 'Tomorrow, don't come with me. Take the girls out for a walk instead.' And I preferred that because it saved me from my father's tedious meetings and errands. Instead, the three of us would go out, have fun, and buy pastries."

"It was beautiful," Aliza said. "A balm for us, who were left behind without knowing where our parents were."

During that conversation, when Aliza mentioned her uncomfortable situation in Lublin and the impossibility of finding a suitable place for her conversion, Oizer came up with a solution.

"I just thought of something. It's evident that you can't proceed with the process in Poland, and even less so in Russia. Not only would it be difficult for you to settle outside the settlement zone, but you wouldn't easily find any Catholic authority. On the other hand, your mother won't allow you to go to Austria. Do you know what the ideal place could be?"

"No, what?"

"Well, Prussia, or rather, Germany nowadays."

"Germany?"

"Yes, sister. The country is predominantly Protestant, but it has a significant number of Catholics, especially in Prussian Poland."

"Well, but I don't know anyone in Prussia, I mean, Germany."

"We can talk to father. The house where we'll be spending some time belongs to a longtime business partner. They're like brothers, and they get along very well, just like their wives. I assure you, if he asks them to accommodate you for a while, they'll be delighted to do so. Don't forget that you're like a daughter to my parents."

The last thing Aliza would have thought of to untangle her situation was Germany, yet the idea didn't seem absurd to her. Oizer told her that the Prussian couple were excellent people and lived in a mansion with several rooms, although they lived alone. They had five children, but some had passed away, and others had become independent, so they would surely agree to receive her.

"It's a fantastic idea," Aliza said. "And where do they live?"

"In Berlin, Mr. and Mrs. Adler, Helmuth and Ingrid."

OOO

Aunt Ruth and her husband went to bid farewell to her at Warsaw's central station. While her aunt found it deplorable that her niece had made such a decision, and she understood that her brother disapproved of it to the point of not wanting to speak to his daughter again until she reconsidered. However, she could tell that Aliza's trip to Berlin was precisely proof that she had changed very little, if at all. As for Aliza, she didn't feel particularly thrilled about separating from the family and embarking on a German adventure with a completely unfamiliar older couple.

At least the Weizmann were still staying at the Adlers' house, so she wouldn't feel too isolated upon arrival. On the other hand, although she naturally missed her parents and siblings, leaving Lublin was a relief for her. She could barely set foot on the street there without feeling scrutinized by passersby and hearing murmurs as she walked by. Undoubtedly, she was madly in love with Karl, but her future mother-in-law was a true harpy.

Oizer and Rachel were waiting for her at Berlin's central station, and it was a relief to see familiar faces in this new and strange city. The reception was warm, as expected, and they took a carriage to the Adler's house. It was in a sector near the Tiergarten, a grand residence surrounded by gardens. Upon their arrival, Oizer's parents welcomed them.

"Hello, my dear Aliza. It's wonderful to see you again," Anya said, embracing her warmly.

"Hello, Anya. I'm so glad you're here," Aliza greeted with a smile.

Jared also approached and kissed her on the cheek.

"Hello, Aliza. How are you?" he asked.

"I'm fine, Jared. And how are you both?"

"Well, enjoying the hospitality of our hosts. Come, let us introduce them to you."

They entered a brightly lit and lavishly decorated grand hall, where Helmuth and Ingrid were having coffee. Both of them were slightly older than Jared and Anya, and they seemed more serious, or at least that was the impression Aliza had. They greeted her cordially but without much warmth, making her even more grateful that the Weizmann were still there.

Her first days in Berlin were pleasant. Autumn was nearing its end, but the temperatures hadn't dropped too much, allowing her to explore the most important and appealing places in the city. Sometimes she went with Oizer and Rachel, while other times she was accompanied by the entire Weizmann and Adler families.

The city seemed as big and bustling as Vienna, but in her perception, the Austrian capital was livelier, more festive, and more carefree. And it wasn't just because of her connection with Karl; she simply felt that Viennese people enjoyed life, while Berliners worked for their lives.

Nevertheless, she liked Berlin. It would never compare to Vienna, but it had its charm with its imposing architecture, good cafes, and beautiful parks. Gradually, Aliza bonded with the Adlers, especially with Ingrid, who was a woman of few words but showed a sweet and generous heart. Helmuth, on the other hand, was stern and serious, but a very kind man who always treated Aliza with sympathy and consideration. His towering height, broad shoulders, prominent paunch, and his thick beard was almost completely white made him stand out. He rarely spoke, and the few times he exchanged a few words with the girl, she never saw him laugh.

He was concentrated on his business and dedicated hours on end to work in his study, where he demanded not to be disturbed, not even by Ingrid. Every Wednesday and Friday, at regular times, a group of friends would visit him, and they would spend the entire afternoon in the gaming room, discussing politics while consuming litres of coffee and smoking so excessively that the room seemed full of fog. On these occasions, his voice could be heard above the voices of his friends. It seemed that he spoke more in those gatherings than throughout the rest of the week.

Ingrid was modest and unassuming, and she spoke a little more than her husband, allowing Aliza to engage in occasional conversations with her. In comparison to her husband's towering stature, she appeared petite. She was a bit overweight and not conventionally beautiful, yet she exuded a certain charm with her sweet smile and had expressive blue eyes. It was through Ingrid that Aliza learned the story of the Adlers, for if it had been solely up to Helmuth, she could have lived in that house for a year without knowing anything more than their surname.

When the Weizmann left, Aliza felt a bit abandoned, not only because she considered them part of her family but also because the house felt empty. The positive aspect was that by that time, she had already established contact with the priest of a parish in the Polish community, who held Jared in high regard since he had once donated wood to build part of the church and the rectory. Aliza attended the church twice a week, embarking on her conversion to Catholicism.

With the Weizmann departure, Ingrid sought more of Aliza's company, and it became customary for them to share afternoon coffee while conversing about many things, including the stories of their respective lives. The Adlers had six children, but two of them passed away at a young age. Among the surviving children, one lived in London, where he worked as a lawyer and was married to an Irish woman.

The next son had emigrated to the United States, becoming a prosperous textile merchant in Philadelphia. He visited his parents every two years with his wife and children. Their daughter had tragically passed away four years ago in an absurd accident when the car she was traveling in veered off the road.

Finally, the youngest son, who had pursued a military career and achieved the rank of lieutenant, met a tragic end in Sadowa. The saddest part of the episode was that the battle had already been decided, favouring the Prussians. The Austrian regiments had surrendered and laid down their weapons. However, a soldier who was unaware of this fact suddenly emerged from behind a house and, upon seeing the blue uniforms of the Prussian cuirassiers, fired without even aiming. The bullet hit the young Lieutenant Adler in the abdomen. His comrades tried to assist him, but they couldn't save him. He died the following day in excruciating pain.

"Since the day we learned of his death, Helmuth stopped smiling," Ingrid confessed to Aliza, her eyes welling up with tears as she recalled her youngest son.

"Oh, I'm so sorry for you both," the girl replied, unable to erase from her mind the image of Karl, also a military man, in the army to which the soldier who killed the Adler's son belonged.

"Not a day goes by without me thinking of him and Maria, our only daughter."

Aliza didn't know how to console her, but she understood the reason why the couple was so quiet and withdrawn.

The days in Berlin began to feel endless, especially as winter approached, even though the approach of Christmas brought some cheer to the atmosphere. At the parish she attended, preparations for this important Christian festival were underway. These events were new to Aliza, but not so unfamiliar anymore due to the lessons she received from the priest for her conversion.

"The 25th of December is very significant in the Catholic faith," the priest explained. "We celebrate the birth of Jesus, that is, his arrival in the world."

Aliza understood that there weren't many differences between Judaism and Christianity. It reminded her of the famous note by Maretska that her mother cherished as a relic, stating that they were sibling religions. In fact, she realized that the Old Testament was practically the Torah, and they shared the same foundation, in addition to being monotheistic religions.

However, there was something in Aliza's mind and heart that remained confusing, and it had to do precisely with Jesus, not so much because he was considered the Messiah, a dogma that Judaism did not accept, but because of something she couldn't comprehend. How was it possible for Jesus, being a man, to be considered God by Christians?

"That cannot be," she analysed. "God is a supreme being. No man can become God."

This topic bewildered her. To her, the divinity of the Virgin Mary would be more feasible than the previous notion. Every night, she pondered on it, and the tribulations of her mind only confused her further. The internal struggle was constant, causing insomnia and loss of appetite. She went to the parish and listened to the priest, participated in the preparations for Christmas, and even joined others in prayer. She sought to consider herself a Catholic in those moments, but as soon as she began her return to the Adler household, she felt Jewish again, which caused her great unease.

The year came to an end, and Aliza couldn't fully settle in Berlin. It was true that Ingrid had grown closer to her in the past few weeks, as Helmuth was away on a business trip to Strasbourg and Paris. Although their conversations were not lengthy, they served as a mutual distraction. Helmuth's absence allowed her to be somewhat more at ease because, even though he spoke very little, his presence in the house made her somewhat apprehensive, perhaps due to his reserved nature, but even more so because of the aura of melancholy he always carried with him, which Aliza found contagious.

The conversion process continued slowly, perhaps because the priest sensed that the young girl was not entirely sincere in her intention to embrace Catholicism. During the celebration of Hanukkah, her soul was more disturbed than usual, even though she miscalculated the dates, forgetting the difference in days between Germany and Russian Poland, where the Julian calendar still prevailed.

In late January, she received the pleasant and unexpected visit of her mother, who arrived accompanied by Jared and Anya. It was a great joy because, despite her age, Aliza remained, in many ways, an adolescent. She was reading passages from the Bible in her second-floor room when she heard the doorbell and greetings in the foyer. She listened, and at that moment, her heart skipped a beat as she recognized her mother's voice. She hurriedly descended the stairs, and there was Sara, wearing a beautiful ochre coat and a hat of the same colour, looking incredibly beautiful.

"Mother," she exclaimed, running towards her.

"My child," Sara replied with the sweet voice that always characterized her.

They embraced each other.

"You've been greatly missed, my little one." "And I've missed you too, mother. You can't imagine how much."

Then she greeted Jared and Anya. Ingrid invited them to come into the living room, coffee was served coffee and they sat down to talk. Aliza took Sara's hands, looking at her with tenderness and love.

"We're glad to see you again," Ingrid said. "Helmuth will be down in a few minutes. He returned from his trip to France with a slight cold, but nothing serious, fortunately."

"He'll have to give up smoking for a while," Jared commented.

"I wish he'd quit for good," Ingrid replied. Then she continued, "And how long will you be staying? I hope it's a prolonged visit."

"Unfortunately, not, my dear Ingrid," Jared responded. "We've come exclusively for an important meeting, looking to diversify the business. Our idea is to join with a French Company that works with architectural wood."

"Oh, I see," Ingrid said with an expression that indicated it wasn't a particularly interesting topic for her.

"I brought Anya so that she wouldn't be alone in Pinsk because Oizer is in Motal, and the boys are studying in St. Petersburg."

At that moment, Aliza interrupted.

"I'd like to ask you a favour to allow me to take my mother away for a few minutes."

"Of course, Aliza. Please, you haven't seen her for several weeks."

"Thank you very much. Excuse us," the young girl said, pulling her mother towards her room.

Once on the upper floor, they entered Aliza's bedroom. Aliza made Sara sit in a chair while she took a seat beside her.

"Mother, you have no idea how happy my heart is to have you here," she expressed with emotion. "But tell me, how are things in Lublin?"

"Overall, things are going well. Everyone sends their greetings to you."

"Thank you. And what else?"

"We miss you a lot in Lublin."

"I miss all of you too, but well, what else has been happening at home?"

"Gabriel is doing well in school. He mentioned that he wants to pursue higher education in economics or commerce."

"He'll excel in whatever he chooses. He's so intelligent. And what else?"

"No, my dear, business as usual."

"Mother!"

"Tell me, my child."

"Don't evade, you understand what I'm asking you!"

"Oh, my dear! He misses you greatly and isn't happy about your departure, but he keeps it to himself. You know he's very proud, and his spiritual principles are very firm."

"But does he ever talk about me?"

"Never. However, he always thinks of you, even if he doesn't admit it. I know him. He loves you with all his soul, but he's resisting."

"Oh, it hurts so much!"

"It hurts me too, my dear."

"Mother, there's something I want to tell you."

"Tell me."

"I'm well advanced in the conversion process. The priest has been very cautious with me, but he has already confirmed that I will be baptized before spring."

Sara's gaze darkened.

"Well, it's what you wanted."

"It's not what I wanted, Mother. You know it's been the circumstances. I couldn't bear to lose the man I love."

"Yes, I understand."

"However, there's something else I want to tell you. I'm telling you because you're my mother. There's no one else in the world to whom I would confess this secret."

"What is it?" She looked at her with concern.

"I'm ready to undergo the conversion, and I'll do it because I know that by doing so, I'll be able to marry Karl. But..."

"But what?"

"It doesn't fulfil my spirit, Mother!" She paused, took a deep breath, and continued. "I feel Jewish. I am Jewish, and I always will be."

Sara held her breath as Aliza waited for some reaction. She said nothing, leaned towards her daughter, opened her arms, and pulled her close, embracing her tightly. Finally, the emotion allowed her to speak.

"My dear daughter, you have no idea how much joy it brings me to hear that confession!"

"That's how it is, Mother. I had to tell someone. I was desperate to do so, and you arrived just in time."

"My heart is filled with joy. God never forgets any of His children. Come, my child, let's pray."

Sara understood that Aliza would never cease to be Jewish. In those moments, she felt the need to speak with a rabbi. She found out the location of a synagogue and asked Anya to accompany her. She didn't want to go with Aliza, as she understood it would be very inconvenient for her. On the way, she shared the news with her friend, and Anya was also overjoyed.

She had a conversation with the rabbi, a wise and experienced elderly man who quickly deduced that this was a situation in which one should not apply pressure. In his opinion, it was preferable for events to take their course. However, as the two women were about to leave, he stopped them and said:

"The young woman will return to the fold."

Sara was struck by the rabbi's words and felt relieved.

Meanwhile, Aliza underwent baptism, first communion, and confirmation simultaneously. She smiled and displayed satisfaction, but internally, she wrestled with deep contradictions. She felt, not without reason, that she was betraying two religions at the same time. She remained in Berlin only long enough to collect the documents certifying her as a Catholic. Once she obtained them, she bid farewell to Helmuth and Ingrid, expressing gratitude for their hospitality, and promising to visit them in the future.

The wedding was scheduled for May in Vienna. Lublin was not the suitable place, as the couple believed that the Catholic hierarchy of the city would be influenced by Karl's mother, who not only rejected the marriage but also distrusted the sincerity of Aliza's conversion. Furthermore, it would be counterproductive to hold the ceremony in the same location where the groom's mother and the bride's father resided, as they detested each other and had made it clear they would not attend the event.

Isaak was immensely delighted when Sara returned from Berlin and revealed the secret Aliza had entrusted to her. However, he didn't budge an inch. He refused to see her upon her return to Lublin and remained firm in his decision not to attend the wedding. This caused great suffering for Sara and her daughter, but when it came to Judaism, Isaak was inflexible.

Except for the father, the whole family travelled to Vienna. The days leading up to the ceremony were hectic. Since other guests would also be attending, they decided that renting a furnished home would be the most practical option. Jared wouldn't allow Sara to bear the cost and announced that it would be the Weizmann gift to the newlyweds.

"Our gift to you, my dear girl, is to ensure that your family, which includes us, is very comfortable in Vienna," said Jared. "Of course, Daddy Jared, they are my family and I love them very much," Aliza replied, giving him a hug and a kiss.

The house turned out to be a spacious and beautiful villa facing the Danube Canal, six blocks away from Stephanplatz. It was actually a grand mansion, almost like a small palace, with nine rooms. Though it might have seemed excessive, it was necessary considering the large entourage of family and close friends.

Jared had planned everything meticulously and hired a complete staff, including cooks and coachmen. From dawn until late at night, the house was brimming with life and enthusiasm. The preparations for the ceremony added to the bustling activity, and the spontaneity of the children brought even more joy. Throughout the day, both adults and young ones laughed and joked. Tatiana and Jana seemed more excited than Aliza herself, and the older ladies, Sara, Anya, Irenka, and Malka, appeared rejuvenated.

However, they missed Isaak. He was the only shadow tarnishing their overflowing happiness. As night fell, a tear rolled down Sara's cheek as she thought about how special those days would have been if Isaak had been present. She suffered in silence, just like Aliza and her sisters.

The men, being a bit more pragmatic, regretted his absence but didn't attribute too much importance to it.

The week leading up to the wedding was particularly special as the weather joined in the celebrations. Every afternoon, they went out together to stroll through the parks and boulevards, then sat down to chat while enjoying some refreshments and savouring the exquisite Viennese pastries. The city had already begun its season of concerts, and they gladly attended them. Karl accompanied them to almost all of these events, feeling so comfortable with his fiancée's family that he didn't want to miss out on any programme, no matter how simple. On one of these outings, they had the opportunity to see the famous Empress Elisabeth in person. Although there was no possibility of greeting her directly, thanks to Karl's connections, they were able to see her up close. Everyone was enchanted by Lisa's grace and beauty, as her subjects affectionately called her. However, Karl stole the spotlight by saying, "My empress is indeed beautiful, but her beauty is overshadowed by that of my future mother-in-law."

The uproar was deafening from all the relatives, and the future in-laws playfully patted him on the back, accusing him of flattery. On the side, Sara blushed even more when Jared exclaimed, "I fully agree with the young man's assessment."

They kept themselves so entertained that the days passed by too quickly. Since the Rothmans were unfamiliar with the protocol of Catholic wedding ceremonies, they had to visit Karlskirche, the church where the wedding would take place, to learn the details and rehearse. Knowing that, according to tradition, the bride enters the church on her father's arm and Isaak would not be attending, Gabriel was chosen to replace him. The young boy wasn't thrilled about the responsibility, but Sara convinced him by making him understand how important and meaningful it was for his sister.

Sara also wanted to take advantage of their stay in Vienna to visit Doctor Frizmann and bring him a gift. She visited him at his clinic accompanied by her children. The doctor was delighted to hear that Isaak had fully recovered and that all discomfort had completely disappeared. He expressed his gratitude for the gesture and sent his regards to his former patient.

Two days before the ceremony, Karl's colleagues hosted a reception at the Hotel Imperial, the same hotel where they had stayed when they went for Isaak's medical consultation. It was a very special night for everyone, filled with great fun and dancing to the famous Viennese waltzes. Naturally, the belle of the ball was Aliza, who thoroughly enjoyed herself, especially when recalling that it was in this very place where Karl had proposed to her a year earlier.

Joy overflowed in that venue, with intoxicating music and a truly special atmosphere. The new commanding colonel of Karl's regiment also had a prominent role, just like the previous year. He was a man of a certain age, who had been married to a Russian woman but had been widowed for three years and had not remarried. He arrived at the party in the company of a lady who also seemed to be Russian, as they conversed in that language. The lady was elegant but rather haughty and rude, openly criticizing the hotel for allowing Jews to enter. It was highly offensive and painful for everyone, including their Catholic friends.

This lady was seated at the adjacent table and, knowing that they understood her, continued with her reproaches and sarcasm, speaking loudly with the clear intention of being heard. The colonel appeared timid or perhaps pretended to be so. Jana wished to put the offensive lady in her place, but Tatiana had a better idea. Taking Robiak by the hand, she passed by Sara and said to her:

"Mother, for once you're going to make use of your charms."

Sara didn't understand what her daughter meant. Tatiana, still holding her husband's hand, approached the neighbouring table and addressed the colonel, saying:

"Excuse us, Colonel, would you be so kind as to grant us a minute?"

"Of course, madame," the officer replied, getting up.

Robiak didn't understand what was going on, while the others watched the scene with intrigue. Tatiana brought the colonel to their table and pointing to Sara, she said:

"Allow me to introduce Mrs. Sara Rothman, the mother of the bride."

Sara had been facing away from the officer's table, so she hadn't been able to see him until that moment. She was visibly surprised by his extraordinary handsomeness. She inclined her head and, making a curtsy, took his hand and kissed it.

"It is a great pleasure, madame."

Tatiana smiled with satisfaction, noticing the impact her mother's beauty had on the officer. Without wasting time, she quickly said:

"Mrs. Rothman would be honoured if you would grant her the privilege of a dance."

Everyone at the table, including Sara, looked up in surprise at Tatiana. She discreetly urged them to support her request. Indeed, both men and women encouraged the colonel to invite Sara. When he offered her his hand, they applauded and exerted pressure on her as well. As soon as they made their way to the dance floor, Tatiana said to the others:

"Now, everyone, let's dance. The goal is to keep the colonel from sitting down again. If necessary, we'll swap partners. Do you understand?" she added, addressing all the women at the table.

No prompting was needed; the colonel was so impressed with Sara that he disregarded his arrogant table companion. He didn't want to part ways with the beautiful blonde with grey eyes. By the time she expressed her desire to sit for a moment, the colonel's friend had already stormed off in fury. Unfortunately, Sara found herself obliged to endure his company for a prolonged period, which was no small sacrifice. He even went as far as to declare that she was the most beautiful woman he had ever seen and that he had fallen madly in love. He proposed marriage, and when she rejected him, explaining that she was a married woman, he replied that he would have to seek solace in suicide for his lovesick woes. Sara called Tatiana and confronted her:

"You sent me a drunkard and a lunatic. He's over there saying he'll commit suicide if I don't marry him!"

Tatiana burst into laughter.

"I'll wipe that smile off your face, just wait," she walked towards the officer and said, "Colonel, please allow me to rest for a moment. In the meantime, would you be so kind as to invite my daughter to dance this piece?"

"Of course, but please wait for me here, divine Sara."

"What disrespect," she whispered to her daughter. "You owe me for this, Tatiushka."

Shortly after, Karl's companions, following an imperial Army tradition, gathered in the centre of the hall. Forming a circle around the bride and groom, they raised their glasses and toasted to their happiness. Sara took advantage of that moment to slip away from the bothersome colonel. Along with Anya and Irenka, she bid farewell and retired to rest.

Finally, the long-awaited day arrived, and the hustle and bustle in the mansion began early. Sara and Irenka were the first to get ready, dedicating themselves to helping Aliza with the preparations. It was a whirlwind of activities, shouts, laughter, and running. The boys played pranks on the other side of the door, where all the women were finishing styling Aliza's hair and adjusting her dress.

"Hey Ali, don't be in such a hurry," Gabriel said. "Karl already regrets it, and right now he's fleeing to Hungary."

"Stop teasing, Gabriel," Sara scolded him. "Go downstairs and wait for us there."

Then Oizer entered the scene.

"Take it easy, Aliza. He left a message that he'll come back when he's a general!"

Robiak approached and said from behind the door,

"What Gabriel and Oizer are saying isn't true, Aliza. The truth is that he was assigned to a military unit in the Balkans, but don't worry, he left three officers for you to choose from."

Sara opened the door.

"And you! A married man with children, haven't you grown up yet? Everyone, get out of here!" And they all, including the twins, descended with laughter. In the garden, Jared, Piotr, Saul, and Carl were waiting, smoking, and savouring a drink. As usual, the men were ready, waiting for the ladies to finish primping.

Carriages arrived at the church, and some guests entered while others conversed outside. Several fellow officers and superiors of Karl accompanied him, engaging in conversation. They all donned their shiny and gleaming dress uniforms. The groom was nervous, and at one point, he was informed that it was time for him to enter and make his way to the atrium. He was not to see the bride until the moment she entered on Gabriel's arm.

The carriage arrived with the bride, accompanied by Sara, Irenka, and Anya. They got down and began to ascend the steps. Aliza looked stunning in her white dress, adorned with a floral crown and chiffon veil, with her mother by her side. On the final steps, Sara greeted a red-uniformed officer, and he responded with a slight bow accompanied by a mischievous smile. Aliza was somewhat puzzled, but she continued ascending. When she reached the top of the staircase, she saw him. He was slightly turned to the side and then turned to face her, standing less than two meters away. The surprise was overwhelming. He approached and opened his arms, and she threw hers around his shoulders, embracing him tightly while tearfully saying:

"Father, you've come to accompany me!"

"Yes, here I am, my little daughter," Isaak said, unable to keep his eyes from getting misty. "And I swear I will never leave you again."

"Father, you make me the happiest woman in the world. I love you so much."

"And I love you, my sweet Aliza, my little and tender daughter." Then he held her at arm's length, looked into her eyes, and said, "I hope you can forgive me for being so stubborn."

"Of course, Dad. You're here with me, and that's enough to forgive you a thousand times."

They embraced once again, this time with Sara, who, of course, couldn't hold back her tears either. The onlookers were greatly surprised and applauded the scene with joy and emotion. It was an extraordinary surprise. Only Karl, Sara, and Anya knew that Isaak would be at the entrance of the church.

Two days before the wedding, Isaak had been in the warehouse, inspecting some materials he had received that morning when he heard someone speaking to him in English.

"You haven't changed a bit, my dear Isaak."

He looked up and saw an old friend at the entrance of the warehouse.

"Andrew!" he exclaimed. "What are you doing here?"

"Well, I came to visit you."

"I can't believe it! What a joy to see you!"

He stepped out from behind the counter and approached his friend, giving him a hug.

"It's a pleasant surprise. Why didn't you let me know you were coming?"

"To be honest, I hadn't planned it. It came up during the trip."

"Whatever the reason, I'm delighted to see you. Wait a moment, I'll give some instructions, and then we'll grab a drink. You have to tell me how a Royal Navy officer suddenly appears in a remote town in Poland."

After Isaak gave instructions to his assistant, they went to the chocolate shop and ordered a coffee each.

"Now, tell me. What brought you here without letting your friend know?"

"I was assigned as part of a military mission to explore the possibility of selling warships to the German and Austrian navies, as well as providing training to their crews. We already went to Berlin, but due to certain inconveniences, the Austrians asked us to postpone the planned meeting in Vienna by a week. Since we were already in Germany, the admiral decided to relocate us to the capital of Austria and wait there until the meeting takes place."

"I see. And then?" Isaak asked, taking a sip of his coffee.

"Well, the journey from Berlin to Vienna can be done via Prague or Krakow, and I thought to myself, if I pass through the latter city, I'll be very close to where an old friend lives. I have a week off, so I requested permission from the admiral to come and visit you. What do you think?"

"Well, Andrew, I think it's fantastic. I never forget everything I learned from you."

"Everything we learned," the officer replied in Russian, showing Isaak that he had also taken advantage of his teachings.

"Very well, you were determined to learn it before you were promoted to captain. I see you've achieved your goal."

"That's right. By the way, I inform you that I've already obtained the next promotion. I'm now a major."

"Congratulations! I'm sure you'll reach the highest rank, just as you've set out to do."

"You'll see, my friend."

"It's lovely to see you, and I appreciate you taking the trouble to come all the way to the ends of Poland just to visit me. By the way, how long will you be staying? It goes without saying that you'll stay at my house. Where is your luggage?"

"I left it at your wife's bakery."

"At my wife's bakery?"

"Yes, I had the address of your house, but when I arrived, I didn't find anyone there. So, I inquired about you, and they sent me to a bakery. They confirmed that it belonged to your wife and said I could find you at your business. We unloaded the suitcases, bid farewell to the carriage, and I walked to your shoe shop."

"Let's go and collect them, and then we'll head home. We have much to discuss."

And so, they did. The conversation continued at Isaak's residence, where he was very candid with his friend, telling him the details of what had happened with his daughter and why he hadn't attended her wedding in Vienna.

"I'm deeply sorry, but there's something I don't understand, and I dare to ask you, relying on our old friendship."

"Of course, what is it?"

"If you already know that your daughter converted to Christianity just to marry the Austrian officer and furthermore confessed to her mother that she still feels Jewish, and even believes she will never cease to be, then why do you still reject her?"

"What do you mean, why Andrew? Because she converted to Catholicism. Isn't that enough reason?"

"Well, it seems like a small matter to me," he shrugged.

"What do you mean? You say that because you're not Jewish."

"Remember that I have Jewish blood."

"Yes, but you're not Jewish."

"Let me tell you something that apparently even you, who are so orthodox at times, haven't considered."

Isaak was intrigued and gestured with his hand for him to continue.

"Alright then, do you remember when I told you on the ship that my grandmother was Jewish?"

"Yes, I remember."

"Perfect. And despite her conversion to Christianity, she raised my mother with all the Hebrew laws and customs."

"Yes, Andrew, I remember that too."

Well, perhaps amidst the frustration caused by your daughter's decision, you have overlooked something as simple within the traditions it is an irrefutable fact that Jewish heritage is transmitted through the mother's womb. Have you forgotten that?

Isaak was a bit confused. Of course, he knew that and hadn't forgotten. Why was Andrew bringing it up? He replied, "Of course, I haven't forgotten."

"Excellent, because then you must accept that I am Anglican, but I am also Jewish because my grandmother was Jewish, and she passed down the heritage to my mother and then to me."

"Alright, but you had an Anglican upbringing from birth."

"Don't believe that too much. Remember that it was precisely on the ship when you wondered why I knew all the Jewish customs and laws so well."

Andrew continued, "If, being Anglican, I can also consider myself Jewish, wouldn't your daughter, who not only still feels Jewish but was born from a Jewish womb and raised in that religion her whole life, be even more so?"

Isaak remained silent. Andrew added, "Listen, my dear friend, based on what you've told me and considering that your daughter converted to

Christianity solely for the sake of marriage, we could say it's exactly the same as if they had demanded that she dye her hair red in order to do so. What do you think she would do with her hair after the wedding? You don't have to answer that: obviously, she would remove the dye to return to her natural hair colour!"

"I understand where you're going with this."

"Ah, finally! It seems that I am succeeding in making you, being so intelligent, open your eyes to reality."

"Yes."

"I assure you, Isaak, as soon as she steps out of that church, your daughter will return to being Jewish in every sense of what it means. I bet the buttons on my jacket that she won't celebrate any Christian festivities, but she will observe the Sabbath, not forget to celebrate Passover, Hanukkah, and Yom Kippur."

"My God, Andrew, I believe you're right!"

"Of course, I am, you idiot! And I'll tell you something else in which I'm also right."

"What is it?"

"If you don't attend your daughter's wedding, you will regret it for the rest of your life."

Isaak looked at Andrew, then stood up and hugged his friend. He then said, "You mentioned that you have to go to Vienna for your military meeting, right?"

"That's correct."

"Well, you have a travelling companion now. We leave tomorrow morning."

"A wise decision. Let's meet up to leave early."

Isaak extended his hand and said, "Thank you, my dear Andrew. I won't be able to repay you for pointing out my mistake in the nick of time."

"Yes, you can."

"Oh?"

"It's quite simple. I love these novel-like events. You're giving me the opportunity to enjoy what will happen in Vienna. What I'm asking is for it to be a surprise for your daughter."

"I don't understand."

"Go rest, and I'll explain the strategy during the journey."

The next day, Isaak packed his finest suit, and they set off for Vienna. On the train, Andrew revealed his plan: for Isaak to meet his daughter at the precise moment of her entrance to the church.

"You describe it as if it were a fairy tale."

"That's it, my friend. You've said it. Let's do it like a fairy tale. Sometimes, one must surrender to romance."

"Very well, I will follow your instructions. It's the least I can do for you."

"I'll take care of everything."

They arrived in the imperial capital as evening fell, checked into a hotel, and set out to locate the family. They had to hurry as they knew the ceremony would take place the next day. They didn't know the address of their accommodation and finding them seemed difficult in a city of one million inhabitants. However, Andrew knew where to start. He put on his uniform, and they went to the Military Garrison Headquarters. There, they found out which barracks Karl served in and made their way there. Upon reaching the guard post, Andrew confidently entered, wearing his officer's rank, and addressed the sergeant who was present, speaking in perfect German:

"Good evening, Sergeant. I am Major Andrew Cronin, from the Royal Marines of the British Navy, an officer in the service of Her Majesty Queen Victoria."

"Ah," Isaak thought, understanding the similarity with English, "when I introduce myself, I simply state my name."

The sergeant stood up from the desk where he was writing a note, put on his cap, stood at attention, and saluted, touching his hand to his temple.

"Good evening, Major. I am the duty sergeant. How may I assist you, sir?"

"Thank you. I am looking for Captain Karl Radetz."

"I will have him called right away, sir."

Indeed, he sent a soldier to fetch the captain.

Karl arrived with the soldier a few minutes later.

"The gentlemen need you, Captain," the sergeant said, pointing to Isaak and Andrew.

When Karl arrived with the soldier, he recognized the red coat of the British officer and noticed the crown on their shoulder insignias, indicating his rank. He saluted, touching his hand to his forehead.

"Good evening, Major. I am Captain Radetz, of the Imperial Army. How can I help you?"

"Good evening, Captain. It concerns a matter that directly and personally involves you," Andrew spoke to him in Russian, then turned to Isaak and said, "As you can see, your future father-in-law is accompanying me."

Karl turned his head and was surprised to see Aliza's father standing next to the major.

"Please excuse me, Mr. Rothman. I hadn't realized you were here," he said, slightly bowing his shoulders.

The young officer's surprise and unease were evident. He had never expected to encounter Aliza's father there, especially knowing that he disapproved of their marriage. Andrew immediately noticed that Karl, despite his composure, was a bit unsettled.

"Don't worry, Captain. Your father-in-law came to Vienna exclusively to accompany you both in the wedding ceremony."

Karl took a deep breath and extended his hand to Isaak.

"It's a pleasure and a great joy to have you here, Mr. Rothman."

"The pleasure is mine, Captain, and I will gladly be present. By the way, my friend here, the Major, has already informed me about the procedure of the ceremony. I know that it requires me to enter the church with my daughter and hand her over to you."

"That's correct, Mr. Rothman. It's tradition."

"Well, since I suppose we won't have the opportunity to talk at the church, I would like to take this chance to clarify something now."

"Naturally, sir, I'm listening," Karl responded.

"I love my daughter with all my heart, and I hope you do too," Isaak continued.

"You can be absolutely certain that I do," Karl assured him.

"I'm glad to hear that because if you ever cause her any kind of suffering, I will find you wherever you may be, and I assure you that you will fear me more than an enemy cavalry charge."

Andrew burst into laughter, leaving Karl unsure of how to respond. The British man put his arms around the shoulders of his two companions and, still laughing, said, "Well, we need to iron out the details. Captain, where can we sit down and talk?"

They went to the officers' mess, where they planned the strategy, as Andrew called it. They decided that Karl would send a note to Sara, asking to speak with her to seek her advice. Since he shouldn't see the bride-to-be on the eve of the wedding, he would ask her to meet outside the house. To avoid suspicion, he would request that she bring someone else along. He also asked her not to mention the meeting to anyone.

Sara was very surprised to receive the note and grew worried. It wasn't something usual, so she quickly draped a shawl over her shoulders, put on her hat, and invited Anya to accompany her. When they arrived at the café, Karl was waiting at the door, wearing a broad smile that reassured Sara.

"My dear mother-in-law, forgive me for making you come like this," he said. Then he turned to Anya and exclaimed, "And thank you for accompanying her, Mrs. Weizmann."

"What is this about, Karl?" Sara asked him.

"It's a pleasant surprise. Please, let's go inside," he replied.

As soon as they entered the café, Isaak and Andrew stood up from their table. Sara, taken aback, exclaimed, "Isaak, my husband! How is this possible?" Overflowing with joy, she approached him and, ignoring the other diners who were watching, kissed him.

They spent over an hour chatting. Sara couldn't hide her happiness as she embraced her husband and kissed him on the cheek. Isaak recounted the details of Andrew's visit, how he managed to make him understand that he was making a mistake and that he needed to be present at Aliza's wedding.

"You will bring her immense joy, my dear, just as you have brought it to me. Her day will be perfect."

"But you know that everything must remain a secret until the hour of the ceremony. It's what Andrew wants, and we owe it to him," Karl replied.

"Thank you, Major. I can never repay you enough for your timely visit," Isaak expressed his gratitude.

"It's a great pleasure for me, but at the same time, I would appreciate it if you called me Andrew. Let's reserve the ranks for the military," Andrew said.

"Well, Andrew, you already have some of my affection for what you've done for my daughter, thank you," Sara said, addressing Andrew.

"Thank you, Andrew." She turned to her husband. How do you say that my love, in English?

"'My love.'"

Sara looked at Andrew and said:

"My love."

Andrew and Karl laughed.

"If you will be gross Isaak!" His friend told him, "What your wife asked you was how to say 'thank you'.

At that moment, Isaak laughed too, slapping himself on the cheek.

forehead and he turned to Sara:

"Excuse me, my dear, 'my love' means my love, because of my clumsiness you end up saying that to Andrew, rather than 'thank you.'"

"Well, Andrew, you already have some of my affection for what you have done for my daughter, so I don't withdraw the previous word and now I say, 'thank you.'"

Everyone laughed and raised their glasses once more. As they bid farewell, satisfaction and happiness shone on their faces. Of course, Isaak left with his friend to the hotel. They had to keep the secret as they had promised the Englishman.

21

Gabriel returned from his sojourn in Warsaw, feeling frustrated and disheartened. After great effort, he had managed to gain admission to the Imperial University's School of Law and Administration. His inclination leaned towards financial studies, and he firmly believed that with a degree in hand, he could dismantle many of the barriers imposed on Jews by the Russian authorities. While he was aware that graduating from a university wouldn't necessarily guarantee success in future business endeavours, he was driven by the desire to prove that Jews could also excel in higher education.

Isaak and Sara shared their son's disappointment, their hearts heavy with sorrow. They knew that Gabriel possessed exceptional intellectual qualities, likely surpassing those of most students at the university. They found it unjust that someone so capable would be hindered from realizing their dreams due to circumstances unrelated to academic pursuits.

With high hopes, the young man set off for Warsaw, enrolling in the university and gaining entry with outstanding grades. He lodged at his Aunt Ruth's house and attended classes diligently. From the very first day, he showcased his remarkable intellect, despite being one of the youngest students in the academic community. Several professors noticed his talents and applauded his efforts and dedication. Yet, even though he encountered discrimination from some teachers and more than a few students due to his Jewish heritage, Gabriel adapted swiftly to the academic rhythm.

Things were going remarkably well in Warsaw. The young lad of merely seventeen years had swiftly adapted to city life and his newfound role as a university student. He devoted himself wholeheartedly to his studies, diligently reviewing the lessons learned each day at his aunt and uncle's house, where he approached his assignments with great responsibility.

With great fortitude, he endured the exclusion that came his way. While there were other Jewish students, his outstanding academic achievements quickly stirred envy among many of his peers, who never missed an opportunity to annoy him. Aunt Ruth advised him to focus on his classes and demonstrate his worth to others through his academic performance. Whenever he witnessed an injustice befall him or any of his Jewish classmates, an inner fury swelled within him, and he found himself on the brink of confronting those who spewed anti-Jewish slogans.

He finished his first academic year with outstanding grades, and he was bestowed with the honour of being not only the top student in his class and faculty but in the entire university. Consequently, he received personal congratulations from the rector and the faculty, along with a special certificate of recognition. Returning home to his parents for the summer, Isaak and Sara couldn't have been prouder when he handed them the certificate for being the top student. His mother, beaming with satisfaction, proudly displayed the document to Irenka and all the workers at the bakeries and chocolate shop.

However, during the vacation, his mother noticed that, despite claiming to be content and enthusiastic, a tinge of melancholy always seemed to surround him whenever he spoke about his life in Warsaw and his activities at the university. The young man sensed that his conspicuous success might lead to even more difficulties, but he chose to set aside his concerns for another time.

He took advantage of those days to spend time with his parents, sisters, and new nephews. Tatiana had given birth to a baby boy, and Jana as well; curiously enough, the two cousins were born barely a week apart. Furthermore, Rachel, Oizer's wife, had given birth to their third child just two months earlier, making the three little ones practically the same age.

The Weizmann were visiting, and as Oizer was considered a brother, conversations often revolved around the three little cousins, who would run around the entire house. Tatiana's son was named Isaak, in honour of his grandfather, while Jana named her boy Aaron. Rachel and Oizer decided to call their new son Jaim Azriel, though everyone referred to him by his first name. From an early age, the three boys very bright and laid the foundation for a lifelong friendship.

Tatiana and Jana were delighted with Gabriel's presence. He had always been the darling of his sisters, and they were proud of him. By the age of eighteen, he had grown into a man with a strong and determined personality, and he had a striking appearance that caught the attention of women. Towering over his father, he had a sturdy build and the beautiful features of his mother, with the same enchanting smile, captivating eyes, and blond hair like a field of wheat. With such a striking appearance, he could hardly go unnoticed wherever he went, and even though he had grown, his sisters still saw him as their little brother, playfully pinching his cheeks.

The girls of Lublin, including the shop assistants at the bakeries, were fascinated by him, much to the amusement of his sisters. However, Gabriel was quite serious and, in reality, somewhat shy. Though he possessed a clever sense of humour and was an engaging conversationalist, he interacted with the opposite gender somewhat awkwardly, often appearing distant. This demeanour, which wasn't entirely genuine, would quickly vanish with a witty remark or a smile, charming the young ladies.

There was one young lady in particular who caught his interest. She was the daughter of a beloved and respected Jewish man in the city, who owned an important printing press that published books in Russian, Yiddish, and Polish. The girl was both beautiful and sweet, and occasionally they had the chance to meet at the park near the market. She was always accompanied by her equally charming older sister. Although Gabriel enjoyed her company and liked seeing her, their relationship remained platonic.

The vacation came to an end, and he returned to Warsaw with enthusiasm to make progress in his studies and the confidence of no longer being a newcomer to university life. Of course, upon his arrival, he had to face those who couldn't accept that a Jew could be the most outstanding student at the university. Besides tasteless jokes, there were constant allusions to his Jewish heritage. However, he adopted the same attitude as in his first year and focused on his studies.

With his attractive appearance, Gabriel also caught the eyes of the girls in Warsaw, including the new assistant at the library. She was a stunning young woman who had a magnetic effect on the students, with almost all of them vying for her affection. However, there was one notable exception: Gabriel. He remained resolute in not letting himself be distracted from his studies or swayed from his goal of becoming the top student at the university once again.

Of course, he had noticed the presence of the beautiful librarian, but he chose to someone else win her. He frequented the library to consult books, not be influenced by the charms of the girl, driven by his determination to advance in his studies and expand his knowledge. Nevertheless, she couldn't help but observe him closely, from the moment he walked in with books and notes under his arm. Usually, she would approach him, asking if she could be of any assistance, and Gabriel would politely decline.

Unbeknownst to Gabriel, the girl, coincidentally sharing the same name as his sister Jana, inadvertently became the reason why he couldn't continue his academic career unimpeded. There was a fellow student who was obsessed with the librarian, but she consistently rejected him. Truth be told, she held a deep aversion towards this student because he was arrogant and overbearing, being the son of the commanding general of the Russian military garrison in Warsaw. The young man presumed he could enjoy privileges at the university, and indeed, he did. Professors and administrators were wary of getting on the bad side of the Russian general and, therefore, tolerated certain liberties from his son.

This young man had his entourage of sycophants, forming a clique that not just anyone could join, though many desired to be a part of. Gabriel, however, had no interest in being part of their circle. His focus was on his studies, and the fact that this young man was Russian only intensified his disdain and rejection towards him.

Since he was a child, Gabriel had harboured a deep animosity towards the Russians. This stemmed from the trauma caused by his father's deportation, during which Gabriel believed him to be dead for three long years. The suffering he endured was immense, and although fate allowed him to be reunited with his father, he could never forgive the people who had caused him, his mother, and his own father so much pain and suffering in his heart.

Jana, the librarian, found herself daydreaming more and more about Gabriel. She was strongly drawn to the tall, young blond man with perfect features who sent shivers down her spine with his mere presence. What made him even more attractive to her was the fact that he was the only student who didn't try to court her. He seemed solely interested in books, which only heightened his allure.

One afternoon, determined to act, Jana waited near the street as Gabriel was leaving the university, pretending it was a chance encounter. She knew that every evening he walked from the campus to his aunt and uncle's house, so she knew the route he would take and positioned herself to intercept him.

"Hello, Gabriel, how are you?" she greeted him casually.

He, lost in his thoughts, was taken aback, and looked at her intently. "Hello, Jana, I'm doing well, thank you."

"Oh, you know my name."

"Of course, it's the same name as my sister."

"What a coincidence. How many siblings do you have?"

Gabriel thought she was asking too much. Why would she be interested in knowing about his sisters? "I have three older sisters. I'm the youngest. Anyway, I must excuse myself now; I need to go."

"Don't worry, I'm heading in the same direction as you. We can walk together if you like."

"How does she know which way I'm going?" Gabriel wondered. Unbeknownst to him, Jana had already found out that he lived with his aunt and uncle on Stare Nalewki Street.

"Sure, that's fine."

Jana attempted to engage him in a more personal conversation, but despite his courtesy, he remained distant and indifferent. The short walk wouldn't have had any consequences if it weren't for the fact that the son of the general learned that the young woman, he was interested in had left the university in the company of Gabriel.

The suitor flew into a rage, and from that day on, his animosity towards the Jewish lad grew even stronger. He continuously harassed Gabriel, emboldened by his group of followers, who gave him a sense of courage. At first, Gabriel paid him no attention and tried to avoid him, but the other persisted in his pursuit.

One day, as Gabriel was leaving class, the Russian boy was waiting outside with his cronies. When he saw Gabriel approaching, he shouted, "Here comes that Jewish guy who thinks he's so handsome, stealing the hearts of all the women."

Gabriel chose to ignore him and kept walking.

"Hey, dirty Jew, are you deaf?" the Russian taunted.

Gabriel stopped and replied, "I'm not deaf, and I kindly ask you not to insult me."

"Hahaha, 'I kindly ask you not to insult me,'" he repeated sarcastically. "He talks like a sissy, that disgusting Jew! I don't know why they let your kind into the university."

"Listen, I'm not offending you, and I don't want any trouble, so let's end things here."

"Oh, I don't want any trouble! Are you so afraid to talk to me?"

"I have no reason to fear you. I just prefer to avoid confrontations."

"Typical Jew, a coward."

"You have no right to insult me, nor any Jew."

"It's not an insult, it's the truth. All Jews are cowards, and Jewesses are nothing but harlots, just like your parents, repugnant Hebrew."

Calmly, Gabriel approached and said, "Do you have any reason to hate Jews?"

"I don't need reasons. They are what they are, and that's that."

"No, it's really not that simple. I think you do need a reason to detest Jews, and I'm going to give you one."

Suddenly, like a bolt of lightning, without giving the Russian boy a chance to react, Gabriel landed a powerful blow that sent him flying more than a meter away, with his mouth bloodied, two loose teeth, and a broken nose. Then, he turned to the others and shouted, "If anyone else wants the same, come closer!"

Nobody moved. Gabriel picked up his books, turned around, and walked away while the Russian boy's friends helped him up and tried to stop the nosebleed.

He arrived at his aunt's house with a throbbing hand and had to soak it in a container of warm water, salt, and vinegar. Yet, he couldn't help but imagine how the other guy's face must have looked. Shortly after, the police showed up, detained him, and took him to a cell where he spent the night. The following day, thanks to the efforts of a lawyer friend of his aunt and uncle, and a hefty fine, he was released. However, that very afternoon, he was expelled from the university. He requested to speak with the rector to explain what had happened and to inform him about the continuous aggressions he had endured from the young man, which were witnessed by others. But the director simply replied, "Only a fool would dare disfigure the son of a Russian general. You'd better look for another occupation because you won't be returning to this university."

Gabriel left the office feeling dejected and pondering the injustice of the circumstances. It was the other man who had relentlessly pursued and insulted him. By chance, he saw him approaching, accompanied by two of his cronies. Gabriel walked towards him, but the son of the general, with his nose bandaged and his upper lip swollen, hid behind his friends, warning him, "Don't come any closer. If you do, the police will arrest you, and this time you won't get out so easily."

Gabriel looked at him with disdain and simply said, "From now on, your crooked nose will always remind you of the Jews, coward."

"You'll pay for this. Someday, I'll get back at you," the other threatened.

The expulsion was a devastating blow to Gabriel, and it kept him withdrawn for a long time. He bid farewell to his aunt and uncle and to Warsaw with bitterness in his heart. He set off by coach for Lublin, just as the librarian was telling the arrogant son of the general that she would never forgive him for causing Gabriel to leave the university. She also declared that he deserved the injuries he had sustained and that she never wanted to see him again.

His parents were also shocked and upset, particularly by the lack of fairness in the university's decision, especially considering Gabriel's exemplary conduct. He had proven to be an outstanding student, demonstrating patience and self-control over several months, enduring constant humiliations stoically. He had only reacted when his dignity was insulted in such a demeaning manner.

For all these reasons, it pained them to see him so dejected, and they tried to console him, to no avail. One day, Isaak suggested to him:

"I've been thinking, son, that you could try restarting your studies somewhere else, perhaps at the Imperial University of St. Petersburg. The twins of Jared study there, and it has a very good reputation."

"In St. Petersburg, father? Forgive me, but there's no way I would study there. In fact, I have no interest whatsoever in visiting that city; just hearing its name makes me nauseous."

"Don't exaggerate, my son."

"I'm not exaggerating. You know I detest the Russians."

"Believe me, I don't have any sympathy for them either."

"Father, my earliest childhood memory was seeing Russian soldiers pushing you while you were burdened with chains. I have never been able to forget that, nor all the suffering you endured unjustly because of them."

"I understand, son, but that is something that's in the past."

"Not for me. Thanks to your courage and determination, you were able to come back to us. It's something I thank God for every day. But if it had depended on the Russians, you would have perished in Siberia years ago. They didn't care about taking my father away from me for three years, and their intention was to take you away from me forever. I also saw my mother suffer, and all of this happened without you having committed any crime."

"What you say is true, but you must understand that not all Russians are guilty of what happened. Like everywhere else, there are good and bad people."

"Well, in Russia, it's hard to find a good person."

"You're being extreme."

"It's not like that; it's what I think."

"Remember that your sister is Russian."

"Tatiana is not Russian; she is Jewish."

"Of course, she is Jewish, but she was born in Russia."

"By accident, but she has nothing Russian about her."

"Oh, my son! Even her name is Russian, and so is her mother tongue. Don't forget that when she arrived home, she didn't speak any other language. But fine, let's leave Tatiana aside. Look at Jared, he's also Russian."

"No, father, he's Jewish too."

"I think you're too fixated on this topic. Perhaps one day you'll understand that not all Russians are evil; that's something that doesn't exist in any country. There are many who are good."

"In any case, the last thing I want is to study in Russia or have anything to do with those people. Remember that my expulsion from the university was because of a Russian."

"Very well, but then, what have you thought of doing?"

"I'm not entirely sure yet. I'd like to start a business; you know that's what I enjoy."

"Very well. Knowing you, I'm confident that you'll make progress in whatever venture you undertake."

"Thank you, father."

He got up, kissed Isaak, and left the room. Isaak remained silent; it was a pity that their son's aspirations been frustrated at the university. Although in his view, obtaining a professional degree was a source of pride and a way to demonstrate that Jews also had abilities, he was clear that success in the business world did not necessarily require higher education. What mattered more was having the right skills, a strong work ethic, and the determination to overcome obstacles.

Gabriel began exploring commercial possibilities. He had no interest in shoes or bread; his parents had already excelled in those fields. Nor was he inclined to establish any kind of store. Finally, he decided that it would be best to venture into large-scale trade, starting at the basic levels.

The only drawback he foresaw was that to develop this entrepreneurial activity, he would have to consider Russia. After all, Poland was part of the Empire and depended on it both in terms of regulation and production. Much to his regret, he began contemplating a trade of Russian products to Central Europe and vice versa.

One day, shortly after the first snowfall, Gabriel was leaving the commercial registration office in Lublin, where he was handling the paperwork for the establishment of a company dealing with various products. Suddenly, he was approached by a group of Russian soldiers, led by a non-commissioned officer, who, looking at a paper he held in his hand, asked him:

"Are you Gabriel Rothman?"

"Yes, that's me."

"You're Jewish, aren't you?"

"Yes, indeed, I am Jewish."

"Come with us."

"Why? Where are we going?"

"Don't ask questions. I don't know the reason; I just follow orders. Come with us."

Gabriel was surprised and intrigued, studying the non-commissioned officer in his dark blue coat, cap of the same colour, and slightly lighter blue trousers. The soldiers all wore the same uniform and carried an extremely long rifle. He knew he couldn't refuse, so he followed them. They walked through the centre of the street for six blocks until they reached the Russian Army barracks. They passed through the guardhouse, where a soldier raised the barrier and let them in, saluting the non-commissioned officer with indifference.

Inside, there was an office with an officer, a non-commissioned officer, and two armed soldiers. The non-commissioned officer who had brought Gabriel presented himself to his superior:

"Permission, lieutenant, I've completed your order."

The officer looked up from some documents he was reviewing, and the corporal handed him the note he had brought. He glanced at it for a moment and gestured for Gabriel to approach.

"Very well, are you Gabriel Rothman?"

"That's my name."

"Perfect, I inform you that from today onwards, you will have the honour of serving in the Tsar's Army."

Gabriel was dumbfounded; he couldn't quite grasp what the officer was telling him.

"I don't understand what you're saying."

"I repeat, from today onwards, you are enlisting in the Imperial Army."

"I still don't understand; I haven't applied to join the Army."

The officer chuckled, got up, and approached Gabriel, saying:

"We're not at a school or a club here; this is the Army."

"I understand that, but I don't want to belong to the Army."

The officer was becoming impatient.

"Look, young man, it seems you don't understand or don't want to understand. You have just been conscripted into the Tsar's Army. We're not asking you whether you're interested or not. Do you expect us to send you an invitation card to your house?"

"No, but it's just that..."

The officer interrupted him.

"Conscription is not voluntary; it's your duty. Mother Russia needs you."

"But Russia is not my Motherland; I am Polish."

Finally, the lieutenant lost his temper, approached him, and shouted in his face:

"And where do you think Poland is? Don't you know that Poland is a province of the Russian Empire?"

"Yes, but..."

"Enough!" he retorted. "I've already informed you that you are now a recruit in the Army, and that's final."

He turned to the non-commissioned officer and ordered, "Get this young man out of here!" Then he continued, "Take him to the others."

The corporal, accompanied as always by the two soldiers, led Gabriel to a room where about thirty young men were sitting on wooden benches. A non-commissioned officer at a table was jotting down information provided by one of them. Two soldiers were chatting casually, leaning on their rifles, by the side of the door. The corporal approached the one who was writing and said, "Sergeant, I've brought another one, sent by my lieutenant."

The non-commissioned officer glanced at him without a hint of emotion and exclaimed, "Very well, have him sit with the others."

Gabriel hadn't fully grasped what was happening yet; the situation seemed unreal, and he wondered if it might be a mistake. He looked at the sergeant taking notes, who appeared like a mechanical figure. He would speak with him and explain that there must be a misunderstanding. He had never requested to join the Army; he was a former student of the Imperial University of Warsaw and was in the process of establishing a business. He had completed the mandatory eight years of school, meaning he had a certain level of education.

He waited until the sergeant called him, walked up to the table, and as soon as he arrived, the non-commissioned officer, without raising his gaze, asked, "Name!"

"Sir, I wish to clarify something."

"We're not here to chat! Name and surname."

"Gabriel Rothman. Look, I must tell you something important."

"I'm here to take your information, nothing more. Date of birth."

"February 23, 1858."

"Age."

"Eighteen years old. Please, let me explain..."

The sergeant raised his head and gave him a withering look, saying, "I repeat, we're not here to engage in conversation! Simply answer my questions. Name of father and mother."

"Isaac Rothman and Sara Rothman. Will you listen to me now?"

The Corporal angrily threw the pencil onto the table, stood up, and roared:

"Do you have any idea where you are? If you haven't understood that you're here to answer questions and nothing more, I'll make it clear with a good thump to that stupid head of yours."

Gabriel remained silent, not knowing what to think. Could they not speak here? Did everyone get enraged instead of listening?

"Religion," the sergeant demanded.

"Jewish," Gabriel replied.

The sergeant looked at him disdainfully and said, "Is this city filled only with the rabble of Jews? We'll have to straighten them out."

Now, it was Gabriel who glared back at him with fury. The sergeant was momentarily taken aback, but he quickly regained his composure.

Just in case, he called one of the soldiers and ordered, "Take this insect away from the table before I smash his face for being disrespectful and a Jew!"

After filling out the forms, the sergeant ordered one of the soldiers to bring the doctor. When the doctor arrived, he made all the boys form a line in front of the wooden benches and instructed them to undress. He proceeded to examine each one carefully, checking their arms, legs, torso, and especially their teeth. The room had no heating, and everyone shivered from the cold.

After the medical examination, the physician turned to the sergeant and reported, "All of them are fit, except for this one." He pointed to a short, blond boy. "He has a disfigured foot and is missing a finger on his left hand. He won't be of any use, not even for peeling potatoes."

Then he approached the table, asked for the forms that the sergeant had been preparing, and began signing them. Meanwhile, the sub-officer shouted, "Put on your underwear." Then, he directed his gaze at Gabriel and said, "Not you, filthy Jew. I'm going to take you down a notch."

The doctor left, and shortly after, another non-commissioned officer entered the room, accompanied by three soldiers carrying canvas sacks. They opened the sacks in the middle of the room, spilling their contents onto the wooden floor: grey shirts, trousers, jackets of the same colour, and leather boots.

"Sokolov," the sub-officer called to one of the soldiers, "sort the forms, separate the ones for the Jews."

The soldier complied and handed over five forms. The sergeant called them one by one, making them step aside. Then, he turned to those who remained, saying, "Choose your uniforms." He glanced at the other group and continued, "The filthy Jews will do so last."

When everyone had picked their uniforms, except for Gabriel, he said, "You have one minute to exchange boots and uniforms according to your size. If you don't manage, tough luck; you'll wear whatever you get, regardless of whether it's too big or too small. Ready... now."

A chaotic scene unfolded as they tried to swap clothing. The sergeant pulled a whistle from his pocket and blew it.

"Finish up and get dressed; the Jew stays put," he declared, pointing at Gabriel.

He walked to the door, opened it. And immediately ordered a soldier to do the same with the windows. A freezing gust of wind swept into the room, chilling everyone. The young men hurriedly dressed, except for Gabriel, who was practically naked and felt his body freezing.

Ten minutes passed, and two barbers entered with their scissors. Finally, the sub-officer ordered Gabriel to put on his clothes, had them all sit on the benches, and signalled to a soldier to close the door and windows. The barbers worked at a breakneck speed, leaving all thirty boys with almost clean-shaven heads. A soldier brought a broom, and the sergeant instructed one of the boys to sweep away the hair that had fallen to the floor.

After a short while, another non-commissioned officer with even harsher features than in charge of the previous activities entered the room. He collected the forms and ordered the boys to line up in front of the benches. Confused and terrified, they stood in line while the two soldiers sneered and laughed. The newcomer called them out one by one, and once they had responded, he began his speech.

"I am Sergeant Vasiliev. From this moment until I hand you over to the training barracks, I will be your boss, your father, your mother, and even your big sister if you like. You will obey me immediately and without a word of protest, or else you'll come to know the sting of my whip," he declared, showing a whip held tightly against his side with his other arm, and I assure you, I know how to use it."

At that moment, he took the whip and lashed it forcefully against the floor, creating a terrifying sound upon impact. Then he continued, "Now, you will all go and sign your forms," handing them over to a soldier who sat down at the desk with them. "Those who don't know how to write will place an 'X' where the soldier indicates."

He then turned to the other soldier and ordered him to fix the bayonet and stand beside the table with the rifle held horizontally. "According to Army rules, the procedure is voluntary. However, the soldier with the rifle will give you a little help if you can't find the spot to sign your name."

Once everyone had completed the task, he lined them up again and continued:

"Now, you are proud recruits of the Imperial Army, and you will have the honour of serving His Majesty the Tsar and Mother Russia. Your service will be for six years, and then you'll move on to the reserve for nine more years, if you're still alive by then."

A chill ran down everyone's spine as Vasiliev continued:

"Now, you'll wait to receive your blankets and personal items. One last warning: you're not soldiers yet; you'll become soldiers once you complete your training period. For now, you are recruits."

He took two steps towards them and pronounced, "But listen carefully, soldiers or recruits, in the Russian Army, deserters are shot."

He turned around and left with the soldier who had collected the forms. A deathly silence filled the air. The soldier who had fixed the bayonet removed it from the rifle and put it back in its scabbard, then said:

"Sit down and don't move a finger; I don't want to have to fix the bayonet again."

Everyone obeyed. Gabriel felt as though he was in a state of limbo. It was a nightmare; it didn't seem real. Just two hours ago, he was greeting Tatiana at the chocolate shop and heading to the commercial office, and now he found himself in a barracks, feeling like a prisoner whose fate was in the hands of Russian soldiers who treated him like animals.

Twenty minutes later, the Lieutenant who had received Gabriel upon his arrival at the Military Garrison entered, accompanied by a corporal. The soldier immediately stood up as if on a spring and saluted the officer, who returned the gesture with a nod. The soldier then ordered the recruits:

"Stand up."

They all complied, and the officer looked them over, noticing that Gabriel and another boy were not wearing boots. He approached and asked:

"Why aren't you wearing boots?"

"The boots are too small for me," replied Gabriel.

"Same here," added the other boy.

"What nonsense," the officer exclaimed. "Is there anyone whose boots are too big?"

"I have bigger boots," said another recruit, raising his hand.

"You all seem foolish," the officer remarked. "Then switch the boots and clothes, come on."

None of them dared to explain that it was the sergeant's fault for only giving them a minute to change. The lieutenant, however, was more patient and allowed them enough time to finish. Then he said:

"You will spend the night here, and the day after tomorrow, you will depart for Smolensk to begin your training." He pointed to the corporal accompanying him and continued, "The corporal will take note of your families' locations so they can come and bid you farewell tomorrow."

When the corporal arrived at the Rothman's house, Robiak, Tatiana, and the children were visiting. Tatiana opened the door and was surprised to see two Russian soldiers. One of them asked:

"Is this Gabriel Rothman's house?"

"Yes, it is," Tatiana replied. "How may I help you?"

"A note for you all, thank you very much, ma'am."

He saluted, bowed, and without saying anything else, turned around and left with his companion. Tatiana, intrigued, quickly went to the living room where her parents and husband were. She handed the note to Isaak, who read it carefully, and then passed it silently to his wife. As she read the contents, she began to sob. Tatiana grew anxious, and Isaak explained:

"Gabriel has just been drafted into the Russian Army."

"It can't be."

"Well, everything indicates that it is true. They inform us that we can go to bid him farewell at the military barracks tomorrow."

"This is an outrage!" exclaimed Robiak. "They didn't give any notice."

"Obviously, they don't give notice; they forcibly recruit," replied Isaak.

"But in previous years, they did give notice," argued Robiak.

Isaak fell silent, as was his habit, and stroked his chin in thought. Then he said:

"In previous years, there was no war."

"Father-in-law, but there is no war now," said Sara anxiously.

"There will be, I suspect," Isaak replied. "The situation in the Balkans is very tense. There have been military movements for several months, and Russia has many interests there."

"Do you believe that war will break out between Russia and the Ottoman Empire?" asked Robiak.

"Not only do I believe it, my dear son-in-law, I think it will be inevitable. For Russia, it's the perfect opportunity to seek access to the Mediterranean. It's an opportunity the Tsar won't miss."

"Yes, that has been a longstanding dream of Russia," agreed his son-in-law.

"And I'm sure Austria will support them; it would be beneficial for Austria and allow them to increase their influence in the Balkans."

"Please," Sara interrupted, "that's not important right now. What are we going to do about Gabriel's situation? We can't allow them to take him into the Army."

"I remember a rule that allowed paying to be exempted from military service," said Isaak.

"Tomorrow, we'll go to the barracks early, and we'll do whatever it takes to bring Gabriel back. It's a pity Carl isn't in Lublin; he would have been a great help."

"Regardless, we have to get him out of there, especially now that war seems imminent," said Sara, still wiping away tears.

The next day, very early in the morning, Isaak and Sara went to the barracks, with Tatiana intentionally accompanying her mother. As soon as they stepped into the military unit, there was a commotion among the soldiers at the extraordinary beauty of the two women. Sara was thirty-eight years old and still retained her natural beauty. She wore a striking grey coat that complemented her eyes, and a straw hat adorned her blonde hair, which cascaded down her back.

Tatiana was no less attractive, her harmonious face and Oriental eyes framed by a typical Russian fur cap. She wore a blue coat, and her shiny black hair stood out against it. The soldiers were captivated by their presence. Isaak's intention was to speak directly to the garrison's commander, avoiding the bureaucracy of the middle ranks. He assumed it would be difficult to gain access to him, but it wasn't as hard as he thought. Sara's tactic worked, as the murmurs of admiration spread throughout the premises and reached the commander's office.

Amidst whistles and compliments, the colonel's aide-de-camp peered out of the window and caught sight of Sara and Tatiana. When the colonel inquired about the commotion, the aide could only respond, "My colonel, two incredibly beautiful women entered the barracks, hence all the excitement."

The officer approached the window and confirmed that his aide-de-camp was right. He turned and ordered, "They truly are a pair of beauties. Find out what they want; it's possible they came to speak with me."

The lieutenant hurried down the stairs and returned shortly, accompanied by the visitors. Sara advised Isaak to let her do the talking, so she explained the situation to the colonel, pleading with him to intervene to prevent Gabriel from being conscripted. The colonel intentionally extended the conversation, clearly with the purpose of spending more time with Sara and Tatiana. He invited them for a cup of coffee and requested Gabriel's file.

In the meantime, he steered the conversation away from the purpose of their visit. He was captivated by Sara, while his aide couldn't take his eyes off Tatiana, not suspecting that she was a married woman. The colonel had shown signs of having the authority to prevent Gabriel's conscription, which greatly reassured Sara, although her husband was somewhat irritated by the officer's exaggerated gallantry towards her.

It seemed that the colonel overlooked the fact that she wasn't alone and was flirting with her unabashedly. Nonetheless, Isaak tried to conceal his unease, knowing that he could tolerate it if it meant that their son would be spared from joining the Army. Moreover, he had long grown accustomed to the admiration his wife garnered.

"I am more than willing to do whatever is necessary and within my power to please such a charming lady," the officer said.

"Thank you very much, Colonel," Sara responded with a melodious voice.

"And don't worry; we'll solve this in an instant."

The recruiting lieutenant arrived with Gabriel's file and handed it over to the colonel, mentioning that it was accompanied by a note. The colonel received the file and gestured for the lieutenant to leave.

"Very well," he said, "let's clarify the situation."

After reviewing the file and reading the note, his expression darkened. He placed the note on his desk and looked up, addressing Sara.

"Oh, my lady, I'm truly sorry, but in this case, there's nothing I can do."

"How so, Colonel? You just told us that my son's situation could be resolved," Sara implored.

"Under different circumstances, I would have had the authority to make a decision, but in this particular case, it's not possible."

"But why?"

"Because your son has been recommended."

"A recommendation?", "I don't understand. Recommended by whom?"

"By a general ma'am, the commander of the Warsaw Garrison."

22

Smolensk felt cold and gloomy, the whiteness of the falling snow only heightened the sensation. From the military barracks, one could see the thin layer of ice covering the Dnieper. Gabriel felt out of place, not because he feared military life, but because he was discontented with the profession he had been forced into. What embittered him the most was being part of the army of a country he detested. It wasn't the rigour of the barracks or the military life that he shied away from, but rather, why did it have to be in Russia? He could have adapted better to any other army.

As he confessed to his father when they said their goodbyes:

"Father, I don't fear being in the army, the strictness of the barracks doesn't intimidate me, but I've never been drawn to military life. Moreover, it distresses me terribly to have to defend a nation I hate, and worse still, perhaps someday die for it. If it were in the Polish army, I wouldn't feel so bad."

He still remembered his father's words:

"Son, when God imposes these trials on us, it's because he has greater joys in store for us in the future. Trust in Him."

The group that came from Poland was joined by others from different parts of the Empire. They passed the guard of the barracks, where some unfriendly-looking non-commissioned officers awaited them on the frozen training ground. They were lined up and one of the officers stepped forward to welcome them.

"Here, you're not in your mother's little house, your lazy lot. You're worth nothing here, and the only word you need to learn is 'obedience.' You only need to utter three phrases: 'what are your orders,' 'as you order,' and 'order fulfilled.' So, now you know. This is the army, and those who survive training will leave here as soldiers."

Everyone looked at him trembling, not just from the cold but also from the fear of what lay ahead. The non-commissioned officer walked along the formation, staring at them with disdain and arrogance, then stopped and bellowed with a thunderous voice:

"I am Sergeant Nikitin! They call me Satan, and you'll soon find out why. You'll never forget me."

The training proved to be very gruelling, not so much due to the strenuous exercises, but because of the sadistic and malevolent pressure exerted by Sergeant Nikitin, the Chief Instructor. He was the typical character who enjoyed instilling fear and relished in others' suffering. His mere presence caused panic, his gaze was malevolent, and his features disproportionate, all of which gave him a fierce appearance. He was well-justified in earning the nickname Satan, and he took pride in being called so. He treated the recruits with extreme cruelty, striking them and using inhumane punishment techniques. To inspire fear, he often declared that his aspiration was to have half of the men end up in the infirmary and the other half in the cemetery.

From the moment of their arrival in Smolensk and throughout the training, they were told that they weren't being prepared for garrison duties or border patrol.

"We leave that to the little customs girls," Satan would say, "you, those who survive the training, will go to fight in a real war."

In fact, everyone in the garrison was convinced that Russia would go to war in the Balkans.

Gabriel's company of recruits consisted of one hundred and twenty men divided into three platoons, and there were four other companies of the same size in the garrison. Recruits had come from all corners of Russia, including Siberia and Central Asia, although surprisingly, the latter were volunteers. Corporal Borisov, their squad commander, said that they joined the army to escape hunger. Some also enlisted following a practice that the law had abolished decades ago but was still being used surreptitiously. They were called "Hunters": men who replaced recruits paying a hefty sum of money to the hunter's family to evade military service.

Borisov was one of the few who treated them relatively well. He wasn't a paragon of kindness, but at least he didn't relish in their suffering. Sometimes he would hit them in front of Satan, but later, in a rather unusual manner in the Army, he would apologize to the recruits. Not publicly, but personally when speaking to one of his subordinates.

He claimed that if he didn't do so, Nikitin would accuse him of being too lenient and indulgent with the lazy ones, as he often referred to the recruits. Borisov surely didn't want to be transferred to some distant garrison. He wanted to remain in Smolensk as long as possible because he was in love with a girl from the city, who was also carrying his child. Indeed, the corporal was a decent human being, perhaps a bit timid and passive for military life, but he duty fully followed orders, and he feared Satan as much as the recruits did.

The training conducted by Sergeant Nikitin, along with the other non-commissioned officers, was truly rigorous. Not only due to the long days of exercises in extreme conditions, but also because of the physical punishments, which all the superiors considered normal. They believed it would toughen the recruits' character and combat spirit. Hardly a day passed without some recruit ending up in the infirmary, either due to the training or the mistreatment.

But it wasn't just during exercises; it seemed that the goal was to make life in the barracks as difficult and unbearable as possible. At times, they were woken up with buckets of cold water, always accompanied by insults that included a wide range of profanities. Formations for roll call, marches to the mess hall, supervising barrack cleanliness—absolutely all daily activities were accompanied by shouting and blows. Gabriel could never understand how these attitudes would turn them into better soldiers.

Discipline was extremely strict, and any disobedience was severely punished with exemplary corrections aimed at deterring others. The cruellest punishment, in Gabriel's opinion, involved carrying a block of ice until it completely melted. Of course, during the winter's freezing temperatures, the only way to achieve this was through body heat, rubbing the ice block against the skin, which felt like being pricked by hundreds of needles.

Upon handing them their rifles, they were told to consider it as their own beloved, and therefore, they could never abandon it under any circumstances.

"A soldier without a rifle is like a king without a crown," declared Sergeant Kuzmin, Satan's right-hand man, who matched him in cruelty to the conscripts. The weapon could never be neglected; doing so meant facing a terrible punishment.

While some recruits couldn't help shedding a tear or two at night, they eventually grew accustomed to the military routine and the demanding training. The bonds of friendship and camaraderie also strengthened, born out of the need for mutual support and the certainty that sooner or later, they might face death together.

Gabriel was not particularly sociable, but thanks to his kind heart and willingness to assist his comrades, he formed a close circle of companions. Gradually, they adapted to the rigorous military life and learned that the treatment they received depended on their individual conduct. Those who fulfilled their duties and obeyed orders without question had no problems.

They gradually settled into their military roles and adjusted to the different types of commanders and instructors. Of course, Satan had earned himself the prize for unpopularity. Most of the recruits would have shot him if they could. His number two might have had a chance to save himself, though after a well-deserved thrashing. There were other officers and instructors with bad tempers or who were overly demanding, like Sergeant Kisilev, nicknamed "the Count", the second-in-command of the Platoon, rumoured to be the illegitimate son of a nobleman from St. Petersburg. He was tall, had a booming voice, and a perpetual scowl. He was known for his meticulousness and excessive use of force, but that didn't hinder him from being an excellent instructor, frequently reiterating:

"At this moment, you may despise me, but in the future, you'll be grateful. The teachings I impart during training will save your lives in the battlefield."

He repeated some unforgettable phrases, such as "it's better to bleed during training than in battle" or the other one: "more sweat in training, less blood in combat." Despite his temper, he was distinguished by his leadership skills, and his subordinates acknowledged it.

Certainly, not all the non-commissioned officers treated them poorly; an example of this was Sergeant Sorokin, the Company's quartermaster and the most senior of the cadre. He acted like a father to the recruits, helping, advising, and encouraging them constantly. He emphasized that the conscript stage was extremely difficult, but once they became soldiers, their conditions would significantly improve. And indeed, they had noticed it - soldiers were treated with much rigour, but unless they committed an offence, they did not suffer any kind of punishment.

Sorokin was beloved by all the recruits, his jolly appearance inspired trust, and he was never heard raising his voice. He even knew when a young lad was on the verge of breaking down and rushed to his aid. He would encourage him, giving firm pats on the chest or back to instil confidence.

"Move on, you can do it, you'll be a good soldier!"

Many times, he shared that he, too, had been a conscript, just like all of them, so he understood perfectly well what they were going through. He reminded them that this phase was fleeting, and of course, the young lads yearned for it to pass as quickly as possible. The conscripts felt sympathy and gratitude towards the sergeant, who, by the way, was a veteran and had earned several decorations for heroic acts in the Crimean War. Merits he never spoke of and would have gone unnoticed by the recruits if not for a remarkable event.

Nikitin often mocked the quartermaster for his leniency towards the subordinates, deriding his behaviour as more fitting for the godmother of soldiers or a member of the Bolshoi Ballet. As it often happens in the barracks, Sorokin became aware of Satan's lack of respect, and one day, when the latter was about to begin shooting exercises with Gabriel's Platoon, Sorokin confronted the audacious sergeant.

"Sergeant Nikitin, I've heard about your inappropriate comments regarding me."

"They must be exaggerations, my sergeant."

"I know they're not, because I know your character."

With that, Sorokin opened his greatcoat, then his tunic, and lifted his undershirt, revealing his bare chest. Two large scars were visible, one on his right side and another diagonally crossing from his collarbone to his abdomen. Instructors and students gazed in silence.

"Do you know what these are?" he said with a strong voice unfamiliar to the recruits, gazing at Satan, "These are wounds received in Crimea, in a real war, Sergeant Nikitin, a true war."

The other man remained speechless, while everyone present held their breath. Sorokin continued, his words carrying weight:

"The day you've fought in a battle, the day you've looked into the face of the enemy, the real enemy who comes to take your life, listen well, that day, and only then, will you have the authority to mock me!"

"But my sergeant..."

"I haven't finished!" Sorokin interrupted, letting his shirt fall onto his chest. "It's easy to mistreat recruits during training. I'd like to see if you're capable of leading them in combat as well."

He turned around and walked away, and no one dared to move. After a few seconds, as Sorokin disappeared behind the barracks, Satan muttered curses under his breath, ordering Kuzmin to continue with the exercise, and then he went after the quartermaster. What transpired between them afterward remains a mystery, but one thing is certain: no more taunts were heard directed at Sorokin.

Another non-commissioned officer who treated the recruits well was Sergeant Zaitsev, the Company's medic. He hailed from a town near Ekaterinburg, in the Urals. His lifelong aspiration had been to study medicine, and he had toiled hard to gather the means to finance his education. Unfortunately, due to social discrimination, he was denied entry into Medical School merely because he was a peasant's son. Undeterred, he pursued training as a medic and volunteered for the Army, where his knowledge was put to good use, assigning him to various infirmaries in the garrisons where he had served.

He was a man of noble sentiments who also offered solace to the recruits. He detested Satan and all the non-commissioned officers who mistreated their subordinates. He shared Gabriel's belief that such treatment did not create good soldiers. Like Sorokin, he always advised the recruits, saying:

"Hold on, lads, this phase will pass soon."

Then, with a prophetic tone, he would tell them:

"Focus on your training and improving your knowledge because you will need it. You will soon smell gunpowder smoke."

He would smile and conclude his speech by affirming, "But fear not, the medic will be by your side to aid you."

Afterward, he would head to the infirmary, which he kept immaculately tidy and meticulously organized. Every shelf, box, and trunk were labelled and classified, just like the drawers containing medical instruments and medications. He reserved a personal space where he kept books, notebooks, and notes in German, a language he studied in his free time. Having been unable to study in Russia, he clung to the hope of one day going to Vienna to fulfil his dream and obtain his medical degree.

Another non-commissioned officer from the Platoon stayed particularly close to the recruits. He was Corporal Ivanov, who not only had the appearance of a boy but was indeed one, having not yet turned sixteen, making him younger than most of the men he led. Nevertheless, his composure and firmness in giving orders and enforcing them were remarkable. He always carried a stick with which he would occasionally strike the slower and more passive recruits, but it was done with the intention of motivating them, never to cause harm. Some even claimed they could hardly feel the supposed punishment.

Ivanov was a good lad, albeit a bit naive and dreamy. He had become involved with the daughter of one of the laundresses responsible for washing the clothes of officers and non-commissioned officers, a task they performed at a small bend in the Dnieper. The corporal was infatuated with the girl, who made no secret that her only interest was to extract a few silver roubles from him every month when the paymaster distributed their wages.

The officers were a separate case altogether. Captain Nikolai Kuznetsov, the commanding officer of the Company, was strict and showed no leniency for the slightest slip-up, especially when it came to matters of discipline. He didn't hesitate to have any recruit whipped for breaking the rules, but at the same time, he genuinely cared about the well-being of his men. He kept a watchful eye on their food, supplies, and medical needs. He firmly believed that "a well-fed soldier can walk barefoot on the snow and scale any mountain." He also repeatedly stressed, as if it were a premonition:

"I need well-trained soldiers because when the time comes, I'll be going to war with you."

Unlike most officers in the imperial Army, Kuznetzov wasn't born into the nobility. His father was a humble carpenter from Samara, whose eldest son possessed great intelligence and a natural ability for learning. Through self-education, he had studied various disciplines and had a vast knowledge of general culture, particularly in engineering, a subject that fascinated him. Additionally, he had studied English and German, languages he spoke fluently. While he held the rank of corporal, his superiors noticed that his behaviour, manners, way of speaking, and both general and military knowledge were far superior to those of any other non-commissioned officer. This led them to support his admission to the Officer School, from which he graduated with top marks in his class. Despite his excellent performance, due to his humble origins, he was assigned to second-tier units far away from Moscow or St. Petersburg.

For Kuznetzov, this turned out to be a blessing. He couldn't bear the idea of working surrounded by officers whose promotions were owed more to noble lineage than military merit. He often referred to them as "not campaign officers but rather champagne officers". Therefore, he gladly accepted postings to remote garrisons. Before fulfilling his duty, he took a short vacation to his hometown, proudly donning his elegant green uniform and displaying the golden shovel insignia with the red line and two stars on his shoulders, the insignia of a second Lieutenant. This sight brought tears of emotion to his humble carpenter father and his simple dressmaker mother, who could hardly contain their pride as they strolled arm in arm through the streets of Samara, accompanied by their son, the officer of the Tsar's Army.

However, his return to the Volga riverside city was not just to visit his proud parents; it was also to fulfil a promise he had made to a fifteen-year-old girl. After stealing a kiss from her, he had given his word that he would return for her. The young girl, now nineteen and true to her promise of waiting a lifetime, if necessary, had become the beautiful wife of the captain, causing many hearts to flutter in the Smolensk Garrison whenever she passed by.

The other officers in the Company were Lieutenants Bukanin and Semionov, both young but equally strict. Gabriel found himself under the command of the latter in his platoon, a man only a year older than him. Much like Captain Kuznetzov, Semionov cared for the well-being of his men. On more than one occasion, he reprimanded Satan for his cruel and degrading methods.

"That won't make them better fighters. It would be more productive to teach them to shoot well," he once retorted one morning.

He often spoke about the possibility of going to war. The custom was for the officers of the conscripts to stay with them in their subsequent postings, except for those who held the rank of instructors, such as Nikitin. The soldiers believed that the real reason he wasn't sent with the former recruits was to prevent him from being murdered by one of them.

Semionov was clean-shaven and had somewhat boyish features, earning him the nickname "Babe" among the non-commissioned officers and soldiers. His father was the wealthiest merchant in Nizhny Novgorod and controlled a significant portion of the trade known as Pomor, between Russia and Norway. The lieutenant was deeply dedicated to studying military subjects, especially Infantry manoeuvres. He aspired to reach the highest ranks in the military hierarchy, influenced further by an uncle who had been promoted to the rank of general just a few months earlier. The pride of being an officer in the Army and the military ran through his veins.

He also kept a close eye on political developments and firmly believed that war between Russia and the Ottoman Empire was inevitable. He would share this conviction with his comrades and subordinates, urging them to prepare because it would happen much sooner than they imagined. He, on the other hand, declared that he wanted to be the first to head to the front, as he aimed to distinguish himself in his career.

"War is the natural state of a soldier," he said with unwavering certainty. "It is there that the mettle and valour of the imperial Army's troops are tested. I will go to war, which I am certain will erupt, and there I will fight at the head of my men, returning with the insignia of a captain."

Bukanin, the other lieutenant, was the opposite of Semionov. He diligently carried out all his duties, but it was evident that he did so more out of a sense of duty rather than conviction. In military units, everything becomes known, and what is not known is often invented. Rumours circulated that he had been compelled to join the Army by an authoritarian father, one of the largest landowners around Moscow. The reason behind this alleged forceful enlistment was that his son had fallen deeply in love with a young and incredibly beautiful peasant girl. They claimed that the girl had become pregnant and, as soon as Bukanin's father found out, he enlisted the help of a friend who was a general, resulting in the young man finding himself at the Officer School just two days later.

Whatever the reason, the young lieutenant's demeanour betrayed his lack of genuine contentment with his role. He was introverted and timid, speaking very little and rarely interacting with others. He fulfilled his duties without going beyond the strict essentials. The non-commissioned officers and soldiers barely respected him; they followed his orders, albeit without much enthusiasm.

As for the higher-ranking officers, the recruits hardly knew them. On rare occasions, they caught a glimpse of them from afar, but as the older soldiers put it, those officers were like God's incarnations on Earth, and a mere conscript had no right to approach within a hundred meters of a major or a colonel. They were seen only from a distance, appearing to levitate rather than walk. However, their mystique was shattered one day when a general arrived from Moscow for a visit. The soldiers observed their immediate superiors hurrying and appearing nervous in the imminent presence of their superior. A fellow soldier of Gabriel remarked:

"Look at them, for one day, they behave like recruits."

"Yes, it seems that after all, they are human too."

Days went by, and the routine of garrison life gradually became second nature to them. As the date for their promotion to private soldiers approached, the conduct of the instructors, except for Satan, of course, became more lenient. Almost imperceptibly, the pressure diminished, and the initial fear dissipated. They had grown accustomed to the methods, customs, jargon, and culture of the barracks, familiarized themselves with the personalities of their superiors, and strengthened their bonds of friendship. Occasional altercations arose among them, but they were rare, as any quarrel was met with severe punishment.

Gabriel stood out from his comrades in several aspects. His surname, so unusual in Russia and even in Poland, led them to call him "the German," and that became his moniker within the Military Canton. Another characteristic that set him apart was his high level of culture; the officers quickly noticed this and began assigning him certain intellectual tasks. He had the discernment to understand that he should not stand out more than any of his superiors or the rest of the soldiers.

He had formed strong friendships with most of the conscripts in his Company, but he was especially close to three young men: one Polish like him, and two Russians. Provowsky, the Polish one, was also Jewish, while Sajarov and Tarasov were Orthodox Christians. The three belonged to the same squad and formed a tightly knit quartet, affectionately nicknamed "the Aces" in reference to the four cards in a deck. They supported each other and shared many experiences within the barracks.

About fifteen percent of the recruits were Jews, but except for a few exceptions, Gabriel was neither a victim of discrimination nor noticed any such prejudices towards his comrades. What was evident, however, was the intent to Russify the Poles and Christianize the Jews. They were not reproached for their race or customs, but their beliefs were targeted; they were obliged to attend religious services and urged to consider converting to the Russian Orthodox Church. They were led to believe that such a conversion would be a necessary requirement for advancing in the Army. For Gabriel, progressing within the ranks of the Russian military held no appeal, and even if it had been his intention, he would never renounce Judaism. He took satisfaction in finding that all his fellow Jews shared the same sentiment, as no cases of conversion arose during his time in Smolensk.

The most pressing concern for Gabriel, in truth, was the knowledge that he was compelled to serve for six years, a seemingly eternal commitment that disrupted all his life plans. He had never contemplated a military career, especially not in the Russian Army, and he felt he was wasting his existence. He longed for his family and lamented not being able to pursue his ambitions or openly express his religious sentiments. He prayed daily, whenever the training activities allowed, but he missed his Kippah and Tefillin.

One late January day, as they were rehearsing for the ceremony marking the end of training and their confirmation as soldiers, Lieutenant Semionov made an announcement:

"The war is now a reality! At this very moment, Army units are heading towards the Ottoman Empire border. We will finally smell gunpowder."

He raised his arms excitedly, fists clenched, while exclaiming:

"We'll have the chance to cover ourselves in glory!"

Glorifying oneself was not among Gabriel's aspirations, so he didn't share the lieutenant's enthusiasm. However, he was fully aware that they would be obliged to go wherever they were assigned. On the other hand, there were those who argued that the newly trained soldiers would be among the last sent to the front in case hostilities broke out.

"They'll likely assign them to rear units for logistical services at most," analysed Sergeant Sorokin one day.

One Saturday, Corporal Borisov arrived, carrying pencils, sheets of paper, and envelopes. He handed them out, saying, "You'll soon be real soldiers, so you've earned the right to write to your families. Make sure to address the envelopes properly."

Gabriel was aware that some of the recruits couldn't write, but he learned that there were many more than he had imagined. Therefore, before composing a greeting to his family, he helped write letters for several of his comrades. Once he finished, he sat down with his own sheet of paper, ready to send a message to his loved ones, but his mind struggled to find the right words. He had thought of so many things he wanted to share with his family on countless occasions, yet at that moment, he felt a blank in his mind. So, he settled for letting them know he was alright, that he loved them deeply, and that he hoped to see them soon.

The following Monday, they received their new uniforms – green jacket, trousers, and cap. Despite everything, Gabriel felt a sense of joy, just like his fellow recruits. The new uniforms symbolized their triumph over the gruelling phase of military training, an experience no soldier ever forgets. They took particular satisfaction in having accomplished it and recovered a sense of identity.

This time, the uniforms and boots fitted properly, tailored to their sizes, and any necessary adjustments were easily made by the barracks tailor.

"What a difference," Gabriel thought as he finished adjusting his new uniform, "It looks like I'm finally a soldier, in an Army I never wanted, but it's what fate dealt me."

He observed his comrades, including some who had shed tears or cursed, now brimming with joy as they strutted around the barracks, proudly wearing their uniforms.

"Look," he said to Tarasov, "it's incredible what this piece of fabric with gold buttons does; they seem to have forgotten the hardships they endured so quickly."

"No, German, they haven't forgotten, and they never will. But it's one of those strange things about the Army. Remember when Sergeant Kuzmin told us that someday, we'd look back on these times with nostalgia and talk about them with laughter?"

"Yes, I remember," Gabriel replied.

"There you have it, in the Army, they don't brainwash you; you do it to yourself."

Gabriel pondered his comrade's words and began to grasp something about the philosophy of the Army, or rather, the philosophy of a soldier.

The ceremony was scheduled for the following Friday. The day before, an event took place that further reinforced Gabriel's belief about that inexplicable behaviour so characteristic of soldiers, which could alter feelings and bewilder anyone who hadn't experienced it first-hand. That afternoon, as they were heading back to the barracks after the final rehearsal for the graduation, they saw the new group of recruits enter through the main gate of the barracks. They all looked tired and fearful, lined up in front of the Instructors and Satan began his speech:

"You're not in your mummy's little house here, you bunch of lazy bums..."

A thunderous uproar erupted from the group where Gabriel stood. It was a chorus of jubilant cheers and mocking remarks aimed at the newcomers, and he found himself, unintentionally, joining in with his fellow soldiers:

"Recruits, get ready to cry!" "They're trembling like little ladies!" "They'll keel over; they don't even have the right to breathe the air!"

Laughter and all sorts of ironic expressions like "Call for mummy!" or "We can bring you a bedsheet to dry your tears!" filled the training ground until Sergeant Kisilev arrived.

"Very well, gentlemen!" he said, clapping his hands, "You're not soldiers yet, and you already think you're generals. Now, back to the barracks to change and then to the mess hall."

Everyone followed the order, still laughing and joking about the newbies.

The ceremony turned out to be more heartfelt than Gabriel could have imagined three months earlier. Contrary to his assumptions, he felt proud to wear the new uniform with the red shovel on his shoulders. His comrades felt much the same way. They got a close look at the major and the colonel for the first time; the latter addressed them from a lectern, expressing in a part of his speech how proud he was of them and how they had overcome the training phase, becoming good soldiers of the Empire. Inwardly, Gabriel thought:

"He's proud of us, but he doesn't even know us. We've never seen him come near the training areas, the mess hall, or the barracks."

To the delight of the new soldiers, they received their first pay, six silver roubles each—it was a small fortune. They had the opportunity to spend the entire afternoon exploring the city. There wasn't much to see or do in Smolensk, but the feeling of freedom was indescribable. Many ended up in one of the two taverns in town, drinking vodka more to keep warm than to get drunk.

Gabriel preferred to stroll through the city. As he made contact with the outside world beyond the barracks, he experienced, for the first time, the sense of disorientation that came from wearing a military uniform. Provowsky accompanied him, and they walked through the streets, speaking in Polish. Near the fortress on the Dnieper, they came across some girls carrying large baskets. Provowsky greeted them with a compliment, and the girls smiled. One of them gazed at Gabriel with obvious signs that she found the young soldier charming. As she passed by him, she simply said: "Handsome soldier!"

Then she ran back to join her friends, who were also laughing, and they continued their way, blowing kisses at him. Gabriel began to realize that to all the residents of Smolensk they encountered on that snowy February day, they were two soldiers of the Empire, two members of the Tsar's Army, who would work and fight if necessary for Mother Russia. However, in his mind, nothing could be further from the truth. He didn't feel Russian, nor did he have any affection for Russia, but there he was, walking in the middle of a street in a city of that country, knowing that he would have to wear that uniform for six long years.

At that moment, he remembered that it was his nineteenth birthday.

23

Eitan savoured his ice cream while observing the bathers who filled Playa Varese, near his son's apartment in the beautiful resort town of Mar del Plata. Next to him, David was enjoying a gigantic double cone of peanut, chocolate, and vanilla ice cream.

"Incredible," said the boy, "Gabriel didn't like the Russians, and he didn't like the army, but he ended up becoming a soldier of the Tsar."

"That's right, son, and there was no escaping it. But before I continue with the family story, let me tell you a bit about Jesus."

"About Jesus?"

"Yes, because he was a very important Jew, and you should know some things that they don't usually teach your Christian friends."

"I want to know."

"First of all, you must be fully aware that not only was Jesus Jewish, but his entire family was too. They even claimed to be descendants of King David."

The boy listened attentively, though he never neglected his ice cream.

"In fact, his real name was Joshua, a Jewish name, which was later transliterated to Greek as Jesus. Don't dwell on that unfamiliar word; what I mean is that in Greek it sounds like Jesus and not Joshua. Do you understand?"

"Absolutely."

"The same can be said about his mother, Mary. Her Jewish name was Miriam. But anyway, what I want you to know is that his roots, his race, his customs, and his culture were entirely Jewish. It's just that he approached certain spiritual aspects differently, but I won't confuse you with too profound ideas. That's not my intention."

David remained intrigued, and Eitan continued:

"I'll tell you something that your little friends here in Argentina probably haven't been told; Saint Joseph, the father of Jesus, and his mother, the Virgin Mary, were born and died in a Jewish home. And not only that, throughout their lives, they followed Jewish customs and laws."

The boy was surprised and asked, "So, could we say that Catholics venerate the figure of a Jewish woman?"

"One could say so," replied Eitan.

"That never occurred to me, Grandpa."

"Don't worry, I assure you that most Catholics who criticize Jews haven't thought about it either."

Eitan gazed at the horizon and then continued, "There's something else I want you to know, something of great significance."

"What is it, Grandpa?"

"I'm referring to the lie that has been spread for centuries, and you must know that it is simply false. You must have heard that the Jews killed Jesus. That's not true, as there is no doubt that the Jewish court that investigated him handed him over to the Romans. You know the story as well as all Christians; Pontius Pilate had the authority to condemn him or set him free. It was he, a Roman, who made the decision. There is one piece of evidence you must never forget: if the Jews had sentenced Jesus to death, he would have been stoned according to the Hebrew laws of that time. You and the rest of humanity know he was crucified, a punishment imposed by the Romans. Explain this clearly to anyone who accuses the Jews of causing the death of Christ."

David understood that he should respond this way if the matter arose again. His grandfather was undoubtedly the wisest man he had ever known, always having the right answer. He told Eitan this, and the old man smiled as he said:

"Oh, my child, engrave these words in your mind and heart: 'all the arguments used throughout history to attack the Jews are based on false premises.'"

24

Gabriel sat next to Sajarov, who dozed off from time to time, taking advantage of the last rays of the sun. In the distance, they could see the sea, its waters fading into the haze of a distant horizon. Closer to them, at the bay in front of the port, several ships were anchored, some belonging to the Imperial Fleet. Gabriel looked towards the boulevard, trying to imagine where his sisters' house might have been in that area. He also thought about how these waters in the distance were the same that his older sister Tatiana had known when they were children. What irony, the first time he gazed upon the sea, it was the same one that the three of them had experienced as little girls.

As the first gas lamps began to light up the avenues, Gabriel woke up his companion.

"Come on, Vladimir, it's getting dark. We should head back to the barracks."

The other man yawned and stretched his lazy muscles before finally sitting up. He looked towards the city centre and then exclaimed, "One of the things I've liked the most about Odessa is its illuminated avenues. I had never seen these gas lamps before."

"Well," Gabriel confessed, "I have seen them before, but not too long ago. I first saw them last year in Warsaw."

"In any case, it's incredible how they light up the streets."

"Agreed, but that's nothing, my friend. They are now testing a new project they call an incandescent bulb."

"What is that?"

"It's a lamp that works with electricity and uses a vacuum to convert electric current into light. Possibly, in the future, not only the streets but also houses will be illuminated with this new invention they are experimenting with."

"I still don't understand; what invention are you talking about?"

Gabriel looked at his comrade, sighed, and replied, "It doesn't matter, let's go, or we'll be late, and you know Kiselev's punishments."

They had been at their new destination for sixteen days; their Battalion had been assigned to the 22nd Line Infantry Regiment. At that moment, Gabriel was certain of two things: there would definitely be a war against the Turks, and Sergeant Sorokin had been mistaken in Smolensk when he said they would only be kept in the rear for logistical tasks. Many units were already near Ottoman territory, and thousands of soldiers were arriving daily at the port of Odessa. The Imperial Fleet's ships were continuously disembarking troops from Sochi and Mariupol, not to mention those arriving by rail. Almost all the regiments that had been stationed in the city when they arrived had already left for the front, so it seemed only a matter of days before they would have to depart as well.

The most enthusiastic of them all was Lieutenant Semionov, who insisted that a unique opportunity was approaching for the brave Russian soldiers to achieve glory, and he would be the first on the battlefield. He would return proudly to show his father and his uncle, the general, his captain's insignia and decorations.

"Even if I just come back, I'll consider myself well-served," said Tarasov, Gabriel's other Russian friend.

Gabriel had sent a telegraph message to his family from Odessa; the message would pass through Kiev and Minsk before finally reaching Lublin. It was much faster than the regular mail, though also more expensive. He simply informed them that he was in the port city and in good health, not adding much more as he considered there was no reason to worry them. The important thing was for them to receive news from him, as they were not allowed to communicate with anyone when they left Smolensk. While in the port, they were authorized to write, but their communications were subject to censorship, even if they were personal messages.

Except for the instructors and Sergeant Sorokin, all the officers and non-commissioned officers who had led them in Smolensk were with them in Odessa. Captain Kuznetzov proved to possess great administrative and logistical skills. More importantly, he had a keen sense of how and where to acquire the supplies to keep his men well-fed and well-equipped; his Company boasted an excellent camp and supply team.

Meanwhile, the soldiers took the opportunity to explore the city, which was truly beautiful. Its avenues, boulevards, parks, and monuments stood out, and its architecture closely resembled that of the major capitals of Western Europe. Much progress was evident, thanks to the incessant commerce, now increased by the presence of troops temporarily stationed in the city before being sent to the front.

"War is always good business for some," Captain Kuznetzov once commented.

Gabriel always went out with his comrades, especially his three great friends with whom he had shared time since the days of Smolensk. Sajarov, Tarasov, Provowsky, and Rothman, the four Aces, were inseparable, and the only times they were apart were when their guard duties prevented them. They entertained themselves strolling along the boulevards or having a beer at bars near the port. The city was teeming with soldiers, and Odessa's young women came out for walks, taking advantage of the good weather and the presence of thousands of admirers.

With his tall stature, youthful face, and good looks, Gabriel was quite popular among the young women strolling or attending bars and restaurants. His companions laughed and preferred to be with him because he attracted the ladies, ensuring they were never lacking female company. Since their arrival in the city, the Army had assigned them extra pay, so they had money to enjoy a few vodkas and have dinner at a nice restaurant now and then.

However, whenever he wandered the streets, Gabriel couldn't help but think of his sisters and the dramatic story they had lived there. It saddened him, but one day, Sajarov, his closest friend, said to him:

"It's true that what happened to them as children was very tragic but think about it - if it hadn't been for that misfortune, they wouldn't be your sisters today."

"You're right, Vladimir, I hadn't looked at it that way," Gabriel replied.

He loved his sisters dearly, including Tatiana, who was the last to join the Rothman family. His comrade Vladimir Sajarov understood him perfectly, for he too was very close to his own sisters. Their story was quite unique. Vladimir hailed from a village near Kazan, where his father worked as a blacksmith and his mother tended to the family's vegetable garden, selling the produce. They had seven daughters, but their father always longed for a son. He persisted in his search until finally Vladimir was born, becoming the darling of his sisters and the pride of his father.

"I understand what you feel, Gabriel," Vladimir told him. "Ever since I can remember, my sisters have been very special to me. They were always spoiling me, just like my mother. Even now, as an adult, she still sees me as a baby and hasn't stopped the habit of pinching my nose when she greets me."

Gabriel smiled as he shared with his friend:

"There's a similarity in the gesture of your mother and that of my sisters towards me. They haven't stopped pinching my cheeks, even though I stopped being a child long ago."

The two friends laughed and made their way back to the barrack, reminiscing about anecdotes of their respective parents and sisters.

When the war was declared, they were still in Odessa, and there was no doubt they would be sent to the front at any moment; they only awaited the order. The preparations of the Regiment progressed, and Kuznetsov's Company was the first to be fully ready to depart. Lieutenant Semionov was burning with impatience and was terribly irritable, so the non-commissioned officers avoided him. However, nearly two months passed before they finally received the order to move. That day was glorious for the lieutenant; he danced like a Cossack in the middle of the improvised barrack, shouting cheers and cries of excitement.

To Semyonov's disappointment, they were stationed in the rear as a reserve unit, spending three more weeks in Bolgrad. Finally, they were ordered to advance and penetrate enemy territory. In July, they crossed the Danube in Galati and entered Romania, rapidly moving towards Bulgarian territory, drawing near to the frontline. In the early days of August, they were in Ruse, where they stayed for three weeks before receiving instructions to head to Pleven to support the Russian troops engaged in that area.

Kuznetsov's Company was able to confirm that the rhythmic tones of military songs and anthems extolling valour and heroism had vastly different sounds from the thunderous boom of cannons, the crackle of gunfire, and the heart-wrenching cries of the wounded. They also realized that the confusion, the scent of blood and gunpowder, or the torrents of mud on their sweat-drenched faces bore no resemblance to the gruelling exercises back at the barracks.

On that 11th of September 1877, Gabriel understood that, regardless of the uniform one wears, war is terrible. Just as terrible was witnessing his good friend Vladimir Sajarov fall by his side, his skull shattered. That very day, Lieutenant Semionov distinguished himself as the bravest of soldiers, living up to the impassioned speeches he had tirelessly given at the barracks. He proved that his words were not mere empty boasts.

True to his promise of being the first in combat and leading his men, he immortalized the phrase he said to his commander before charging at the Turkish trenches with his platoon: "Captain, today my troops will be the first to be covered in glory or die."

With great courage, he led the assault, and his men, including Gabriel, followed him without hesitation. Semionov achieved his dream and returned to Russia decorated and bearing the captain's insignias. Both the medal and the four-star epaulets rested on velvet atop his coffin.

The Turkish firepower was relentless, knocking down the Russians like dominoes. Just a fraction of a second after Lieutenant Semionov was hit, Gabriel felt as if he had collided with a wall. The last thing he saw was a thick black cloud; then darkness and absolute silence enveloped him. At that precise moment, Sara was tallying up accounts with the bakery clerks. Suddenly, she felt a shiver.

"What's the matter, Mrs. Sara?" one of the girls asked. "Are you feeling alright?"

"Yes, yes, I'm fine. It's just that I felt something strange."

Without apparent reason, tears welled in her eyes. She sighed and said:

"Let's finish for today. We'll check the remaining tasks tomorrow. Close up the bakery; I'm going home."

Sara walked anxiously along the pavement, unable to grasp what was happening, but feeling herself on the verge of collapsing. Thoughts of Gabriel flooded her mind, and she had an overwhelming perception that something had happened to her son. The sensation was dreadful. She quickened her pace, veering towards the shoemaker's shop. Upon arrival, Isaak grew concerned seeing her dishevelled face.

"What's the matter, my love?" he asked, rushing towards her.

"I don't know, I have a premonition about Gabriel."

"A premonition?"

"Yes, I believe something bad has happened to him."

"Calm down, my love. Let me get you some tea."

He made her sit down and brought a chair to sit beside her.

Sara clasped her chest with her hand, and her husband held the other hand, saying, "You must calm yourself, my dear. He's fine. If something had happened, they would have notified us."

"But how long do they take to notify when something happens to a soldier in a distant war? In a war so far away?"

Isaak remained silent, and she continued:

"Read the news that comes. They always talk about the large number of Russian and Turkish soldiers dying every day, but they report it much later. We haven't heard anything from Gabriel since the telegram he sent from Odessa over four months ago."

"You must calm yourself, my love. It's just a mother's premonition, you understand?" Isaak repeated, though he couldn't hide his own worry. Having a son at war was one of the harshest trials that could be imposed on parents.

"Yes, a mother's premonition, do you get it? We have to do something; we need to find out."

"But how do we do that? We don't know anyone; we have no contacts."

"Send a telegram to Jared. He knows many people in St. Petersburg. Oizer too, he travels there frequently; he must have some acquaintances."

And so they did. Oizer brought forward a planned trip to the capital to inquire at the Ministry of War, where he knew a colonel with whom he had conducted business in the past. Unfortunately, the endeavour proved fruitless. The course of the war in the Balkans was not very favourable for Russia at that moment. The great disorganization and chaos prevailing on the front made casualty reports unreliable, often too delayed, and sometimes non-existent, limited to mere numerical figures without detailing names.

Back in Pinsk, Oizer had the idea to pass through Smolensk. After all, it was there that the Garrison where Gabriel had served was stationed, and they might know something. At the Guardhouse of the barracks, he was informed that the entire unit to which Gabriel belonged had been sent to the Balkans and attached to a Regiment, and therefore, the war reports related to that Battalion were not sent to Smolensk. Only the training and logistics staff remained there to prepare new groups of recruits. Disappointed, he was walking back to his carriage when he heard someone calling him.

"Oizer? Oizer Czemerinsky?"

He turned around and saw a military man approaching, but he couldn't recall ever meeting him before.

"Are you Jared Czemerinsky's son?"

"Jared Weizmann, formerly Czemerinsky, that's right."

"I thought it was you. Do you remember me?"

Oizer studied him carefully.

"Of course, I remember now. You were the one in the cart accident."

"That's right. I had a minor ankle injury, but if it wasn't for your father's timely intervention, and, well, your help too, I wouldn't be here to tell the tale."

"How have you been? I remember you perfectly, but I've forgotten your name."

"Ivan Sorokin, sergeant."

"Yes, of course. How have you been?"

"Very well. Now, I'm mostly involved in logistics tasks. But tell me, what brings you to Smolensk?"

"I was inquiring about a soldier."

"Which soldier?"

"One who was here and got sent to the Balkans."

Sorokin looked intrigued and invited him to the NCOs' cafeteria to discuss the details.

"I understand now. We haven't received any notification, but the parents are worried."

"Yes, it's been four months without any news, and his mother has a bad feeling about it."

"It's not easy to find out about a soldier at this time and getting a response can be quite slow. What's his name?"

"Gabriel Rothman."

"Hmm, I think I remember him—the one with the German last name, tall, and blonde, right?"

"Exactly, Ivan. I would be deeply grateful if you could inquire about him. Gabriel is like a brother to me."

Sorokin clicked his tongue as he thought, then said:

"Well, any attempt to find out has to go through Odessa. My nephew is also a sergeant and coincidentally works in the communications centre at the Army Headquarters in that city. If anyone can help us, it's him. I'll send him a telegram right away, asking him to inquire with the personnel officers at the front."

"You have no idea how much I appreciate this, Ivan."

"You have nothing to thank me for. I owe my life to your father and to you. I'll do everything in my power to try and find out how your friend is doing."

He left Jared's address in Pinsk and bid farewell, hopeful that they could get some information about Gabriel.

Three weeks later, Sorokin kept his promise and sent a telegram to Jared's house. The message was brief:

Line Soldier Rothman Gabriel —First Battalion, Regiment 22, Fifth Army— "Missing in Action" In Leven, September 11, 1877.

Jared immediately relayed it to Lublin. When Sara read the telegram, she fainted and lost consciousness. The tragedy was devastating for family and friends; everyone who had known Gabriel deeply mourned the news. When Aliza received the telegram in Vienna, she had such a sudden nervous reaction that she had to be hospitalized. Tatiana and Jana wept uncontrollably, while Isaak was so crushed that he locked himself in his room, refusing comfort from anyone.

The rabbi visited the Rothman family, trying to alleviate their pain. Sara thanked him for the gesture, offered him some tea, and they sat in the living room with the daughters and their spouses. Isaak came down to greet the rabbi, and at that moment, Sara, who had cried until she had no tears left, exclaimed:

"The note is very clear—it says, 'Missing in Action,' it doesn't state that my Gabriel is dead. I pray to God that He returns him to me alive."

Everyone listened to her with unwavering attention, detecting a glimmer of hope in her eyes. Jana and Tatiana stood up and hugged their mother. She turned to the rabbi and made a request:

"I beseech you to lead us in a prayer, imploring God for the return of my son," Sara pleaded.

Robiak looked at Saul with a face of incredulity, then approached and whispered in his ear:

"I, too, would like to believe that nothing has happened to him, but according to the message, he disappeared three weeks ago. Don't you think he would have turned up by now if he were alive?"

25

He had an unbearable headache: everything seemed to spin around him. His throat was parched. He heard someone speaking, but the words seemed to come from beyond the grave, incomprehensible and distant.

"Look, it seems he's thirsty. Give him some water, Ionela," said one person.

"Help me lift his head," another voice chimed in.

They raised his head gently and moistened his dry lips. Then Ionela brought a pitcher and let the liquid flow. The man coughed and opened his eyes slightly, only seeing shadows. The two girls settled him softly onto the pillow, and after a while, he managed to open his eyes again.

"Come, Ozana, I think he's finally waking up," said one of the girls.

The other girl approached and looked at him attentively.

"You're right. Hello, can you hear me?"

But the man didn't respond; he blinked a few times and observed them, his gaze distant and dreamlike, like that of a sleepwalker. One of the girls said to the other:

"Look at him, Ozana, he opened his eyes again. They're lovely, aren't they?"

"Shh, he's coming to his senses. He might hear you," Ozana whispered.

At that moment, the man tried to sit up, but weakness prevented him, and he collapsed back down. One of the young women advised:

"Take it easy, don't exert yourself."

He didn't understand the words and placed his hand on his throbbing head, feeling the bandage on his forehead.

"No, don't remove the bandage."

With a bit more awareness, he gazed at them, intrigued. The two girls smiled at him. Then, he slowly turned his head, examining the room, trying to determine where he was. A few moments later, he lowered his head again, feeling like it might explode. As consciousness returned, he also felt pain on his right side and leg. He closed his eyes briefly, took a deep breath, and opened them again, looking back at the two young women with evident curiosity. Finally, one of them asked him in a rough Russian with an odd accent:

"What's your name, Russian?"

"I'm not Russian, I'm Polish."

"You're not Russian?"

"No."

"What's your name, then?"

"I'm Gabriel Rothman, Private Rothman."

When Lieutenant Semionov gave the order to advance, the soldiers followed, shouting at the top of their lungs. Tension reached its peak, and their only thought was to reach the Turkish trenches and take them by blood and fire. They ran as if desperate, getting closer and closer to the Ottoman soldiers with their olive-green uniforms and distinctive caps. When they had covered about half the distance, the lieutenant ordered:

"Fire! Fire at will!"

All fired their rifles simultaneously, and hell broke loose as Turkish bullets grazed their sides. They threw themselves to the ground, seeking shelter behind the small mounds of terrain. Reloading their rifles, Semionov split the platoon in two, sending Sergeant Kisilev with half the men to the left flank while he took charge of the right. With courage in his voice, he rallied them:

"At my command, we will advance! Ready? Let's show these Turks what Russian soldiers are made of."

Gabriel adjusted his jacket, and Sajarov, his good friend since Smolensk, who stood beside him, said fearfully:

"We are made of flesh and bone. I hope we come out of this intact today."

Trying to reassure him, Gabriel replied:

"Don't worry, Vladimir. You'll see, we'll make it through this."

Just then, Semionov shouted, "Ready, attack!"

They rose, shouting, and ran after the officer. Gabriel had barely taken three steps when a bullet struck Sajarov in the forehead. Blood and bits of his companion's brain splattered onto Gabriel's face. He turned to look at him, but Sajarov's body had been blown into the air, lying lifeless on the ground. His mother would never again pinch his nose when greeting him, and his sisters, who spoiled him, along with his father, who had waited so many years for a son, would never see him again. Nevertheless, Gabriel pressed forward, the explosions getting closer. He witnessed the lieutenant falling, and shortly after, he felt a blow that knocked him down.

When he regained consciousness, he felt freezing cold, as if he were on an ice floe. Absolute darkness surrounded him, his mouth was dry, and an overwhelming thirst tormented him. He would have given anything for a sip of water. His entire body ached; it felt as if a cart had run over him. Distant murmurs reached his ears, but he couldn't grasp what was being said. He looked up and saw the sky adorned with stars, the pale crescent moon shining in the firmament. He tried to sit up, but he was too weak and sore. He began to crawl with difficulty, his eyes gradually adjusting to the darkness. The faint moonlight allowed him to make out the surroundings of small mounds.

He continued crawling but stumbled upon something blocking his path. Feeling with his hands, he realized it was the cold and lifeless body of a soldier. He kept moving forward among dozens of stiff bodies, able to identify them as Russians, his comrades from the Second Platoon. He resisted looking at their faces to avoid recognizing them, yet the words of Lieutenant Semionov came to his mind: "Today, my troops will be the first to cover themselves in glory or die." Indeed, they covered themselves in glory... and died.

He tried to find a rifle, but not a single weapon was in sight. He crawled for about fifteen minutes before stopping due to the unbearable pain in his head and knee. Thirst consumed him, and at that moment, he noticed that the murmurs sounded closer. He remained still, listening attentively; it was a group of men conversing in a low voice. He couldn't understand their language, and fear crept in. He wanted to keep moving to distance himself, but he didn't know which direction to head. Exhaustion took hold, and he decided to rest for a moment, lying on his back while gazing at the sky and the moon. In that instant, he recalled a phrase his father had once said: "The crescent moon, the horns face east." He wasn't sure if the moon was waxing or waning, but regardless,

he knew that if he followed the direction of the horns, he would move
east or west. The Turks were to the north, so it was crucial to avoid that
direction. Thus, he continued crawling, relieved to hear the murmurs
becoming more distant.

After about twenty minutes, he noticed he was nearing a forest,
where he would find more shelter. When he reached the edge of the
trees, he tried to stand, but a sharp pain shot through his right knee.
He found a branch that served as a makeshift walking stick. With great
difficulty, he managed to move further away from the battlefield, arriving
at the end of the small woods and stepping out into an open and sloping
area.

The moon had hidden behind a cloud, intensifying the darkness. He
descended the terrain, stopping a little further ahead to listen once more.
He thought he recognized the sound of running water. Descending a bit
more along the slope, he discovered, to his joy, that there was indeed
a small stream at the far end of the field. Enduring the pain in his leg
and supporting himself with the improvised stick, he reached the brook.
Slowly, he lowered himself and lay down by the bank, submerging his
face in the water and desperately drinking the restorative liquid. At that
moment, he had no idea that he had sustained three wounds from
bullets, leading to significant blood loss.

After quenching his thirst, he felt somewhat rejuvenated. He crossed
to the other side of the stream and let himself fall onto the ground to
rest a little. Then he heard voices approaching, speaking in an unfamiliar
language. Cautiously, he hid behind a bush and held his breath. He
managed to make out that there were three soldiers who collected water
from the brook and then returned from whence they came. He emerged
from his hiding place and took the opposite path, advancing a short
distance before the tormenting pain caught up with him. He sought
shelter beneath a bush and tried to sleep a bit. His slumber was sporadic,
and he remained that way until dawn. Once again, he suffered from
intense thirst and overwhelming weakness. He noticed he had a fever
and felt dizzy. Nevertheless, he pressed on as best as he could until he
reached the edge of a road. He collapsed to the ground again, attempting
to stand up, but the dizziness prevented him. In that moment, he fainted.

The elderly Romanian peasant and his nine-year-old daughter found the soldier unconscious by the roadside and took pity on him. He was semi-conscious but accepted some water from them. They lifted him onto their cart. The cart driver recognized him as a Russian soldier. Although it was unlikely, they would encounter Turks, as the Romanian Army had taken control of Grivitsa and the surrounding area, he took precautions by removing the soldier's uniform and hiding it. He covered the soldier with a flour sack cloth and set off for Nikopol on the banks of the Danube. They arrived in the afternoon, and Gabriel was shivering and delirious due to his high fever.

The peasant's wife, who had been waiting for him in the village, attended to Gabriel by placing cold cloths on his forehead. She then bandaged the wound on his head, covering the injury on his skull. She also dressed the wound on his leg and said to her husband:

"We must take him to Alexandria; if he isn't seen by a doctor, he will die."

"Agreed," he replied. "I brought him from the frontline; taking him a bit further won't change anything. Besides, he's in no condition to return to his unit. Let's go, my dear."

In Alexandria, a doctor examined him, treated his wounds, and, not wanting to leave him abandoned, accommodated him in one of the rooms of his own house. The doctor had to depart for Leven as he had to fulfil his service period on the frontline. Thus, he entrusted the nurse from the small clinic in the town to attend to the soldier's daily care.

Gabriel spent nearly a week in a semi-conscious state, being fed small sips of soup. Finally, on the fifth day, he began to regain awareness and saw two young women attending to him.

"I am Ionela, and she is my sister, Ozana," said one of the girls.

He didn't reply as he still felt weak and disoriented. He had no idea where he was, and his memories were muddled. He closed his eyes for a moment and took a deep breath.

"I think he has fallen asleep again," said Ionela.

He opened his eyes again.

"No, he's awake," confirmed her sister. Then she greeted him, "Hello."

"Hello," he said weakly. "Where am I?"

"In Alexandria, soldier."

"Alexandria? Where is that, and how did I end up here?"

"You're in Romania. They brought you wounded from the frontline."

"I don't remember anything."

"You've been unconscious for five days."

Gabriel tried to sit up a bit and looked at the two girls, then his gaze wandered around the room before he asked:

"And who are you? You don't seem like nurses."

The two girls laughed, and finally, Ozana said:

"No, we are the daughters of Alexandria's doctor, and we know a thing or two about nursing. But don't worry, a real nurse comes every day to take care of you."

"And why am I here?"

"A peasant found you near the frontline; you needed a doctor, and he helped you."

He began to recall, but his memory only reached the moment he was drinking water from a stream.

The next day, he tried to get up. He felt very dizzy and weak, but he managed to take a few steps, although he couldn't properly support his right leg. The nurse came to treat his head, knee, and side wounds. She advised him not to put weight on his leg yet and provided him with a crutch. She spoke only Romanian, so one of the young women or her mother translated for him. While they didn't speak Russian fluently, they managed to hold a conversation as they had lived in Galati, near Bessarabia.

He remained very frail and only consumed liquid food. The doctor's wife, Doína, entered to greet him.

"Good afternoon, my name is Doína. I am the lady of the house and the mother of these two girls. How are you feeling?"

"I feel a lot of pain, both in my head and leg, but I suppose I am improving because I felt worse yesterday."

"What you need is rest. The nurse will continue with the dressings; the most important thing is to avoid infection, especially in your leg."

"It is an honour to meet you, ma'am, and to have the opportunity to thank you for the care you are providing. Please excuse any inconvenience I may have caused."

Doína was surprised by his language and manners, which were quite different from those of an ordinary soldier.

"You express yourself very well, and don't worry, we do it with pleasure. My husband is a doctor, and we take care of anyone in need with great care."

Ionela approached Ozana and whispered something in Romanian:

"Especially if he is as handsome as this soldier."

The two sisters laughed, and the mother scolded them:

"Girls, it's not the time for jokes. Let the soldier rest; he is already enduring enough pain."

She instructed them to leave the room, and she followed suit, saying to the wounded soldier:

"We'll leave you to rest; the nurse will come later."

He managed to sleep for a few hours. When he woke up, the pain bothered him, and he tried to sit up, but he felt dizzy. Nevertheless, with great effort, he managed to sit on the bed. He realized that part of the dizziness was due to not having stood up for so many days. Just then, the nurse entered to tend to his wounds. Usually, one of the girls would enter the room to act as a translator, but this time, there was none of them.

Gabriel couldn't understand what the nurse was saying, but he saw her smiling, and he thanked her more with gestures than words. Speaking Russian would be of no use. She was a young and very kind girl, seemingly a bit shy, but extremely attentive. That day, after finishing the dressing, she did something unexpected: she leaned in and gave him a kiss on the cheek. Immediately, she blushed and hurriedly left the room. He was surprised, as this didn't seem like typical behaviour for a nurse.

"What could she have said in Romanian?" he wondered.

That evening, the doctor returned and entered to check on him.

"Good evening, soldier. How are you? I am the doctor, Mihai. What's your name?"

"Good evening, doctor. My name is Gabriel Rothman. Thank you very much for your care. I hear that you saved my life."

"You have nothing to thank me for. It's my duty, and I am glad to have been able to help a Russian soldier."

"I'm not Russian, doctor."

"It doesn't matter; you are part of their Army, and we are very grateful for what you are doing for our country. Thanks to you, there is hope that a dream that has persisted for over three hundred years may finally come true. It seems that we may free ourselves from the Ottomans at last."

"I hope so."

"Well then, let's see how your wounds are healing. Let's start with your head."

He approached and removed the bandage, examining the wound with his fingers.

"You were very lucky. The bullet made a groove along the skull bone without splintering. Had it been otherwise, some fragments could have penetrated the brain. A few millimetres more, and you wouldn't be here. It's healing well, and the inflammation is beginning to subside. I believe that in three days, the headaches will stop."

"Thank you. It still hurts quite a bit, but less than yesterday."

"Tomorrow it will hurt even less. Now, let's look at your side."

He examined the side wound and seemed satisfied.

"This one is also much better. There were some splinters in this area, but it's healing well. Now, about the knee."

He lifted the sheets and observed the leg, palpating it. Gabriel felt much pain and winced.

"This wound is the most severe, which is why it requires two dressings daily. We cannot risk any infection. It's best not to stress the knee, no walking for now, not even within the room."

"Understood, doctor. Thank you so much for everything. Can I ask you a question?"

"Yes, of course."

"It's about the frontline. Could you please tell me how things are unfolding there?"

"Sure," Mihai replied, pulling up a chair and sitting by his side. "The situation is unstable. The Russians have been trying for several days to break through the Turkish resistance and take the city, but they haven't succeeded yet. They haven't even managed to reach the outer trenches that the Ottomans have around the city."

"I know those trenches well; it's where I got wounded."

"It seems that the battle will last for several more weeks, and the outcome is still uncertain. The Romanians have made significant advances; they took Grivitsa and still hold it. Our troops have been successful and are protecting your Army's flanks quite well."

"I truly hope things improve."

"We'll see, soldier. I must be on my way. I need to support the medical teams at the frontline every week, so when I return, I have a lot of work to catch up on in the village. I'll drop by for a moment after dinner tonight."

"Thank you very much, doctor, to you and your family. I won't be able to repay what you've done for me."

Gabriel was truly indebted to that family; the nurse and the two girls attended to him diligently, supporting him in every way he needed. Ionela was particularly special; she loved sitting on a chair beside him, eager to hear about his life and experiences in the Army. The girl was watchful whenever the nurse arrived and didn't like leaving them alone together. The nurse seemed bothered by Ionela's constant presence. On more than one occasion, she asked Ionela to leave, which she did reluctantly and returned quickly. Gabriel couldn't understand Ionela's attitude until one day, while the nurse was changing his bandage and caressing his hair—a simple massage from the temples to the centre—Ionela entered and confronted the nurse. They had a heated argument, and though Gabriel couldn't understand their Romanian words, he deduced the nature of the dispute from their gestures. He confirmed it when the nurse left.

"That nurse is shameless," Ionela complained, visibly angry. "How dare she touch your hair like that?"

Gabriel looked at her and smiled. "Touch my hair how?"

"Just as she did, I told her she should come to do the dressings, not to caress you."

He chuckled. "And why are you bothered by it?"

"How can I not be? I don't like how flirtatious she is with you."

Gabriel observed Ionela, and for the first time, he saw her as a woman. At seventeen, Ionela had an angelic face, dark hair, beautiful green eyes, thick eyebrows, long lashes, prominent cheekbones, and a lovely mouth. She wasn't tall, but she had an attractive figure, and most importantly, she was very sweet and tender. However, she also had a strong character, as he witnessed when she reprimanded the nurse.

Gabriel's physical appearance made him very attractive to women, but he had always focused on other interests. While he had noticed them, his priorities had always been his studies, his great passion, and later the Army, where he was forced to serve, but which took up all his time. He hadn't had a girlfriend or thought about it. However, now, noticing Ionela's jealousy toward the nurse, he realized that she had feelings for him, and as he contemplated her, he discovered that the feeling was mutual.

She didn't speak Russian very well, but they could understand each other. Besides, she was pleasant company because she showed a genuine interest in getting to know him and his past; giving him the opportunity to reminisce about better times and forget, even for a little while, about the war and his involvement in the Army.

The next day, Ionela entered with the necessary items to perform the routine procedures and change the bandages. Gabriel looked at her with surprise and asked, "Are you going to do the dressings for me?"

"Yes, from now on, I'll take care of changing your bandages," she replied.

"What about the nurse?"

"She won't need to come back; I'll handle it."

"Did you tell her not to come back?"

"Exactly. I can take care of you."

"But she's a nurse."

"So what? I can do dressings too; remember, my father is a doctor, and I've learned from him."

"I don't doubt that, but..."

"And why do you want that nurse to come back? Has she enchanted you or something?"

"No, of course not," he said, laughing.

"I hope not, because she can't be trusted."

"What do you mean?"

"She confessed to my sister that she really likes you."

He burst into laughter. He knew he had a way of attracting women, but it was a different story when it came to pursuing romance, given his priorities and even his shyness.

"And does that bother you?"

"Well, yes, it does bother me. We were the ones who welcomed you into our home and protected you."

"I'm very, very grateful for that, not just to you but to your parents and your sister as well."

"You don't have to be; we do it with affection. We don't forget that you Russians are helping us liberate ourselves from those wicked Turks."

Gabriel looked at her and thought to himself that, in his particular case, he had been forced into the war against his will.

"So far, I haven't been able to help much. In my first battle, I got wounded."

"Just with that, you've done quite a lot," Ionela said while changing the bandage on his forehead.

Seeing Gabriel's beautiful blonde hair, she felt the urge to caress it and, for a moment, understood why the nurse had done so. However, she became upset at the thought of the nurse and snorted in annoyance.

"What happened?" he asked. "Is something wrong with the wound?"

"No, I just remembered that shameless nurse," she replied.

He laughed again and said, "Anyone would think you're jealous."

She looked up, stared at him intently, and retorted, "You silly boy!"

Gabriel was a bit taken aback and didn't know what to say. At that moment, Ozana entered and commented, "You look good playing the nurse. Come, let me help you support his leg."

They finished the procedure, and then both girls sat on either side at the foot of the bed.

"I can't find the words to express my gratitude to you and your parents," he said.

"I told you that you don't have to," Ionela replied. "You've already done enough for our country."

"Agreed," added Ozana.

"Well, I feel very embarrassed, but I need to ask you for a favour," Gabriel said.

"We're listening," said Ionela, leaning closer to hear him.

"I actually have two favours, but first, I want to know how far we are from the front."

"Why?" asked Ozana. "Do you want to go back?"

"No, but I'm a soldier, and at least I should inform my superiors about my situation. According to my calculations, it's been ten days since the battle where I was wounded."

"As you said, where you were wounded, not just one wound, but three," pointed out Ionela. "First, you need to recover."

"But I must find a way to send a message."

"Well, the front is a two-day journey from here, but you have to cross the Danube, and with this war, finding a way is not easy. Besides, you could encounter Ottoman soldiers at any moment. You're safer here."

"Thank you, Ionela, but it's not about safety; it's about fulfilling my duty."

Ionela looked at her sister and exclaimed, "As my father says, soldiers are brainwashed: 'duty!' I suppose your duty is to heal first and then figure out what to do, right? Or do you plan to walk around with that leg as it is? Haven't you noticed how swollen your knee is?"

"Yes, but..."

"But what? Did you hear that my father removed a bullet from your leg? And not just that, he also took one from your side, and another grazed your head. You survived by a miracle, and now you want to go back to the front as if nothing happened?"

"You're right, but I still need to send some message."

At that moment, the girls' mother entered, a woman of very kind and cheerful character.

"What's going on? Who's planning to go to the front?" she asked.

"This crazy soldier," Ozana exclaimed, "he says it's his duty."

Since she spoke in Romanian, he didn't understand, but the lady said, "Let's speak in Russian so he doesn't feel left out." Then she addressed

Gabriel, "My daughter concludes that you're crazy for wanting to return to the front, and I agree. It's unnecessary."

"It's my obligation, otherwise, I'd be considered a deserter."

"Oh, my boy! A deserter is someone who flees from combat. Your case is exactly the opposite; you charged at the Turkish trenches, and they nearly killed you. But fine, we need to be practical and weigh the situation."

Gabriel wondered what Sergeant Kisilev or Captain Kuznetzov would consider being practical under the situation. He was a soldier, and he had the duty to report in. The lady continued:

"There are several aspects to consider: first, you have three wounds, and before returning to your military unit, you must be in optimal physical condition. It would be absurd to attempt to cross territories alone where you might encounter the Turks. Second, with your medical condition, you wouldn't be useful on the frontlines; instead, you would become a burden to your detachment. Trust me, field hospitals are not very pleasant. Remember that my husband is a doctor and has to do shifts there."

Gabriel acknowledged that the lady was absolutely right. However, he remained convinced that he had to report in, and he conveyed this to them.

"All right, my husband returns the day after tomorrow for his rest period. Five days later, he will be back at the front. We can send a message to your commanders with him, although it's not certain they will receive it, as I don't know what kind of communication exists between the Russian and Romanian troops there."

"I thank you very much for your help. Please understand that not only do I have to return to my unit, but I also can't continue to impose on your hospitality. I'm a burden to you."

"You're not a burden!" Ionela clarified hurriedly.

Her mother confirmed it:

"So don't worry; we're happy to help an allied soldier of Romania." She looked at her two daughters and added, "Besides, I see that Ionela and Ozana are happy to have you here."

They blushed under their mother's keen gaze.

"Thank you again, ma'am," said Gabriel, "and the same to your family; everyone has been very generous to me."

"Relax, you can stay here for as long as you want; the important thing is that you recover."

The lady left, followed by her daughters, but just as they were about to go, Gabriel called for Ionela.

"I apologize, do you remember that I said I needed to ask you for two favours?"

"Of course."

"It's been several months since I communicated with my family."

"With your family?"

"Yes, my family lives in Poland."

"You have family in Poland?" Ionela asked, becoming very serious.

"Of course, everyone has family."

"Are you married? Are you referring to your wife and children?" the girl asked, furrowing her brow.

Gabriel looked at her and smiled, noticing the anxiety on her face.

"No, Ionela. I mean my parents and sisters."

The girl let out a big sigh, and her eyes lit up.

"Oh, I see. For a moment, I thought... well, how can I help you?"

"I need to send them a message. It's possible that the Army has already listed me as missing in action, and if so, my family might receive wrong information. They would think I'm dead, you understand?"

"Perfectly. What I'm not sure about is how the mail works from here to Poland, but I'll find out today."

"Thank you. Can I ask you one more question before you leave?"

"Yes, tell me."

"Do you see that brilliant sun?" he said, pointing to the window.

"Of course, the sky is clear, and the weather is very pleasant. We should take advantage of it before summer ends."

"Would you like to enjoy it with me?"

Ionela raised her eyebrows, unsure of how to interpret the question.

"I mean," Gabriel continued, "if you'd like to go out in the sun with me. I won't suggest going for a walk, as your father advised me not to walk just yet."

The girl asked expectantly, "Is that an invitation?"

"Exactly, even if it's within your own home."

"Of course, yes, but it would have to be in the back, in the orchard. I hope walking there won't harm you."

"We'll go slowly to avoid any harm, and I'll also apply the healing method used in the Army for these cases."

"What is it?"

"Walk next to a beautiful girl, it improves any wound."

Ionela laughed joyfully, and her cheeks turned rosy.

The young woman arranged two benches in the meadow by the orchard, and they slowly made their way there. Gabriel leaned on her arm, and when they arrived, they sat down. They began to converse; Gabriel told her about his sisters and how they had come to live with his family. The sun hid behind some clouds, and the wind picked up, so they decided to go back inside the house. On the way back, he felt a slight pain in his knee, so he rested with his leg slightly elevated. Ozana arrived, and as had become customary, the two sisters sat at the foot of the bed, continuing the conversation.

The following day, the sky was clear again, and the sun shone brilliantly. Gabriel dared to take a longer walk, so Ionela guided him to Vedea Park, located very close to the house. Gabriel leaned on the crutch while the girl held his left arm to help him maintain balance. It was evident that she was happy. They sat for a few minutes, and he told her about his life in Poland and how his father had achieved an incredible feat, worthy of being recounted in an adventure book. The girl couldn't take her eyes off Gabriel as he spoke.

The next morning, they returned to the same park to bask in the breeze that flowed from the river. Ionela was captivated by Gabriel's tales and couldn't help but feel that her own life paled in comparison to his adventures. She relished listening to him, gazing at him with starry eyes, especially when he recounted pleasant memories, causing his grey eyes to turn a captivating shade of blue, accompanied by what she deemed the most beautiful smile she had ever seen.

Ionela entered the room to tend to his wounds. The injuries on his side and head had healed perfectly, but his knee remained inflamed and painful. Before changing his bandages, she said, "I've been informed about how you can send a message to your family, the quickest way possible. Here, I've written it down for you."

"Please, do explain," Gabriel requested.

"The best way is to send a note to Brasov. There, it'll be converted into a telegraphic message and sent to Sibiu, then to Timisoara, followed by Budapest, Vienna, Brno, Cracow, Warsaw, and finally, to Lublin. That's the entire route. Some of those places I had never heard of before; the gentleman at the post office wrote them down for me."

"Quite a journey! Did they mention how long it would take for the message to reach them and the cost involved?"

"Six to seven days, and don't worry about the cost."

"But I do worry; it must be quite costly. The note will pass through Romania, the Austro-Hungarian Empire, and then Poland, which means the Russian Empire."

After a brief pause, his eyes lit up. "Wait, of course! How didn't I think of it before?"

"What is it?"

"My sister, Aliza, lives in Vienna. I can send the message to her; it'll be faster and more economical. After all, Brasov is Kronstadt, isn't it? And that's already part of Austria."

"Much better, you can draft it right away."

"I'll do it immediately, but I need you to lend me the money to send it. In the note, I'll ask my sister to send something to repay you."

"Think nothing of it; the crucial thing now is to let them know your situation."

"Thank you, Ionela. Please come closer."

She approached the bed, and he took one of her hands in his, gently squeezing it before planting a kiss on it. The girl blushed and hastily left the room, momentarily forgetting about the bandage change.

He drafted the note, informing Aliza that he was safe, that he had been wounded but was recovering well in the care of some extraordinary people who had saved and taken him in. He asked her to inform the rest of their relatives in Lublin. Upon finishing it, he realized he didn't know his sister's address in Vienna, so he addressed it to Captain Karl Radetz at the Western Military Garrison in the Austrian capital.

The injuries improved significantly; Mihai's excellent intervention and subsequent care allowed for a very satisfactory recovery. The bandage on his head had been removed, the side wound had almost completely healed, and the knee injury, the most delicate of all, would take some time to fully recover. However, the pain had considerably diminished.

Strolls in the park became a regular occurrence. Gabriel replaced the crutch with a rustic walking stick Ozana had found in a nearby grove, making his walks much easier. Although both of them knew he no longer needed the support, Ionela still held his left arm, supposedly to ensure he didn't lose his balance. They ventured further, reaching the river, and Gabriel continued to share passages from his life, such as the one that occurred in Warsaw, which disrupted his studies. She, in turn, spoke about her dreams, her desire to travel and explore other countries, including grand capitals like Vienna and Paris. She was a simple girl with a kind heart.

He treated her with chivalry, displaying great gentleness and kindness. She found herself increasingly drawn to him, not just due to his physical beauty but also because of his sweetness and innocence, combined with a strong and decisive character that greatly appealed to her. Ionela, on her part, was hopelessly in love, and as expected, her mother had noticed, as the girl couldn't help but gaze at him whenever he spoke to them.

Doína was concerned; she believed Gabriel was a charming young man with extraordinary qualities, but she knew that being a foreign soldier, he would eventually return to his country, and she feared that her daughter would be hurt. She expressed her worries one day.

"You must take things slowly, Ionela. It's not advisable to fall in love with that young man."

"Mother, it's too late for that."

"No, my dear. Later, you'll suffer greatly. He's an exceptional man, and I understand why you're attracted to him, but his life isn't here."

"Do you think I haven't considered that? But it's beyond me, you
can't imagine. His mere presence overwhelms me. He's my first thought
in the morning and my last at night. I'm happy just knowing I can see
him every day."

"Oh, my dear, you're going to suffer."

"I know, mother, and I want to be happy for as long as I can."

That's how Ionela lived, and every time her eyes met Gabriel's, she
felt time stand still. Knowing that he was nearby became the source of
her greatest joy, and their evening walks in the park were the happiest
moments of the day. On the very afternoon she had spoken to her
mother, they sat on a bench by the river when Gabriel announced that
he would tell her the story of a famous battle he had studied in the
barracks. It surprised her a bit since they rarely discussed military topics,
nor were they of her interest. Nevertheless, anything Gabriel spoke about
fascinated her, so she prepared to listen intently to the tale.

He began to talk about the Battle of Sedan, where they had to
capture a hill. He gently took her shoulders and made her stand up
straight.

"Let's suppose you're the hill," he said with a smile. Then he continued
seriously, "The French troops advanced from this side." He moved his
right arm along her side to indicate the movement of the troops.

"And the Prussians advanced from this other side, and both groups
started climbing the hill, firing their weapons."

Gabriel raised both of his hands in hopping motions, simulating the
troops scaling the mountain. Then he said, "Both armies reached the
summit."

At that moment, each hand cupped one of Ionela's cheeks, and he
said, "And there was a tremendous explosion in the centre."

Simultaneously, he kissed her on the lips, very softly but lingeringly.
Ionela remained still, feeling a literal explosion inside her. She held her
breath; it seemed that the kiss reached straight to her heart, and she
became acutely aware that she would love that man for the rest of her life.

At that precise moment, eight hundred kilometres away, in a military
barracks in the capital of the Austro-Hungarian Empire, Major Karl
Radetz received a telegraph message from Budapest. As he opened it,

he noticed that its initial origin was from a place he had never heard of before: Alexandria-Romania-Ottoman Empire.

Thirty minutes later, he burst into his home like a whirlwind, shouting for his wife, who was feeding their little son.

"Aliza, my love! Where are you?"

She hurriedly left the child on the carpet and stood up just as her husband entered the room.

"I have great news for you!"

She looked at him with questioning eyes, and he exclaimed, "Gabriel is alive!"

"How? Is he alive?"

"Yes, my dear, he is!"

"Oh, my God, tell me, please!"

Karl raised the telegram in his right hand and waved it in the air. "I just received this telegraph from him."

Aliza snatched the paper and read it, tears filling her eyes. When she finished, she embraced her husband.

"Thank God, my little brother is alive," she said between sobs.

Karl handed her a handkerchief to wipe her tears. The child looked up at them from the carpet, not understanding what was happening with his parents. Aliza picked him up, giving him a kiss and saying, "Everything is fine, my love."

"Why are you crying, mama?"

"Tears of joy, my darling, because I'm very happy."

Karl gently caressed the child's head and embraced his wife once more. Then she remembered, "But it says he was wounded, that he's injured."

"He's recovering; it can't be too serious. The important thing is that he wasn't lost in action."

"Yes, you're right, my love. We must inform my parents immediately."

"Of course, get ready; we're going to the telegraph office right away."

They walked down the street, and Aliza felt overwhelming joy, squeezing her husband's arm as she repeated that she was the happiest woman in the world. Countless memories of her brother flooded her mind, and the heart-wrenching agony she experienced when she was told

he was missing came rushing back. She gripped Karl's arm tighter and
said, "I am so happy, my love, so happy... And mother will be too."

The next day, as the evening fell, Isaak slowly made his way home. For
some strange reason, he felt unusually tired that day, so he left the store
earlier than usual. There was no particular reason for it, and it hadn't
happened in the days prior, even though he had not slept well since
Gabriel's disappearance.

The tragic event caused him double pain - the sorrow of a father and
the suffering of a husband, as it tore his heart apart to see Sara's despair.
She had stopped laughing and almost stopped speaking altogether.
Nothing could lift her spirits, not even the frequent visits from Tatiana,
Jana, and Irenka. Isaak suffered for both of them.

As he walked along the street, he gazed at the trees starting to shed
their first leaves. A memory from years ago in Bialystok came to mind,
an autumn afternoon when he explained to Gabriel the cause of that
phenomenon. The recollection brought tears to his eyes, and he
absentmindedly gazed into the distance. He was so lost in thought that
he didn't hear the postman, who had to call him repeatedly, saying, "Mr.
Isaak, Mr. Isaak, a telegraph message for you."

He snapped out of his reverie, received the message, thanked the
postman, and decided to open it at home, as he was just a few steps away
from the entrance.

Upon opening the door, he felt the cold and darkness that
surrounded a household in mourning, where sadness and pain had
reigned for several days. It was a place where it was impossible not to
remember the presence of their beloved son and all the shared
experiences with him. Isaak knew that somewhere in the house, his wife
was engulfed in tears. At that moment, he felt that life had lost its
meaning and that it would only find purpose if he ever had the chance to
see his beloved Gabriel again.

He left the envelope that the postman had just handed him on the
hallway table, then hung his overcoat and hat on the coat rack before
setting out to find Sara and greet her. At that moment, he remembered
the note and retraced his steps. He approached the window, seeking

some light, and checked the sender – it was Aliza from Vienna. He opened the letter and read:

"Father, mother, I have wonderful news. Gabriel is alive. He is injured but recovering. He wrote to us from Romania, and we have already replied. Aliza".

Isaak's entire body trembled, and he couldn't react; he seemed frozen. He read the note again, pausing several times at the phrase "Gabriel is alive." Unable to contain his emotions, he burst into tears and hurriedly ascended the stairs, calling out to his wife:

"Sara, Sara!"

His emotionally charged voice echoed throughout the house. She came running out of the room and saw him ascending the stairs as if possessed. He reached the landing and said, his voice choked with tears:

"Gabriel is alive! Our son is alive!"

Sara let out a scream and covered her mouth with her hands, struggling to breathe. Isaak approached her and embraced her, then showed her the message.

"He got in touch with Aliza, and she sent us this telegraph."

Sara could hardly process the news, and her husband handed her the paper. She read it with profound emotion and then looked at Isaak, tears streaming down her face. They embraced once more.

"God heard my prayers!"

"And your heart was right."

Isaak raised his arms to the sky with clenched fists and nearly shouted:

"Thank you, Hashem, thank you!"

In that moment, he felt everything brighten again, as if the sun had burst into their home, making it once more a happy and radiant place.

Sara continued to read and reread the note, and Isaak wiped away his tears and said:

"We have to inform our daughters, let's go, come on."

She got up from the chair where she had sat to read Aliza's message countless times. She hurried to the bedroom, quickly changed her shoes, donned a shawl and hat. When she came back down, Isaak was already waiting, wearing his overcoat and holding his hat.

They didn't walk; they ran through the streets. First, they went to Tatiana's, and Isaak repeatedly rang the bell. When she appeared at the window, intrigued, Sara shouted:

"Tatiushka, Gabriel is alive, alive, alive...!"

Tatiana jumped with joy and rushed down, opening the door to embrace her parents. The three of them practically danced together on the street, overwhelmed by their happiness. Finally, she asked, "How did it happen? Tell me, where is he?"

"He's in a village in Romania, he's fine, recovering from some injuries," Isaak said, and then continued, "Come on, daughter, we must tell Jana."

"Wait for me, of course, I'm coming with you."

She rushed inside the house, urgently called Robiak, and shared the great news, asking him to take care of the children. He came out and hugged his in-laws, overjoyed with the good news.

Parents and daughter ran to the bakery managed by Jana since Sara decided to stay at home after Gabriel's disappearance. Jana was with the shop assistants, checking some orders, and she was surprised to see her parents and sister rushing in. All of them stared at them, puzzled, but before anyone could react, Sara shouted, "Gabriel is alive!"

Her daughter, like Tatiana, jumped with joy and ran to embrace her parents.

They immediately went to share the good news with Irenka, who naturally believed it was a reason to celebrate with a party. They decided to gather everyone at home to share the joy of the event. Isaak first went to the rabbi to inform him and thank him for his prayers. He also invited the rabbi and his wife to join the entire family, including Carl and Irenka. The atmosphere was filled with jubilation, and amidst the excitement, Sara announced, "Tomorrow, I'll leave for Vienna."

Everyone fell silent, looking at her. Sara continued, "My Gabriel is alive, and that is the most important and joyous thing, but he's injured, and I have to go see him."

They remained silent, and finally, the rabbi broke the silence. "But Sara, he's in a remote village in Romania."

"I don't care; I must visit him wherever he is."

"Remember that Romania is at war and part of the Ottoman Empire, whose soldiers are enemies of Gabriel."

"That won't stop me; I have to see my son."

At that moment, Isaak intervened. He walked toward her and took her hand, saying, "What you want to do may be reckless, my dear. But it's the kind of recklessness one must embrace in life."

Sara looked at him with deep gratitude as Isaak continued, "A few days ago, we thought Gabriel had died, or at least that's what events seemed to indicate. If ten seconds after receiving the note informing us of his disappearance, someone had told us that he was alive, our first instinct would have been to go to see him, even if he were on the other side of the world. Why should things be any different now?"

The others listened attentively and in silence. Isaak continued, "On the other hand, there was someone who listened to their heart, and it told them that Gabriel was still alive."

Then he turned to Sara and said, "I will go with you."

Everyone applauded and excitedly approved the decision. Immediately, they started writing notes for Gabriel. They didn't know how serious his injuries might be, but there was only one thing that mattered – he was alive.

The next day, Isaak and Sara set off for Vienna. They arrived at Aliza's house, where it was very emotional for her to share the joy with her parents. She also told them that she had already made the decision to go with them to visit Gabriel. Karl had advised her not to do so since Alexandria was located in a war zone, but he had come up with a solution. Just then, Karl arrived, and after the customary greetings, he invited them to have a drink in his small study. He shared with them, in strict confidence, that Austria had significant geopolitical interests in the Balkans.

"Between us, Austria is using Russia to strengthen its power in the Balkans," Karl said.

"I've thought the same," Isaak replied. "What's your perspective?"

"It's quite simple. Russia is doing the difficult work for Austria by pushing the Ottomans out of the region."

"I agree."

"In any case, let's get back to our purpose," Karl summarized. "The news that Gabriel is alive has brought immense joy to everyone. We don't know the details, but we've already written to him, asking for more information about his condition. Based on our calculations, we should receive his response tomorrow."

"We also sent him a money order," Aliza interjected. "He's in great need of money, and there's no such service at the post office in the village where he is. But we sent it to Bucharest."

"Thank you very much, Karl, and you too, my dear," Isaak said. "I will repay you later."

"Don't worry, father-in-law. It's the least we could do for Gabriel," Karl said reassuringly.

He then began to explain, "The village where he is located is very close to the war zone, about eighty kilometres from Pleven, where the bloodiest battles are taking place. Although Alexandria and its surroundings are reportedly under the control of the Romanian Army, we can't rule out the presence of Ottoman soldiers. In conclusion, it's not a safe area."

The in-laws looked at him with great anticipation. Karl spoke with authority, using military terms, and they followed his words attentively.

"Alright, I have a map here that I sketched out to scale of the area we're interested in. Let's move to the dining table to examine it," Karl suggested.

He took out a paper from his leather briefcase and led the others to the dining room. Once there, he unfolded the map and showed them the important locations: the frontline, the positions of the Russians and the Ottomans, and the areas where the most significant battles were taking place. It was a detailed military briefing. Finally, with the tip of his pencil, he pointed to the spot where Gabriel was.

"He's here, in Alexandria, about forty kilometres north of the Danube."

He looked up and saw the expression on Sara's face. "Yes, my dear mother-in-law, it's the same river that runs a few blocks from here, but sailing its waters is neither the fastest nor the safest way to get to Gabriel."

He turned back to the map and pointed to another location with the pencil.

"My esteemed brother-in-law is just two days away from this city."

Isaak leaned forward and read the name of the place indicated by his son-in-law.

"Kronstadt."

"Exactly, and that town is already within the territory of the grand Austro-Hungarian Empire," Karl announced proudly.

"Hmm, I see," exclaimed Sara.

"You'll understand that I would never allow my beloved Aliza to go and see Gabriel in Alexandria, in Ottoman territory. And I would advise you not to do so either. However, I would have no objections if the meeting were to take place in Kronstadt."

"Well, if Gabriel has the opportunity to travel there, it would be perfect," Isaak said.

"Exactly, we sent him a telegram, inquiring about his medical condition and whether he's capable of making his way to the Austrian border," Isaak exclaimed.

"Very well," Karl responded, "but once at the border, will he have a chance to cross it without any problems? I imagine it must be heavily guarded given the current circumstances."

"Everything is perfectly calculated. The Ottomans have long lost control in that area. Of course, the Austrian troops exercise strict vigilance, but it helps to have a major from the glorious Imperial Army in the family," Karl said with bombastic eloquence.

After the anguish they had endured with the news of Gabriel's disappearance, they couldn't help but smile at Karl's grandiose way of speaking. He continued, "Major Hasler, my fellow classmate, currently serves in the military garrison in Kronstadt. I have already sent him a telegram to arrange for Gabriel's reception and organize all the logistics for the meeting, including accommodation. He speaks Russian fluently and is just waiting for the precise details. I know him well; he is extremely meticulous and will ensure that everything goes perfectly. He'll do it with great pleasure, not only due to the strong friendship between us but also because I saved his career during an embarrassing incident involving a young lady."

Aliza caught Karl's arm, asking, "Which young lady are you talking about?"

Karl smiled, "A young lady with whom he had a romantic encounter, not me, my dear wife."

"Ah, and why were you the one who saved him? What did you have to do with the woman?" Aliza inquired with curiosity.

Karl chuckled again, and this time, Isaak joined in, taking Aliza's arm and pulling her close, giving her an affectionate hug. "I didn't know you were so jealous, my dear daughter."

He then released her, planted a kiss on her forehead, and turned to Karl. "It seems you've contemplated and organized everything down to the finest detail, my son. I thank you deeply," Isaak said, extending his hand.

Sara, Aliza, and Karl all noticed the use of the word "son."

"Thank you very much, father-in-law. Now, I'd like to invite you to honour me by accepting an invitation to dinner, but first, let's stop at the East Station to buy three train tickets to Kronstadt. We'll keep the reservation open until we receive a response from Gabriel and can finalize the details. I intend to accompany you, of course, but I haven't yet received authorization from my superiors."

"Thank you for everything, Karl," Sara said.

"You're welcome. Now, I suggest we get ready to go to dinner." He then turned to Aliza. "Please inform the nanny to take care of the little one and get yourself ready. At dinner, I'll tell you the anecdote about my colleague and the famous lady. If I don't, my wife won't let me sleep tonight."

Everyone laughed, and Sara was filled with ecstatic happiness at the prospect of seeing her son soon.

26

Autumn began with strong gusts of wind, but the weather still felt very pleasant, inviting them to continue their daily walks, which were occasionally joined by Ozana and Doína. They had grown very fond of Gabriel, who, despite moving with difficulty, had become an efficient helper, taking on maintenance tasks. He displayed great skill in any work he undertook; he repaired roofs, designed a rainwater collection system, built with his own hands a pump, fixed the fences around the garden, and reinforced the structure supporting the attic of the house.

In addition to his practical abilities, he possessed a great wit that never failed to make his companions laugh. Gabriel had a strong character, but also a fine sense of humour. On another note, he had regularized his situation in the Army. The message had reached Captain Kuznetzov, who ordered him to remain in Alexandria during his convalescence and carry out intelligence operations in the entire area. He had to send regular reports every Wednesday, delivered by the same carter who had rescued him. In the end, Doína's instincts were right, returning to his unit would have been more of a burden than a help. Moreover, Kuznetzov had more significant concerns than recovering a wounded soldier.

The only problem was that the weekly reports required him to travel within a twenty-kilometre radius, along the route from Bucharest to Ghimpati. The Army did not provide him with the necessary resources for his movements, so Doína's brother lent him a horse on the condition that Gabriel covered the expenses of its feeding and care. He already owed Ionela money for the cost of the telegram he had sent, but he had to rely on her generosity again to maintain the horse. As expected, she provided him with the sum he needed, understanding that as long as he had this mission, he wouldn't be reintegrated into his Unit on the front.

The romance with Ionela was like a dream, and with each passing day, Gabriel fell deeper in love. He never tired of admiring the beauty of her olive-green eyes, especially the tenderness they conveyed. Every glance from Ionela pierced his heart, and her lips were irresistible to him; he couldn't resist stealing kisses whenever the opportunity presented itself. She, of course, adored these affectionate gestures, though always mindful of preserving their secret.

During their walks along the riverbank, they could unleash their passion, kissing each other passionately, expressing the intense love that consumed them. Ozana acted as their confidante and matchmaker, genuinely appreciating Gabriel, and enjoying mutual trust with them. The three of them would joke together, fully embracing the joy of their youth.

For Ionela, Gabriel was the most handsome man in the world; she likened him to the most beautiful Greek statues. This opinion was shared by Ozana, Doína, and all the women in the village who admired him when he rode through the streets on horseback or went on his customary strolls with the sisters.

He had also established an excellent rapport with Mihai, spending hours conversing about the course of the war and what awaited Romania if they managed to defeat the Turks. During these days the doctor was wounded in the leg by a piece of shrapnel while attending to some casualties at the field hospital in Grivitsa during a bombardment. He had been evacuated to his own house for convalescence, and now it was he who lay in bed, receiving daily visits from the nurse for his dressings. During these moments, Ionela would be like a tigress, marking her territory and not allowing the girl to approach Gabriel if she wasn't present.

The response from Aliza and Karl arrived, requesting more specific information about his medical condition and the possibility of meeting them in Kronstadt. They asked him to inform them of the date to coordinate the encounter and also informed him about the postal order to be claimed in Bucharest. Gabriel felt comforted knowing that his family was already aware of his situation, so they wouldn't worry. Of course, he was unaware of the communication they had received from the Russian Army reporting him as missing. The news of his sister's visit excited him even more, and he felt relieved about the money, as he had been staying at Ionela's for some time, relying on her family's support, which made him feel embarrassed.

Except for Mihai, they all went to Bucharest, leaving before dawn and arriving in the capital around nine in the morning. Gabriel claimed the postal order and immediately replied to his sister's message. Then they went to a store where he bought some clothes and shoes, as he had been wearing clothes borrowed from Mihai. After that, he treated the three ladies to lunch and went for a stroll in the city centre, which Gabriel found charming with its beautiful architecture. He was walking better now, though still using a walking stick, and as it had been from the start, Ionela held his left arm, less to help him keep his balance, but rather to discourage the young women who glanced at her boyfriend.

Upon receiving the new letter from Aliza and Karl confirming the day and location of the meeting, Gabriel was overjoyed to learn that Isaak and Sara would also be there. He proposed that Ionela accompany him to introduce her to his parents. The girl felt a bit nervous, but he reassured her:

"Don't be nervous; they are the kindest, most cordial, and down-to-earth people in the world."

"Well, if they are anything like you, I believe you," she replied. In her heart, she felt fulfilled that Gabriel wanted his parents to meet her, as it was a significant step. She was deeply in love and never wanted to be separated from him. However, she expressed her concern:

"I'm worried that they might consider me insignificant for you, just a simple girl from a Romanian village."

"Oh, please don't say that! Once they see your grace, beauty, and personality, they'll understand that you are the perfect woman for me."

"Gabriel, I love you so much," she said, thinking that her beauty was probably the least important attribute for his parents. Then she added, "In any case, you know my mother would never allow me to travel alone with you."

"I've thought about it, and that's why I'd like to ask her to come along too," Gabriel said.

"That would be wonderful, but another issue is that Kronstadt is Austro-Hungarian territory, how do we enter without passports?" Ionela questioned.

"My brother-in-law is in the military, and he has already arranged my entry, which should include my companions as well," Gabriel reassured.

In the end, Doína agreed, and Mihai gave his permission. Ozana pleaded with her father to let her join as well.

"Oh, father, please say yes! I would love to explore that city," Ozana implored.

"All right, daughter, go with them," her father granted.

The four of them set off for Kronstadt, embarking on a journey that was a thrilling adventure for the women, as they had never before left Romania. The prospect of exploring Austro-Hungarian territory was exhilarating. Karl's instructions were clear - upon reaching the border control post, they were to identify themselves, and they would be guided from there.

After two days of travel, they arrived at the border, where they encountered a checkpoint manned by customs officials, police officers, and military personnel. The customs agent spoke Romanian, so Doína acted as their translator. Unfortunately, the official had no knowledge of who Gabriel Rothman was, and he refused to allow them to proceed. They spoke with the police officer standing nearby, but he also did not recognize the visitor's name. They even inquired with a young Army corporal in a small adjacent office, but he too had no information or instructions about Gabriel, resulting in their passage being denied.

Gabriel felt disconcerted, as Karl's note had assured them that someone would be there to guide them. He was unsure of what action to take when they noticed a soldier sprinting towards them. The soldier communicated with the police officer, who then pointed towards Gabriel. The soldier approached and asked in German:

"Are you Gabriel Rothman?"

"Yes, I am," Gabriel replied in Russian.

"Please wait here," the soldier said.

Although Gabriel didn't understand the soldier's words, he comprehended the gesture, indicating that he was to wait there. The soldier rushed back to where he had come from, and midway, he conveyed some information to another military personnel, who was hurrying towards them. The corporal in the office immediately came out, stood at attention, and saluted the new arrival. The latter returned the salute and then approached Gabriel, who was in civilian attire. As he reached Gabriel, the soldier stood at attention, saluted him with military precision, and spoke in a rough Russian with a noticeable German accent:

"Lieutenant Kerst, Mr. Rothman, it's a pleasure to greet you," the officer said with a courteous nod.

The women exchanged glances, surprised to see a Lieutenant addressing Gabriel, a mere soldier. Even Gabriel found it peculiar, but he didn't mention it. He simply replied, "Thank you, the pleasure is mine."

"I will escort you to the hotel. Do you have your passport with you?" Lieutenant Kerst asked.

"Unfortunately, I lost it," Gabriel replied.

"Very well, come with me."

At that moment, Lieutenant Kerst noticed the women. Their beautiful eyes caught his attention, and he paused, briefly admiring them before turning back to Gabriel. "Are the ladies with you?" he inquired.

"Yes, they are," Gabriel confirmed, pointing to them. "They are my wife, my mother-in-law, and my sister-in-law."

Upon hearing the word "wife," Ionela's eyes widened, but she concealed her emotions as best as she could, feeling an undeniable sense of happiness.

"Perfect, no problem at all," the lieutenant said, putting them at ease.

He then addressed the Police officer in German before turning back to Gabriel. "Please follow me, and I'll escort you to the hotel."

They got into an elegant carriage and crossed the border, passing through picturesque countryside before entering the city. The young women were thrilled to experience being in another country for the first time. Ionela remained enchanted with the promising sound of the words "my wife" on Gabriel's lips.

Doína, too, felt content. Her daughters looked joyful, and she relished the journey to a country they had heard so much about but never visited. However, what pleased her even more was the fact that Gabriel wanted to introduce Ionela to his parents—a positive sign indeed.

They arrived in the city centre, whose architecture resembled scenes from a fairy tale. Near the Council Square, they found the hotel, where a small group of military personnel stood at the entrance. As the carriage came to a halt, two soldiers opened the doors and assisted the women to alight. When Gabriel stepped out, an officer, clearly of higher rank, approached him.

"Good afternoon, Mr. Rothman," the officer greeted in Russian. "I am Major Hans Hasler, the commander of Kronstadt Military Garrison. I extend my warm welcome to you and your distinguished companions."

"Thank you, it's a pleasure to meet you," Gabriel replied, choosing not to clarify his rank, and it seemed the officer was unaware that he was addressing a mere private.

"We had information that you were coming alone, but it poses no inconvenience. We'll promptly arrange accommodation for the ladies," Major Hasler assured him.

"Thank you, you are very kind," Gabriel replied.

The major gave instructions to the lieutenant who had received them at the border, and the luggage was taken into the hotel.

"While they finish preparing your rooms, allow me to invite you for a drink," the major offered, leading them to the hotel bar.

The place was splendid and elegant, and the attentive waiters swiftly pulled out chairs for the ladies as the commander sat with them.

"I appreciate your kindness, Major," Doína initiated a conversation.

"It's my pleasure, madam. Mr. Rothman is the brother-in-law of my best friend in the Army, and it's an honour to host you all," the major replied politely.

Meanwhile, Ionela leaned closer to Gabriel and whispered softly, "It sounded so beautiful when you said, 'my wife.'"

He turned his gaze towards her and said nothing, but his eyes spoke volumes, leaving Ionela's heart aflutter.

They engaged in lively conversation; the major was courteous with Doína and Ozana, allowing Gabriel to have a private chat with Ionela on the side. He informed them that the train from Budapest would arrive around four in the afternoon, giving them some time to rest before heading to the station.

"I'll leave you to rest," the officer said, rising from his seat and then addressing Gabriel, "It has been a pleasure to meet you, as well as your wife and charming companions."

With a bow, he took his leave, and Ozana playfully told her sister how well she played the role of a married woman, causing Ionela to blush, while Doína appeared contemplative.

They retired to rest for a while and prepare themselves to head to the station. Gabriel was pondering over the major's kindness but wondered who would foot the bill for such an upscale hotel. Upon reaching the reception, the bellboys were ready to accompany them to their rooms. To their surprise, there was one prepared for Doína and Ozana, and another for the supposed married couple. Gabriel found it amusing and had to suppress a smile. They entered their room, closed the door behind them, and approaching Ionela, he said, "Come, my wife, what do you think of our room?"

"Oh, Gabriel, I'm so embarrassed!" she replied, blushing.

Despite her embarrassment, he embraced her and kissed her. As always when Gabriel did so, she felt as if the ground was shaking beneath her feet. After a few seconds, Gabriel said, "I'll carry your luggage. Let's go to the other room before your mother has a heart attack."

Promptly, they were picked up in the carriage and driven to the station. While Romania had some railway lines already, it was the first time for the three women to be in a terminal and witness the arrival of a train. The imposing locomotive expelling steam and making a thunderous noise was a grand spectacle for them. They tried to hide their amazement, but it was particularly novel for the two young women.

They were accompanied by the major, the lieutenant, and a few soldiers. Finally, the train came to a complete stop, releasing steam with a great clamour that startled Ionela and Ozana. As the train doors opened, passengers began to disembark. Gabriel rushed towards his father when he saw him.

"Father!"

Isaak was helping Sara, who then stepped down and immediately opened her arms to receive her son, who was limping slightly and using a stick. The three of them embraced in a long-awaited hug, and Sara couldn't contain her tears. At that moment, Karl came down from the train and offered his hand to Aliza, who was carrying their little son. She handed him over to Karl and ran to where her parents and brother were. She hugged Gabriel, filled with joy, and a tear rolled down her cheek. Karl approached his brother-in-law and gave him a couple of pats on the back before greeting his comrade.

Meanwhile, the three women observed the scene from a distance. Ionela leaned towards Ozana and said, "Now I know where Gabriel got his good looks. Do you see his mother?"

"You're right, she does resemble him. What a beautiful woman," replied Ozana.

"Well, my darlings, you're absolutely right. Mrs. Rothman is very lovely," confirmed Doína.

"Look, mother, the same eyes and the same hair as Gabriel," remarked Ionela.

At that moment, the young man, whom Sara was caressing and holding by the arm, exclaimed, "Father, mother, Aliza, please come. I want to introduce you to the people who saved my life. I'll tell you all about it." Lowering his voice, he continued, "To cross the border, I had to claim that they were my wife, mother-in-law, and sister-in-law. They are very kind people and speak Russian."

He led them towards the women and made the formal introductions, "Doína, Ionela, Ozana, I would like to introduce you to my mother."

"It's a great pleasure to meet you, ma'am," said Doína.

"The pleasure is mine, and please allow me to take the liberty of giving you all a hug. My son just told me that you were the ones who saved his life, and I will never be able to thank you enough."

She embraced each of them, saving Ionela for last. When she hugged the girl, both women sensed something special – perhaps Sara with her intuitive sense and Ionela with her inner desire to be hugging her future mother-in-law. Unintentionally, Ionela held her tightly, and Sara noticed.

Aliza approached and embraced them as well, expressing her profound gratitude. Then, Isaak stood before them and posed a question that any parent might face, not knowing how to answer: "What does one say when standing before the person who saved their child's life?" He took a deep breath and added, "Forgive me for breaking any protocol, but the right words haven't been invented yet." He then hugged them too.

The atmosphere was undoubtedly euphoric, and shortly Major Hasler invited everyone to get into the carriages and head to the hotel. The two newly arrived couples settled into their rooms and later gathered for a lively dinner. The two old comrades from their military days added a humorous touch to the reunion, recounting a myriad of anecdotes from their time in the service. Throughout the evening, Sara constantly caressed Gabriel on one side, while on the other, Aliza held on to him and occasionally teased him with the typical gesture that she, Tatiana, and Jana had always done, which Gabriel detested – squeezing his cheeks. Lieutenant Kerst, who had noticed Ozana's fresh beauty, sat beside her and, in his rustic Russian, tried to engage in a conversation.

The dinner extended into a celebration as Hans brought in an orchestra and ordered more champagne. The waltzes began to play, and couples formed on the dance floor. No one remained seated, and the gallant Major invited Doína to dance. The lieutenant, no longer struggling with his Russian, enjoyed dancing with Ozana. Sara danced with Isaak, Aliza with Karl, and, of course, Gabriel with Ionela. Despite having to lean on his cane, she supported him without hesitation, and they swayed gracefully to the waltz.

At last, Sara noticed something more than just gratitude between her son and the beautiful green-eyed girl. It wasn't merely the dancing; she had sensed it earlier, the way she looked at him. While they danced, Sara mentioned to Isaak:

"My love, I believe our Gabriel is in love."

"What do you mean?"

"That's precisely what I mean – he's in love."

"But how? I don't understand."

"Could it be that with age, your sharp intelligence is fading, my beloved? Have you forgotten what it's like to be in love?"

"Of course not, I'm in love with you."

"Well, Gabriel is in love with that girl, and it seems she's even more in love with him."

"But how do you know? Has he said anything?"

"I don't need him to say it, I just know."

"I think you're exaggerating, Sara. They're dancing a bit closer than usual because he can't support himself well."

"The dance is beside the point, my dear. It's not the waltz that tells me they're in love."

"And then why is it?"

"I saw how they looked at each other, especially her at him."

"Just based on a look?"

"Yes. Do you know why?"

"Why?"

"Because she looked at him with the gaze of love."

"And how do you recognize such a gaze?"

"It's one that pierces the soul."

"We should study what those gazes are."

"Do you remember how you looked at me the first time you saw me?"

He stayed silent for a moment, then looked into Sara's eyes and kissed her.

"Alright, my love, but we're in public."

They enjoyed three unforgettable days in Kronstadt. As Karl had predicted, Hans proved to be an excellent host, arranging outings, dinners, dances, and visits to clothing stores. Gabriel and his parents happily reciprocated by giving gifts to Doína and her daughters to cover all the expenses the family had incurred while taking care of him.

The farewell was naturally a sad one, but they took solace in the knowledge that Gabriel, who had been on the verge of death, was now recovering and happy. On the second night during dinner, Sara told Isaak that Gabriel had confessed to being in love with Ionela. She made it clear to her husband:

"It wouldn't be surprising if they decided to get married. Gabriel hasn't proposed yet, but it could happen. You should know that the girl is an Orthodox Christian, but she assured me that if she had to leave her religion to marry Gabriel, she wouldn't hesitate for a second."

"Dear God," Isaak sighed, "I have four children, and three of them have chosen non-Jewish partners."

The previous day, while the men were enjoying some beers, the women had gone shopping. Sara and Ionela walked together, and at a certain moment, Sara said:

"I know you're in love with my son."

The girl became quite shy and didn't know what to say.

"Don't worry, there's nothing wrong with falling in love with a man."

"Mrs. Sara, I don't know what to say."

"To start with, call me Sara."

"Alright, Mrs. Sara, I mean Sara. It just feels strange to address you like that."

"You'll get used to it. Now tell me, how much do you love Gabriel?"

The young woman didn't respond.

"Speak, my dear."

Ionela remained somewhat apprehensive.

"Talk calmly."

"Oh, I don't know how to put it into words. My feelings can't be expressed with mere words. I love him deeply; he's the finest man in the world."

"I know that perfectly well. I've known him since the day he was born."

"He possesses so many qualities; he's exceptional. Besides, there's no man on Earth more handsome, and I could see where he inherited it from."

Sara smiled.

"Thank you for the compliment."

"You're so beautiful, Mrs. Sara."

"You are beautiful too. And your eyes are so expressive; I know it was that gaze that made Gabriel fall in love with you. He told me himself."

"He said that? He confessed it? He's so special. I fell in love with him from the very moment I saw him. You can't imagine what that feels like, Mrs. Sara."

"Believe me, I do know. It happened the same way to me."

Now it was Ionela's turn to smile as she tried to imagine what that encounter between Gabriel's parents must have been like.

"Confirm something for me, Ionela. Do you know he's Jewish?"

"Of course, Mrs. Sara."

"You keep insisting with 'Mrs.' I hope someday you'll get used to it. Well, do you know that Jews can only marry women of the same religion?"

"Yes, I'm aware of that, Sara."

"You're a Christian, right?"

"I'm an Orthodox Christian, but if Gabriel were to propose to me, I would convert to his faith. My love for him is above everything."

"Come here, my dear."

Sara pulled her into an embrace. Ionela's heart was racing, as she understood that she had just received Sara's approval for marrying Gabriel.

The train picked up speed towards the west, and everyone on the platform watched it until it disappeared around a bend. Then, Gabriel and his three companions boarded their coach and headed back to Alexandria to collect their belongings. Major Hasler bid them farewell at the hotel's exit, and they all thanked him profusely for his attentive care. Lieutenant Kerst accompanied them to the border, promising Ozana that he would write to her and improve his Russian or learn Romanian for her sake.

In Alexandria, they resumed their routine of strolling together and continued to relish their sublime feelings. One day, a note arrived for Gabriel, ordering him to report to his Unit. It was stationed in the Grivitsa sector, very close to the area where he had been wounded and lost his dear friend Sajarov.

Gabriel had to confront the reality of being a soldier again, while Ionela felt as if darkness had enveloped her life. From the moment she learned that Gabriel had to return to the front, her countenance turned sad and melancholic. He tried to console her, assuring her that due to the lingering knee injury, they wouldn't send him to the front lines. He was likely to be assigned administrative tasks in the rear.

However, Ionela couldn't resign herself to the situation and wept in her room at night. For her, it was as if a crystal ball had shattered, and her romantic novel had reached its end.

"I fear losing you," she said tearfully, sitting on a bench in the park.

"You won't lose me; I've told you before. They won't send me to the front," Gabriel reassured her.

"It's not just that; I'm terrified you'll forget about me."

He embraced her tenderly and kissed her.

"That will never happen."

"If you go far away, you might meet other girls."

"You are the sole owner of my heart; trust me."

"I trust you, but not other women. You're so handsome that there will be hundreds chasing after you."

"Don't talk nonsense."

"Nonsense? Do you think I don't notice how they look at you? Here in Bucharest, in Kronstadt, everywhere."

"I will come back for you, I promise."

"If I lose you, I'll die, Gabriel. I'll wait for you for eternity."

The day finally came for him to depart. He donned his uniform and checked his military ID, which he had kept safe, semi-destroyed and still stained with blood. He bid farewell to Mihai, expressing gratitude for saving his life when he arrived, almost lifeless, at that house. Then, he extended his hand to Doína, thanking her for being like a mother to him. He hugged Ozana, who had been both a friend and a sister, and finally, he embraced his beloved Ionela, promising her:

"Ionela, I'm going to the front, but my heart stays here with you. I'll return for you to place it back in my chest."

"I told you, and I'll say it again, I'll wait for you for an eternity if necessary. I'll look down the road every day, hoping to see you return," Ionela declared.

They shared a passionate kiss before he boarded the cart of the same peasant who had transported him from the front to that place. The cart, which had once been creaky and dilapidated, was now new and modern – a gift from the grateful Polish soldier who never forgot that, without the carter's help, Gabriel would have perished, bleeding by the roadside.

27

"Hey, look who's back from the dead!" exclaimed a soldier while cleaning his Berdan rifle, surrounded by about eight comrades doing the same.

"Yeah, look!" chimed in another. "It's the German."

Gabriel approached, walking with the aid of the cane he still used, more as a precaution than a necessity since he could now bear weight on his leg without pain from his knee. Better safe than sorry, he thought, wanting to avoid any setbacks. He greeted each of his comrades from what used to be his platoon since the days of Smolensk, glad to see Tarasov approaching. They embraced warmly.

"My old friend, it's so good to see you again. We thought you were dead, but Kisilev told us you were injured and recovering while doing intelligence work."

"Something like that."

"Where were you wounded, German?" asked another of the soldiers.

Gabriel bowed his head and touched the scar on his scalp, then lifted his uniform to reveal another two scars, showing them to his comrades.

"Three wounds, you're lucky, buddy," remarked another companion.

Gabriel scanned them with his gaze and inquired, "And the rest of the platoon?"

"Hospital and mass grave," replied one of the soldiers.

He turned to Tarasov. "Provowsky?"

His comrade shook his head. "I'm sorry, Gabriel. Only the two of us are left from the quartet."

"Yes, Gabriel, the platoon and the company have been decimated. Did you hear about Semionov?"

"Yes, of course. I was just behind him when I saw him fall, a second before I was wounded."

"Of the one hundred and twenty of us in the company, not even half remain. They've sent reinforcements and new officers to Captain Kuznetzov."

"New officers?"

"Yes, because apart from Semionov, Lieutenant Bukanin also fell. Corporal Ivanov died two weeks ago; a bullet tore through his abdomen, and he was left in the trenches when we had to retreat. Despite his screams, no one could go to his aid. It was a terrible loss, just like the departure of all the others."

Gabriel could not help but think that while he danced and enjoyed himself in Kronstadt, Corporal Ivanov, a mere sixteen-year-old boy, was dying, bleeding and suffering, in the midst of unimaginable pain. He also remembered Bukanin, who never liked the military and had been forced into the Army.

Since his knee recovery wasn't complete, he was assigned to the Logistics Support Unit located in the Opanets sector, behind the troops facing Pleven. The hostilities in that area were almost at a standstill, as the Russian commanders had decided to besiege the city instead of trying to capture it. The Turks attempted to break the siege several times, leading to occasional skirmishes that needlessly wore down soldiers on both sides.

One night, he found himself near the medical tents. By the dim light of a feeble lantern, he was writing a letter to Ionela, unsure of how or when he could get it to her. Two fellow soldiers were engaged in a hushed conversation, leaning on their rifles. Suddenly, they heard a commotion, and Gabriel hastily stashed the paper and pencil into his jacket. He stood up, grabbed his rifle, and hurried toward the area where the two soldiers had been just moments ago. They were now running ahead, and one of them yelled:

"The Turks, the Turks are coming in!"

Almost immediately, gunshots rang out, growing in intensity with each passing second. Amidst the darkness, confusion reigned, and it was hard to discern whom or what they were firing at. However, as their eyes adjusted to the dimness, they managed to make out a group of Ottoman soldiers running from Pleven towards the right bank of the Vit River.

Without hesitation, he grabbed two bags of ammunition and joined his comrades in the front trenches. A sergeant arrived with another large group of men and started leading a counterattack towards the river sector, where some Finnish soldiers were already engaged in combat. The sergeant decided to take his men to the right flank. Gabriel joined that group and took up positions. More soldiers arrived, and a lieutenant appeared, assuming command. He regrouped them all and ordered a frontal assault.

He had completely forgotten about his knee discomfort, and under the command of the lieutenant and the sergeant, he ran alongside the other soldiers to the riverbank. A hail of bullets came from the makeshift Turkish positions, but their attack was so strong that the enemy couldn't hold their ground. They advanced with greater speed, and at that moment, Gabriel felt a blow and something warm running down the left side of his chest. He reached a small depression and, following the lieutenant's orders, dropped to the ground along with other soldiers. The officer had been wounded in the leg and was moving with difficulty. Other comrades were also wounded or had already fallen.

Only Gabriel and another soldier were still able to fight when a group of Turks approached, intending to surround them. Despite the darkness, they could distinguish their cloth caps and fierce, dark-skinned faces painted in camouflage. Gabriel had no time to feel fear; he fired his rifle, hitting a Turkish soldier. His comrade handed him another loaded rifle, and he fired again. In this unplanned duet, driven by the urgent instinct to save their lives, they formed a perfect tandem. Gabriel shot, dropped the rifle, and his companion handed him another loaded one. They continued this sequence, not knowing how much time had passed. Together, they managed to repel the attack and force the Ottomans to retreat.

At that moment, five soldiers led by a corporal arrived. The lieutenant, lying on the ground, ordered Gabriel to cross the mound and pursue the few Turkish soldiers who were already fleeing towards Pleven. Then, he turned to Gabriel and the other soldier and said:

"Come on, come on, follow the corporal, don't let the enemy regroup." They quickly got up and ran after the corporal's group, chasing the fugitives. However, they heard cries for help coming from the left flank. The corporal turned and saw Turkish soldiers closing in on a trench where a group of Russians were stationed. The enemy was about to surround them. Without hesitation, the corporal directed his men towards the trench. With all the firepower they had, they managed to push back the Turks, who, upon realizing that the entrenched soldiers were receiving reinforcements, chose to retreat and join those who were already fleeing.

They reached the trench where their comrades greeted them with relief and joy. They embraced each other warmly – those who had endured the enemy siege and those who came to their rescue. The former were grateful to those who saved them, and the latter were satisfied that they were able to do so. At that moment, someone shouted:

"Hey, German! You are here?"

Gabriel turned and was surprised to see his company commander, Captain Kuznetzov.

"Are you, my Captain?"

"Of course, I am! A commander should be by the side of his men."

"I feel proud to be one of your soldiers, Captain."

Kuznetzov, who used to be so cold and distant, approached and extended his hand.

"I'm proud that one of my men saved our lives. If you hadn't arrived, those Turks would have surrounded us. As you can see, there were only six of us left – Sergeant Kuriev and me."

Gabriel returned the salute, shaking hands with his superior, and replied:

"You exaggerate, Captain. Knowing you, I'm sure you would have held them off."

"I don't think so. We were almost out of ammunition. I'm filled with pride seeing your performance, soldier."

"You trained us well, Captain."

They retraced their steps towards the trench where they had repelled the enemy a few minutes ago. The lieutenant and other wounded soldiers were still there. Seeing them approach, the officer asked:

"What's your name, soldier?"

"Rothman, sir."

"And yours?"

"Sukov, sir."

"I congratulate you; today you've covered yourselves in glory. It's an honour to have fought alongside you."

With some difficulty, the lieutenant got up, and Sukov assisted him – his leg was shattered. Once he was on his feet, he exclaimed:

"In addition, I thank you; you saved my life and the lives of these wounded men. Let's go and help them," the lieutenant said.

They assisted the other soldiers in the trench who had sustained various wounds, while Sukov went to find a medic. Although three of these later perished, seven soldiers who had been incapacitated survived thanks to Gabriel and Sukov's actions. If they hadn't repelled the Turkish attack, the enemy would have overrun the trench and killed everyone there. Not only had they saved eight comrades in that trench, but astonishingly, they had also accounted for sixteen Turkish soldiers.

The medic arrived with several soldiers to attend to the wounded. Gabriel asked if they had water, and one of them handed him a leather flask, which he brought to his lips, drinking in large gulps until almost empty. The soldier looked at him and said, "Drink it all; I have more, and you've just been in combat."

He drank the last drop and returned the flask, only then noticing that his hand was covered in blood. The wound on his shoulder had caused blood to trickle down his torso and arm. Opening his jacket, he felt the paper he had tucked into his pocket – the half-finished letter. It was now almost entirely soaked in blood, rendering it impossible to send. Yet, he kept it as a memento, a reminder that he had survived that battle.

However, one who didn't survive that night was Sergeant Zaitzev, the battalion medic. While attending to a group of wounded soldiers, he was hit in the thigh. Ordinarily, such wounds weren't fatal, but he had the misfortune of the bullet piercing his femoral artery, causing him to bleed out in less than five minutes. He was aware that death was imminent. Leaning against a log, the last thing he did before losing consciousness was to remove a crucifix hanging around his neck and hand it to his assistant, whispering in a feeble voice:

"Please, make sure to deliver this to my mother in Ekaterinburg. She herself placed it around my neck, hoping God would protect me when I enlisted in the Army."

Then, he began to weep weakly until his sobs faded away. In his backpack under the field hospital cot lay notebooks and study materials for the German course he had been taking. He had mastered the language enough to fulfil his dream of studying medicine in Vienna.

The next day, Gabriel and Sukov visited the recovering wounded in the field hospital. Joy permeated the camp; the Turkish nocturnal action had been the last attempt to break the siege, and there were rumours that Osman Pacha, the Ottoman commander, had been taken prisoner by the Romanians.

The lieutenant was lying in a bed, pale but with a decent appearance. He greeted them with evident gratitude.

"How are you, lieutenant?" asked Gabriel.

"Given the circumstances, well, soldier."

"And your leg?" Gabriel inquired.

The lieutenant didn't answer immediately, but his eyes moistened. He took a deep breath and said with immense sadness, "It seems I won't lose my leg, soldier, but the war is over for me, as well as my military career."

"What happened?" asked Sukov.

"My knee is shattered; I won't be able to walk normally again. At least, there's no sign of infection yet, and the doctors said amputation might not be necessary."

The soldiers moved closer, one on each side of the bed, breaking protocol to comfort their superior.

"Lieutenant, at least you're alive," Sukov said. "More than three thousand comrades fell last night, and they can't say the same."

"That's right," Gabriel affirmed. "Three thousand Russian families will soon be in mourning, unable even to bury their loved ones."

"Thank you for your comfort, lads, and especially for your actions last night. If you hadn't been in that trench, I would be one of those three thousand men."

He lifted his hands to shake theirs, and in that moment, a friendship that would last forever was born.

Naturally, Captain Kuznetzov and Lieutenant Saskarov reported on the heroic act of soldiers Rothman and Sukov, who had accounted for sixteen enemy soldiers, saving the lives of a lieutenant and seven soldiers of the Empire. As if that wasn't enough, they were immediately involved in an action that saved the lives of another officer, a non-commissioned officer, and six more soldiers. A week later, in a snow-covered field, they were decorated for their valour and for embodying the highest qualities of an imperial soldier of His Majesty the Tsar. They were praised for taking out sixteen enemies and saving the same number of Russians. Gabriel thought that it wasn't something to be overly proud of.

However, he humbly accepted the prestigious Order of St. George, not so much for risking his life but for saving the lives of several comrades. His Company Commander, Captain Kuznetzov, approached and shook their hands, congratulating them.

"You must feel deeply honoured to wear this decoration. I have witnessed it being bestowed upon officers and non-commissioned officers, but it's the first time I see it awarded to private soldiers. Personally, it brings me great satisfaction, for I was directly benefited by your heroic acts. Congratulations, you are a source of pride for the entire Company."

"Indeed," Gabriel thought to himself as he looked at the black and yellow-striped medal, "it seems that everyone else feels prouder of me than I do myself."

Three weeks later, he was sitting in a small café in Odessa, where he had been transferred. The fierce battle in Pleven had re-aggravated his knee injury. The higher-ups had decided to move him to the Headquarters of the port city, a logistical support centre for the war. Now his work involved managing the accounts for some of the supplies sent to the front, which had shifted southwards. The general consensus was that the war was nearing its resolution, with a great Russian victory on the horizon.

"But at what cost," Gabriel pondered.

Captain Kuznetzov's company had been almost entirely decimated. On the very night of the battle in Pleven, Sergeant Kisilev had died, and later, during a simple skirmish as the Russian army marched towards Sofia, Tarasov had been wounded. Fortunately, the injury wasn't fatal, and they were evacuated to Odessa, enabling them to be reunited once again. They were the only survivors of the famed Four Aces. As for the officers and non-commissioned officers who had been with them in Smolensk, most of them now lay under the Balkan soil. His memories took him back to those days of harsh training.

"It was tough," he reflected, "but it forged us and allowed us to create unbreakable bonds."

Undoubtedly, the bonds forged by soldiers go beyond death. "And such is life," he continued his thoughts, "surely Satan will continue to sleep peacefully at night and mistreat recruits during the day."

Taking a sip of coffee, he closed his coat tighter to shield himself from the cold and returned to his task of writing a letter to Ionela. "...I miss you immensely, I need you so much, I see you in the face of every girl from Odessa I come across..."

Two weeks later, Ionela's response read: "And just how many Odessan girls do you come across daily?"

Gabriel burst into laughter upon reading the note; he had forgotten how jealous his girlfriend could be.

The war had come to an end with the defeat of the Ottomans, but the Russian troops remained in the Balkans, even near Constantinople; talk of an armistice was in the air. Gabriel continued his duties at the logistics headquarters, which gradually shifted its focus from the frontlines to the interior of Russia. The efforts were now centred on the soldiers' return and the dismantling of the administrative machinery that had supported the war effort.

Gabriel accompanied Lieutenant Saskarov to the station, where he was departing for his hometown of St. Petersburg. There, a disappointed father awaited his son, who had been discharged from the Army due to a lifelong leg injury, and a mother who preferred her son to return, even if without his legs, but alive. Gabriel understood wounds all too well, having received four of them during the conflict. His knee injury was improving, but he realized it would bother him for many years, perhaps for the rest of his life. He no longer needed a cane, but the discomfort lingered, especially in the winter.

They bid farewell as if they had been old friends, with no distinction of military rank. They hugged, and as Saskarov boarded the train, he said, "I await you in St. Petersburg; you must come visit me someday."

"If I ever go, the first thing I'll do is come to say hello," replied Gabriel.

Shortly after, Gabriel received orders to relinquish his position and prepare to join a group returning from the war to Smolensk. Part of the group consisted of the remnants of Kuznetzov's Company, with him now bearing the insignia of Major. Additional contingents of soldiers trained at that Garrison joined them. The major had been the only officer from the Company to emerge unscathed from the war. He recognized Gabriel at the Odessa train station.

"Hello, German, what are you doing here?" he asked.

"I've been working here for the past few weeks, Major. Now I've been ordered to return to Smolensk."

"That's right. We're all heading there to regroup and reform the Company. Some will be assigned to different Units, while others will be discharged."

"Discharged, Major?" Gabriel's eyes lit up.

"Yes, those who have completed the mandatory six years of service, as well as those with physical scars or those who have distinguished themselves with extraordinary actions."

Gabriel's heart raced; he met two of the requirements. He had his knee injury, along with three other wounds, and he had received the highest decoration. Suddenly, the future seemed to open up before him, presenting a joyful opportunity to leave the Army. This realization filled him with enthusiasm during the journey to Smolensk.

Returning to the barracks where he had endured his first bitter military experiences evoked an ambiguous feeling in Gabriel. On one hand, there were memories of the harsh treatment and the shock that came from enduring such demanding training. On the other, there was the nostalgia for the comrades lost in the war. Out of the forty young men who had comprised Lieutenant Semionov's Second Platoon, only twelve had returned. Apart from Corporal Borisov, all the officers and non-commissioned officers had perished in the conflict.

A fresh group of recruits was now undergoing training in the yard. The once fearful lads had transformed into hardened and seasoned soldiers. Some of them leaned against a palisade, observing the exercises, and heeding the shouts of Sergeants Nikitin and Kuzmin. One of the soldiers exclaimed, "It's incomprehensible; those two sergeants who are so rough and overbearing here, have no idea what real war is like."

"You're right," said another soldier, "we've seen that even the toughest and most demanding training can't compare to a minute on the front lines."

"That's why the Army never progresses," commented the first soldier, "we're trained by those who have no idea where or when they'll send us, especially that damn Nikitin. Just wait and see, I'll set him straight."

"Hey, what are you going to do?" Gabriel asked him.

"I'm going to give him a piece of my mind."

He approached where the recruits were, trudging through the snow, enduring Nikitin's pressure and shouts. The others followed him, and when he was close enough, he yelled, "Hey, Satan, don't you think it's about time you stopped shouting and went to a real war?"

The others were surprised but soon burst into laughter.

Nikitin turned and came at them furiously, brandishing his whip.

"What do you think you dogs are doing?"

"These dogs have fought like true soldiers for Mother Russia, something you can't claim."

"It's true, all you know is how to mistreat recruits. We'd like to see you on the front line."

He reached where they stood and raised his whip threateningly. The first soldier faced him defiantly.

"Dare to touch me, and I'll knock you out right here in front of your recruits."

"This warrants a court-martial; you can't talk to me like that."

Gabriel remembered the incident with Sergeant Sorokin, the Crimea veteran, and decided to repeat the scene. He stepped forward, took off his overcoat, and then his tunic.

"Do you know what these are?" he said, showing him the scars on his shoulder and side. Then he pulled down his trousers to reveal the knee scar.

Satan and everyone else, including the recruits, stared at him in silence. Gabriel continued, "These are war wounds, received in the heat of battle, not in training areas. You know how to mistreat but not how to fight. Don't you dare say anything to those of us who risk our lives for Russia. We can teach those recruits more in ten minutes than you could in a whole year."

His comrades cheered and hoorayed, then they all left, taunting Satan, who was red with anger and couldn't recover.

"Well done, German, you repeated history with that wretch," his comrades said, patting him on the back.

Kuznetzov, who was now the second in command of the Garrison, stared at each of them, then walked around them with his hands clasped behind his back.

"I won't deny that it amuses me to see you put Nikitin in his place, but rules apply to everyone. I could order you to be flogged or impose a more severe punishment, but you are veterans, and we fought side by side in Bulgaria."

He stood in front of the soldiers again and said sharply, "Three days of solitary confinement for all, two more for Buganin for being a loudmouth, and five more for Rothman for the spectacle."

Gabriel had already served six of the eight days of bread and water confinement when Kuznetzov's assistant came to fetch him, leading him to the second commander's office.

"Come in," the officer said.

"At your orders, Sir?" Gabriel said, standing at attention before his superior.

"Rothman, I've called you here to inform you that your request for discharge from the ranks of the Army has been accepted, considering your physical ailments and your brilliant performance on the front lines."

Gabriel felt immense joy and could only say, "Thank you, sir."

"I regret it; you're an excellent soldier, but I understand it's what you wanted. Under these circumstances, there's no point in keeping you in confinement. Proceed with the process of military discharge and turn in your weapons and equipment."

He stood up from his chair and extended his hand, saying, "Thank you, soldier, for what you've done for the Army and for Mother Russia. And thank you personally for what you did for me. I wish you the best of luck."

"Thank you, Sir, for your teachings and your example," Gabriel replied.

Then he saluted, with the joy of knowing that it would be the last time he made that military gesture. He left the office, still in disbelief. His enlistment had begun abruptly, and now it was ending just as abruptly, bringing his Army experience to a close.

As he rode in the coach on his way home, he pondered the strange feeling of nostalgia he experienced when handing over his uniform and bidding farewell to his comrades at the barracks. It was an unexpected sensation for someone who had been forced into the Army and never liked being part of it. The next morning, he woke up at the inn in Minsk where he had spent the night, feeling like an orphan yearning to be surrounded by the military environment. Before continuing his journey, he went to the post office and sent a telegraphic message to Lublin, letting them know he was on his way.

He decided to deviate slightly from the route to visit Jared and Anya in Pinsk, as well as Oizer and Rachel. It was a delightful surprise for the Weizmann family, and Gabriel was overjoyed to see them. Like the girls, he considered them as his second parents, and Oizer was like an elder brother. He found him in Pinsk, together with Rachel and their five children. The family had grown considerably.

"I returned to Pinsk with Rachel because Motol is not the best place to raise children, as you can see, the family is growing," Oizer explained.

"I can see that," Gabriel replied, "you certainly don't waste any time."

They all laughed, and Oizer continued, "Besides, there was no reason for me to stay there. The businesses have shifted towards transportation and the timber trade, so I need to spend more time in the Brest sector. Besides, we're closer to my parents here."

"You're a good representative of Jewish traditions, unlike my sisters, who between the three of them have as many children as you and Rachel," Gabriel teased.

Gabriel stayed with the Weizmann for two days before continuing his journey to Lublin. As expected, his arrival was a grand event for the family. They gathered at their parents' house to celebrate his return, and Tatiana and Jana, who hadn't seen him in a long time, sat on either side of him, holding his arms and caressing his hair, even inspecting the scar from his shoulder wound.

His parents were brimming with joy to have their son back, especially because he had left the Army with such honour. They spent the evening conversing until late at night, bombarding Gabriel with questions and asking him to recount all his experiences. He obliged, omitting the harshest and bloodiest parts of his stories, yet still unable to avoid the darker aspects, such as the loss of his comrades.

The next day, Irenka and Carl, along with Tobias and his wife Sara, came to visit. They wanted to greet the war hero who had returned home. As they chatted, the rabbi arrived, having closely followed all the events surrounding Gabriel's time in the Army and his experiences in the conflict. Irenka informed them that she was planning a grand celebration at her residence to mark Gabriel's return. Sara jokingly remarked, "How peculiar, my dear friend, I didn't know you enjoyed hosting parties at your mansion."

"It's a new trend I want to start, as I'm organizing very few social gatherings lately," Irenka replied with a smile.

Everyone presents chuckled playfully. "You are cordially invited," Irenka continued, "it will be next Saturday, once the Shabbat is over. Please join us, Rabbi."

"With pleasure, thank you," the rabbi responded.

"We hope you and your wife, as well as your niece, will attend. It's good for her to meet people, especially since she's recently arrived in Lublin," Irenka added.

"Thank you very much, I'll ask her if she'd like to come," the rabbi replied.

"That sounds perfect," Irenka said. "I'll invite the cream of Lublin's society, as this is just a family gathering for now."

"And where they serve very little wine," Carl interjected.

Everyone laughed, and Isaak got up to fetch more bottles, joking that one invitation a year was enough, lest Carl bankrupt any host. Meanwhile, Gabriel shook his head to avoid his sisters pinching his cheeks. It was a joyful occasion – the family had endured difficult times, but things were now going well. The only thing that had been missing was the presence of the son.

The next morning, Gabriel discussed his future plans with his father. "Father, I need to resume the business affairs I had on hand when I was drafted."

"Of course, my son, tell me about them."

"I will restart the process of establishing a trading company for goods between Russia and the rest of Europe."

"That's a good idea, and you have my full support."

"That's precisely why I wanted to talk to you. I need to request a loan."

"Of course, my son. Not only that, I will provide you with a sum to help you start your project."

"Thank you very much, Father, but with one condition."

"What's that?"

"It's a loan, I'll pay back every single rouble."

"That's not necessary, you're my son, and you need an initial boost."

"Thank you, father, but it will be a loan."

Isaak looked at him with deep affection and then smiled, saying, "Alright, as you wish."

"Thank you very much, father. I will resume the necessary formalities tomorrow."

Irenka had organized a lavish event to celebrate Gabriel's return. Neither he nor his parents really desired such a celebration, but they agreed to it to please Sara, who had become a true sister to Irenka. The house was brightly lit with gas lamps and lanterns that Carl had brought from Germany, installed by a specialized team. When the Rothmans arrived, there were already several guests who warmly greeted Gabriel, though most of them were strangers to him. Being rather shy, he didn't feel very comfortable in that environment and preferred to slip away, finding the perfect spot on the terrace in the fresh April breeze. There, he struck up a conversation with his brother-in-law, Saul, who was also seeking refuge from the bustle. However, they couldn't escape the whirlwind that was Irenka. She arrived with a young lady and approached Gabriel, saying, "Come, Gabriel, I want to introduce you to Janelle, the rabbi's niece, and a charming young lady."

Gabriel approached and looked at the girl; she was surprisingly beautiful. Her features were proportionate and harmonious, with fair skin, dark eyes, and brown hair.

"Pleased to meet you, Janelle. I'm Gabriel."

"The pleasure is mine, and of course, I already know your name. Moreover, I know that the gathering is in your honour."

"A somewhat inaccurate observation; the party is simply because I arrived in the city, and our dear hostess never misses an opportunity to throw social gatherings."

"Well, the excuse of your arrival was perfect," Irenka chuckled, then turned to Saul and said, "Darling, would you accompany me for a moment, please?"

It was obvious that her intention was to leave the young couple alone. Gabriel invited Janelle to take a seat.

"Thank you, Gabriel, you are very kind."

"With pleasure."

"It's always a privilege to sit next to a war hero."

"I see you know more about me than I would have imagined, but I'm afraid to disappoint you – the real war heroes I know all rest beneath the Balkan soil."

They had been conversing almost all night, and the fact did not go unnoticed by anyone. The girl was truly captivating, and what Gabriel loved was that she possessed a deep cultural background and great fluency in holding engaging conversations, aside from her evident beauty.

Isaak was pleased to see how well his son and the rabbi's niece had connected. He knew Gabriel perfectly and understood that it wasn't easy for a girl to bond so quickly with him. Gabriel had never really had girlfriends; his priorities had always been elsewhere. The only one he had known was the Romanian girl, undeniably pleasant, but as he once told Sara, she was too foreign and, moreover, a Christian. Janelle, on the other hand, was Jewish.

Naturally, Sara also noticed the chemistry between Gabriel and the young woman. She also noticed how Isaak looked at them with delight. She pulled him aside and asked, "What do you think?"

"About what?"

"Don't pretend with me, about the rabbi's niece."

"Oh, she's a delightful girl. I had the opportunity to speak with her some days ago. She's a great conversationalist and very intelligent."

"Alright, but don't dodge the topic. I notice you're content seeing her talking to Gabriel."

"I'm pleased they're becoming friends."

"And what pleases you the most?"

"As I said, she's an admirable girl."

"She certainly is, but we should see what Gabriel thinks."

"He surely feels the same as me; otherwise, he wouldn't have spent so many hours talking to her."

"Alright, let's wait and see what happens. Remember, he has a girlfriend."

"Yes, the Romanian girl."

"Exactly, I don't know if he's forgotten her, but he seemed very much in love when we met in Kronstadt."

"It might have been a passing fancy; you never know."

"That's what you would like, but you can't fool me."

"Well, yes, my dear, I must admit that's what I'd like."

"Anyway, maybe we're getting ahead of ourselves; he'll have to follow his heart's desires."

"Yes, I hope his heart leans towards a Jewish woman."

"Even better if it's the rabbi's niece, right?"

"That wouldn't be lamentable at all; quite the opposite."

"Now we'd have a rabbi in the family."

"Sure, but it's not the same."

"I too would prefer a Jewish woman for Gabriel, but not necessarily as a priority."

"I don't understand you."

"No, my dear, I definitely would prefer a Jewish girl in my son's life, but if he truly loves her and she makes him happy."

The truth was that Sara valued Ionela. In her motherly heart, she felt that Ionela would be a worthy wife. She also knew that the Romanian girl genuinely loved Gabriel, not just for his physical attractiveness. She was also aware of something that Isaak couldn't ignore, which was that Ionela was willing to abandon Christianity to be with her son.

"It will be what his heart decides, not the religion of the girl he chooses," she thought to herself. "If his feelings for Ionela were merely a product of the special circumstances during the war, he'll forget her, and that will be that. But if he truly loves her, he'll go back for her."

"Why so pensive?" Irenka asked, interrupting Sara's thoughts.

"Nothing special," Sara replied.

"It is something special. Don't think I haven't noticed that you're keeping an eye on Gabriel and Janelle. Not just you, Isaak and half the room are doing the same, and Tatiana and Jana can't take their eyes off them."

"It's not common for Gabriel to spend so much time with a girl, especially as he just met her."

"You're right. One of his secret admirers told me the same thing."

"Who? One of the girls from the bakeries or the chocolate shop?"

"No, everyone knows those girls are fascinated by Gabriel. I'm talking about another woman."

"And what did she say?"

"She said Gabriel was a waste."

"What do you mean?"

"Just like that. She said, 'he's perhaps the most handsome man in Poland, and no woman can remain indifferent to his physical attributes, but he seems uninterested in women.'"

"What are you implying?"

"Calm down, my dear Sara. I'm not implying anything. I've known Gabriel since he was a child, and I know what he's like. I'm just passing on the comment."

"Well, whoever that woman is, she's audacious and ignorant."

Irenka laughed. "Don't get angry. It's nonsense."

"In any case, and I say this with motherly wisdom, Gabriel is or at least was deeply in love with the Romanian girl I mentioned."

"Well, lucky her if she managed to conquer your son's heart, because not only is he very handsome, but he's also a man of great qualities and commendable feelings."

"I know. Who do you think raised him?"

"But it's not just a matter of upbringing; some things are inherent."

"And whose blood do you think runs through his veins?"

Both friends laughed and changed the subject.

The family's talk began to centre around Gabriel's interest in Janelle. He seemed captivated by her. He would invite her for walks in the park and to have a drink at the chocolate shop. They would spend hours there talking, much to the envy of the shop attendants. They couldn't fathom how they could discuss topics they often didn't even understand. The workers weren't accustomed to hearing about subjects like trade with the United States, the decline of the Ottoman Empire, or items with such exotic names as the electric light bulb and the internal combustion engine.

Gabriel hadn't wasted time; he had already registered his trading company and was in contact with his future partner in Russia, Ivan Saskarov. Together, they would manage the import and export business. To finalize the details, Gabriel would travel to a city he had once sworn to never set foot in. But circumstances change, and so do times. The restrictions on Jews prevented them from settling outside the settlement area and registering businesses. However, there were certain exceptions, and one of them was having served in the Army. So, after all, Gabriel would benefit from his involuntary conscription.

The extensive conversations with Janelle had to be postponed due to the trip to St. Petersburg to meet with his future partner. Jana convinced Saúl to allow her to accompany her brother; they would stop by Pinsk to greet the Weizmann's, which was a great incentive. She also had the desire to return to the city she had visited several years ago, in the company of Jared and Oizer.

So, at the beginning of May, the two siblings set off for Pinsk, where they spent three days at the Weizmann's' home, reminiscing about the days they had lived in St. Petersburg. It was delightful to be with such dear friends again. They continued their journey and arrived in the imperial capital with pleasant weather and a clear sky. Iván was waiting for them at the station, and as soon as they greeted each other, Gabriel introduced his sister Jana.

"This is my sister Jana," and turning said, "Lieutenant Saskarov."

"Delighted, ma'am, it is a pleasure to meet you. By the way, the lieutenant thing is now history."

"I know, Mr. Saskarov. My brother has already told me that you retired from the Army," Jana replied.

"That's the nature of the job. Anyway, let's head to the carriage; you'll be staying at my house, of course."

The two men, once superior and subordinate, had formed a friendship that began in Odessa and continued through correspondence; through which they had enveloped the project of starting a business together. One favour Iván asked of Gabriel was not to refer to him as "lieutenant" but to call him by his first name. They would be partners, but above all, friends, and Gabriel gladly accepted. It seemed that both of them felt the need to put their military experience behind them one because the injury he suffered had cut short his aspirations and those of his father, and the other because his military service had been against his will.

They quickly adapted to their new conditions; the uniform and the war became part of their past. One peculiar thing they had in common was that both were wounded in the right knee and left with lifelong disabilities. Though Gabriel's impairment was barely noticeable, Iván needed a walking stick to get around and experienced sharp pains when the temperature dropped.

Iván's residence wasn't very large; however, this was compensated by a lush garden surrounding it on all four sides. The interior was tastefully and elegantly decorated. As soon as they arrived, they were greeted by Iván's wife, Olga, whom he introduced to Gabriel and Jana before settling them into their rooms. That evening, Iván invited them to dine out and take a stroll through the splendid city. For Jana, it was a wonderful experience to roam the boulevards and avenues where she had walked as a child with Aliza and Oizer. Both she and her brother were amazed by the spectacular gas lamps that illuminated the city.

The next day, Olga and Jana went out to continue exploring the city and do some shopping, while the two men sat down to finalize the details of the company they were about to establish. Gabriel had already registered the business in Lublin, but for practical reasons, the headquarters had to be in St. Petersburg, and that was the main reason for their visit.

The company was formally established in the commercial registry of St. Petersburg under the name "Saskarov and Rothman Associates." After completing the legal procedures, they began specifying details, such as the logo for the new partnership.

"My dear Gabriel, we will start with the export of rye and barley flour. I have contacts here in St. Petersburg, and you should establish your own in Germany and Austria and determine the most suitable imports for Russia," Iván explained.

"Understood, Iván. As soon as I return to Lublin, I will head to Berlin. I will take advantage of the connections of a family that are close friends of mine and trade wood between Pinsk and Germany. After that, I'll go to Vienna, where my brother-in-law, who is an officer in the Austrian Army, will assist me. He has good connections in the city," Gabriel replied.

They shook hands, sealing the beginning of what they hoped would be a prosperous venture. Later, they planned to involve soldier Sukov, the other hero from that night in the trenches of Pleven. He lived in Novgorod, a three-hour train ride from St. Petersburg, and would handle all matters related to transporting the goods.

After completing the necessary formalities, they said their goodbyes and headed back to Lublin. Jana thoroughly enjoyed her time in the city, exploring many places with Iván's wife and buying small gifts for the whole family, including one she wanted to send to Aliza as a reminder of their time together in the capital of the Russian Empire.

As soon as they arrived in Lublin, Gabriel sought out Janelle to resume their delightful conversations, which seemed to make time fly by. Isaak was pleased to witness their interaction, as he harboured the hope that something deeper would develop between his son and the charming rabbi's niece. There were days when he left the shoe store solely to pass by the chocolate shop to see if they were there, engrossed in conversation. On more than one occasion, he found them indeed there, and exchanged warm greetings.

He felt that he had already compromised enough when he allowed Tatiana to marry Robiak, who was Catholic. Not to mention Aliza's conversion, which she had accepted out of love for her daughter, but from which he had not fully recovered. He knew that Gabriel was a devout Jew, faithfully observing the traditions of his religion, so he did not wish for love to once again interfere and potentially distract his son from his duties. On the other hand, he yearned for a formal relationship between Gabriel and Janelle. She embodied everything a Jewish wife should be.

Sara, on the other hand, was less certain about the situation. She knew that Gabriel still wrote to Ionela, but in a ratio of four to one since he received more letters from the Romanian girl than he sent. She sympathized with the young woman, knowing she was deeply in love. However, she also understood that she couldn't intervene in this matter. She only hoped that her son would make a decision soon, although she realized that he was completely focused on achieving success in the businesses he was organizing.

Gabriel spent only two days in Lublin before heading to Berlin to speak with Helmuth, Jared's business partner. He hoped that Helmuth, in turn, would help him connect with beer merchants and large German bakeries to whom he planned to sell rye and barley flour. When he arrived in Berlin, they warmly welcomed him; he and his wife Ingrid fondly remembered Aliza.

"Your sister is a delightful woman," Ingrid said. "We grew fond of her when she spent some time with us here."

"I know. She always speaks of you with great fondness."

As gracious hosts, despite their serious and reserved nature, they attended to Gabriel with great pleasure and took the opportunity to catch up on Aliza's life in Vienna. He was careful not to touch upon the topic of his participation in the Balkan War, as his mother had warned him about the tragedy of the couple with the death of their son in Sadowa. Other than that, they thoroughly enjoyed Gabriel's company and cheerful conversation.

Helmut was of great help as he knew a good number of entrepreneurs not only in the capital but throughout Germany, from Strasbourg to Munich. In addition to providing him with contacts, he personally accompanied Gabriel on business trips to several cities, and the three weeks proved very fruitful for the future of the enterprise. Once back in Berlin, Gabriel wanted to invite Helmut and Ingrid to dinner at a luxurious restaurant in the city. The conversation was lively, and at one point, Helmut said:

"I have witnessed the meetings we've had with several entrepreneurs, some I knew, and others I didn't, but you have handled them very efficiently."

"Thank you very much, Herr Helmut."

"I have been discussing with Ingrid and considering your commercial future, and I've come to a conclusion."

"Quite intriguing. And what is that?"

"That you will have great success in your business endeavours."

"Even more intriguing, Herr Helmut. And what makes you think so?"

"You possess three essential qualities. First, you have the knowledge and intelligence to develop businesses; in fact, you are visionary and innovative."

"Quite a statement. I think your appreciation is somewhat exaggerated."

"Not at all. Remember, I have been in the business world for many years. The second quality is that you persevere; it's obvious that you don't give up easily, and that paves the way to success."

"Well, to some extent. And the third?"

"My wife says you are very handsome, which opens many doors. But beyond that, it's the fact that you have something the Spanish call 'angelic.'"

"Angelic?"

"Yes, it's a virtue difficult to describe. It's like an aura that may not be immediately perceptible, but it makes you likable to everyone. Some also call it charisma. Do you understand?"

"I believe I do."

"It may seem trivial, but I have been in the commercial field for many more years than you have lived, almost as long as your father has. I can assure you that half of successful businesses are achieved through the emotional aspect, and being likable to others promotes those emotions."

"Well, thank you very much; I wasn't aware of that."

28

The maid, upon hearing the bell, went to open the door and saw a young woman with a lovely face and a fresh and vibrant demeanour.

"Good morning, may I see Mrs. Aliza Radetz, please?" the visitor said in very broken German and with a peculiar accent.

"Good morning, whom shall I announce?" asked the maid.

"Ozana Kerst."

"One moment, please. Mrs. or Miss?"

"Mrs. Kerst."

The maid led her to the study where Aliza was reading some Yiddish manuscripts. She interrupted her, saying, "Excuse me, Mrs. Aliza, there is a Mrs. Kerst at the door, asking for you."

"Mrs. who?"

"Kerst."

"I don't remember any Mrs. Kerst. Let's see who it is."

She went to the door with the maid, and upon seeing the visitor, she looked at her carefully until she finally remembered.

"Ozana," she said at last, "forgive me for not recognizing you earlier. What a pleasant surprise. Please come in."

Aliza greeted her with a kiss on the cheek and led her to the study, asking the maid to serve them tea with rolls.

"What a delightful surprise. Tell me, what brings you to Vienna?"

"I arrived a few days ago, Aliza, and now I live here."

"Have you settled in Vienna?"

"Yes, I'm with my husband."

"Ah, you're married! Tell me, who is the lucky man?"

"Lieutenant Kerst of the Austrian Army. I don't know if you remember him; he was with us when we met in Kronstadt."

"Of course," Aliza smiled, "I remember he couldn't take his eyes off you and didn't let you go for a moment while we were dancing in the hotel salon."

"Now he's, my husband. They transferred him to Vienna, and he'll soon be promoted to Captain."

"Congratulations! I'm glad, and we'll have time to spend together. Consider this your home."

"Thank you so much, Aliza, you're very kind."

"And your mother and sister, how are they?"

"They're fine, carrying on with their lives."

She fell silent and lowered her gaze. Aliza sensed something was amiss and asked, "What's wrong? Has something happened to them?"

"Truthfully, Ionela isn't well, and it pains me to see her like this."

"Is she ill?"

"Let me be honest, Aliza. I came to greet you, and I'm delighted to see you, but the main reason for my visit is precisely to talk to you about my sister."

"Tell me, Ozana, I'm listening."

"She's very sad and depressed. Mother says she doesn't even have the energy to eat properly."

"Why? She seemed so happy and radiant when we were in Kronstadt last year."

"She was very happy back then because she had Gabriel by her side."

Aliza hesitated about what to say next. She knew her brother well and remembered him confessing his deep affection for Ionela in Kronstadt. Could Gabriel have forgotten her?

"But don't they exchange letters? I know my brother has been very busy, but I assume they correspond."

"They do, Aliza, but it's been over two months since he last wrote to her. This morning, I received a telegram from Ionela telling me she's sent him four letters without getting a reply."

"Oh dear, I'm so sorry to hear that, Ozana. I know Gabriel has had many commitments lately; he was in St. Petersburg, and now he's in Germany. It's possible that's why he hasn't been in touch."

"Maybe. It eases my mind to know he's been traveling, and I hope that's the reason. But my sister is desperate; you can't imagine how much she loves Gabriel, and it's been over eight months since they last saw each other."

"I have some news for you; he's in Berlin and will be coming to Vienna from there. We will host him at our home, so we'll have the chance to talk and find out what's going on in his mind and heart."

"It's good to know. I hope I can have a conversation with him."

"Leave me your address, and I'll let you know as soon as he arrives. I swear I hope it's all just because of his busy schedule and nothing else. Ionela is a wonderful girl, and it would hurt me if she had to suffer because of my brother. However, I want to make one thing clear: I know him very well, and if his heart didn't beat for your sister anymore, he would have let her know."

"I hope so. You give me hope."

Gabriel bid farewell to Helmuth and Ingrid, thanking them for all their attention and essential support for the establishment of Saskarov and Rothman Associates. He got into the coach and headed to the station to catch the train to Vienna. He felt satisfied as the contacts he had made, and the terms of negotiation bode well for the company's future. As the train sped through the Bohemian plateaus as he hoped for success in Austria. He took the opportunity to study the German course books he had started since returning to Lublin.

By late afternoon, he arrived at Vienna's central station, where Karl and Aliza were waiting for him. He greeted them warmly, as well as their little nephew, who bore a striking resemblance to Karl. That evening during dinner, he shared his business plans and his trips to St. Petersburg and Berlin. He also spoke about his war experiences, something that Gabriel didn't particularly enjoy but discussed due to Karl's keen interest in military matters.

At coffee time, Aliza took his arm and led him to the study, apologizing to her husband. Gabriel couldn't understand her insistence. They reached the study, and she practically pushed him onto the sofa, sitting beside him, and confronted him.

"Gabriel, what's going on with Ionela?"

"With Ionela? Nothing."

"What do you mean nothing? Do you still love her?"

"Of course, I love her."

"Then why haven't you written to her?"

"I have written to her."

"When was the last time you did?"

He paused, then said after a moment, "About a month ago, before leaving for St. Petersburg."

"A month? Let me tell you something; that girl is distressed. She can't even eat properly because you've abandoned her."

"No, for God's sake. I've been traveling, but she knows I love her."

"She knows I love her," Aliza imitated his tone, "listen, my dear brother, it's not enough for a woman to know you love her. You have to tell her constantly, especially when you're living far away. How can you go a month without writing to her, especially when she sent you four letters during that time?"

"Four letters?"

"Yes, four."

"How do you know?"

"Ozana told me. She's living here in Vienna, married to an Austrian lieutenant."

"Well, I never!"

"She also told me that Ionela is on the brink of despair, thinking you've forgotten her or replaced her with another woman. Tell me, Gabriel, do you still love Ionela?"

"Of course, I love her with all my heart. In fact, my eagerness to get the business running is because I want to marry her."

"Well, you're quite the blockhead, Gabriel. A simple telegram saying 'I love you' would have been enough to spare her so much suffering. Why is it that men often take things for granted?"

Gabriel fell silent, and his eyes clouded.

"But well, what matters is that you still love her. Now you have to tell her. Tomorrow morning, you must send her a telegram."

"No, I won't do that."

"What do you mean?"

"I'll do something better. Tomorrow, I'll travel to Romania, I'll go and visit her."

Aliza was thrilled. Like Sara, she cherished Ionela and felt saddened by the girl's distress.

"And what about your business meetings?"

"I'll postpone them. She comes first; there's no point in pursuing business if I don't have the woman I love by my side. I'll go to Alexandria and ask her parents for Ionela's hand."

"That's my brother!" Aliza said, getting up and pulling him up for a hug, then pinching his cheeks.

"Alright, alright, Aliza," he said, shaking his head.

"Very well, now get ready because we're going out," Aliza said.

"Where are we going?" Gabriel asked.

"To Ozana's house. I won't wait until tomorrow to share the good news with her. Besides, these summer nights are perfect for strolling around Vienna."

Indeed, the night was cool and pleasant. Karl didn't accompany them as he had some pending work at home. Once they arrived at the Kerst residence, Aliza rang the bell insistently, and Ozana opened the door.

"Gabriel!" she exclaimed, throwing herself into his arms.

"My dear sister-in-law, how are you?" Gabriel replied.

Ozana, still holding onto him, turned her gaze towards Aliza, who said, "Everything is perfect. He'll be your brother-in-law for many years to come."

The girl let out a joyful squeal and hugged Gabriel even tighter. Then she led them inside, greeted the lieutenant, and convinced him to join them for a walk and some drinks. during their conversation over coffee and pastries, Ozana persuaded her husband to allow her to accompany Gabriel to Alexandria and take the opportunity to visit her parents. For obvious reasons, Aliza offered to go with them, and the plan was set.

They arrived at Kronstadt Station, which brought back pleasant memories for all three. They immediately made their way to the border and took a coach to Alexandría. They spent the night in Targoviste and continued their journey the next day. At one point, perhaps recalling the unforgettable surprise she received on her wedding day when she found her father waiting on the church steps, Aliza said to Ozana, "Let's give Ionela a nice surprise. When we arrive at your house, you go in first and then signal us to follow."

They reached Alexandria at dusk. Ozana went ahead and rang the bell, while Aliza and Gabriel hid from view. They heard the commotion caused by the presence of the daughter and sister. At one point, Ozana said, "I haven't come alone; I'm accompanied by some friends whom I'm going to introduce to you."

She approached the door as Doína asked, "Why didn't you bring them in?"

At that moment, Ozana peeked at the door and gestured, and Aliza and Gabriel entered. Ionela's cry of joy resounded throughout Alexandria. She didn't care that her parents were present; she threw herself into Gabriel's arms. She couldn't speak due to her sobs, but she held him tightly. Finally, she managed to articulate words and said, "My love, my Gabriel, you have no idea how happy you make me."

Then, as a show of having lost all reserve and modesty, she cupped his cheeks and kissed him on the mouth.

He felt a bit embarrassed, gently moving her aside, and addressed her parents, "Mihai and Doína, I have come to Alexandria because I wish formally to ask for Ionela's hand."

She couldn't hold back any longer, hugging him again and crying tears of joy. Then she hugged Ozana and Aliza, while Gabriel shook hands with his future in-laws. It seemed as if he hadn't even considered that Ionela was Christian. Aliza thought that issue would be addressed later; for now, it was a time of celebration that shouldn't be marred.

Ionela was once again completely happy, accepting Gabriel's explanation about his silence being due to his full dedication to establishing the company and securing their financial situation before getting married. They strolled through the park and by the river once more, this time accompanied by Ozana and Aliza. Seated on the same bench where they were on the day Gabriel left to return to the front, he spoke to her:

"Do you remember what I told you in this very spot on the day I left?"

"Of course, you promised you'd come back for me."

"And here I am, my beloved. I've kept my promise. I'll never stop loving you."

"And do you remember what I told you in response?"

"That you'd wait for me for eternity."

"And, as you see, I've kept my promise too. I'll love you for the rest of my life."

They shared a tender kiss amidst the teasing from their respective sisters. At that moment, Aliza approached them, taking Ionela's hand, and said, "Excuse me, Gabriel, I'm stealing her away for a few minutes."

Ozana sat next to him and said, "Thank you, Gabriel, for making Ionela so happy. She fell in love with you from the moment she saw you, even though you hadn't seen her because you were unconscious."

"I remember those days. When I started to wake up, the first thing I saw were her beautiful green eyes. Since that day, they've been imprinted in my heart. You know, what will always bind me to Ionela is the tenderness in her gaze."

Meanwhile, Ionela and Aliza walked hand in hand through the park.

"Ionela, there's something you need to consider," Aliza said.

"What do you mean?" Ionela asked.

"You know that Gabriel is Jewish. To marry him, you'll have to embrace our religion."

"I thought you were Catholic," Ionela replied.

"No, my dear sister-in-law. I converted to marry Karl, but I've never stopped being Jewish. As you can see, my situation is exactly the same as yours."

"Aliza, I had already told your mother that if I have to renounce my religion to marry Gabriel, I will. Forgive me, and may God forgive me, but my beliefs don't come before my feelings. Nothing stands in the way of the man I love."

"I'm glad to hear you say that. You should prepare yourself because the process is not usually easy or quick. The sooner you start, the better. You'll have to do it in Bucharest."

During their farewell, Ionela felt nostalgia but at the same time was filled with great inner excitement. This time was different; she wouldn't live in uncertainty anymore because Gabriel wasn't going to the frontlines, and he had asked her to marry him. She felt like the happiest woman in the world and was determined to start her conversion process to Judaism right away.

Back in Vienna, Gabriel made all the contacts necessary to expand the future sale of barley and rye flour. For this, he had to travel to Salzburg, and Karl requested permission to accompany him because although Gabriel's German was improving, it still wasn't fluent enough to finalize deals worth hundreds of thousands of florins.

He returned to Lublin very satisfied, sharing the progress of his projects and the details of the negotiations he had conducted in Germany and Austria with his father.

"Well done, son. I see that you're establishing your path, and I congratulate you," his father said.

"Thank you, father. If everything goes smoothly, we should start seeing the first profits next summer."

"With your work ethic, I'm sure that will be the case. Let's go to the sitting room; I've invited the rabbi for lunch, and he should be arriving soon."

As expected, the invitation had a double intention, and the rabbi arrived with his wife and niece. Gabriel was delighted to see Janelle again, and naturally, so was his father, especially when the two young people retired to a corner to have a more private conversation. Isaak looked at them with a pleased glance.

They sat close to each other, and Janelle asked him, "How was your trip?"

"Very good. I managed to establish several valuable contacts for our future business."

"That's great. Congratulations. And how was Vienna? You met with your sister; I assume."

"Of course, I visited her. She's my sister, and I adore her. But that's not all; you know what else?"

"What?"

"I went to Alexandria!"

Janelle placed her hand on Gabriel's forearm and asked, "Did you go to see her?"

"Yes, with all the traveling and business matters, I had neglected to write to her, and she was very sad. My sister scolded me, so I decided to visit her, and Aliza accompanied me."

"Oh, how I envy you, Gabriel! What a lovely surprise for Ionela. I can imagine she was overjoyed."

"Definitely. As soon as she saw me, she threw herself into my arms, not caring that her parents were present. But do you know what made her even happier?"

"I don't know; tell me."

"I formally asked her parents for her hand in marriage."

"No way! But what about the religion issue? Have you decided on that?"

"Aliza spoke with her, and she's going to start the conversion process."

"I'm so happy for you. Too bad I can't say the same for my situation. You know that if my parents find out I'm in love with a Lutheran German, they'll have a fit," she said, glancing at the rabbi who was chatting with Isaak. "And my uncle, let's not even talk about him."

"I understand, my dear friend. It's exactly the same situation as Aliza's."

"Let's change the subject. No need to spoil the night for me. Let's focus on being happy with your news. By the way, did you see how the Congress of Berlin ended?"

"Very favourably for us Jews. The British are the only ones who truly think of us."

"Agreed, although we must admit that it's thanks to Disraeli's good efforts."

"Indeed, he is undoubtedly a great politician, the only Prime Minister of Jewish descent that Britain has had," Janelle acknowledged.

"Regardless, we have much to be grateful to them for," Gabriel affirmed.

"There is no better nation in Europe; the English are a special breed. They never give up, and when they set their minds to something, they always achieve it," Janelle added.

"Oh, I almost forgot to tell you some news I learned recently. I'm not sure if you've heard about it. Do you know an American inventor named Edison?" she asked.

"Of course," he replied. "He was involved with the electric light bulb."

"Exactly. Well, he has patented an invention he calls the phonograph," Janelle said.

"What is that?" Gabriel inquired.

"It's a device that can record sounds from the environment and then play them back," she explained.

"Incredible! The sciences are progressing at great speed," Gabriel remarked.

"That's right," Janelle agreed.

Meanwhile, Isaak waited, hoping that something important would come out of these conversations. Well, something important had already emerged, a beautiful friendship.

29

The wedding was splendid; Ionela looked radiant, as all brides tend to be, and Gabriel looked very elegant in his black suit and hat. Sara felt overjoyed, but nostalgia crept in as well. She remembered the restless and lively little boy who used to play with wooden carts, and she couldn't pinpoint the exact moment he had grown into a man, assuming the responsibilities of a husband. She felt that now, she and Isaak were finally alone, though she was fortunate that all their children, except for Aliza, lived in the same city.

As she looked at Isaak, he still appeared as handsome as the day she had met him, but the years had left their mark. Small streaks of grey adorned his temples, and dark circles had formed under his eyes. Yet, his physical and spiritual strength remained intact, along with his convictions and adherence to all customs and traditions. He couldn't quite recover from the fact that their children had chosen partners outside the community. Gabriel had been the last, and even though Ionela was now Jewish, Isaak still wasn't entirely convinced.

Nevertheless, to be fair, he couldn't complain. His youngest daughter had filled his heart with unexpected joy. Four days previously, when she arrived in Lublin to attend her brother's wedding, and they were all gathered at Irenka's house, where a reception had been organized for the guests, Aliza called him aside and said:

"Father, I want to tell you something. Could we go to the study?"

"Yes, daughter, let's go," he replied, intrigued.

Once in the study, he was eager to know what she had to say.

"Tell me, what is it?"

"It's something I know will please you," Aliza said, approaching him.

"Well, I'm listening, my dear."

"You know that I converted to Catholicism only to marry the man I love, but I have never stopped being Jewish."

"I know, my dear."

"I think it's also important for you to know that we do not celebrate Christian holidays in our home, except for Christmas, which is more of a social tradition than a religious one."

"That sounds fine, my dear."

"You should also know that, on the other hand, we do celebrate all Jewish holidays, without exception."

Isaak was taken aback; he seemed to understand and not understand at the same time.

"You celebrate all our holidays?"

"Yes, Father. Rosh Hashanah, Pesah, Purim, Hanukkah, Yom Kippur—every one of them."

At that moment, Isaak recalled the premonitory words of his good friend Andrew Cronin on the day when, thank God, he convinced him to attend Aliza's wedding.

"Did you hear me, Father?" she asked, bringing him back from his thoughts.

"Of course, my daughter."

"We also honour Shabbat and observe the Jewish dietary laws."

"How happy I am... But... What does Karl think about all this?"

Aliza looked at him with a typical expression of disbelief.

"But what's the matter, father? You are usually so perceptive. Did you lose track of the difference between singular and plural?"

At that moment, Isaak, who had been hoping that his suspicions were true, finally understood that they were. However, he exclaimed:

"It can't be!"

"Yes, it can, Father. It wasn't easy; it took a lot of time and patience, but it's true."

"Oh, God, what joy! Are you sure?"

"Absolutely, Father. He's, my husband."

"And is it from the heart?"

"He's even willing to give up his military career, and you know what that means to him."

"Daughter, you have given me immense joy."

"I knew you would feel that way, Dad."

"My child, I love you so much." He stood up from the armchair and said, "Come here, give your old father a hug."

"You're not old; you could still win over more than one heart."

They embraced again, and at that moment, Sara entered the study, noticing Isaak's teary eyes, and she addressed Aliza:

"Have you told him?"

"Yes, mother."

"You knew?" Isaak asked.

"Our daughter told me this morning, but I thought it was her place to tell you."

Isaak raised his eyes to the sky and exclaimed:

"Thank you, Hashem. You never abandon your people, and your people never forget you."

"Let's return to the living room; Tatiana and Robiak have just arrived," Sara said, taking each of them by the arm.

As with all important occasions for the Rothmans, both joyous and sorrowful, the whole family gathered, accompanied by their loyal friends. Besides the hosts, there were those who had arrived in Lublin to attend the wedding: the Weizmann, including the now young adults, Piotr and Malka, Tobias and Sara.

Even visitors from as far as St. Petersburg were present; Ivan was there with his wife Olga, and Sukov, still unmarried. They were strangers to most, but Gabriel and Jana took it upon themselves to make them feel at home, not leaving them unattended for a moment and integrating them into the family.

Mihai and Doina were also present, along with Ozana and her husband, Captain Kerst. Ionela was the only one missing, following the Jewish tradition that forbids the couple from seeing each other for seven days before the wedding. However, her brother was there, seizing the opportunity to visit Poland and attend the event. To be more precise, he was more interested in the gatherings and parties, as he was a brawler and a big fan of liquor. Embarrassingly, after a few too many drinks, he started praising the great beauty of the charming lady with gray eyes and blonde hair like the summer fields.

When they took him out to the terrace for some fresh air, away from the other guests, he coincidentally found Tatiana conversing with Ozana. The indiscreet man began to praise the exotic beauty of Tatiana, the woman with raven-black hair, improvising unrhymed poetry.

Gabriel decided to intervene, saying, "Wait, I know how to calm him down, and don't get jealous, Robiak. Who asked you to marry such a beautiful woman as Tatiana?"

"Ohhh, my beloved little brother," Tatiana responded, approaching, and pinching his cheek.

"I hope none of my sisters teach Ionela that ugly habit."

"Not a bad idea; I'll ask Jana and Aliza about it."

Gabriel seated Ionela's uncle in an armchair and said, "Let's have a toast with vodka." He went and returned shortly with two glasses filled to the brim.

"Now, uncle, let's show everyone what men are made of. Let's drink down in one; there's no stopping halfway."

He handed a glass to the uncle, then raised his own and made them clink together. The onlookers observed sceptically, as the glasses were huge. Could they really drink all that liquor in one go?

"Cheers!" Gabriel said and started drinking from his glass.

The poor uncle made a supreme effort and downed all the vodka, then stared straight ahead, his eyes rolling back, and collapsed. Gabriel, who had only consumed water from his glass, left it on the table and, along with Robiak, lifted the man, placing him on the terrace's sofa.

"Wow, Gabriel, I didn't know you were such a good drinker," Ivan said, having watched the scene with disbelief.

"I'm not, my dear friend. My glass was filled with water."

Everyone burst into laughter, and Ivan added, "But you practically knocked him out."

"That's because I added some caffeinated tea to his vodka, which they use as a relaxing drink. Not only he will rest for a few hours, but he'll wake up refreshed tomorrow."

Indeed, the uncle slept soundly for the rest of the night without further bothering the ladies.

Meanwhile, Ionela was at the hotel, reminiscing joyfully about the time she first met Gabriel. She had arrived with her family three days earlier and had not yet seen her future husband, but she had met the rest of the family. Sara had come with her three daughters to visit her. They warmly embraced, and Ionela immediately remembered the hug they had shared in Kronstadt.

"What joy to see you again, my daughter. You seem more beautiful every day," Sara said.

"Thank you so much; it's a great compliment coming from you."

Ionela was delighted that Sara called her "daughter."

"You already know Aliza, but not my other two girls. This is Tatiana, my eldest daughter."

Tatiana came forward and embraced her. "Welcome to the family, Ionela. I would have liked to meet you sooner, but I'm glad you're here, and I know you'll be happy with Gabriel. He's the best man in the world."

"Thank you, Tatiana; your words are as beautiful as you are."

"And this is Jana, my second daughter," Sara said, introducing her.

Jana also approached and hugged her. "I also welcome you. I'm sure we'll get along very well."

Ionela shed a few tears, and Sara was moved. "I know you'll be nervous; the day after tomorrow will be one of the most important days of your life. Dry your tears, and let's have a talk."

"Thank you very much, Mrs. Sara. I am indeed nervous, but my tears are of happiness for meeting my two new sisters."

Tatiana and Jana approached once again and embraced Ionela, then sat down to talk. Ionela quickly bonded with her new sisters-in-law; she was a tender-hearted girl, and Gabriel's sisters were three good-hearted women. In truth, all the Rothmans were kind, honest, and upright individuals, and the entire Lublin community attested to this.

On the appointed day, Gabriel was extremely nervous. He was accompanied, as tradition dictated, by Isaak and Mihai, while Ionela stayed with Sara and Doina. Like Isaak's experience with Aliza's wedding, the mother of the bride was also uneasy about her daughter's change of religion. However, she was perfectly aware that there was no force on Earth capable of convincing Ionela otherwise. As a mother, she knew that Ionela was deeply in love with Gabriel, and as a woman, she understood why because he was a decent man, chivalrous, highly educated, an excellent worker, and of impeccable conduct. It was evident that he truly loved her daughter.

Naturally the marriage and subsequent celebration took place at Irenka's house; it was the second Rothman wedding to be held there, following Tatiana's wedding to Robiak. Sara had lost count of how many parties and gatherings she had attended at her best friend's home.

The rabbi arrived, and the ceremony commenced. It was emotional when Ionela handed the Tallit to Gabriel, and they shared a kiss. As soon as he broke the glass, the celebration started with dancing and music, with the men on one side and the women on the other.

The newlyweds settled into a small house very close to where Jana and Saul lived. Gabriel was overjoyed with his wife, and she grew closer to her mother-in-law and her sisters-in-law. She bonded particularly well with Tatiana, who taught her to perfect her Russian and started teaching her some basic Polish. She also developed a strong rapport with the rabbi's wife, whom she visited frequently, demonstrating wonderful integration into the community. The rabbi's wife remarked, "She is a better practitioner of our religion and our customs than many other Jewish women in Lublin."

Gabriel worked diligently to expand the business, traveling extensively between St. Petersburg, Berlin, and Vienna. On some occasions, he took Ionela along, and she was fascinated by these three capitals due to their size, activity, and progress, which were so different from her hometown of Alexandria and even from Bucharest. The first time she arrived in St. Petersburg with her husband, she could not believe that so many beautiful and imposing buildings could exist in one place. She admired the bridges, parks, buildings, and boulevards of the imperial capital. The soft and pastel colours of the architecture caught her attention, and the Winter Palace appeared majestic to her.

Ivan's wife took her shopping at the department stores on Nevsky Avenue, and for the newlywed, it felt like being part of an enchanted tale. Gabriel affectionately teased her, saying that if he always took her on his trips, all the company's profits would be spent on her shopping. He loved seeing her so happy and being able to wear sumptuous dresses and magnificent hats while strolling through the city streets.

As Gabriel had predicted, by the mid-1880s, Saskarov and Rothman Associates began to generate profits, which continued to grow in the following months. The three partners, including Sukov, the former soldier who now held a 20% stake in the company, wisely reinvested the dividends in transportation infrastructure and warehouses. By the autumn of that year, they began transporting part of the cargo by railroad and the rest with their own carriages.

Additionally, they began to diversify and expand the range of goods. The first step was to bring back finished products from German factories, a country at the peak of a great industrial revolution. Machinery and tools filled the goods waggons of the train on their return journey to St. Petersburg. They later expanded the range of products, adding wool, leather, and furs to the barley and rye. Although still in small quantities, it was undeniable that the business was progressing.

Around the same time, Ionela shared the good news with Gabriel that she was expecting a child. The joy was immense, not only for the soon-to-be father but also for the future grandparents. Isaak was overjoyed; as a devout Jew, he aspired to have a large family. However, it seemed that his three daughters did not share the same desire: Tatiana had only two children, as did Jana, and Aliza had one. Thus, he hoped that Gabriel would be more inclined to have a larger number of offspring.

In December, taking into account the difference between the Julian and Gregorian calendars, Karl and Aliza came for a family celebration of Hanukkah. Ionela found it delightful, as despite getting along well with her other sisters-in-law, she had always felt a special affection for Aliza. The whole family gathered at Sara and Isaak's house before beginning the commemoration, and joy filled every room with children's games and laughter from the adults.

"It's a blessing to have all our family gathered," Sara said to her husband, observing their daughters and grandchildren.

"Yes, my love, it's a joy, especially because most of them are nearby."

"And how the family has grown," she added, looking at her sons-in-law and daughter-in-law.

"You are right, but it's not as Jewish a family as I would have wanted. I still wonder why only Jana married someone from our community."

"You are mistaken, my love. I think you have much less insight than I do. Saul is not only a very authentic Jew, a source of pride for us, but he's also a rabbi now, and that makes us even more esteemed. But let me tell you something: none of the others disappoints us. Look at Robiak; he is a practitioner without a doubt. I would say he's more observant of our laws and customs than many Jews in this city."

"You're right, and that's something that fills me with joy. I've discussed it with the rabbi as well."

"And speaking of our daughter-in-law, you will agree with me that Ionela is almost as Jewish as I am. It's evident that she sincerely feels it and practices our customs with naturalness and true conviction. I must confess that even I have been surprised. The rabbi's wife has also told me that she has grown fond of the girl."

Isaak looked at his daughter-in-law; he had also come to love her. Due to Gabriel's frequent travels, Ionela spent a lot of time at home, sharing time with Sara, who felt happy to have such pleasant company. Ionela was very down-to-earth, though she had a strong character that occasionally showed when her jealousy was awakened by other women who flirted with her husband.

"And then there's Karl," Sara continued, "which is perhaps the most significant case. It's true that he hasn't converted, but every day he identifies more with Judaism. Look, he celebrates our holidays with us, adheres to our dietary laws entirely, and see, despite being a gentile, he wears the kippah. I believe it's only a matter of time. Aliza tells me that he already visits the rabbi at the synagogue near their home in Vienna."

"I must confess, my love, that this young man's case has brought immense joy to me. There is an important difference compared to Ionela and Robiak, and that is that they converted to marry our children. In contrast, Karl was already married when he decided to embrace our religion, which means that he did so on his own accord, not just to achieve a goal. Not to mention that he is risking his military career. Do you understand?"

"Of course, my love, I understand. But you must admit that it was a result of the efforts of your youngest daughter."

"You are absolutely right," Isaak said, smiling.

At that moment, Isaak stood up and walked over to Aliza, who was conversing with Ionela, and without a word, he embraced her. His daughter was surprised, but pleased, and returned the embrace to her father.

"I love you very much, my dear," he said.

"And I love you too, father," she replied, a bit puzzled.

Isaak noticed her confusion and clarified, "This hug is for what you've achieved with Karl, making him a full member of the family and the community."

She looked into his eyes and smiled; words were unnecessary. Then Isaak turned to Ionela and embraced her too.

"And this, my daughter, is because I am very happy that you are as Jewish as us, just as our grandchild, who is on the way, will be."

Right at that moment, the doorbell rang, and Ionela had a hunch, saying, "It must be Gabriel. According to his telegram, he should be arriving around this time."

She rushed to the door, and indeed, it was her husband returning from Berlin. She embraced him tightly, and everyone was delighted, going to greet him. Now the whole family was complete to begin the celebration of Hanukkah.

"You've arrived just in time, son," Sara said, hugging him. "The sun is about to set."

Then she turned to the women and said, "Let's get everything ready to fry the latkes."

Meanwhile, Isaak brought out the Hanukkiah and prepared for the ceremony. The women returned from the kitchen, and then Saúl, as the rabbi, had the honour of placing the candles. Afterward, Isaak took the menorah to the window in the living room and proceeded to light the first candle. The singing followed, and then Sara and Tatiana brought the trays with the delicacies. Love and joy filled this united Jewish family.

30

Isaak rubbed his hands together after removing his gloves to search for the keys to his home. That day had seen the heaviest snowfall of the winter so far, and he noticed how the cold seemed to affect him more with each passing year. Memories flooded back of those nights, particularly those freezing dawns in the barren forests of Siberia during his escape. It was precisely towards the end of that incredible journey that he met his good friend, now staying at his house with his wife, Mary.

Indeed, Andrew Cronin, now holding the rank of a colonel, was on his way to Italy, with plans to embark on Venice, and then onwards to Constantinople. There, he had been appointed as the deputy head of the British military delegation to the Sultan of the Ottoman Empire. He had previously held the same position in St. Petersburg, and it was there, through one of those peculiar twists of fate that life sometimes brings, that he encountered Gabriel.

One day, while strolling with Mary and their three children through the Summer Garden, they crossed the avenue on their way to the Marble Palace. Suddenly, the youngest of their children recklessly dashed to the other side of the street, oblivious to a fast-approaching carriage. A man passing by rushed to the child's rescue, pulling him away from the wheels just in time. It was a terrifying moment, and Mary let out a horrified scream. Andrew hurried towards the scene, where the man had already helped the little one to his feet. But when Andrew arrived and saw the tall, blond man before him, he couldn't believe his eyes.

"Gabriel! Is it really you?" he exclaimed.

Initially, he didn't recognize him, but after a few seconds, placed him.

"You're Andrew from my sister's wedding in Vienna, aren't you?" he said, extending his hand to shake while holding his son with the other. "Thank you, Gabriel, you saved my little one."

At that moment, Mary arrived, terribly worried, and embraced the child in her arms. "Are you alright, my dear?"

"Yes, mother."

"What an agony, dear God!" She then turned to Gabriel. "Sir, I can't thank you enough."

"There's no need for thanks, ma'am," he replied modestly.

"How can you say that, Gabriel?" exclaimed Andrew. "You saved our boy."

Mary looked at her husband, puzzled. "Do you know him?"

"Yes, Mary, he's the son of a great friend."

"What a fortunate coincidence. I'm grateful for your timely intervention."

Afterwards, they invited Gabriel to dine at their residence. Mary grew fond of him, never forgetting his heroic act. This was one of the reasons why, on their way to Constantinople, they decided to spend a few days in Lublin visiting the Rothmans. They wanted to greet both Isaak and Gabriel.

Isaak entered the house, hanging up his coat, scarf, and hat. He then entered the living room where the British couple was enjoying tea with Sara. Andrew and Mary's children were reading and playing in the study.

"Good evening," greeted the newcomer.

"Hello, my dear Isaak. You've come just in time to join us for tea. Sara bakes delightful pastries," responded Andrew.

"She's been an expert baker for many years," added Gabriel.

"Gabriel is coming to dinner with us tonight," said Sara.

"Oh, Gabriel!" exclaimed Mary, then turned to Sara. "I adore him, you know why."

"Yes, I heard about what happened," replied Sara.

"We'll be delighted to see him again," Andrew remarked with a smile.

Laughter filled the room as they reminisced. Soon, the focus turned to Andrew's new position in Constantinople.

"Now, my dear friend, you're more of a diplomat than a military man," remarked Isaak.

"Well, what can we do? The British Empire doesn't want wars, at least not ones worth the trouble. There's always somewhere to fight, but for now, apart from minor skirmishes in some African colony, there's no major confrontation that would require Queen's approval for Colonel Cronin's military expertise."

"I see," added Sara. "I suppose if she ever needs them, she'll send you a personal note, handwritten by her."

"Of course, delivered by the royal messenger, or, according to our modern times, the royal telegraph operator."

"Not even that," said Sara with a smile. "It will be through that new invention they call the talking telegraph, it's quite incredible."

"I've heard about it," said Andrew. "In the United States, they've created a device that allows a person to speak to another person who's hundreds of meters away, even several kilometres. They call it a telephone, and I believe it could have significant military applications."

"Very well, and changing the subject, what will your role be in Constantinople?" asked Isaak.

"As you said, my dear friend, to endure the wretched life of a diplomat, representing England at the Sultan's court."

"To Great Britain," Mary corrected him.

"Apologies, my dear." Then he turned to their hosts. "You should know that Mary is Scottish, not English."

"With great honour and pride," she replied.

"In any case, I must sacrifice myself daily, representing the entire British nation," he said, smiling at his wife, "or, to be more precise, the United Kingdom of Great Britain and Ireland, at the dreadfully dull dinners, strolls, meetings, and parties organized by Sultan Abdul Hamid."

"What a name," said Sara.

"It truly sounds like a tedious job," Isaak sarcastically added, and everyone laughed.

"At these events, I must assure the Sultan that England, pardon me, Great Britain, continues to support him, while keeping my Russian friends at a prudent distance."

"How ironic," Sara remarked. "You come from St. Petersburg, where you assured the friendship of England and Russia against potential enemies, and now you're off to the Sublime Porte to secure the same friendship against potential enemies from the other side. Oh, God, international politics."

"You've put it quite well, my dear Sara. Countries have no friends, only interests."

"Well, I wish you much success in this challenging mission," Sara said, then turned to Mary with a teasing voice. "And to you, I hope you don't suffer too much through all these social events."

"Speaking seriously, the mission is a bit more complicated and delicate than it may seem," Andrew replied.

"It must be," Isaak concurred.

"For instance, we have to finalize several matters concerning the establishment of British military bases and troops in Cyprus. By the way, my dear Isaak, one of the tasks I've been assigned is to advise the ambassador on matters related to the rights of Jews in Palestine."

Isaak's eyes widened with great interest. "As you hear, part of the peace treaty from the Russo-Turkish War stipulates that the rights of Jews residing in the Ottoman Empire, particularly in Palestine, must be respected. It was England who imposed that condition."

"May God protect England for all eternity!" Isaak exclaimed enthusiastically.

"And our dear former Prime Minister Benjamin Disraeli, it was he who imposed that condition," Andrew added.

At that moment, the doorbell rang, announcing the arrival of Gabriel and his wife. Andrew and, especially, Mary welcomed them warmly. Mary embraced Gabriel and kissed him on the cheek, then took him by the arm, leading him to the study to greet the children, especially little John, whom Gabriel had saved a few months ago in St. Petersburg.

Ionela, his sweet and unassuming wife but terribly jealous, took Gabriel aside during coffee time.

"What's the deal with that woman? Why so affectionate and warm towards you?"

"For heaven's sake, my love, she's a married woman."

"And does that mean she can't like you?"

Gabriel burst into laughter and proceeded to explain the reason why Mary held him in such high regard and trust. Ionela seemed satisfied with the explanation.

"I see," she said. "However, a kiss on the cheek would be enough, not such an embrace and handshake."

-ooo-

A month after Andrew and Mary's visit, Isaak was inspecting the extension work at the warehouse. The business had flourished, necessitating the acquisition of another building to accommodate another workshop for making and repair. He had found a suitable location five blocks from the main establishment. It was necessary to expand the original business, since he had diversified the products, he no longer designed and marketed only shoes but also various leather items such as wallets, belts and jackets.

Carl rushed into the store, breathing heavily, clearly having run there.

"Isaak, Isaak, have you heard the news?"

"Hello, Carl. No, what are you talking about?"

"They've assassinated the Tsar!"

"What? I can't believe it."

"That's right. They killed him while he was traveling in his carriage on a street in St. Petersburg."

"Good Lord, what a calamity! Gabriel is in St. Petersburg right now. Come with me to the post office; I'm going to send him a telegraph."

The two friends left, discussing the incident. The Tsar Alexander had already survived several attempts on his life carried out by extremist groups. Isaak lamented the news, as it was not only a crime against a human being but also Alexander II had liberalized many anti-Jewish regulations, alleviating some of the pressure imposed by the authorities on the Jewish community.

Naturally, the news spread like wildfire. Throughout the Empire, people talked only about the terrible assassination of the Tsar. Isaak returned home to share the unfortunate event with Sara. She was in the living room, having a conversation with Piotr and Malka, who were visiting.

Everyone was deeply shaken by the news, and Sara immediately became concerned about Gabriel. However, her husband reassured her, informing her that he had already sent a message and that Gabriel would surely respond within a few hours. However, that didn't happen, as all

465

the telegraph offices in St. Petersburg were overwhelmed, transmitting messages to the entire world.

In any case, given the circumstances, Sara had decided to have Ionela with them so that her daughter-in-law wouldn't be alone, especially in her pregnant state.

Only the next day, in the afternoon, they received a response from Gabriel. He was safe, but the city was in turmoil, with constant patrols by the military and the police on the streets.

The news outlets continued to report more details about the assassination attempt. It was noted that the attacker was allegedly Polish. It appeared to have been a senseless action in which a man had thrown a bomb at the Tsar's carriage wheels, which had fatally injured several guards and passersby. The emperor himself had been somewhat dazed but seemingly unharmed. After disembarking from the carriage to assess the damage, another terrorist had thrown a second bomb, which had caused his death.

"If this version is true, it's incomprehensible that the Tsar, after surviving one bomb, got out of the carriage," said Isaak.

"Even more so," exclaimed Piotr, "that his security detail allowed it, instead of protecting him by taking him away from the scene."

"And they say they captured the assassin, who is Polish," Malka added. "Oh God, I hope that doesn't lead to reprisals against our country."

At that moment, Carl and Irenka arrived at the house, just as shaken as everyone else in the Empire. They confirmed that the assassin was a Polish man belonging to a terrorist organization, and its members were already being arrested by the Russian police, thanks to the information he had provided.

"However, Isaak," Carl continued, "I came here because I heard that some news outlets are spreading rumours that he is Jewish. They even have a name: Ignacy Hryniewiceky."

"What?" inquired Piotr. "Could you repeat that?"

Carl read the name again. "That surname is undoubtedly Polish, and quite uncommon. I once knew a man with the same name, a young man who worked at my sawmill during the summers to help pay for his studies at the college in Bialystok. It would be quite a coincidence."

"It cannot be," said Carl, who had continued reading the communication. "It seems it's not a coincidence, Piotr. It says here that he is from Bialystok."

"It must be the same person," asserted Piotr. "Then, the Tsar's assassin worked at my sawmill."

Malka turned pale. "Oh no, Piotr, what if they come after you?"

"Well, that was over five years ago. Besides, it's not certain it's the same person, although everything points in that direction. I remember that after graduating from the Gymnasium in Bialystok, he moved to St. Petersburg."

Everyone fell silent for a moment. Malka furrowed her brow with concern at the thought that the man who had murdered the Tsar had worked with her husband. She feared that if they traced his history, they might lead back to his origins in Bialystok and possibly involve Piotr. He noticed her distress and tried to reassure her.

"Don't worry, my love. As I said, many years have passed, and he wasn't the only student I had during the summers. Regarding this event, there's another point that catches my attention. They say the assassin is Jewish, but the man we know is not. He's a Catholic."

Isaak looked at his friend and didn't say anything, but a strange sensation ran through his body.

As the days passed and more details emerged, Isaak became increasingly interested in knowing the origins of the terrorists from an organization called Narodnaya Volia, who had been arrested for their involvement in the Tsar's assassination. However, he couldn't find any official reports confirming that any of them were Jewish, and this fact troubled him greatly. Why then was there a rumour spreading, stating with certainty that the assassin was Jewish? It was something he couldn't quite grasp, and it filled him with unease. One night, unable to sleep, Sara noticed his restlessness.

"What's troubling you, my love?"

"I don't know, something has been on my mind for a few days now."

"What is it about?"

"They say the Tsar's assassin is Jewish, but that's not true, and I don't like it at all."

Sara immediately understood his concern. She sat up in bed, lit the lamp, and turned to Isaak.

"They're blaming a Jew, and you think they'll end up generalizing and accusing everyone else, don't you?" she asked after thinking for a moment.

"Exactly," he replied.

She nodded, understanding his concerns. "Do you feel the situation will escalate?"

"Yes, my love, and I suppose you know what I'm thinking."

"Of course, that this inexplicable feeling has happened before," she said. "It happened in Ostrow when you sensed something was about to happen. And later in Bialystok when I had a premonition that trouble was coming. That's what I feel now."

"Then we must not waste time; we need to take action as soon as possible," Sara declared, convinced that if her husband had a premonition, they should heed the signs.

"Agreed, my dear. Tomorrow we'll start organizing our affairs to be prepared for any unforeseen events," Isaak responded.

And so, he did, taking pre-emptive measures against any potential harm to the Jewish community. Early the next day, he went to speak with the rabbi, sharing his concerns and alerting other rabbis in Lublin. Then he visited Jana's bakery and asked her and Saúl to join them for dinner, as they needed to discuss an important matter. Afterward, he went to Tatiana's house and extended the same invitation. On his way, he stopped at the post office and sent a telegraphic note to Aliza, requesting that Karl open an account for him at East Bank and send him the corresponding number as soon as possible.

That night, they gathered at home, and Isaak spoke candidly to his daughters, daughter-in-law, and sons-in-law. He shared his concerns and past experiences, stressing the need for them to be prepared to face adverse and potentially dangerous situations.

"Don't be surprised if violent actions against Jews arise in the city," he warned.

"Forgive me, father-in-law, but honestly, I don't think that can happen," Saúl exclaimed. "We are far from St. Petersburg."

"I agree with Saúl," interjected Robiak. "It's true that a Pole was responsible for the fatal bomb, but I don't believe it implicates the whole country."

"During the uprisings in '63, a few Jews participated in the riots, but many who didn't suffered death or deportation, myself included," Isaak recalled those dreadful days. "Believe me, once violence erupts, it's difficult to control."

Isaak then turned directly to Saúl and said, "And in that year, St. Petersburg was as far away as it is now."

"Well, father-in-law, what do you think might happen? What should we prepare for?" Saúl inquired.

"There's a troubling detail: the Tsar's assassin was a native of Bialystok, which will lead the authorities to focus on Poland. Worse still, there are claims that the perpetrator was Jewish, and this falsehood has spread throughout the Empire, with rumours of several other conspirators being Jewish. According to what Piotr and Gabriel have told me, that's not true, but it doesn't matter, they're blaming the Jews."

"I understand your concern," Robiak said, "but do you think it will affect us here in Lublin? We are well-known and respected."

"Eighteen years ago, I was well-known and respected in Bialystok, and I was Jewish," Isaak reminded them.

Sara, who had been present but hadn't spoken, interjected, "When these anti-Jewish riots occur, it's usually not so much out of hatred or animosity towards us, but rather a desire to seize our property."

Isaak nodded, acknowledging his wife's insight. The two sons-in-law fell silent, considering the gravity of the situation, but thinking their parents-in-law's concerns might be exaggerated.

"Okay, we'll stay alert," Saúl said.

"It's not just a matter of staying alert," Isaak replied. "We need to take action starting tomorrow."

Tatiana and Jana had listened attentively to the entire conversation. Finally, Tatiana spoke on behalf of both of them. "My love," she said to Robiak, then turned to her brother-in-law Saúl, "Jana and I have experienced violence against Jews, and we fully trust our parents' insights. If Dad recommends taking urgent measures, it's wise to heed his experience."

The following day, Saul and Robiak, more compelled by their wives' insistence than considering it necessary, telegraphed Karl to open bank accounts in Vienna on their behalf. They planned to travel later to sign the necessary documents and transfer their savings to the Austro-Hungarian capital. The amounts weren't substantial, but according to Isaak, it was wise to protect their savings. The three families decided to gather their most valuable possessions from each house, not just for their cost but for their sentimental value, and secretly store them at Irenka's residence.

Gabriel returned from St. Petersburg and confirmed his father's fears. The rumour that the Tsar's assassins were Jewish agents had indeed spread widely. These accusations were false; in fact, none of the individuals arrested for the attack were Jewish. Nevertheless, animosity against Jews was growing throughout the western part of the Empire.

"I understand your concerns, father, and I share them. We must be very cautious. I'll be traveling to Berlin in the next few days, so I ask that you host Ionela in your home during my absence," Gabriel said.

"Of course, son," Isaak replied.

"As soon as I return, we'll assess the situation. If we find it necessary to leave Lublin for a while, we mustn't hesitate. We could temporarily settle in Vienna or Berlin. I agree with you; I don't want to put Ionela at risk, especially in her condition."

"I'm relieved to hear that you agree with my assessment. It's undoubtedly better to stay away from Russia for a while, at least until things calm down," Isaak agreed.

Several days passed, and Saul and Robiak were seriously underestimating Isaak's concerns when they began receiving reports of isolated protests against Jews in other regions of the Empire. However, they dismissed them as mere local disturbances, without any significant political or social consequences.

Everything changed at the end of April when they received news of a massive anti-Jewish uprising in the town of Yelizavetgrad. As was often the case, Carl, who was well-informed and received telegraphic updates from various places, came to Isaak's house to share the latest developments.

"It was a highly aggressive uprising, my dear Isaak. Many Jews were killed and injured within the community. Women were violated, and Jewish properties and belongings were destroyed or stolen. It was a horrifying ordeal."

"When did it happen?"

"The night of the 16th to the 17th. It was so severe that the governorate had to send in the Army. They've even given these violent acts a name - they call them Pogrom; you know that word in Russian means devastation."

"Yes, Carl, devastation for our people. At this point, it doesn't matter if the rumours are false; the mobs have turned their words into actions. You know what worries me the most?"

"What is it?"

"That violence travels faster than the telegraph."

"You're right. Anti-Jewish riots have spread throughout the Jerson governorate, especially in the northern sector, towards Kiev."

"In other words, closer to us."

A few days later, they learned of another Jewish massacre, this time in Kiev. Isaak couldn't wait any longer; he gathered his sons-in-law once again to take decisive action. Following Gabriel's suggestion, it was preferable to suspend their businesses and leave Lublin for a while.

"You're aware of the news from Kiev and the surrounding areas. It's time we took decisive action before it's too late. These riots can spread across Poland at any moment," Isaak said.

"Agreed, father-in-law," said Saul. "I must admit your fears were not unfounded."

"What do you suggest?" asked Robiak.

"The best course of action is for us to leave Lublin for a while. We should close our businesses and temporarily settle elsewhere, preferably outside of Russia."

"But we make our living here; our savings will only last for a while," argued Saul. "In my case, I have a community that I can't abandon."

"I don't disagree," said Isaak. "You're right about your duties as a rabbi, but you'll agree with me that it's safer for Jana and the children to leave Lublin."

"Of course, I have no objection. I would continue overseeing the bakery," said Saul.

"Very well," continued Isaak. "Robiak, I believe you should temporarily close your business. I would advise you to move the carts outside of the city and keep them safe."

"Indeed, father-in-law. I've already thought about that. I'll transfer two carts to my assistant, and he'll supervise the carters. I'll secure the other three in a friend's barn outside of the city."

"That sounds good, lads. Gabriel will be here next week, and we'll further advance our plans."

The next decision was where they would settle, at least temporarily. Isaak had already considered this matter and made the necessary arrangements. He, along with Sara, Jana, and the children, would go to Berlin to Helmuth's house, as Jared and Anya would also be staying there for safety. When they consulted Ingrid, she happily agreed to receive them all. The couple felt quite lonely in their eight-room mansion. Aliza would host Tatiana, Robiak, and the children in her house in Vienna, although it might be a bit cramped, but they would make it work. Ozana would welcome her sister and Gabriel.

Isaak was becoming more anxious for his family to leave the city. He started sensing a certain animosity in the air, and it troubled him. He believed that sooner or later, the anti-Jewish demonstrations would reach Poland, which is why he pressed for a faster departure. Jana was the first to leave, as Jared and Anya made a stop in Lublin on their way to Berlin. They spent two days at Isaak and Sara's house before traveling with Jana and the children. Saul accompanied them to get them settled in the German capital before returning to Lublin. Sara didn't want to leave just yet, as she was awaiting Gabriel's return and didn't want to leave Ionela alone. She also planned to travel with her husband.

The management of the bakery was entrusted to the oldest of Jana's assistants, with Saul taking charge of supervision. According to the plan, he would be the only family member remaining in Lublin due to his responsibilities as a rabbi.

Two days later, Gabriel arrived and was delighted to see that Sara had already organized the entire residence for their absence. All valuable objects had been stored at Irenka's house, the furniture on the ground floor was covered with sheets, and the suitcases were ready.

"I see you have everything perfectly prepared, mother. We can start our journey now," said Gabriel.

"Oh, my dear! If it were up to your father, we would have left several days ago," replied Sara.

"I believe his decision is right. If nothing happens, we can consider this as a period of rest and return to resume normal life. Well, mother, I'll head to the cellar to put everything in order, then I'll come back to go with Ionela to her house and pack our things. We'll leave this afternoon."

Gabriel left and headed to the cellar, contemplating the need to coordinate well with his two workers to manage the warehouse during his absence. He considered that he could come periodically to check on things. In any case, it wouldn't affect him much since he had to travel frequently to Vienna anyway, and Ionela would be happy to spend some time in a city she loved and in the company of her sister.

"We'll be back in a few weeks," he thought to himself.

At that precise moment, he heard the first gunshots. He stopped in his tracks in the middle of the street and listened carefully to locate their source. Then, more shots rang out, accompanied by shouts coming from the city centre. Gabriel quickly changed direction and headed at full speed towards the commercial avenue where his mother's bakery, along with several other Jewish businesses, were located. He was certain that this was the epicentre of the events, knowing that she wasn't there, but the shoe shop of his father, Isaak, was nearby, and he rushed towards that street.

As he approached, the voices of the crowd grew louder and louder, and he could clearly distinguish anti-Jewish slogans and chants: "Drive the Jews out of Lublin," "Down with the assassins of the tsar," "Let's get rid of these Jewish dogs."

Gabriel prayed that the mob hadn't reached his father's shop. When he turned the corner, he saw a large crowd coming towards him, hurling objects at shop windows and violently entering the establishments. Some carried revolvers and fired into the air or at the entrances of the shops, while others wielded clubs, pikes, and even axes. His heart sank as he realized that the furious mob had already passed Isaak's shoe shop. But almost at that very moment, he saw his father coming towards him at full speed, pursued by two ruffians armed with sticks and a third brandishing a dagger in his hand.

A trickle of blood ran down Isaak's right temple, but otherwise, he seemed fine. Gabriel sprinted towards his father and, like a cat, pounced on the man carrying the dagger, violently knocking him to the ground and immediately delivering a kick that shattered the man's face with the heel of his boot.

Meanwhile, Isaak, feeling supported by his son, turned to face his other two pursuers. One of them managed to strike him hard on the left arm, but he reacted swiftly, leaping onto the assailant and wrestling him to the ground. After leaving his first opponent groaning with a bloodied face, Gabriel spun like a top and lunged at the third aggressor, who was about to bring down his club on his father's head. Gabriel made him stumble, grabbed the piece of wood from the man and dealt him such a blow to the head that he felt completely motionless, his skull seemingly crushed.

Isaak had already subdued his attacker, who was now writhing on the pavement. He got up just as Gabriel urged him, "Let's go, father! The mob is coming!"

Indeed, a large group of men was approaching them, some pointing in their direction. Isaak and Gabriel sprinted away, taking advantage of the fact that the gang of criminals coming towards them had momentarily stopped to inspect the three men lying on the ground. They ran until they reached the next corner and turned left. Just then, they heard someone calling out to them in distress. They turned around and saw Robiak hurrying towards them.

"Come with me to my house. There are also disturbances in that area, and Tatiana is alone with the children," said Robiak.

They were about to follow Robiak, but Gabriel stopped Isaak. "No, father, I'll go with him. You go home. Ionela and my mother are there alone."

Isaak went in that direction while Gabriel and Robiak ran towards Robiak's residence. It was true; disturbances and anti-Jewish slogans were also present in that area. As they approached the street where Robiak's house was located, they felt genuine dread, for several Jewish families resided in that block, and their homes were being attacked. They continued forward, arriving at the entrance of the house, where they noticed it had already been broken open. A few policemen and soldiers were present, but they were doing absolutely nothing.

They entered the hallway and quickly climbed the stairs. Just at the landing, a Russian non-commissioned officer and a soldier stood motionless while shouts echoed from the upper floor. As they entered the room, they found around ten to fifteen men, some looting objects, and others destroying the furniture. Gabriel delivered a powerful blow to the jaw of the first man he encountered and turned to Robiak.

"The children, the children!" he cried, pointing at them.

The two little ones huddled behind a chair, clinging to each other with terror-stricken faces. Robiak rushed to them, throwing himself to the floor to shield them, while Gabriel dealt with another assailant who attempted to attack him. At that moment, he discovered with horror that several men on the other side of the room were surrounding Tatiana with the intent to violate her. They had already torn part of her clothes, pinning her against the wall. Gabriel realized that he couldn't take on so many men at once, so he spun around and rushed back to the stairs. The non-commissioned officer and the soldier were still there, completely oblivious to the screams and destruction.

"Please, help me!" Gabriel pleaded with the non-commissioned officer.

But the soldier remained immobile and merely replied, "I have no orders."

"I implore you! They're going to rape my sister!"

The corporal simply turned his head from side to side, and Gabriel didn't hesitate. In an instant, he lunged at the soldier, pushing him down the stairs. As the soldier rolled, he dropped his gun, and Gabriel took advantage of the corporal's turned back to snatch the revolver and push him down the stairs as well. Then he re-entered the room. His sister was almost naked, pushed against the carpet, with one of the men trying to mount her while others held her limbs.

In that moment, Gabriel's mind switched to a soldier's mindset. He saw the wretches as Turkish soldiers, even imagining them in their olive-green uniforms and cloth caps. Instinctively, he covered the distance to his sister in three strides, aiming at the head of one man holding her by the foot and pulling the trigger. In a fraction of a second, he turned and shot the man in the forehead who was pressing down on her hand, and finally the despicable man attempting to rape Tatiana. The man was getting up and received the shot in the chest.

The rest of the thugs immediately rushed towards the exit and huddled on the stairs. Meanwhile, the non-commissioned officer, accompanied by three soldiers, tried to climb up. In that state of confusion, Gabriel went to the door, dropped the revolver, and raised his arms, surrendering to the first soldier entering the room. Tatiana had gotten up, trying to cover herself with her torn clothes, and Robiak emerged with the children from behind the chair. As the non-commissioned officer entered, Gabriel, with his arms restrained by two soldiers, said:

"Corporal, I beg your pardon for having taken your revolver, but I had to save my sister's life and honour."

Although the non-commissioned officer's eyes were fiery, he initially remained speechless. Then he looked into Gabriel's eyes and asked:

"Why are you calling me corporal?"

"Because I'm a discharged soldier of the glorious Tsar's army, corporal. I am a war veteran against the Turks, decorated with the St. George's medal."

Gabriel hoped these words would prevent the corporal from reacting violently, and they had the intended effect—the non-commissioned officer was stunned and didn't take any reprisal against him. He went with a soldier to the three men lying on the floor, the soldier knelt to check them.

"These two are dead, corporal. The other one is wounded, but I think he's in bad shape."

The non-commissioned officer turned to Gabriel.

"Well, you clearly have the hands of a veteran. Only a veteran wouldn't hesitate to do this in a matter of seconds. You'll have to come with us to the barracks."

"I understand perfectly."

He then made the gesture of standing at attention before a superior and said, "I respectfully request a favour, corporal, not as a man but as a soldier."

"Do you think you're in a position to ask for favours?" The corporal looked sceptical, but he continued, "Fine, tell me."

"Allow my sister, brother-in-law, and nephews to accompany me. If they stay here, they'll be at the mercy of the mob."

The corporal looked at Tatiana, who had finished adjusting her clothes, and then at Robiak and the children.

"I'll grant it, but only because you're a veteran."

Gabriel nodded in gratitude. At that moment, he recalled a passage when he had watched a captain galloping into the distance, who had also granted him something significant. And indeed, as soon as they were escorted by the Russian soldiers, the mob entered the house and without concern for the wounded man, they looted and destroyed it. Robiak, Tatiana, and the children would have surely met a tragic end.

Isaak ran at full speed, deeply worried as he noticed that the groups of rioters were beginning to move towards the residential neighbourhoods, including his own. The street still appeared calm as he rushed into his house, where Sara already had a suitcase and two sacks in hand. She rushed towards him and embraced him.

"Thank God, my love! Have you seen Gabriel?"

"Yes, dear. He went with Robiak to rescue Tatiana and the children. The mob is going mad, destroying everything in its path. The shoemaker's shop must have been wrecked and looted."

"Oh no!"

"The thugs are moving towards the outskirts. I'm certain they'll reach here soon, so let's not waste any more time."

"Let's go!" Sara urged Ionela. "Hurry, my dear."

Isaak took the suitcase, and they hurriedly left the house.

"Let's go to Irenka's house," said Sara.

"Agreed."

They walked at a brisk pace, turned the corner, and headed towards their friends' house. Halfway there, they saw a group of hooligans coming from a side street, chanting anti-Jewish slogans. Without hesitation, they broke into a run. A few meters ahead, Ionela tripped, spraining her ankle and fell heavily onto the street, showing signs of pain. Sara turned to help her, but Isaak yelled at her:

"No, keep running, find a place to hide, but don't go into Irenka's house."

Immediately, he tossed the suitcase aside, picked up Ionela, and carried her on his back, running as fast as his legs would allow.

"Hold on tight to my chest and don't let go for anything," he told his daughter-in-law.

Fortunately, they managed to put enough distance between themselves and their pursuers to enter a house's garden without being noticed. Isaak gestured to Sara to jump over the wall and help him receive Ionela on the other side. They entered the property, and Isaak swiftly carried Ionela to the back of the house. Then they ran through the yard, reaching the perimeter fence. They crossed it and moved through a field covered with dense bushes. Shielded by the vegetation, they advanced around three hundred meters to a small stream. Crossing it, they climbed a hill until they reached a point where a small grove began. They disappeared into the woods, taking cover behind the trees.

Isaak gently placed Ionela on the ground and rolled to the side, completely exhausted. He was breathing rapidly, trying to catch his breath, and Sara also sank to the ground, attempting to recover herself. They remained hidden there until nightfall. Ionela was in intense pain from her sprained foot and abdomen. Isaak lifted her up and carried her again; cautiously, they left the woods, making their way down to the stream. Under the cover of dusk, they re-entered the urban area and reached the back of their friends' house.

Irenka was horrified and deeply concerned. She was immensely relieved to see them arrive.

"Thank God, Sara. This is terrible, you can't imagine the news. Although they say the situation is now under control. Come, sit here, they'll bring you some coffee."

"Thank you, Irenka. Have you heard anything about Tatiana, the children, or Gabriel?"

"We haven't dared to go out. The only thing I've heard is that there was immeasurable destruction. Even those savages came through here; it was terrifying. I saw them armed with axes and picks."

At that moment, Ionela started feeling sharp pains in her abdomen. They quickly brought her to one of the rooms, and Sara tried to give her some apple tea, but she refused. The pain only grew worse, and later, Sara noticed that her daughter-in-law was bleeding. Carl hurried to fetch the doctor. The physician examined the patient, but there was nothing more to be done. Ionela had lost the baby. Undoubtedly, the cause had been the hard fall she suffered while fleeing from the enraged mob.

The doctor administered a sedative and stayed with her for several hours until she finally fell asleep. After bidding farewell to the doctor, they sat in the living room, deeply affected by the news. Isaak felt incredibly frustrated.

"My God, I knew this was going to happen. Why didn't I take action much earlier?"

"Don't blame yourself," Carl consoled him, "You did take action and acted ahead of events. Remember, you sent Jana to Berlin already, and you had planned to leave today."

The doorbell rang at that moment; it was Robiak with Tatiana and the children. Sara and Isaak sighed in relief to see them, but their anxiety grew as they learned the details of what had happened at their house and heard that Gabriel was detained in the Army barracks. Sara broke down in tears, and Tatiana tried to comfort her.

"Mother, take solace in knowing that Gabriel managed to persuade the Russian officer to escort us out of the house; otherwise, they would have killed us."

"Oh, my dear Tatiushka," she said, embracing her.

Then, she called her grandchildren and gathered them in her lap, showering them with kisses.

Tatiana chose not to tell her mother that Gabriel's capture was a result of him shooting three men, killing two of them. She also decided to keep the reason behind the incident to herself. With her mother already burdened by the loss of Ionela's baby and Gabriel's predicament, Tatiana took her father aside and shared all the details with him. Isaak immediately called for Carl and Robiak.

"I'll go to the barracks tomorrow and see what we can do," Carl said reassuringly. "According to Robiak's testimony, it was an act of self-defence to protect a woman and two children. Let's remain calm; I'll speak to the military commander. I know him."

"Oh, dear Lord, Carl!" Robiak added. "The barracks' chief is no longer in command. New troops arrived from somewhere in Russia, and now there's a colonel leading them."

"Nevertheless, I'll talk to him; we'll come up with something to help Gabriel," Carl assured.

"We should inform Sara about the situation," Isaak suggested. "Sooner or later, she'll find out, and she has the right to know."

Learning about Gabriel's severe predicament, with the likelihood of a murder charge, further shattered Sara.

"Oh, God!" she lamented. "Why does this have to happen to us? What crime have we committed? It's so difficult being Jewish."

Isaak approached her and said, "Calm down, my love. It's undoubtedly tough to be Jewish here, but remember, we always overcome everything and find a way forward. Have faith; things will get better. In the end, the Lord never abandons us."

He tried to put conviction into his words, but deep down, he felt like he was pretending. He was still angry at himself and ashamed before his wife. It was the third time such a thing had happened, and he had lacked the strength of character to insist on moving the entire family out of Lublin earlier. On the other hand, he understood that Gabriel was in serious trouble, and he doubted even Carl could easily extricate him. This was no longer a baseless accusation from the old scoundrel Marinowsky.

The next day, Carl went to the barracks and returned with bad news. Gabriel was still detained, along with seven other Jews accused of various crimes during the riots. The Police had filed the appropriate charges, and they were processing the necessary documents to transfer the prisoners to their jurisdiction for trial. The most serious charge was against Gabriel, as he was accused of three counts of homicide, since the man he had wounded in the chest had bled to death without medical attention.

Sara collapsed, and Tatiana did the same. No one dared to tell Ionela, who was still deeply affected by the loss of the baby. Nevertheless, Isaak insisted that she needed to know, as it would be worse if she found out through other means. The news was a harsh blow for Ionela, who fell into a state of semi-consciousness. Later, she wept uncontrollably, and no human power could console her.

"Two days ago, I had everything - my Gabriel and our child," she sobbed on Sara's lap, "and now I have nothing. I lost my beloved husband and our baby."

Everyone was heartbroken, but the most affected, besides Ionela, was Sara, who refused to speak with anyone and repeatedly blamed their Jewish identity. She even questioned her faith, and Isaak struggled with how to handle the situation. For their safety, they couldn't leave their residence, but they called for the rabbi, who spoke to Sara and managed to bring some sense back to her. The house was enveloped in an impenetrable cloak of sadness. They all sat in the living room, silent and despondent. Ionela sobbed constantly, while Irenka tried to coax them into eating, but none had any appetite. That was how they were when the doorbell rang, and the butler came in with news:

"It's a Russian Lieutenant with two soldiers. He's asking to speak to Mr. Isaak."

-ooo-

Gabriel found himself in the exact same compound where he was recruited, and memories of those days flooded back as if they had occurred just yesterday. Signing the forms, receiving the uniforms, enduring the jests of the veteran soldiers—all of it played before his eyes. Lost in his thoughts, he heard someone exclaim:

"German, German! Is it you?"

He looked towards the voice at the door and saw a soldier in uniform, adorned with sergeant's insignia. It took a moment for Gabriel to recognize him.

"Could it be? Corporal," he paused, glancing at the insignia again, "My apologies, Sergeant Borisov."

"The very same, German! What are you doing here?"

"It's a long story, Sergeant."

"Let's head to the cafeteria, and you can tell me all about it," Borisov invited, reflecting the camaraderie that goes beyond ranks, forged among soldiers who have fought together in war.

However, the non-commissioned officer in charge of guarding the prisoners refused to let them leave. As Borisov was outranked by the other sergeant, he couldn't insist, but he sat next to Gabriel and listened to his account.

"I understand completely, German, and I assure you, I would have done the same."

"Thank you, Sergeant, and I must say, if the situation arose again, I would do it all over."

At that moment, Borisov got up and said, "You know, I believe there's someone else who will be interested in your story. I'll be back in a few minutes."

Gabriel didn't comprehend, but Borisov left the compound and returned five minutes later, accompanied by a lieutenant who addressed the guarding sergeant:

"Sergeant, this man must come with me."

"My apologies, Lieutenant, but under orders from my superior, I cannot let any of these men leave."

"Well, I'm giving you the order to let him come with me."

The guarding sergeant felt the obligation to follow his superior's orders, but he didn't want to upset the lieutenant. Ingeniously, he found a solution.

"Please, Lieutenant, let me come with you."

The officer shrugged. "Fine, let's go."

The sergeant gave instructions to the soldiers at the door and left with the other three.

They headed towards the second floor climbing the stairs, leaving Gabriel intrigued. They arrived at the commander's office, where the lieutenant went in first and emerged almost instantly.

"You may enter, before my colonel," he said to Gabriel.

Upon entering, Gabriel almost stumbled backward. Before him, behind the desk, proudly displaying the insignia of a Lieutenant Colonel on his shoulders, stood none other than his old company commander, Nikolai Kuznetzov.

"I can't believe it!" Gabriel exclaimed, unable to conceal his surprise.

The indescribable sense of camaraderie imprinted in the hearts of those who have been through military service took over, and Gabriel stood straight, saluting.

"Good morning, Colonel."

Kuznetzov turned around his desk, approached Gabriel, shook his hand, and placed the other hand on his shoulder, saying, "I'm thrilled to see you again, German."

"And I'm delighted to see you too, Colonel. It feels unreal that you're here."

"Come, let's sit down," Kuznetzov said, taking Gabriel by the arm and leading him to the sofa.

The sergeant guarding Gabriel was incredulous; how could a prisoner, facing justice, be so familiar with the colonel? Kuznetzov noticed the sergeant's confusion and explained:

"I see you're surprised, Roskov." He gestured towards Gabriel and continued, "This man you see here is a hero of the Motherland, who fought like the best soldier and did more for the Tsar and our army than all of us here combined."

The sergeant's eyes widened, and he looked at Gabriel again. The colonel continued:

"He singlehandedly took down sixteen enemy soldiers and saved the lives of sixteen of our own, including yours truly, isn't that right, Borisov?"

"That's absolutely correct, Colonel," the sergeant confirmed.

Roskov continued staring at Gabriel, utterly incredulous.

"Borisov knows it well," Kuznetzov went on, "because he was with us in that war. Oh, and by the way, for everyone to know, our friend here holds none other than the Order of St. George."

The sergeant stood there with his mouth agape, just like the lieutenant aide; their surprise was immense. A soldier with the Order of St. George? Then the colonel said to the sergeant:

"Well, Roskov, from this moment on, I relieve you of your duties as the custodian of this soldier of the Motherland. The German is now under my care; you may leave."

The sergeant had nothing more to say; he saluted militarily and left the office. Kuznetzov called for a bottle of vodka and told Gabriel:

"Now, you're going to tell me what happened in your life and how you got into this mess."

They conversed for more than two hours, and finally, his old commander said:

"Well, German, if I'm here talking to you, it's because four years ago, you saved my life. I believe it's time to return the favour. I could tell you that you're free to leave, but that would be sending you into the clutches of the city's police. You must leave Lublin and go as far away as possible."

"Actually, I was planning to travel to Vienna, Colonel."

"That sounds like a good plan; the further, the better. I'll arrange your departure from the city."

"Thank you very much, Colonel. May I ask for one more favour?"

"Of course, tell me what it is."

"My family is here in Lublin, and they're in danger."

"Where are they?"

"I'm almost certain they must be hiding in the house of some friends."

"How many are they?"

"My mother, my father, my sister with her husband and two young children, also my wife, who is pregnant."

"Ah, the girl you met during the war?"

"The very same, Colonel."

"Don't worry; I'll make sure that you and your family leave Lublin without any trouble."

"Thank you very much, Colonel; I'll be grateful to you for the rest of my life."

"You don't have to thank me; this doesn't even begin to repay the debt I owe you."

Gabriel had no words to reply, but his gaze indicated a special feeling. A phrase his father had told him once came to his mind, "Not all Russians are bad; there are good Russians too."

Clearly, they became anxious. Carl instructed the butler to show the officer in, and he entered, standing before everyone with great formality. He performed a military salute and then a bow to the ladies.

"Good afternoon, I am Lieutenant Olaf Safin. I come with a message and instructions from the Garrison Commander, Colonel Kuznetzov."

The name sounded familiar to Ionela. The officer continued, "The Colonel wishes to inform you that Mr. Gabriel Rothman is his special guest at the barracks."

All of them looked at the officer, almost holding their breath. He went on, "Furthermore, given the circumstances he and your family are facing, he has arranged for two carriages so that you can leave the city as soon as possible, escorted by a military detachment that I will have the honour to command."

No one knew what to say, still trying to grasp the lieutenant's words. Eventually, it was Ionela who asked, "Are you telling us that Gabriel is alright? That he and we will leave the city with a military escort?"

"Exactly, Miss," replied the officer. "I have come to inform you so that you can prepare to depart."

Sara approached the officer and inquired, "Lieutenant, are you assuring us that my son is the colonel's special guest? He is not detained?"

"Certainly, he is the colonel's guest."

"But... I don't understand. Does my son know the colonel?"

"I am unaware of the details, ma'am, but I assure you they are very good friends. I say this because of the great respect my colonel shows him and the instructions he has given regarding all of you."

No one knew how to react at that moment; they all looked at each other. Finally, Isaak spoke, "Lieutenant, thank you very much for your visit and the excellent news you've brought. Could you please advise us on the next steps?"

"Of course, the transportation is being prepared. In approximately an hour, I will return in the company of Mr. Rothman."

At that moment, protocol was broken. Isaak shook the officer's hand, and the same was done by Robiak and Carl. Then Sara, Ionela, and Tatiana approached to greet him, taking his hands, which left the young man bewildered. As soon as he left, the four, joined by Irenka, embraced each other and could not contain their tears. Sara stepped aside for a moment, took her husband aside, and said:

"I'm sorry, my love, for my attitude."

"Don't worry; you see, God can send us many trials, but He recognizes those who love Him well. He never forgets His people."

As the officer had indicated, he returned with two carriages and an escort consisting of a non-commissioned officer and eight soldiers. The reunion with Gabriel was very emotional. They decided not to tell him about the loss of the baby yet, but rather when they were on their way. They bid farewell to Irenka, who was sobbing because she understood that it would be a long time before she saw the family she cared so much for again.

"Lublin will seem empty without you."

"Let's hope things improve, my dear Irenka," Sara said. "You can visit us; thanks to the railways, it's much easier and more comfortable now."

They left a city where they had enjoyed happy moments and endured bitter ones, but nostalgia overwhelmed them all. After living there for almost eighteen years, they were now becoming refugees with an uncertain future. The efforts of so many years to succeed in the bakery, the shoemaker's shop, Gabriel's trading business, all were going to waste.

As they passed the urban centre of Lublin, the greedy mob, worse than birds of prey, had completely looted and destroyed the two bakeries, the chocolate shop, the shoemaker's shop, and the warehouse. They had also ransacked Isaak and Sara's house, leaving it completely empty.

At least, on this occasion, thanks to Isaak's foresight, they had some savings safe and sound, as well as all the tools, supplies, and most of the merchandise from the shoemaking business. They had also safeguarded all their valuable belongings, stored in the cellar in Irenka's house. Nevertheless, it was still frustrating that their entire economic downfall was merely due to the simple fact of being Jewish.

"We have lost our material possessions," said Sara, sitting on a bench at the Garwolin inn where they were staying, halfway to Warsaw, "but we have the most precious things—our love for God and all our loved ones alive and healthy. We will recover from this."

"I am glad to hear you speak like that, my love," said Isaak, and then continued, "that is the greatness of our people, we always bounce back. It's much harder for us than for others, but we are a special race; nothing and no one can break us: 'the children of Israel may fall a thousand times and a thousand times they will rise again.'"

31

For Gabriel, learning about the loss of the baby was a painful blow. Nevertheless, he felt the need to console Ionela, who understandably was in a state of deep depression. The company of Tatiana became a great comfort to her sister-in-law; she didn't neglect her for a moment during the journey and kept her occupied, trying to divert her mind with optimism towards the future. The truth was that dramatic as everything that had happened was, given the circumstances, they had fared better than other Jews in Lublin and the Empire.

Thus, Gabriel ruminated in silence, as memories flashed through his mind, pondering life's paradoxes. He had never wanted to be in the military, let alone the Russian Army. Although his time in the service had involved living through the horrors of war, it had brought him many benefits afterwards. Thanks to it, he met Ionela, established the import-export business with Ivan, reacted as a soldier to save Tatiana from degrading humiliation, and saved her and her family from certain death. Finally, they all managed to escape from Lublin by the fortuitous encounter with Borisov and Kuznetzov. Despite everything, he felt grateful to the Russian Army and had no regrets about having belonged to it.

They arrived in Warsaw, and before bidding farewell to Lieutenant Safin and the escort, Robiak and Tatiana bought some gifts to offer them. It turned out that the non-commissioned officer who accompanied them was the same corporal who agreed to escort them out of their house when he detained Gabriel. Later, they visited Ruth, Isaak's sister, who held great affection for Gabriel since his university days when he lived in their house. They spent the night there and the next day headed to the railway station to continue their journey—some to Berlin and others to Vienna.

Sara felt deeply dejected; having three of her four children living in the same city had become a comfort to her. The shock of recent events, the knowledge of losing their sources of livelihood, and having to abandon their house in Lublin—the very house they had bought and furnished with so much effort—caused her immense distress.

The farewell at the Warsaw station was filled with tears and promises to see each other again soon. Isaak and Sara departed for Berlin, while the others sat on benches, awaiting the train that would take them to Vienna. Tatiana said to Gabriel:

"Beloved brother, amidst all of this, I haven't had the chance to thank you for what you did."

"Tatiushka, I know it was a tragic and shocking event, but I had no choice. I couldn't allow them to inflict such terrible harm upon you."

"Indeed, it was shocking, but not at all tragic. Forgive me for what I'm about to confess, and may God forgive me, but I'm glad you killed those three wretches."

"Sister, you should know that I have no regrets, and I wouldn't hesitate to do it again. Let me tell you something."

"Tell me, Gabriel."

"During the war, I killed many Turks. It was my duty as a soldier, and I had to do it, or else they would have killed me. However, they were young men, just like me. They all had mothers, sisters, wives, or children waiting for them at home. Surely, they were good human beings with hopes and dreams, but circumstances dragged them into the war, just like me."

Tatiana listened intently, and Gabriel continued:

"None of them had caused me harm, unlike those wretched men who were willing to do grave harm to a woman I love with all my heart."

Tears welled up in Tatiana's eyes as she leaned towards her brother, embracing him tightly and planting a kiss on his cheek. Gabriel returned the hug, showing all the love he had just spoken of. Meanwhile, he thought of the absurdity of this incongruity: for killing Turkish soldiers, he had been decorated, but if he had done the same to three criminals, he might have been sentenced to death. Moreover, there was probably a pending criminal complaint against him, preventing his return to Lublin, perhaps even Poland and the Empire altogether.

Ionela, of course, continued to be devastated. As there were still two hours until the train departure, Gabriel suggested going with Robiak to fetch coffee and pastries for the two women and the children. They had just risen to head to the cafeteria when a very beautiful girl approached, saying:

"Gabriel, Gabriel Rothman, what a surprise!"

She came closer and embraced him. He was taken aback, and when he recognized her, he looked at her with puzzlement.

"Hello, Jana, how are you?"

"I'm doing well. I'm so glad to see you. What brings you to Warsaw?"

"I'm passing through on my way to Vienna with my wife and my sister's family."

"With your wife? Did you get married?" There was a tinge of disappointment in her eyes.

"Yes, that's right."

"Oh, how I regret it!" She interrupted herself, realizing the inappropriateness of her comment, and then added, "It was nice seeing you, and I wish you luck."

She continued her way. Ionela witnessed the whole scene and stood up, addressing her husband:

"Who is that girl?"

"She used to be the university librarian."

"Why did she hug you so familiarly?"

"She crossed a line. I never gave her that level of familiarity."

"And what did you have to do with her?"

"Absolutely nothing."

"Oh, really! You even remembered her name."

"Darling, because she shares the same name as my sister."

"And she looks very beautiful. Did you like her?"

"Oh, my love! I swear there was nothing between us. I know she liked me, but I was never interested. Back then, I was deeply immersed in my studies. Unfortunately, that girl had something to do with my expulsion from the university."

Ionela recalled the episode because Gabriel had told her about it. Tatiana and Robiak were laughing, as Ionela's jealousy had momentarily made her forget the sadness she was engulfed in.

Finally, the train arrived, and they boarded it towards the Austrian capital. It was comforting to see Aliza and Ozana again, even though the circumstances were unfavourable. The first few days were not easy, as there was a prevailing sense of frustration due to the awareness that the situation was unjust. Many years of effort and sacrifice lost in an instant, all because of a false accusation, taken advantage of by miserable individuals who stole the fruits of their labour. Gabriel and Robiak felt defeated and disheartened.

But perhaps the one who was most affected was Isaak; he fell into a state of lethargy that was unexpected in a person who had overcome countless difficulties before. However, once again, the entrepreneurial spirit of a woman resurfaced.

"I'm losing my spirits, my love," he confessed one night on the terrace of Helmuth's house in Berlin. "First Ostrow, then Bialystok, and now Lublin. Since we got married, we've started from scratch three times and managed to establish prosperous businesses, but three times everything has been taken away from us. And you know what's the worst part?"

"Tell me, my dear."

"That I have never harmed anyone; I haven't committed any crimes. I have worked honestly and diligently all my life."

"My husband, you don't need to tell me. No one knows it better than I do. But look, just as we've recovered before, we'll do it again. I know it's terribly unfair; our only sin is being born Jews. But precisely because of that, we carry a special mark of our lineage. We never give up, and we have the ability to overcome anything."

"Oh, Sara, I don't know if I have the strength for it anymore."

"Don't say that my love. You are the pillar of the family, and I know you'll lead us forward once again. We will restart our businesses, and you'll see that we will succeed, just like we have in the past."

"I don't have the same energy anymore; the years are beginning to weigh on me. In a short time, I'll be fifty."

"There are four more years until then. When you turn fifty, we'll have our businesses again. Think that at least this time, we have some capital to start with, and our children are already independent."

Sara noticed that, for the first time, her husband was overwhelmed and disillusioned. For several days, she tried to console and encourage him, but she couldn't lift his spirits, and instead, he grew more and more despondent. Furthermore, he felt very uncomfortable at Helmuth's house; he was aware that this wasn't just a courtesy visit, and his pride made him increasingly desperate as he felt like a refugee. Not even the presence of Jared, his good friend, could pull him out of the abyss he seemed to have fallen into. Sara began to seriously worry, until Jana found a solution and spoke with her one day:

"Mother, don't think I haven't noticed the state of despondency my father is in. Saúl feels the same way, like a stranger, and he's getting desperate with this situation. We've been here at Ingrid's for two weeks, and we can't keep depending on her generosity. I think it's time to take some decisions."

"What do you propose, daughter?"

"We are a strong family. The first thing we need to do is come together again to move forward as a unit."

"I like what you're saying. You know what? Let's call Isaak and Saúl, and you can present your proposal to all of us."

And so, they did just that. Sara called the men, and taking advantage of the warm evening, they gathered on the terrace. Jared and Anya were invited as well, as they had been considered part of the family for a long time. Jana began her lengthy speech:

"We find ourselves in this deplorable situation because of soulless individuals driven by anti-Semitism and greed. Lamenting and being despondent won't change the circumstances anymore. We must act as Jews and demonstrate that nothing can defeat us because we are a resilient people. Throughout the centuries, we have developed great tolerance for suffering, but at the same time, an unparalleled capacity to overcome it and find joy again."

Everyone present was mesmerized, listening to her speak with such authority and wisdom. She continued:

"Those who attack us are driven by the vilest human emotions—hatred, pride, greed, envy. They may outnumber us, but they will never destroy us because, in the end, God never forsakes us. Other nations might succumb to despair and become beggars, but not the Jews. We weep in the face of injustice, but as soon as our tears dry, we rise and work tirelessly until we recover once more."

No one dared to interrupt Jana; Saúl thought that if she were a man, she would have been a great rabbi. He felt immensely proud of her. His wife continued:

"Even the greatest disasters don't defeat us. If the Egyptians, Babylonians, Greeks, and Romans couldn't do it; therefore, the representatives of an Empire sick from within will certainly not succeed. Do you know why I say this? Because it was the sons of Russia who murdered the czar. I don't predict many more years for the reign of the czars."

They continued to look at Jana with anticipation. She pressed on:

"The ideal would have been to return to Lublin and pick up our life there, but that is not feasible, at least not now, given the current circumstances. I believe that Poland is a closed chapter for us, and we must consider a new family chapter somewhere else. Since we can't sit idly without trying anything, I think it's time to make decisions. The Rothmans are entrepreneurs, especially when we work together. The first thing we should do is explore the possibility of starting a business outside of Russia, and I believe Vienna is the ideal place. The language barrier is a challenge, but it can be resolved. Gabriel and Aliza already speak it, and the rest of us will learn. Vienna has the advantage of being the home of my three brothers and their families."

Isaak and Sara looked at each other and then turned their gaze back to their daughter.

"We have some savings," she continued, "and Carl could help us sell the properties in Lublin, gathering enough capital to start our bakery and shoemaking business in Vienna. Gabriel and Aliza can begin the process of obtaining the necessary permits from the local authorities. What do you think?"

"Daughter, you leave me speechless. There is nothing more to add, only to tell you how proud I am of you," Isaak said.

Sara stood up, walked towards Jana, and embraced her while saying, "I completely agree with your father. I am proud of you too."

"So, is the proposal approved?" they all responded almost in unison, including Jared and Anya.

"Thank you, but there is one more thing pending, and this is the most important and unchangeable part," Jana said, as they all looked at her, waiting for her to continue.

"It's about a journey."

"A journey?" Sara asked. "Where, and with whom?"

"Both of you, mother, together with father."

"How?" Isaak asked.

"Before I answer, let me tell you that it will be arranged considering that neither of you is working at the moment. I must also inform you that it will be funded by all four of your children. Saúl and I have contributed, and so have Gabriel, Aliza, and Tatiana. We've pooled our savings to gather enough resources."

"But, my dear, I don't understand— a journey?"

"Yes, mother. We know that the English officer, your friend, is in Constantinople. It's the perfect opportunity for our father to fulfil a lifelong dream."

Isaak stared at her, his eyes filling with tears. Jana approached him and said:

"Yes, father, it's now or never. All your children have decided for you; it's the least we can offer you after a lifetime of sacrifices to provide the best for us. Your English friend is already aware and organizing the details."

"My little girl, my little girl," Isaak said with tears, "I don't know what to say."

"I do know what you can say father. Please repeat it with me: 'this year in Jerusalem.'"

-ooo-

And so, the family got together in Vienna. As soon as they arrived, Saúl and Jana began to study German, while everyone else adapted to their new reality. For Gabriel's safety, he couldn't enter Poland or Russia. His company had lost the merchandise stored in the warehouse in Lublin, but it was necessary to continue with the import and transport business. The solution was to have Robiak replace Gabriel in supervising and managing activities within the Empire. As a Catholic, Robiak faced no restrictions in moving throughout Russia, unlike Jews who were prohibited.

Thanks to Karl's good offices, now a lieutenant colonel, Robiak managed to create a small transport company in Vienna and transferred the three carts he had saved from the riots. They also started the procedures to set up a small bakery, to be managed by Jana and Tatiana. To reduce costs, they rented a large house not far from the Danube canal, where the three families would reside while they achieved economic stability. As always, some lose and others win, and Aliza was the happiest because she had all her relatives close again.

One evening, when the whole family had gathered for dinner at their youngest daughter's home, Isaak took Karl and Aliza aside.

"Allow me a moment; I want to make a confession," he said, with a serious expression.

Both his daughter and son-in-law looked intrigued. Aliza asked, "What is it, Father? You seem quite serious."

"You know that I didn't approve of your marriage, and you also know the reason for it," Isaak said, looking at Karl, and then continued, "Time has proven how wrong I was. I don't say this because you've embraced our religion," he said, directing his gaze back to Karl, "it's not the most important thing for me right now. What matters is that you've proven to be an extraordinary man, that you truly love my daughter, and you've made her happy, which in turn has brought joy to my heart. So, I can only say: thank you, my son."

Karl couldn't hide his emotions; he approached his father-in-law and hugged him. Aliza joined them, overflowing with happiness.

Two months after their arrival in Vienna, and with the bakery already open, they were all gathered at the central station. Isaak looked rejuvenated, and Sara appeared more beautiful than ever. The tragic events in Lublin were fading into the past, and everyone smiled with renewed and genuine happiness.

"My children," Isaak said, "the remaining years of my life will never be enough to thank you for this gesture you've made towards me."

"Father," Aliza said, taking his hands, "do you remember when you saw two little girls shivering in an alley?"

Isaak looked at her, and tears welled up in his eyes. Aliza hugged him and concluded, "There's nothing more to say."

"Agreed," Gabriel interjected, "because I believe that we are even happier than you are, Father."

"We love you so much, father," Tatiana said, as the four of them approached to embrace that good and decent man who had been the best father they could have hoped for.

At that moment, the whistle announced the imminent departure of the train. It was a flurry of hugs and good wishes. Sara, standing by the train window, blew kisses to her children and grandchildren. She looked beautiful in her blue dress and round straw hat. Beside her, with a childlike smile on his face, Isaak waved his hand in farewell. On the platform, their son and three daughters felt immense happiness, knowing that their father was embarking on fulfilling the dream of his lifetime.

Seven days later, their dear friend Colonel Cronin welcomed them at a dock near the Galata Bridge in Constantinople.

"Sara and Isaak, welcome to Constantinople," Andrew said warmly.

"Thank you, my dear Andrew. It's a pleasure to see you again, especially under these circumstances," Sara replied.

Andrew and Mary's house was a grand mansion, close to Dolmabahçe Palace. It was spacious, well-lit, surrounded by extensive gardens and terraces. They settled on one of the terraces to have tea.

"You've chosen the best time for this trip," Andrew said. "June in Constantinople is cool and pleasant. Palestine, on the other hand, is always hot, but I don't think you'll mind much since you'll be fulfilling your dream after all these years."

"It could be a boiling cauldron, and my husband wouldn't care," Sara added.

"I agree with you. I never forget our conversations on the ship coming from Hong Kong. Even then, he spoke of this dream," Andrew reminisced.

"Oh, Andrew! He had that dream even before we got married," Sara said affectionately.

"In any case," Mary interjected, "I'm glad that Isaak's dream was the reason for your visit. I'm delighted to have you here."

"We feel the same, dear Mary. It's so lovely to see you, especially after all the trials we had to endure in Lublin," Sara said.

"Forget it all. We're far away from Poland now, and we're going to enjoy ourselves," Andrew said. "This city is fascinating; it's like being in two worlds at once."

"It will be interesting to explore it," Isaak remarked.

"Indeed, my friend. We'll have time to do that leisurely later, after your return from Palestine because the ship departs the day after tomorrow."

"The day after tomorrow?" Isaak exclaimed.

"Yes, Isaak. I must go to Cyprus, so I'll accompany you until the island. I don't have authorization to travel to Palestine, but everything is perfectly organized."

"Andrew, when I met you on the ship, I never imagined that you would be the one to make my old dream come true."

"Well, that's how fate wanted it. Traveling to Palestine isn't easy; the Ottomans are very strict with Jewish immigration, but you know they want to maintain good relations with England."

"And we European Jews will always be grateful to the British," Isaak said.

"Very well said," Mary chimed in, "to the British."

Andrew laughed heartily. "I always forget to speak correctly at home. Forgive me, my beloved Scotswoman. Well, Isaak and Sara, let me explain the plan. We'll go to Cyprus, where I'll remain to attend to some duties related to my position, while you'll travel to Beirut. From there, you'll journey by land to Jerusalem, and the return will be from Haifa to Cyprus, where we'll all reunite and return together."

Isaak felt like he was dreaming, and what his friend was describing seemed unreal. On his lips, it sounded as if Andrew was saying, "Tomorrow we're going to Cracow and then to Vienna," but no, it was Jerusalem. Emotion overwhelmed him.

"As I was saying," Andrew continued, "I can't go to Palestine, but you'll be accompanied by a gallant lieutenant of Her Majesty's Army. He'll travel incognito but with diplomatic status, just like you. Moreover, he'll carry all the credentials and authorizations of none other than Kusuk Mehmed Said Pasha, with his signature and imperial seal."

Isaak and Sara looked at Andrew without comprehension.

"Could you translate that for me, Andrew?" Sara asked. "It sounded like the name of some exotic Oriental dish."

Andrew burst into laughter and then explained, "Oh, my dear Sara! If they heard you say that at the palace, it could cost you your head."

Isaak and Sara continued to look at him with questioning expressions. Finally, Andrew stopped laughing and clarified, "Kusuk Mehmed Said Pasha is the Grand Vizier, the most powerful man in the Empire. A document with his signature could make all of Palestine kneel at your feet."

"I understand now, and I appreciate it very much," Isaak said, "but it's not necessary. I'm content just to be able to see Jerusalem."

"Now, we'll leave you to rest. You must be exhausted from the journey. We'll have dinner at eight, and tomorrow, we'll finalize everything related to your adventure."

The next day, they packed their luggage and enjoyed the pleasant company and conversation of Andrew and Mary. They didn't venture out to visit the city since they had planned to do so upon their return from Palestine. They retired early, and very early the next morning, they set sail for Larnaca on the island of Cyprus. As soon as they arrived at the dock, a young officer in a red and green uniform, looking no older than eighteen, approached Andrew. He stood at attention in front of Andrew.

"Good morning, Colonel, Lieutenant Jack Miller, reporting as per your orders, ready for the assigned mission."

"Good morning, Lieutenant."

"With me, sir, is Sergeant Roberts, my adjutant."

The non-commissioned officer stepped forward and saluted his superior. Andrew introduced Isaak and Sara to them, and then they proceeded to embark.

The journey was quite pleasant, even though it was a cargo transport ship with only a few simple yet comfortable cabins. The weather and winds were favourable. It was Sara's first time traveling on the high seas, while Isaak, experienced in maritime adventures, was impressed with the steam-powered navigation.

Three days later, they arrived at the port of Larnaca, where they spent two nights. On the third day, Andrew bid them farewell at the dock, and they boarded a much smaller vessel, exclusively designed for cargo transportation, without any cabins. The documents and credentials carried by Lieutenant Miller began to take effect. The captain, with ceremonial gestures, kindly offered his own cabin for the distinguished visitors to rest during the voyage to Beirut.

This leg of the journey was a bit more eventful, but they reached the port without any major incidents. The lieutenant immediately contacted the military authorities in the city, who received them kindly upon seeing the documents. A Turkish officer who spoke some English became their liaison and translator, and they were accommodated in comfortable and elegant rooms at the military barracks. Miller informed them that they would spend one day in Beirut and depart for Palestine the next. Isaak's excitement was mounting, and he constantly showed his emotions to Sara, who smiled tenderly and caressed her husband's hair.

The following day, they visited the city with the lieutenant, the sergeant, the Turkish officer, and some soldiers as their escorts. They felt like important figures, which they did not particularly enjoy. Sara's beauty stood out in the group, especially her blonde hair, which, despite being pulled back, revealed a few curls. Her face, though showing the marks of years gone by, remained strikingly beautiful. The Turkish officer who accompanied them stole glances at her, as did the men and women they encountered.

They visited the fortress of Beirut, the streets, and squares, as well as the market, filled with typical oriental products. The contrasts in the city caught the attention of Isaak, Sara, and the English soldiers. There were people dressed in European fashion, but the vast majority wore white tunics, complemented by chilabas or the fez, those strange caps that looked like an upside-down bowl. It was equally unusual for them to see a large number of women with their hair and faces covered, with only their eyes barely visible.

They departed from Beirut in a carriage escorted by Turkish soldiers and headed towards Haifa. Isaak thought that if it weren't for Andrew's position, it would have been very difficult for them to visit Palestine. During the journey, they encountered Bedouins and desert nomads, experiencing the novelty of meeting the slow and steady camels. They encountered military checkpoints twice, but as soon as they spoke with the lieutenant leading the escort and showed the official documents, they were allowed to continue without delay.

They spent the night in Haifa, and the next morning, they set off for Jaffa. This part of the journey was shorter, and by the end of the day, they arrived in the city famous for the story of Jonah. Isaak was overflowing with excitement, and by this point, his anxiety barely allowed him to sleep. There, they rested in a true oriental palace, and their room seemed straight out of the tales of One Thousand and One Nights. As the evening fell, they sat on the terrace adjoining the alcove, with a view of the sea. The sun set on the horizon, painting the sky with shades of red and orange. The refreshing breeze from the west gently stirred Sara's hair.

Isaak gazed tenderly at Sara while enjoying a refreshing drink and said, "You know, I've always dreamed of seeing Jerusalem, but that longing would have been incomplete if I couldn't share it with you. I thank God that you are here with me."

Sara returned his gaze, expressing all the love she had professed to him for over twenty-five years. She extended her hand to intertwine it with his and replied, "Yes, my love, God has blessed us to be together, here in the land He gave to our people. This incomparable experience wouldn't have been the same without you by my side."

Isaak reflected on their beloved daughter Jana's wise words, realizing that she had organized everything and communicated with Gabriel, Aliza, and Tatiana to plan this journey. "Our daughter is truly beautiful," he said. "At this moment, I understand that whatever we lost in Lublin is inconsequential as long as we are together. With our four exceptional children and our beloved grandchildren, what more can we ask for from life?"

"You're right, dear," Sara agreed. "We are fortunate to be alive, healthy, and united. When we return to Vienna, we will work hard, and I assure you, in no time, we will recover all that we lost. The most important thing is that we have each other."

"And the only additional thing I would ask for, I'll have tomorrow," Isaak said joyfully. "I am so happy and deeply grateful to God. Let's pray."

He put on his Tefillin and directed his gaze toward the city he would visit the next day. All his life, his eyes had been fixed on that place, but never his feet.

The much-anticipated day arrived, and Isaak was so anxious that he didn't want to have breakfast; he hurriedly climbed into the coach. Before departing, Lieutenant Miller asked him to step down for a moment to introduce him to a European who would be traveling with them to the Holy City. The man was of medium height and build, and he approached Isaak, extending his hand and speaking in perfect English with a distinctive accent, "Pleased to meet you, sir. Luigi Fiorillo, I am a photographer."

"The pleasure is mine, Mr. Fiorillo. Where are you from?" Isaak inquired.

"I'm Italian, and I specialize in photographing people and landscapes of the Near East. I'm going to Jerusalem, just like you, and then I'll head to Egypt."

"Ah, you must be familiar with these regions."

"I have some experience."

Sara arrived at that moment, and Isaak introduced her to the photographer. Fiorillo kissed her hand and explained that he was a photographer. Isaak thought it would be wonderful to have a visual memory of their visit to Jerusalem.

Fiorillo said, "It would be an honour to take a photograph of you both."

"The honour will be ours," Isaak responded.

The day would be unique and unforgettable for Isaak, etched into his memory for the rest of his life. Around noon, they entered the Holy City, and Isaak's eyes welled up with tears as he tightly held Sara's hand. Passing through the Damascus Gate, they headed towards Jaffa Gate, the only entrance wide enough for the coach. Isaak was so overcome with emotion that he hardly noticed the poverty around him, the dusty road, or the difficult heat. Tears streamed down his face, and Lieutenant Miller observed him with some surprise. Fiorillo explained to the British officer that the Holy City had that effect on Christian visitors but even more so on Jews.

They got down and started walking through the narrow streets. The peak moment was when they reached the small hill that offered a splendid view of the Western Wall in all its glory. At that moment, Isaak completely broke down, feeling that his life was justified solely by experiencing that unforgettable instant. He wanted to hold onto it forever. Overwhelmed, he wept profusely, holding Sara's hand even tighter as he knelt down to kiss the ground.

After composing himself, Isaak requested a favour from Fiorillo, "My esteemed friend, I beg you to take a photo of my wife and me as we stand before the Western Wall."

"With pleasure, but it would mean capturing you from behind," Fiorillo replied.

"Exactly, that's how I prefer it. Afterwards, you can take as many front-facing photos as you like."

The photographer shrugged and began preparing his equipment. Once Fiorillo had completed his work, they descended to the Wall where they found some Jewish worshippers praying. Isaak greeted them in Yiddish, exchanged a few words, and then prepared himself to experience the longed-for moment. As he touched the Wall with both hands and began his prayers, he felt his spirit flowing out of his body.

32

Eitan was reclining in his favourite armchair in the study of his son's house in Buenos Aires, with David sitting nearby, listening to his grandfather speak.

"When he touched the Wall with both hands and began his prayers, he felt his spirit flowing out of his body," Eitan recounted.

"How moving! He fulfilled his dream," David exclaimed.

Eitan's philosophical side came to the forefront, "It has been the dream of all Jews, from all times and places."

"It was an extraordinary tale. Please continue, I want to know what happened next - with Isaak and Sara, with Gabriel, with the daughters, and with everyone else."

Eitan smiled, "Be patient, David. I will certainly narrate the events that followed, starting with the birth of Ionela and Gabriel's son, Yosef, my grandfather."

"That will be very interesting. When will you tell me? I want to know so much more about my family's history."

"Soon, my child. I will share more about our ancient ancestors and more recent forebears, their adventures, and misfortunes. But most importantly, do you know what it is?"

"No, tell me."

"It's the story of how our family grew closer and closer to *Eretz* Israel."

33

First, he prayed standing and then kneeling, kissing the stones of the Wall as tears streamed down his cheeks. He thanked God for allowing him to live that moment, and images of his life flashed through his mind: when he was a young boy dreaming of this day, when he met Sara and married her, still dreaming of this day, when he had Gabriel, when he was a prisoner in Yakuts and still dreaming the same dream, when he escaped his captivity and continued to dream of this day, when his children grew up, and he never stopped dreaming of this day.

Sara also approached the Wall and offered her prayers with deep fervour and gratitude. Her happiness was beyond words. When they finished praying, they looked at each other with tenderness, and she said, "I feel so blessed to have witnessed the fulfilment of your dream that I would trade everything I have for this glorious day."

"And I am happy to have shared it with you, my beloved wife. From this moment on, I am fully aware that my life has had meaning and will continue to do so for the rest of my existence."

They embraced, conveying all the love and joy they felt. When they parted, Isaak confided, "Can I tell you something?"

"Of course, my love. I'm listening."

"When I was praying at the Wall, I had the sensation that my spirit left my body, and my soul soared above the land of Israel. I felt so close to God and understood something."

"Tell me, what is it?" Sara asked.

"... *That the path to heaven runs through Israel.*"

GLOSSARY OF TERMS

BAR MITZVAH: Ceremony through which the transition from childhood to adolescence is celebrated. It takes place when the boy turns thirteen and from thereon, he acquires religious responsibilities.

BAT MITZVAH: Same as above but for girls. In his case it is when he turns twelve.

ERETZ ISRAEL: The land of Israel.

HAFTARAH: Reading of the second part of the Tanakh or Hebrew Bible.

HASHEM: Literally means "The name", it is used to refer to God without naming him.

HANUKKAH: Festival of lights that commemorates the miracle of the oil in the lamps in the temple of Jerusalem and the rebellion of the Maccabees against the Seleucid Empire.

CHANUQUIÁ: Candelabrum of nine candles that are lit, one each day on Hanukkah.

CHEDER: Traditional Jewish elementary school.

KIPÁ: Ritual cap used by Jewish men, as a signification of the presence of God.

LATKES: Festive dish that is served on Hanukkah, it is a fried pasta with various ingredients.

MENORAH: Chandelier with seven arms. One of the main symbols of the Jews.

MEZUZAH: Parchment that contains two verses of the Torah written and is housed in a small box attached to the right jamb of the porches of Jewish houses.

ROSH HASHANAH: Jewish New Year. It is celebrated between September and October.

SHABAT: Holy day of rest for Jews. It begins at dusk on Friday and ends at dusk on Saturday.

SHALOM ALEJEM: Traditional Jewish greeting that means "Peace be upon you." It is usually answered with the phrase "Alehem Shalom."

PESACH: Festival that commemorates the liberation of the Hebrew people from slavery in Egypt.

PURIM: Festival that celebrates the salvation of the Jewish people, due to the intervention of Esther, avoiding her annihilation in Persia.

YOM KIPUR: Known as the day of atonement, forgiveness, and repentance.

TALIT: Religious accessory in the form of a shawl used by Jewish men.

TALMUD: Work that collects Jewish laws, traditions, customs, stories and legends.

TANAJ: Set of the twenty-four canonical sacred books of Judaism.

TEFILIN: Little leather boxes that store passages from the scriptures of the Jewish religion. Men place them to pray, one on their forehead and another on their arm.

TORAH: Holy book of the Jews.